CW00760020

The Covenant of Shadows

SILVER

Book Three

Kade Cook

SILVER

This is a work of fiction. Names, characters, places and incidents are either the product of the author's imagination or, if real, used fictitiously. All statements, descriptions, information and material of any other kind that may be contained within this novel is solely for entertainment purposes only and should not be considered as accurate. Other names, places and events are products of the author's imagination and any resemblance to actual events or places or persons, living or dead, is completely coincidental.

All rights reserved. No part of this book may be reproduced in whole or in part in any form.

Copyright © 2018 Kade Cook

Cover by AWeeDram Covers

Edit by Kayla Krantz

Proofed by Stéphanie Di Cesare

E-book ISBN: 978-0-9948678-7-2
Paperback ISBN: 978-0-9948678-8-9

First Edition October 2018

Theo & Quinn Creative Works
Shediac River, New Brunswick, E4R 6A7, Canada

www.kadecookbooks.wordpress.com

To Continue the journey click here:

https://www.amazon.com/Kade-Cook/e/B01M64VACI/

Acknowledgements

First and foremost, to you the courageous readers in my ARC team of the Skeleton
Crew,
who took the chance to pick up SILVER,
Thank you from the bottom of my heart.

Without all of you, who told their friends, left a review, tweeted or shared it on
Facebook, I could never have gotten this far without all your support and
encouragement.

To my incredibly talented graphic artist, Jenna McLean, and my wonderful editor, Kayla
Krantz, my biggest hugs and thanks for all their hard work. Without them this would
never have been possible.

To Donna, Jenna, Denise, Brenda, Doris, Shanda, Nik, and Peggy, you are all amazing!
Thank you for beta reading SILVER, and helping me get the draft copies out there.
Our chats about imaginary people, the cast of stars we see as the characters and your
undying belief in me, are what keeps me inspired. You are my heroes.

I want to give a big hug out to Jo-Ann
for her unending support and belief in my journey.
And finally, I want to thank **YOU** for reading this. Without the support of readers like
you, I would still be just a dreamer. You are the reason why dreams really do come true.

So, Thank you.

For Jenna, James, Kaidyn, Liam, Meagan,
Channy man and sweet baby Kain.

May they know
That I love them dearly.
In this world
And
In all those that follow.

FELLOWSHIP HIERARCHY

ZEPHYR – *AIR*: ELDER VAEDA KARRIN

EGNI – *FIRE*: ELDER ARRAMUS URIE

HYDOR – *WATER*: ELDER CASPYOUS WILEY

EORDEN – *EARTH*: ELDER KALEB DIMIRI

ISA – *ICE*: ELDER ASHEN GRACIE

DERKAZ – *DARK MAGIK*: ELDER CIMMERIAN COLE

BORAGEN – *BORROWERS*: ELDER ETHAN BORNE

SCHAEDUWE – *SHADOW WALKERS*: ELDER ORRORYN REDMOND

VINDERE – *REINCARNATE/MEDIUMS*: ELDER ARIAH FELLOWS

ARGUROS AUCYEN – *SILVER MAGE*: ELDER CERA ARGRYIS

SILVER

In a world filled with chaos and calamity,

The smallest act of kindness can forge bonds

That shine like beacons in the darkest of hours.

Prologue

Truth and Hope

From within the shadowed halls, the tension in the air weighs heavily with the mournful concern of those who sit, quietly pondering over what remains of their once powerful and absolute regime.

So many barren seats surround the High Table—an obvious display of loss in the aftermath of an intricate web woven by devious spiders who unleashed a sinful plan upon them all which costed some their loved ones.

"Is there really any sense in being here?" Ariah exhales from her small perch, glancing at Ethan. "I mean, Orroryn is somewhere within the Veil, Vaeda is dedicated to Tynan's aid with…" She bites her tongue, sensing the tension around Ethan build as the obvious reason is bared and his concern brought forefront to the space.

Ethan lifts his head to the sound of her voice, pulling away from the inner privileged dialogues that hum beneath the surface of the table. His mind reels in the unrelenting questions bombarding the silenced room around him. So many decisions to be made, so many doubts to be put to ease, but with so much unrest within the people, even *he* is questioning the future of the Realm.

And his heart aches for his friends, one in particular.

Such a tragedy her life has become.

Ariah pushes forward with her course of concern. "...and with Cimmerian and Caspyous being incarcerated within the Guardians watch..."

"Yes, Ariah, I know how it looks." He exhales. "But we must remain resilient, a show for the people that the Elders are still maintaining order within the Realm. Even within the chaos, there must be a display of command." Not knowing when or how this will be sorted out, Ethan—as well as the others—knows that without direction, disarray will quickly follow. Regardless of all the loss that has occurred, they must persevere to maintain order. "This is our liege and our obligation to the Realmsfolk."

Ariah lowers her eyes and nods, knowing he is right.

Arramus leans in, engaging the already disheartened conversation at play. "Since we must push forward, a starting point is needed. So, Ethan, what do you suggest we do?"

All those in attendance straighten their backs and still their wandering minds to listen for the much sought-after answers. As the Eldest of the group, Ethan feels the sudden urge for guidance on his shoulders, the inevitable duty of direction his role plays. Raising his head from his steepled hands and pushing back his own cloud of dismay, Ethan inhales, eyes darting around the room. There are no easy answers he can give. There is only the truth and trust that the universe knows what it is doing.

"We gather ourselves as best we can, seek out the rest of the Elders for an immediate decision on council, and then" —Ethan rubs the edge of his chin and pauses— "we hope for a miracle."

Chapter One

The Man in the Mist

A faded daydream of a faraway world drifts in and out of Gabrian's thoughts as soft grains of sand sift through her toes. Her bare feet press small indents into the seemingly endless shoreline of Erebus and a warm breeze tickles against her skin, making her smile as she lifts her face to the grey sky above her, soaking in the invisible sun. Her pace is slow and unhurried but Gabrian's course is predestined by her beautiful Gargon escort gently coaxing her onward, their fingers entwined.

Gabrian opens her eyes and drops them, lingering over Eva whose presence somehow does not leave a mark on the edges of the pristine beach. She takes brief notice but lets the thought go, consumed once again within her whimsical state of wandering. Such trivial things are of no concern to her—at least not here.

Eva's form drifts in and out of the mist as they promenade along the shore until Gabrian notices a string of tension in the air from her escort. In the distance, a figure dressed in white flowy cotton fabric cuts through the fog. The edges around his form are sharp and pristine rather than faded like the edges of the others she has seen here.

A slight hitch in Eva's step draws Gabrian's attention as they continue their direct collision course with the figure. The closer he draws near, the more familiar he seems to Gabrian. She chuckles at the absurdity of it. They are in Erebus; certainly she knows no one here.

A couple of feet in front of them, the man halts. "May I have a moment, my dear?"

13

Unsure of whom he is speaking with, Gabrian remains silent and hears the soft, hollow echo of Eva's silent words of protest ring through her mind.

"Don't worry, you will see her again if she so chooses," the familiar stranger hums, a tender smile blossoming on his lips.

Eva peeks up at Gabrian, eyes holding a sincere sadness that Gabrian doesn't understand as her hand is freed from its entanglement with Eva's

Gabrian steps to follow her, the loss of her company pulling on her like an invisible string attached to her soul, gently tugging, sweetly coaxing her to go.

"Come take a walk with me," the man lulls out, interrupting her pursuit of the Gargon, and softly beckons her to follow him instead.

Gabrian steals one last glimpse in Eva's direction then turns to tail the man, skipping a few steps to catch up. "Do I know you?"

He only grins at first then replies coyly, "Do you think you know me?"

Gabrian twists her brow at the queer answer but continues trailing her new companion in silence.

Her awkward expression causes him to give a slight chuckle. "I am Rhadamanthys, the eastern keeper of Erebus."

In her clouded state, Gabrian tries to retain the name. "Ra Daman…" The word forms queerly in her mouth but she continues, "I'm sorry. Could you say that again?"

His chuckle grows louder as she tries to say it again. "It is alright. You may call me whatever part of my name that sticks with you. That way it will be easier for you to remember."

Odd, Gabrian thinks but his logic makes sense.

The further they walk, the more distance is placed between themselves and the mist. Gabrian begins to have flashes of memories, more lucid and familiar, which had been void since her arrival into Erebus. More and more they come, bombarding her, vivid distractions cutting through her once calm mind. Swirling within them, she becomes lost, unaware that she has stopped moving to digest what's happened to her.

"Are you alright?" His soft words hum across his lips, delicately breaking her from her entrapment of visions.

Gabrian blinks hard, returning from her internal journey, and presses a curve to paint her lips. "Yes, no…" she offers, lifting her eyes to meet his. Her mouth flattens, letting the corner of her lips drop. The golden sheen of his irises catch her attention, burning brightly against the hazy world they drift in. "I am feeling a bit peculiar all of a sudden."

His cheeks rise, and his golden eyes pinch at the edges, watching her dissect the situation of her mind. "They are your memories," he offers her. "The images running through your mind are small coherent pieces of your life trying to break through the bonds this dimension tends to forge upon the consciousness of souls."

"Memories?" She glances around, face contorting and eyes searching for clarity. "These images and strange sensations…these are mine? These are my feelings?"

"Yes, my dear. Don't let them worry you. It is just your thoughts clearing." Rhada smiles and extends his elbow, offering it to her in an invitation to continue on their journey.

Gabrian's eyes glance down briefly at his chivalrous offer then accepts, slipping her hand through the loop of his arm as they continue on their uncharted trek.

"The Gargons who dwell here have an uncanny ability to enchant those harboring in the mist. They can captivate every thought and delude any ability to reason. They deluge the soul to drown, so to speak, within their own creation of euphoria. It is an unnatural state of being, but a necessary gift they allow during the transition from one status of existence until one reaches the next." Rhada's words sing out slow and delicate in effort to allow her to ingest his explanation without sparking her natural reaction of fear. "In turn, they cast you into a dream-like state that helps keep everything in check, so to speak." He narrows his eyes, observing Gabrian's reaction to all this, and at her slow nod of comprehension, he continues. "And, that strange physical feeling of loss you felt as Eva left you to me was just her suggested illusion diffusing from its hold over your mind."

Gabrian's eyes shutter as he speaks his truth and her mind grasps at the slivers of understanding still melding in the toxins of the dead. Watching her struggle as her conscious fights against the compelled delusion, he continues his deliverance of truth. "It was necessary for me to distance you from her spell. I need your ability to think clearly in play to resolve what we need to discuss. I need you to be able think for yourself without influence."

Still floating, Gabrian stares ahead, lost within the nothingness, but her eyes begin to blink rapidly. Bits and pieces of what she is being told gathers, and she forces them to mesh together in order to grasp hold of any understanding. Between the continual flood of emotions prickling and gnawing at her, and the complex replay of dramatic visions dousing her brain in fuel and setting it ablaze in torment, her attention to what she is being told is strained.

"Did you like your life, Gabrian?"

The simplistic sharpness of the question shreds through her chaotic turmoil like a knife, stopping her in her tracks, and snatches her back immediately. Her eyes narrow. She has to grip hold of the words to hear them. "My life?" she whispers, raising her head to look at him.

"I need you to try hard to focus," Rhada says, only letting his sight drop in a brief side sweep of her presence. "Did you like your life?" he repeats, returning his gaze forward—his tone gentle but firm.

Finally gathering enough distance to break free from the hold of the fog and its incessant shroud, her mind becomes her own again. Gabrian's eyes blink with clarity as she gazes across the vastness of the clouded shoreline. Colours form, taking contrast in their surroundings. "I think so. Or at least I believe I did once." Her bottom lip quivers and a solemn tear breaks from the corner of her eye to slide down the side of her pale cheek. "Well, before the bottom of it fell out and I ended up becoming the monstrous screw up and nightmare that came with it."

With a huffy chuckle, the stranger nods his head. "Ah, yes, Cera certainly did make a mess of things, didn't she? Undoubtedly, it was all done in regards to your best interest. But, as we both know, sometimes things are better left to their own devices."

All her memories, bad and good, rush back to her at the sound of her birthmother's name. Gabrian halts, disrupting the smooth pristine placement of the white sands at her feet. "Wait a minute, you know Cera?"

Rhada looks down at her, his face warm and inviting, to give her a quick golden-eyed glance painted in humor. A cheerful smirk curls upon his lips. "We have met a time or two."

Gabrian turns and grabs onto his white-cotton sleeves, pulling him into an unavoidable stop. "But we are in Erebus? How could that be? Is she dead too?" she pants, eager for his reply.

But he only steps around her, continuing his journey without her, and offers her no solace, only a crooked grin His eyes meet hers, granting a strange otherworldly dilation in his passing.

She gasps, watching a straight black line jet out from the center of his eyes, widening across the golden hue of his irises, and flaring out before returning as if never born. Gabrian staggers, nearly tripping over herself with the memory of why the man seems so familiar. "The stairs," she stutters, stumbling over herself, "you are the young man on the stairs. The one who disappeared into thin air the night I went to the college to speak with Cimmerian on the night of my attack."

With a golden wink and a grin that doesn't break his stride, he peeks over his shoulder. "You have a very good memory."

Chapter Two

Decisions

Pushing her toes hard against the sand, Gabrian rushes forward and blocks Rhada's path. "I don't understand," she argues, bunching the edges of his cotton sleeves in her fingers. "None of this makes any sense."

Rhada lets out a long heavy sigh. "There is so very much you do not understand." He drops his gaze and gently reaches up with his hands, grasping her wrists. His otherworldly touch sets her skin to chill and the hair on her arms stands in their embrace. But she does not falter. His eyes twitch, and his mouth curls sweetly at her. "Something I intend to remedy."

Gabrian stares deeply at him, grasping at his clothes once more. "What is that supposed to mean? How?"

Rhada looks out across the water. His eyes fill with the reflection, the array of colours prismed and dancing on its easy edges. "Well, Gabrian, that depends on which path you chose to take next."

Gabrian shakes her head. Riddles and lies, deception and delusion roll around within her, waking her up to the reality of where she has come from and what has suffered. Rhada lets go of her wrists and motions forward, pulling free from her surrendered hold on his sleeves. "Come, we have much to discuss," he says, leaving Gabrian to her decision.

She glances back at the mist from which they came, almost wishing she could return to its easiness, but her conscious—well awake and unrelenting as ever—forces Gabrian to dart after her new acquaintance, eager for answers.

His words spill out the moment she reaches his side. "Do you want to know?" he asks, his mouth impishly sweetened at one corner, already knowing the answer as she nods.

"Yes, tell me."

"Very well then." Rhada nods, his face barren of humor. His features look aged as his lips part to relinquish his wisdom upon her youthful soul. "Ultimately, it is your decision but I, being the judgement of eastern souls of who enters Erebus, feel it is not your time to pass. The scales of balance have been breached, and I am afraid an awful evil has managed to fracture its delicate plates. I cannot be certain how deep the infection has been spread, but I fear, if left untended, worlds as we know them will be left forsaken from the contamination."

With narrowed eyes and her chin draping as his words spill out, Gabrian takes them in, however convoluted they sound. "But what does this have to do with me?"

"Unfortunately, sweet child, everything," Rhada delivers to her, voice low and sullen.

Such queer words, she thinks, her eyes searching through the meaning. "I don't understand. What do you mean?" she pleads, her grip firm now, pulling tight against his sleeves.

"Even I cannot divulge this forbidden liberty of matters spoken. My tongue is bound to its limits of truth and knowledge. It is your will and choice of direction on the path taken now that will allow you this revelation," he offers, his golden hue shimmering around the edges of his long black lashes, casting an enchanting glow across his cheeks. "So, answer me this child, search the innards of your soul. How do you feel at this very moment?"

Gabrian swallows, pulling hard through her memories, drowning within her torn and mixed emotions, and tries hard to choose the right words to say. She opens the gates to let everything in, seeing the faces of all those she loved and still loves, and answers him with merely a whispered phrase. "I feel like I am coming undone. Like I am being pulled in a thousand different directions at once."

He cups her trembling arms and gazes on her with adornment. His face is soft and serene but shadowed in a moment of sadness as he smiles. "Then you, my dear, are not ready for this side." Sliding his grip to the tips of her fingers, Rhada gives a gentle squeeze and lets them drop. "It is done," he announces, stepping away, and utters something to himself undecipherable by her.

"What is done?" she huffs, her eyes wild as she seeks understanding. "What does that mean?"

"It means that you must be brave now. The worlds are counting on you, so you must believe. You must reach deep inside of your very essence and you must fight."

"I am sorry, but I really don't understand."

Rhada's lids close, and he inhales. "It is time. Are you ready?"

"Ready? How can I be ready when I don't even know what is going on?" she garbles at him.

"You are going home."

"Home?" Her heart flutters at the sound. *Home,* she hums inside, caught somewhere between sadness and joy.

The mist around them shifts and the colours dancing across the ocean's flesh sparkle and intensify, cascading in fireworks across the sheen of Rhada's eyes. Winds roll across the water, throwing Gabrian's hair to float all around her face.

"But first we must undo what has been done." Rhada lifts his hand and cups her cheek gently. "I am sorry for what I must do now. There will be suffrage on your part, please forgive me, but you must find a way to persevere. You must fight." His words are mournful and hushed in his warning. "Do you hear me? Fight for all you hold dear."

Not understanding much other than the fact that she is going home, Gabrian nods and forces her eyes to meet his. Rhada's golden eyes of judgement swirl. The center of his pupils pulse as a thin line of blackness spears out either side—pulling the center clear across until it devours all that remains—opening some kind of internal anomaly. She gasps, seeing beyond what his human facade appears to be and into a depth beyond explanation, a state of eternal existence emanating within.

"Now, close your eyes," he whispers, hands gently cupping the side of her head, thumbs resting on her lids to coax Gabrian to lower them. He delivers one last tender grin as she does as she is instructed. Gabrian inhales, listening to the soft soothing waves of his voice. "Look through the darkness to find the light within for it will be needed to restore peace. Let them find you, and he will save you. Draw on his strength, and his love to pull you through to the other side."

In the darkness, the cryptic instructions begin to ring hollowly through her ears. She presses open her eyes to question his instructions, but before the words can leave her mouth, everything around her gives way. Her body is weightless and floating within the vast empty space between where she had just been and nowhere at all.

Chapter Three

From Erebus we fall

In the painful silence that fills the Shadwell home, Tynan and Vaeda sit sipping the bittersweet taste of raspberry wine clasped between their fingers. Vaeda gazes lovingly at her host, running a delicate touch along his shadowed jawline, and feels the roughness of it nibble at her skin.

His heart tightens with her touch, caught delicately within a web of pain that he cannot extinguish. Softening his face, his mouth plays the fool as it twists into a gentle upward fold.

"Did Ethan say there was any change?" Vaeda knows what is on his mind so there is no sense making idle chatter about things he has no interest in. Direct and to the point is better, welcomed to Tynan, even if the words cause him to flinch.

"No," he drones, lifting his glass to his lips. "He says that he cannot find her, but I am not ready to hand her over to the keeper of Erebus and his judgement. I know she is still in there somewhere. Gabrian is much too stubborn to give up." His voice cracks under his words. "She cannot give up, I will not allow it."

Vaeda rubs his arm and gives it a tender pat, lifting her own glass. "Yes, well, if I have learned anything about the girl, it would be that." Vaeda allows a soft chuckle to escape, easing back into the impending silence.

*

23

A soft voice whispers to Gabrian as she floats within the void. "Surrender Egni." And she screams as her body explodes into a bright orange flare, engulfed with pain.

*

A loud shriek rips through the room, echoing off the walls as it strikes out at them for the bottom of the stairwell entrance. Tynan's wine glass shatters on the floor, spilling its contents as his body falls into the shadows, leaving Vaeda alone with her thoughts. He reappears in the same breath, rigid and alert, at the side of Gabrian's bed upstairs.

Another ear-piercing wail exits the small decrepit remains of her earthly form as her extremities lunge out, clutching at the blankets with her fingers curled into claws and feet twisted and strained. A crimson glow flares out from her body, bursting with heat as it brightens the room.

Laying his hand on the pale clammy surface of her forehead, he feels the fire that burns under her flesh. Ripping back covers, and gathering her into his arms, Tynan gently cradles her heated body against his own just as Vaeda enters the room. He pushes past her, entering the bathroom and cries out his plea, his eyes wide with fear. "She is burning up. You must find Ethan and Arramus."

Vaeda gasps, stepping aside when she feels the heat.

"Bring them to me. Please, quickly," he adds.

She nods and swiftly eddies her hand in the space between them, hearing the urgency in his voice, and creates a portal of air. She slips within the folds of iridescent fractals and is gone.

Thrusting the shower lever upward, he steps into the frigid blast of water with Gabrian still nestled in his arms, and settles onto the shower floor, letting the downpour of icy pellets work their Magik against the feverish heat.

Tynan feels his niece flinch in his arms as her flesh reacts, but instead of cooling her off, her own Magik rebels against the assault and ignites in a multitude of intense heat waves. Each surge increases in temperature as it hits and turns every droplet of water into steam, sizzling on contact, and hazes the air around him, coating the glass shower frame with its clinging vapors.

Tynan grits his teeth. His flesh feels the intensity of the battle raging inside of her and he begins to smell the stench of burning flesh—his. He cries out as the flames consume him. His eyes glaze over, but still, he refuses to falter. Panting and clenching his teeth, he releases a guttural growl as he bears down hard, jaws aching under the pressure.

His eyes roll back into his head, revealing the white stained with crimson streaks, as his skin blackens from the barrage of Egni Magik refusing to let go.

He cannot let go.

The cold bite of mist stings on his face and urges Tynan to opens his eyes. Water drips from his lashes as he stares upward. The fire within Gabrian's soul releases from her body and pulls away. The heat is gone. Tynan greets its departure with a loud exhale of relief and slumps back against the wall, slowing his breath, and looks down. His arms are charred and black but still clutching onto his niece who remains limp and pale in his hold.

*

Once more, the voice whispers within the darkness of Gabrian's mind, her body still and no longer aflame. "Surrender Derkaz." Her eyes shoot open, irises swirling of violet, and in the sting of black Magik exiting her soul, she screams as sizzling strings of purple toxins slither and snake across her then strike, choking her, smothering her, sucking at her life force. She struggles, kicking out and clawing at the invisible force strangling her within the darkness.

***

In the stillness, his senses detect something new as the room takes on an eerie purple glow, sifting through the haze of mist. The violet flare snuffs out the remains of Gabrian's red hue, bringing with it a stinging layer of painted toxic fumes that waft on the air and catch in Tynan's lungs. He coughs as they enter, searing his airway, making him gasp for breath. Tynan unbinds one of his arms and covers his mouth with his sleeve, pressing it tight against his face just as the watery air on the other side of the shower bubbles in front of him.

Shadows outside the shower door play tricks with his eyes, making him think help has arrived. But his sight is mistaken. Vaporish visions of Gargons harbor within their folds nearby, threatening to breech the Veil between Earth and Erebus as Gabrian's Magik thins the barrier between the two divides.

A swirl of light appears, mixing with the clouded dark vapor, and washes away bits and pieces of the Gargons' trickery. Vaeda steps out of the bend of air followed by Ethan and Arramus. An eruption of coughing takes over the silence as they cover their faces when they come into direct contact with the hovering toxins tainting the air.

Tynan suffers a breath and inhales to expel his warning to them. "Stay back. It is toxins of black Magik."

"Botah." A hushed word slips across Vaeda's lips, and immediately, she is transformed into sparkling dust while Ethan's body shivers. His flesh reacts to the attack, attempting to repair itself from the continual invasion of dark toxins.

Arramus releases his human form and shifts. His skin colours to an autumn hue, warming to his internal temperature, and melds his form into the fiery Magik that dwells within. He steps inside the bathroom on the tile floor, not as affected as the others by the deathly fog.

"What is going on?" Ethan croaks out between coughs.

With a shallow inhale, as the toxins seep into his mouth, Tynan replies, "I don't know." His words come out a chalky whisper under the duress on his vocal chords. "One minute she is burning up alive," he muffles out through the cloth in his sleeve, followed by a handful of coughs, "and the next thing I know, all of Erebus breaks loose." He coughs again, and stares at them through bloodshot eyes.

Vaeda's mirage glides closer to where Tynan and Gabrian lay, trying to assess the oddity of the situation, and she gasps, lifting her hand to cover her sound. The beautiful Shadow Walker she so desperately adores is merely no more than a shell of a man cloaked in sunken blacken skin that is wearing thin. Tynan's flesh shows of festers, puss oozing from them in the erosion of toxic mist seeping around them from Gabrian's form.

Tynan lifts his weary bloodshot eyes and sees all that he has become in Vaeda's gape, but he does not care about himself, only the child killing him in his arms.

***

"Surrender Isa," Gabrian hears in the void just before the slivers of soul-numbing pain tears through her limbs, and she lets out a pain-filled shriek.A bright pristine collage of whiten-blue shards of light burst forth across Gabrian's body, her violet swirl now replaced by a haunting and deep royal blue.

***

Arramus steps to the shower, feeling helpless to aid the Schaeduwe Guardian. Droplets of water from the shower sizzle and mist as they fall from the head. He turns to look at the mess of souls huddled on the floor of the tub, surrounded in a violet haze. Then it shifts colour as toxins withdraw, slowly dissipating and retreating from the chamber. The mist that clung to the glass walls around them whiten and scatter.

They reach for the glass, growing fingers as they vein out in an array of icy shards.

The walls become a canvas of Isa art. Layer by layer, it devours the room, burying it beneath an icy wrath as Gabrian's body sparks in a lethal borealis of Magik. Stalactites form under the soaking cloth draped across Gabrian's flesh and frozen crystals of whitened strings of Isa Magik attach to everything around her. Each and every droplet of water that had once run free is now captured and imprisoned, her uncle as well.

Tynan's blackened, tattered skin fades under the assault. Clutching hold of his flesh, it snakes rapidly all over his body, covering him in a web of ice, sharp and deadly. He bellows as the frost creeps into the crevasses of his wounds, digging deep and prying them apart as they expand within the cell of his existence. The coldness of death has taken a new shape. His skin, tendered from fire and unworldly toxins, cracks against the frozen kiss and tears at the seams, releasing crimson tell of the unspoken abuse.

The Elders are helpless to aid and only watch the display of violent chaos taking place within the frozen glass walls. Arramus pushes out a wave of his own fiery Magik in hopes to hold back the frozen cloak encompassing the shower, but it is no use. The warp of Isa Magik is too absolute. It feeds off of his attempt and thickens its assault on Tynan's prison.

As the warm crimson laces over the fractals of frozen life, banding together in his desperate claim to live, Tynan cries out. His voice is filled with a mixture of emotional and physical torment, and Arramus halts his aid. It is only making the situation worse.

*

The voice softly whispers once more in her ears, and she cries out, "No, no more, please." But her plea is lost within the void as hushed words are spoken. "Surrender Boragen."

A surge of energy bursts forth, in a speckled array of exit points all over her body. Her life force sways around her in a light, smoky cloak sheared by each spear of light. Tears leave a trace of her pain down the sides of her temples as she feels it depart her soul.

*

In the midst of Tynan's torment, Gabrian's eyes open almost in response to her uncle's plea. Her pupils dilate in a black rage. Her jaw drops and a wispy current of light grey smoke exits her mouth and rolls across her lips. It twists and winds in an elegant dance, closing in on her uncle.

Tynan's eyes narrow. He winces from the tyrant of pain ravaging him from within, watching the spectacle of illusions in front of him with uncertainty of what the hell will come next. Clutching Gabrian closer, he braces for the worst.

As the smoky aura floats and lingers across his mangled flesh, the sharp jagged edges of the constant pulsing pain eases and dulls, no longer tormenting from within. The barrage of constant torturous waves slowly subsides, smoke swirling and clinging to his tattered skin. The white frostbitten and broken crust darkens as heat is returned to the ends of his flesh. It meshes the crevasses and melds the cells back together, leaving nothing in its soothing wake but dried blood and a glistening path from his lids to his chin where Tynan's tears run freely down his face.

The room is silent. Eyes dart frantically over each other but no sound escapes to ease the void of noise. They jolt and cover their ears as pain shrieks from Gabrian's mouth, and she wrenches her body upright, rigid under her sudden duress. Her eyes flare out in a golden hue then dim again, shifting to an icy blue. Her head tilts to gaze at her uncle and she lifts her sallow hand to cup his chin. Pressing the edge of her lips to curl upward, she looks up at him, making his heart burst with pain.

He smiles back at her and starts to speak just as all colour bleeds out of her eyes. Nothing remains but a vacant cloud of blue as her body collapses once more into Tynan's arms. Gabrian's skin cracks and melts away in blisters and sores, pocketing with the puss of ruin. The weak grey aura flares timidly and returns itself to its owner before finally letting go of its hold on her—disintegrating before its master stiffens in one last shudder in the Schaeduwe's arms.

No aura, no movement. No breath.

Tynan roars, searing his throat with his angst and bounds up out of the shower, laying her body on the floor. Barely able to see her through his tears he yells out, "Ethan, help me."

Ethan rushes to the girl's side on the floor and lays his head over her chest, listening. Only the sound of one heart beats in his ears, his own. He stills himself and closes his eyes, searching. Rushing his mind to open to listen for her thoughts, hoping he grasps at fragmented memories— wishing they were real—but he shakes his head, finding nothing. He quickly draws energy strands from his hands and wraps them around her still form, over and over again but the girl's body does not respond to his gift.

Lifting his head to look upon a devastated Tynan, his lips tremble. "We will get her back, I promise!" Ethan's eyes are wild with fear as he rolls up his sleeves. "Even if we have to do this the old-fashioned way, I'll bring her back."

Tynan stands back and nods, letting Ethan have his space. His tears run and his fists pump, trying to contain his angst of a probable dark reality. Vaeda slips to his side and touches his fisted hands. It remains clenched but then releases and tenderly entwines around her touch, thankful for the gift she has given. She pats his arm then with one small tender squeeze, lets go and lowers to the floor beside Ethan now pumping hard against Gabrian's still heart.

Pinching Gabrian's nose she donates a special gift, breath of Zephyr.

Once.

Twice.

Three times Gabrian's chest is lifted.

Nothing.

"Ethan," Vaeda cries out, urgent to give life back to the girl below her. "It is not working, try again. Use your energy." She slides back, allowing Ethan to hover over where she had just shadowed as he readies for another attempt to start Gabrian's heart. This time, he surrounds his hands with his own life energy and readies it for impact on the compression.

*

Floating aimlessly with the darkness all around her, the weight of the toxins press the surface of her skin, searching for an opening to absorb her back into Erebus. There is no pain. She can hear the whispers, voices speaking riddles—not making any sense at all—but she doesn't care. It is peaceful again, and she smiles.

From the wall of darkness, a familiar voice pierces the stillness of silence as Rhada appears and whispers to her, "You must fight for it." The weight of knowing their meaning breaks her serenity.

Ethan pumps hard on her chest, sending a jolt of his life force behind it.

Her stomach dips as the blow hits her, and she begins to fall, sinking deeply into the darkness below, unable to stop it. Falling, falling, her arms sway at her sides, weightless in her descent. Her body flushes as a sudden rush of heat consumes her, growing warmer and warmer. It swallows her up and the air around her, feeling the flesh melting on her bones.

Wishing for air to reach her lungs, she remains still, unable to move but feels the fire so close. The sting of its teeth tears into her flesh, searing it, and flooding her with pain.

Ethan pumps her chest again, sending a larger bundle of energy with it.

Rhada speaks again as the blast comes, "You must fight for it, Gabrian."

The heat of the fire within her is lost in the blast, and she falls again, feeling the coolness of the void of fire. Her breath slows as she falls. Moist vapours shine and sparkle in the space above her, leaving white puffs of crystals in its place. The shrill sound of glass breaking pierces the silence as her body crashes through the divides of Magik slicing at her. Her mind screams out but her body remains still. No sound escapes her lips. It tears through her veins, stripping her of every ounce of Magik it had contained, and lets her fall once more.

"But you must fight for it." The words echo in her ears, over and over, and voices chant the words until they stick inside her head. Something shifts within her. A sweet scent catches in her nose—the smell of grass, of summer blossoms, of life.

There is so much white essence clouding around her, that it tempts her, scattering her thoughts with the sting inside of the unrelenting pain of hunger. Her smoky grey aura swirls madly around her, sealing in all the pain, all the suffering, and all the chaos within. And she falls again, within the void, suffocated with silence, and floats aimlessly into the darkness.

There is no pain. There is no Magik rippling within her veins, only loneliness.

The pull of sadness drapes on her skin, clinging to it and seeping into her heart, twisting inside her chest. The taste of its bitterness bores through her. It is real sadness. Gabrian's lips quiver as faces of her life float by, each one pulsing with an aching devotion to her heart, tender smiles of the taken, and all those who still remain in wait of her return.

But you must fight for it.

Rhada's words caress her and she stills within the memories of all that she has lost, all she has been through, all that could be. Tears trickle down, warming her temple once more as she mouths the words, "But I must fight for it."

Ethan grits his teeth and lends a large drain of his life force in his hands as he strikes down on Gabrian's chest once more. "Come on, Gabrian, fight!"

Sharp pain jolts through Gabrian as the bottom of her world drops once more. Air rushes into her lungs, and she gulps, feeling life violently thrust back into her body. Claws of mortality tear through, assaulting her vision as her eyes rush open, back from the subtle hues of the underworld and into the light of day.

Chapter Four

Sorting through the Wreckage

"There is something not right with the child." Ethan rubs the stubble of his shadowed jaw, slowly treading a path in the pine floor of Gabrian's home. He glances every few moments out the French doors at the ocean as if seeking its counsel for the phenomenon resting quietly in her bed upstairs.

Tynan meets his words with a growl from the kitchen above. "She is alive, Ethan. That is all that matters." The words are edged in warning as they slip over the Schaeduwe Guardian's lips. After all they went under and witnessed of the girls return, her existence, in whatever form, is a blessing—one of which Tynan ensures to make them understand.

"Yes, of course it is," Vaeda coos, lightly touching the side of his arm with the hopes of stilling the nerves of her affections. "I think Ethan is just concerned for her wellbeing as we all are."

Tynan's eyes shoot her a cool glance, thinking no one here can even come close to understanding what the magnitude of her existence means. She is all he has left in this world. She may not be of blood but by the spirit of the Realm, she is his family by choice, a choosing just as important to him if not more so.

Ethan stops his miniscule journey in front of the French doors to address Tynan's concern. "All I am saying is, something is off. She is in there. I know she is. I have felt her mind." Rushing his fingers through his peppered hair, he turns to consult the ocean again. "It is just that she has no traceable aura."

"But isn't that a trait of your Boragen Fellowship anyway?" Arramus hums, entering into the conversation from the corner chair of the living room. "A part of your cloaking ability to mix in, undetected, with the humans? That was Gabrian's first telling of being part of the Realm. Maybe that is all that has happened. She is cloaking herself, a survival instinct of sort."

Ethan peeks at the large Egni Elder over his shoulder. "To mix in and take on the colour of humans is one thing, to not have an aura at all is quite another."

"I have no aura," Tynan admits lifting his cup to his lips and eyes the others, still stiff from angst riling within his soul. "Maybe somehow the Magik has shifted in her from the horrific ordeal she has just suffered. Maybe the ancients have graced her with our Magik."

"Maybe," Ethan mumbles, letting out a sigh and returning to the ocean. "I honestly do not know. The girl has been through hell and back, literally, and it shows on the shell her soul now wears. But what I do know is, the Gabrian who has returned to us from Erebus, is not the Gabrian who entered in."

Chapter Five

At the Garden Gate

A vaporish form appears just beyond the garden gate. His face is void of the usual pompous smirk instead appearing sullen, marked with concern. With no way to find information, and no way into the house, Adrinn lurks at the edge of the wards Cera had placed around her home and hopes for a miracle. "You must be alright. I need you, Gabrian," he whispers into the shadows and fades into the night.

Chapter Six

Mirror, Mirror

Tynan enters the room and draws near the bed. His mouth smiles, but his eyes glaze over with dew as he looks at Gabrian. Gently reaching out, he tucks a strand of loose hair behind her ear and cups her cheek. "How are you feeling?"

Gabrian peeks at him through strained eyes. The light hurts. It stings her pupils but refusing to lay in darkness anymore, she had asked her uncle to leave open the curtains beside her bed. She forces a smile. The simple act punishes her with pain, but she cannot let him see it or he will make her drink the vile-tasting muddy tincture Kaleb brings fresh to the house every day. "I am good," she croaks out over a raw throat. "Much better today," she lies.

Gabrian sees *all* the truth in her uncle's eyes each and every time he enters her room.

"Can I get you anything?" Tynan sweeps the room, his eyes tracing over every detail of it. He has kept it immaculate—no dust, no clutter, and everything is pristine, way better than she ever kept it—but that was typical of him. "Or are you hungry? I can bring you up something, I just..."

"No, I am fine, Uncle Ty." She breathes out, triggering a slight coughing fit from the small depletion of oxygen in her lungs.

Her body is a wreck. She has been lying in this bed in this room for what seems like an eternity and her recovery is slow—deathly slow. But Ethan and Kaleb both assure it is to be expected from the otherworldly travels she had gone on. A round trip to Erebus and back is excruciatingly hard on one's body, not to mention soul.

Lifting from the side of her bed, Tynan straightens her covers and nods, his mouth still holding strong to his façade and gentle smile. "Alright then, I will be back in a while to check..." He stills his words and corrects them. "...to see if you need anything."

Gabrian plays his game, mirroring the same pressed smile as his, and glances around the room, spying something. "Oh, could you pass me my journal?" she squeaks out. Nearly bored silly within the walls of her confines, the thought of maybe expelling a little of the internal garbage whirling around in her head may aid in the healing process—at least it couldn't hurt.

Tynan hurries himself back inside her space and returns to her side. Reaching out across the bookshelf, he retrieves her leather-bound journal and sets it on her lap. "Now, don't tire yourself out, okay?"

Seriously? How can writing in a book tire someone out? Gabrian mutters internally but after he leaves, she understands and swallows her sharp words completely. Her fingers ache to the bone only after a few seconds of pressing the pencil to the paper. Just writing the date is a chore. Dropping her grip on the pencil, she drops her hand and lets it rest on top of the scribbling. "What the hell happened to me?"

Grinding her teeth and letting her stubbornness kick in to take over the fight against the soreness of her digits, Gabrian begins to write.

I used to believe that everything happens for a reason, but today, when I awoke, my beliefs faltered.

SILVER

Once I lived in what I thought was happiness and moderate success in life, but found it only to be a façade of the reality that was waiting for me, leaving me unguarded and vulnerable.

Being the human, I thought I was, I fought to get back up, to punch my way through the best I could, using human faith that some higher power was helping me through.

But I am not human, nor was I ever.

My existence is an atrocity to anyone who comes near.

The parents who raised me are dead.

My rightful birth parents—well, they might as well be for the convoluted mess that is.

My heart has never been so weary and without hope, and without Shane. I am the reason my shadow has fallen. I cannot even begin to express in words how much I long for the subtle scent of summer. All I have left are the torturous memories of what I have done and this shelled soul that was left behind.

I should be grateful that I am alive, but I cannot even find a fraction of that in the fact my hopes to return to a life, a body without Magik, have come true. I am buried alive too far down within a world which requires the cursed Magik to survive.

I feel cold. I feel alone.

I have become a ghost amongst the living.

Under the slow but constant pressure, Gabrian's fingers burn. Setting the pencil down on her mental scribblings, she flexes them to ease their strife. Licking her lips, dry from mouthing the words as she writes them down, she reaches for the cup on the nightstand.

Empty.

Needing a drink, but not wanting to burden her uncle with her needs, Gabrian clutches the glass and slowly slides her legs to hang over the edge of the bed. Biting her lip, she fights through the heavy ache and soreness of her inactivity. She does not even know how long it has been since she actually moved. All she knows is that her body is blatantly rebelling against the act, sending slivers of sharp pain through her appendages and back as she moves.

Sliding forward and touching her toes to the floor, Gabrian readies herself to make the estimated ten step journey to the bathroom in search of some tap water. The absence of any kind of activity has wreaked havoc on her physical condition. Each step, calculated and slow, wrenches at her back and her calf muscles are taut, threatening to cramp. Gabrian can already see white orbs of vertigo dancing in her eyes as she closes in on her destination.

Eight. She reaches the doorway, clinging to its frame.

Nine…only one more step. Her hand braces the wall beside her.

And…ten.

Gabrian sets down the cup and grasps tight against the porcelain base. Though panting, she cheers, coughing out her victorious feat in reaching the faucet.

Turning the tap, her tongue feels heavy and thick as she anticipates the taste of the cool liquid soon to be captured. Raising the half-filled glass to her mouth, Gabrian catches a glimpse of something unrecognizable, a distorted image, and freezes, horrified by what stares back at her from the mirror.

Chapter Seven

Unveiled Deception

Buzzing whispers hiss around the walls of the High Table. Those who remain of the Elders is bleak to not only the Elders themselves but the Realmsfolk crowding into the Covenant of Shadows. Never before has such devastation occurred from within the very foundations of the Realm's hierarchy.

"Cimmerian Cole, please rise," Orroryn growls out. His words boom across the hall, bouncing off the marble walls encompassing them and destroying the sting of hisses that bite at his ears from the onlookers. He clutches at the large table, bearing the weight of his turmoil within his grasp, and his olive fingers pale in his conviction to stay in control.

Of all of whom he thought he could trust in this world, it was the Elders of the High Table and now two of them have been brought to stand judgement in front of their peers for unthinkable sins against their own kind.

Even the ex-Elder Caspyous was an unlikable man at times, in a million years, Orroryn would never have guessed that he would to succumb to such murderous acts—in cold blood no less—yet he did. And now, Cimmerian, a level-headed, by the book, peer and friend is rising to stand before him to be heard for his crimes against humanity, against Orroryn's most sacred and protected world. Madness unleashes within Orroryn's already broken heart.

Cimmerian does as commanded and lifts his eyes to the Elders staring back at him from around the table, the table he had sat by for two thirds of his life and swore to defend its honour right along with those who sat there now as his equals.

And now he stands before them in judgement.

His heart had led him to his own destruction. Pushed to deception by a venomous fiend in addition to being hell bent on getting his own way, Cimmerian became blinded of his own sworn oath to manifest the wants of the heart.

He knows all these ugly truths.

"How do you find yourself to the charges of cohering with a known Vampire, a criminal of the Realm?" Orroryn stares at him, hurt and broken from the deception, but doesn't move from his position.

Cimmerian holds his chin high, ashamed of the company he had kept but resolute to his reasoning for committing the act. "Guilty," he offers with a low admitted plea.

Buzzing echoes through the walls at his reply. "How do you find yourself to the charges of kidnapping a daughter of the Realm and holding said child captive until her demise due to neglectful judgment of magical misconduct?"

He swallows back the bite of remorse pinching off his wind as his mind replays the nightmare which unfolded at his hands and the resulting anguish he had caused her. Cimmerian shuffles and forces his chin to remain in place. "Guilty."

Gasps echo in unison from the people. Orroryn gathers himself for what he is about to ask. "How do you find yourself to the charges of willingly opening an unauthorized portal to Erebus and allowing a youngling to enter into its..." His voice breaks, and a tear escapes down his cheek. He tries to refrain from leaving his post as co-holder of the table to rush forward to shake the very life out of his peer for his selfish wants and disregard for safety. This was his son, this was his life. How could Cimmerian do this? But he does not move. Even though Orroryn understands the reason why he did it, it still does not excuse the Elder's actions. Clearing his throat, he continues. "…into its uncharted borders alone… un-warded no less?"

Cimmerian flinches at this, and his eyes search the Elders for understanding. "Guilty," he grunts out.

Tears unleash over Orroryn's cheeks, causing many eyes at the table to glaze over. So many lives are involved, so many undoings have been done. It is such a shame to watch the Covenant being broken apart by matters of the heart. Unfortunately, most desperate measures which cause a soul to lose its moral conviction are indeed committed at the mercy of a heart's claim to sanity.

Vaeda wipes the dew from her eyes, thinking of Tynan—who refuses to leave his niece's side—and resigned from his post temporarily until she is well enough. Vaeda feels the pain resonating off of not only Orroryn but Cimmerian as well in their undying devotion and love for their children. "For the love of the Realm, Cimmerian, what would make you folly in your judgement like that? You know the creatures that harbor between the divides of Erebus. You know there was likely no return from such a journey."

The Elder's weepy gaze irritates Cimmerian's already fragile façade. He was lied to. Not only by Adrinn, who had upped the ante of the game to get him to play, but by the Elders as well. She had no right to look upon him with pity or righteousness.

"I beg your pardon, but in my defence, Lady of Zephyr, brothers of Schaeduwe and Boragen, I was not properly informed of the situation I was put under." His eyes no longer simmer in sadness but in bitterness of their betrayal. "I was directed to do his bidding. The boy, Shane, released upon me the indisputable decree of the Guardian of the Silver

Bloodline. As oath taker and Elder of the High Table, I was not at liberty to challenge him. Orders, governed by supreme chain of command, are followed orders."

The gasps overtake the room and the hall fills with the uproar of uncoherent broken questions. This knowledge of utmost secrecy between Orroryn, Vaeda, Ethan, Ariah, and Cimmerian was out, unable to be pulled back in. All the lies that had been spoken, hiding the real truths of the skeletons kept so neatly locked in the closets for so long, had been released from their captivity—unveiled and ugly for all of the Realm to see.

Vaeda and Orroryn bow their heads under the weight of their own guilt. He is right, and they know it—he had no other choice or risk further conviction to his crimes. "Your uncontested admittance of guilt is clearly noted and will bode well for our final judgement against you," Vaeda hums out her speech, cupping her hands on the cold table in front her. Her eyes smoothly dart around the High Table, regarding the other Elders as they shuffle in their chairs and eye each other as she delivers her final judgement.

In her peripheral, she catches the nodding heads of the Realmsfolk mumbling their approval in the background. "Due to the severity of your crimes, Cimmerian Cole, you must be held accountable." Vaeda straightens, willing herself to continue. "We as the Elders of the Covenant of Shadows charge you guilty for crimes against the innocent of the Realm. That being said, due to the revelation of new circumstances brought to light, another trial is necessary to be held at a later date in order to revise the severity of the sentence carried out. You will be held until further notice."

A cloak of Guardians step out from their positions and clasp hold of the back of Cimmerian's arms. He gasps, voicing a heart-wrenching plea, "My daughter! What about Symone? I just got her back, and I cannot leave her! She needs me."

The sadness rings out through his broken voice, and they all sink within his desperation. "We understand your concern, but you are to be immediately escorted to the hollows of the Shadows." Orroryn glances once at his peer and lowly utters his reply. "Rest assured, she will be housed, cared for, and taken under our protection as she is a daughter of the Realm."

Cimmerian releases a loud sigh, aching to look at her face just once more before incarceration but will not contest. She is back, safe and sound. There will be no more lies, no more conspiracy games, and the devil he sold his soul to can rot in the deepest holes of Erebus for all he cares.

Chapter Eight

From Within the Monster

Jolted by the sight of the creature staring back at Gabrian through the mirror, the glass drops from her hand and shatters against the porcelain basin. Meeting the reflection of what is left of the body she possesses grips her in a trance.

Her eyes, clouded in a blue mist set deep within purple sockets, are fixed upon sunken grey cheeks. Her lips, chapped and crusted, are merely two chalky lines painted across her mouth. A tarnished yellow and brown hue creeps up to cling on her flesh at the edge of her collarbone. Pulling the neck of her nightshirt down, Gabrian gazes at the fading black bruises given to her by Ethan's violent and determined efforts to start her heart again.

Her wide, unearthly eyes skate upward, bypassing the frightening horror that is her face, and freeze on the scattered clumps of hair—or what remains of it on her scalp. Each piece is connected by red, cracked scar tissue.

Tynan's pitiful stares strike her and the way his mouth quivers when he speaks, his continuous referral to her as a survivor. Gabrian is numb. She doesn't see a survivor. All she sees is a monster looking back at her.

SILVER

Her hand lifts to touch the edge of a fallen strand of hair—one last effort to feel, to see if it is real—and she hopes it is just a nightmare she can wake up from. A hue of crimson drapes her wrist, colouring the pale canvas of her paper-thin flesh and catches her attention from the glass horror show.

Gabrian pulls her arm in close.

Blood.

A small deep gash running crossways on her wrist is the culprit of the colour works. She stares at it with dull eyes, consumed in a messy mental state numbed by the reality that is her life. Once more, she dances from one hideous feature to the next, feeling empty and undone. Dropping her eyes to the mess of glass and blood growing in the sink below, she reaches down. Her fingers gather around a shard of crimson-painted glass. Once more, she looks up and eyes the useless creation gawking back at her from the other side of the mirror. Gabrian turns her back to it and slides down to the floor, the painted shard still in hand.

Tears well up in her eyes, blurring her messy world within smeared colours. Gabrian's heart pounds under her ribs. The sound of it drums in her ears, drowning out the world around her as she lowers her lids, releasing the levy of moisture on the edges of her lashes.

Within the whirling chaos of her mind, a familiar voice whispers to her from the darkness—a faint, familiar voice from the shores of Erebus, calling her back, filled with a promise to ease her pain, to end this suffering. Gabrian's fingers tighten around the glass dagger, its edges pressing into her skin.

She remembers the beauty within the depths of Erebus, the peace she felt walking along its shores. No pain, no stares of pity, no helplessness and hideousness to deal with, just soft words and unrelenting waves of love and kindness from beyond. Her cheeks glisten with the bounty of her pain as it escapes from within her soul. Gabrian hears another murmur of encouragement, a sweeter song of beckoning, and a subtle nudge to leap toward what she knows awaits on the other side of that blade.

This is not about the loss of her beauty, nor the absence of her Magik. It is deeper than that. She has become something weak, a burden on the hearts of those who love her even more than she had been before. Gabrian's heart plummets to the edge of no return, lingering in despair as she pictures her uncle's face, remembering the empty caskets of her parents, clutching to the pain on Shane's face when she pushed him away.

No more.

She pinches her shaky hand on the bloodied glass. There would be no try, no cry for help, just an end to this silent misery. Opening her eyes, she wipes the blur from her vision enough to see the crimson tell of her opening to the other side. Gabrian's lips tremble but the decision is made. Inhaling a slow deep breath, she presses the glass into the wound. Angling it a way that will ensure the deepest and deadliest cut, she bears down and readies to set everyone free from her curse.

"This is not who you are."

Gabrian gasps, and hurriedly wipes the tears away, clearing her vision.

She is not alone.

Chapter Nine

Heart to Heart

Still clutching her means of escape tightly in her hand, Gabrian whips her head around. The embarrassing sting of being watched in her darkest hours jars her back from its depths and interrupts the call from the dark side of her mind—muting Eva's sweet beckoning.

Blinking away her tears, she swipes away the remainder of the blurry film distorting her view with the back of her bloodied arm, leaving a streak of rouge to stain her face. Gabrian pinches her eyes in search of the intruder. From the corner of the bathroom, leaning against the wall, stands the tall blond-headed Rhada wearing a narrowed gaze of worry.

Gabrian snuffs at the moisture running from her nose and stares at him blankly. The depth of her despair numbs her concern for her blood-soaked appearance. "What are you doing here? Am I dead again?" she drones out, confused.

Lowering, Rhada clutches her bleeding wrist and points it to face her so she can see it clearly then raises his eyes to meet her dismal stare. "Is this really what you want?"

Gabrian looks away from him and the bloodstained skin. Trails of her sins run onto the floor in front of her and what she was about to do. Her fingers still clutch to the glass in her other hand. "I…" she whimpers and tears return to wash down her cheeks, rushing to her trembling lips. "I just want to stop the misery my existence seems to cause everyone I love. And this pitiful excuse of a body." Her voice spikes, trembling as she waves her bloody hand over her form. "Just look at me. I am nothing, useless to help anyone. I have no Magik. My return is causing more suffering than if I would have just let go." Her voice trails off into a mumble.

"My dear child." Rhada twists his lips to curl into a gentle smile and softly grips her hand. "Your last breath on this Earth was taken weeks ago. That Gabrian has walked upon the shores of Erebus. The girl I look upon now has been reborn, a child of the Universe untangled and stripped clean from the mess you were first brought under and made whole again, untainted and pure. Your return from the mist changed things, surely you must have felt it. You and your gifts, would not be as they once were before."

She nods, remembering the pain, and hears her Uncle's cries as he held her along with her own screams as it all came undone. "I know, but I didn't think it would be like…" She lets her head fall back, inhaling a quivering breath. Tears fill her eyes, distorting the sharp edges of the reality around her. "…like this."

She lifts her head and peers through her blurry eyes to look at Rhada's form still kneeling in front of her. Even through her blurred vision, she still sees the pity in his stare. "I can see what I am in your eyes. Even Uncle Ty can barely stand to look at me."

She remembers why she decided to return but cannot grasp what good she can do for the world like this. She is nothing. Especially in a world built of Magik. Even though she had wished for so long to just be normal again, a non-Magikal human being again, she is empty without it. Her mind is too quiet, deafening almost. Gabrian's world seems too big for the pathetic shell of a ghost she had returned as.

"You told me I was needed, convinced me to come back to help. How can something so pitiful be of any good to anyone?"

Rhada grins, his eyes sparkling with hope. "You must try to understand that you, your gifts, will not be as they once were before."

"But that is just it. I have no gifts at all," Gabrian tries to say but her words are garbled, caught in her upset and tripping on her dismay. "I heard them all talking. I don't even have an aura anymore."

Her body tremors under her duress, sobs breaking her words into pieces of high-pitched whimpers that are barely comprehensible. The dark burden of her despair sinks in her chest, pulling her down into a dark well of sorrow. "At least if I am gone, everyone I plague can mourn then move on with their life. I would no longer be a hindrance to anyone."

Rhada lifts a hand to cup her cheek, thumbing away the moisture falling, fed by her misery. "You, my dear, are nothing of the sort." He leans in to place his soft warm lips on her forehead, gently cupping the back of her head, and kisses her. Leaning back and looking her straight on, he continues his plea. "You are a miraculous and wondrous seed in waiting. All you need is a place to grow and a little hope does not hurt either," he softly hums and rises to his feet, gathering a small towel from the top of the sink and lowers himself again.

Laying the cloth over the open wound, he presses gently, holding it onto her wrist. "Do not dwell upon what lies on the surface. You must seek solace deep within. Everything else is of little concern."

Letting go of her wrist, Rhada makes an obvious glance to her other hand and notices the shard of glass still tightly bound within her fingers before rising to his feet.

Gabrian watches her friend, desperate and wanting to absorb some of the faith he has so openly expressed in her importance. "Find your hope, Gabrian," he whispers to her once more, his voice fading into a hollow echo.

"Rhada, wait…" she chokes out, but he is no more. Only her will is left to keep her company. The darkness which offered to consume her is wiped away as a band of mental light flips the switch on within her, subsiding the wave of sorrow she was drowning in. The uncharacteristic impulse no longer carries any weight as she stands up from the floor and throws the shard of glass into the garbage.

Gabrian turns to stare down the reflective monster looking back at her and glares at it. Turning on the tap, she places her wrist under the rush of cold water, slowing the bleed, and clears the mess of her moment of darkness away down the drain. She replaces the bloodied hand towel with a new one and lays it across her wrist then searches under the sink for the first aid kit to bandage up the cut.

A white cloth wrap decorates her arm and Gabrian grins at it, pleased enough with her handiwork. She cleans the sink from the debris of her almost self-inflicted tragedy. Once unsoiled, she splashes her malformed face with the brisk spray of water and pats it dry with a clean cloth, forcing herself to face the unsettling reflection in the mirror—to look past the surface and seek the soul waiting within.

Gabrian's heart drops as the two meet and cringes for a moment. Her mind reels to the last time she stared this hard into the looking glass with so much turmoil. It seemed like a lifetime ago.

Maybe it was.

She is not the same girl she knew then, nor the same soul. All she knows is that she chose to stay and so stay she shall even from within a monster's shell.

Chapter Ten

On the Loose

Feeling the pressure beneath her fragile façade building, Gabrian wipes the dew blurring her vision and hobbles to her closet with a new determination and a new desire. The smell of stale sweat mixed with the coppery scent of her indiscretion reeks from her pajamas, nearly gagging her, so a quick change of clothes is in order.

Slowly riffling through her belongings, she pulls on a pair of grey track pants, a white tee, and her black hoodie. Easy as pie but the socks give her a battle. Gabrian sits on the side of her bed, breathless and nearly exhausted.

"This is ridiculous," she huffs, the pounding of her pulse thudding in her ears. She had remained still for far too long; it's time to get back to plain old Gabrian, and back to the girl she knew before the Realm had claimed her. She may not have any Magik but she still has her hell-bent stubbornness and her brains, and they scream at her to gather her life back, to sort out a plan and to run.

Even if it means shuffling her decrepit remains of a body down the road only a couple feet, she needs to claim back her life, step by step. Hurrying as best she can before Tynan returns, she changes the bandages on her arm, giving the cut a bit more padding in case it opens. Gabrian glances one last time in the mirror. Inhaling a deep defiant breath, she glares at her reflection and points to the monster staring back. "This isn't over," she growls, turning her back to it. "Not by a long shot."

Grabbing a toque from the top shelf of the closet, she slips it on over the patchwork of hair on her head and stands pondering a dilemma just brought to mind—her uncle Ty. Her self-designated babysitter, who is all consumed in his pity and protection for her well-being, no doubt will protest her wanting to go from bedridden mess to instant athlete needing to leave the house for a run. Without question, this is going to be a no go.

Her eyes dart around the room and she taps a bony finger against her chalky pale lips, trying to conjure up a plan of action. A loud caw destroys her silent pondering, not to mention scaring the crap out of her. Her heart nearly jumps out of her chest. On the ledge of her window, in his finest black suit, sits her trusty stalker.

No, not a stalker, not any longer.

He is her friend.

He had come to sit there every day since her return.

Her heart warms, thawing the ice that had encased and hardened it. Theo's ebony sheen drapes in a prismatic silhouette against the low setting sun, bringing her eyes to water and a sprig of joy to dance in her soul, urgently aware of how much this black-winged bird has been a life line. Theo's shiny black beak taps gently on the pane of glass separating them. His head tilts as he gazes at her, watching and waiting on her.

"Hmm," she hums twisting her lips into a crooked grin, eyeing the bird. "Clever bird, aren't you?"

Theo has just given her the answer.

The window.

Her uncle is soon to make his rounds with an offering to bring her some soup and everything else under the sun to make her more comfortable. Gabrian knows she must make a quick exit, severing any possibility of his interference in her grand scheme of escape.

Turning the latch on the top of the window and lifting the frame from the bottom, her biceps ache. Her forearms threaten to force a strike and quit but she grits her teeth and pulls with all her might upward on the old pane of glass, hoping it will give and trying hard not to make too much noise. Theo rattles a happy gurgle and jumps from the ledge, flying off to the nearest branch to take up his watch there.

The window creaks and she groans in her strife to open the stubborn pane but she lets out a curse, pressing her last remains of energy into her efforts, and finally, it gives in to her demand with a quick release and a face-plant by Gabrian into the half-lifted glass.

"Bugger, bugger, bugger," she hisses, rubbing the ache now burning across her cheek and into the bridge of her nose. Blinking away the pain, she grins just the same at her success. The security of the window has been breached and it is now open. A delightful waft of fall's warm breath brushes over her flesh, tickling on the way by as it waltzes through the opening of the window into her room and washes away the oxygen-deprived air around her, cleansing it.

Gabrian cannot help filling her lungs with the gift, inhaling deep enough to make her cough. Unhealthy and tired lungs are to fault. Cheating death of its claim comes at a price. And with no Borrower Magik to heal her this time, Gabrian's journey to recovery is going to be a long one but she is ready.

With one last peek over her shoulder at her room, Gabrian's hands tremble a bit. For the first time in her life, the absence of security is now profoundly all around her. Her level of courage dips as she moves forward. A longing for her mom and dad's gentle watch, for the warm blanket of Shane's arms around her, even her uncle's constant check-in's that smother her in the knowledge of the perverse mess her life is tightens the strings of muscles in her shoulders in her vast awareness of how the world really is.

The void is maddening, biting at her from the inside, and so she makes good on her attempt at escape. She slides her small body through the frame of her window and grips the side of the ledge, looking down at her dangling limbs. *Do it, Gabrian, let go. It's not that far.* Her fingers give way before her mind does. The eight-foot drop hits hard as the ground rushes up to meet her and crumples her into a searing ball of mess below the window.

Son of a—that hurt.

An encouraging caw from above helps remind her why she is there and suffering. Gabrian blinks away the tears blurring the world and pushes the pain jolting through her body into fuel for her mission. Edging up onto her elbow, Gabrian lifts her skeletal form from the ground and rolls her weight over onto her legs. Pressing her hands on her knees, she pants through the masochistic discomfort until it slows.

Gabrian gathers in her breath, slow and steady. The clean scent of rain clinging to the damp air is sweet and refreshing but warns of what is to come, giving her the cue it is time to go.

If she manages to get away and do this, there is no more looking back. It is time to take control, human style. Lifting to her feet, she brushes off the cluster of twigs and bits of leaves scattered over her clothing. Hearing echoes of footsteps taping upon the stairwell from inside the wall of the cottage, she curses. *Crap, it is now or never.*

Gabrian scuttles forward across the lawn. Her body fights against the first few steps but she manages to shuffle her way to the main road and onto the sidewalk. Stopping to catch her breath, she meets the horrified gawks of two frightened pedestrians hurrying to get away from her. The strange reaction punches her in the chest, making her hands lift to touch her face. Gabrian forgot she must look like nothing short of a monster out of a horror film.

Gabrian's heart sinks but only for a moment. A disgruntled barrage of caws aimed at the hurried walkers makes her look up and grin. "I know, right? Maybe they are not big horror movie fans," she jests, glancing over her shoulder at them.

They snicker under hushed tones, staring back at her over their shoulders like she is some crack pot on the loose, and standing in broad daylight making conversation with the local ravens no less.

An approving cackle forces her to grin even more, but there is no need in giving everyone a heart attack or reason to be afraid of her, not to mention a dead giveaway of her location to her jailer. She tugs the edge of her toque down to set on the bridge of her nose, just hovering above her eyes, and pulls the top of her hoodie up over her head.

Time to do what she has run away to do.

With every hit her foot makes with the earth, it jars through her. Gabrian's mind whispers pleas for her to stop the madness but lets her stubbornness kick in and take over her will, muting out the negative influence bouncing around in her head. She pushes herself to just take one more step, then the next, then the next, then it happens.

She remembers what comes next.

Her muscles begin to respond, pushing away the sluggishness of the decaying slumber, drowning her painful memories with it.

Chapter Eleven

Beach Bound

After a couple miles of Gabrian's therapeutic rhythm, she feels the endorphins take over and she lets them, gratefully getting lost in their powerful healing. A loud honk blasts from a passing truck, bursting her bubble of serenity with a sharp jolt to her nerves. She jumps sideways, losing her footing on the side of the road, and tumbles down into the ditch.

Physically and emotionally a tangled mess, Gabrian struggles to reclaim her control. Upside down and resting in a damp mess of brush with the ditch looming above her, she lies still, listening to the sound of concern-filled shrieking caws from above that accompany the rapid thud of her pulse pounding in her ears.

She lays still for a moment, tired. Her body aches to remain unmoved. Taking in a large breath of air, she rolls to her side, feeling a sharp tug on her head that holds her in place. Gabrian's hand searches for her captor and realizes she must find a way to unravel what remains of her hair from the sharp clutches of brush.

A cool wetness on her scabbed head from her bony hands covered with mud, makes her sigh, trying to be thankful it is not blood. She stares at the fragility of her hands, twisting them in front of her as the endorphins slow her euphoric state, and she resurfaces back to the real world, pulling free what remains of her hair from the bushes.

Detangled, she sits upright. A damp breeze kisses at her bare scalp, sending a shiver through her. Her muddied fingers graze over exposed tuffs of hair and she searches the brush to find a group of dogwood switches proudly displaying her wears. Concerned rattling caws draw her attention to the side of the ditch where a very distraught ebony stalker inquires of her wellbeing. Retrieving her borrowed toque and placing it back on her head, she sits quietly among the brush.

"I am okay, Theo. It's gonna be okay," Gabrian's voice trails off into a whimper as she buries her head in her hands. Her body trembles as tears well up in her eyes. Her mind whirls through images of varied painful memories, devouring her newfound determination and shoving it back down into her darkened vortex of chaos. The heaviness of her mere mortality is all too clear.

How could she miss the Magik and all it entailed? How? She is back, a human girl with just her brain to take on the world. This is what she wanted. Why in the hell is she so sad?

Her heart spikes with adrenaline and her veins sting, making her want to tear her skin off. No longer able to stand the consumption of self-pity, she growls, frustrated, and forces herself to her feet. "Ugh, there is no Magik. Okay? It is gone, so get over yourself," she scolds and pushes her legs to move forward, digging her way out of the ditch. "Stop. Being. A. Victim!" she yells out and darts forward as fast as her wobbly legs will allow down the side of the road, hoping to convince herself—hoping to outrun her fears—and praying to whatever higher power listens to her. She will find the hope Rhada told her to find.

Unsure of how long she has been running, obsessed and clinging to the hypnotic rhythmic of steps in her search, Gabrian sees a clearing in the trees up ahead and heads for it. Her steps slip, dragging from exhaustion. She is no longer running on fuel form her pent-up anger and feels eager to take a rest.

She staggers onto the soft cushion of worn dirt leading toward the beach. Golden grains of crushed sand crunch beneath her steps until she reaches the dark edges of the shore and drops down to her knees, denting the smooth surface under the weight of her fall.

Gabrian's heart pounds in her ears, keeping time with the soft rolling hush of the waves as they rush in to meet her, silencing her heavy breath and sending a gentle breeze to sooth her soul. She settles down on folded legs and lets her eyes drift unfocused, surfing the wakes of whitecaps as they line up to welcome her arrival. Gathering a few more deep breaths, her lungs relax, and her heart returns to a normal pace, silent once more beneath her chest.

The corners of her lips curl as she rolls back, relieving her legs of weight, and rests her backside on the sand. The familiar song of the water wraps her within a trick of time. Memories of a life lived so long ago, of dancing barefoot in this very sand, carefree and giggling, watched over by her ever-loving parents lingers. A hollow empty ache echoes all around her, longing for those stolen moments once more—a world where Gabrian's life made sense and her parents were still with her.

Pulling her knees up in front, Gabrian lays her head on her arms. She tries to create a safe place at the back of her mind—a place where it doesn't hurt so much—but today she does not have the strength to keep the memories at bay. She swings her arms out, pounding her fists into the sand, and yells out against the roar of the waves, releasing the last ounces of frustration. Tears smear the world once more, and she feels lost, alone, and very, very, human.

Once the levy of tears is empty, and having depleted every ounce of energy on feeling sorry for herself, the reality of Gabrian's overspending of her body's willingness to serve brings her back to the real world with a sharp sting. Blinking away the blurry remains of her self-loathing, she sees the repercussions of her jaunt and groans. "Great. Just great."

Untying the laces of the crimson-painted runners, she winces, slipping off the shoe to assess the damage that lies within. Skin that used to be seasoned for the constant pound against the asphalt is now a mess of torn flesh. The red show of blisters forming on the sides of her feet announce their mistreatment loud and clear.

She slips off the other shoe and notes its level of defiance thinking, *At least my wrist hasn't bled through its binding,* which releases an unhinged giggle to surface. *Nicely done, Gabrian.*

Sighing, she drifts once more over the water and pushes to her feet. Rolling the edges of her pants up to meet the sharp bony defines of her knees, Gabrian reveals thin skin covered with bluish veins. Wiggling her toes, covered in sand and blood, she steps into the water, waiting for the mighty Atlantic to cool and cleanse her aching feet.

She breeches the surface and waltzes further into the water. Her skin tingles in the salt-kissed openings of her wounds. Flesh pimples rise to the temperature of the water but not in the way she had expected. Instead of the bite of cool artic trails, she is met with strands of tempered bath waters, warm and inviting her in, urging her to step forward, and surround her entire body within its delicious embrace.

The enticement of the strange euphoric liquid clinging to her body pulls at her senses, each step rewarding her with a gift of pleasure the further she lingers into the deep dark water. No longer caring about getting her clothes wet, she wades out. Her body tingles, swooning to be engulfed entirely. Gabrian lowers her lids and allows herself to lose her inhibitions within the warm rapture.

In the soft lull of the rushing waves and the hushed whispers of the ocean wind, Gabrian retreats from her moment of bliss. A strange lyrical voice echoes clearly over the delightful white noise, beckoning her mind awake. Her eyes rush open and she twists in the water, searching across the harbor for the source of her disturbance. Something moves just ahead within the waves—a blurry mirage of light and darkness combined together.

Gabrian wipes at her eyes, a trickery of light, and blames the wetness in her vision for the strange mirage. Giving her head a shake and finding nothing, she shuts the world out once more, hoping to let the pull of the water caress her skin once more and return her to her newfound favourite place.

Denied.

The strange entanglement of sound, closer and even more adamant, strikes an irritation in her serene moment. She is jarred back to reality, studying her surroundings. "Is someone there?" she calls out, knowing in this Realm that anything which seems impossible is more than likely to be possible.

For the moment, alone in the water, she scans the surface to make sure. A sigh of relief escapes her and a frown forms from a little disappointment. After being exposed to so many wondrous things this last year, nothing really surprises her anymore.

She lowers her head and rests her eyes on the waves, watching the water as it laps up against her. Ragged strands of her hair brush along her face. A soft breeze skirts in off the water, racing with the small whitecapped waves. It carries a strange lyrical whisper to tickle against the inside of her ear.

"Ghee-Breah-In," the song sings.

She twists around quickly, heart lurching in her chest. Water swirls in her wake as she gasps, trying to dissect the strange call of her name over the rushing of the waves. Narrow eyes dart across the nothingness in front of her. She searches for any unexpected visitors but only sees the ebony mark of her faithful guide perched on a large piece of driftwood on the beach. She studies his expression, searching for any signs of upset or distress but he is still, watching her every move. Noticing her full attention on him, he sings out a gentle rumbling coo, an assurance that all is well.

Her heart slows, sure that Theo will alert her to any danger as he so faithfully has in the past. He is her black knight, her ever seeing eyes in the sky.

The uneasiness subsides and her lips curl into a smile as she turns back to the vast openness of the water and stumbles. She is not alone. Nope, she is very much indeed, not alone.

Chapter Twelve

Reunion of Souls

Escorted from the confines of his holding area, Cimmerian appears just outside of the Mount Desert Island Hospital in Bar Harbor, accompanied by two Guardians of the Realm. His palms sweat and his heart thrums as they make their way into the building. Their boots clack on the tile floor, announcing their arrival. He inhales gradually and slows his nerves, wanting to use his Magik to rush to her side.

But it is not allowed.

Under his sentence, he is to abstain from the use of Magik and hereby deemed mute as a mage. His overall admittance to the outside world will be judged in an upcoming trial, but for now, he is given special visitation rights due to the fragile state of his daughter's health. The Covenant of Shadows' Elders are dead set on him being punished for his crime but they are just. All who remain around the High Table have soft hearts that understand everything he has done. Cruelty is not part of their ruling and to deny him this would indeed be a cruelty.

Cimmerian hastens his steps, turning the corner of the hospital under the warning of the nurses to keep the visit quick. He will oblige the rules, all of them. From now on, there will be only his compliance to hopefully ease the judgement that will come down on him. Praying to the gods his time within the Hollows of the Shadows will be short, he is not sure how long he will be able to take the constant whining and complaining of Caspyous.

Rolling his eyes, and giving his head a good shake, Cimmerian pushes out the irritation in his mind when he reaches his destination. His heart lurches in his chest—the desire to look at her nearly kills him.

"You know the rules," the Guardian hums low and un-daunting as he places a hand on Cimmerian's arm.

The Elder stops, meeting his gaze, and nods in acknowledgement of the conditions laid down to the unsupervised visit. "Yes, thank you for bringing me, Morgan," he whispers, low and unruffled.

He has no desire to mess up his visitation rights nor cause anymore unnecessary stress. He just wants to make sure she is alright and be the father he has longed to be for the last twenty-six years.

Thrumming loudly under his ribs, Cimmerian's heart twists within his chest. A large dry lump in his throat chokes his breath as he pushes against the door. The monitor welcomes him as he slips inside the dimness but that is all. The girl he came to look at is still lost to this world, caught somewhere in the darkness between Earth and Erebus.

Wrapped in wires and tubes, Symone lays still under her blankets. Her skin is thin and blanched, her body frail, and her heart struggles to keep her blood moving within.

But she is here, he thinks and smiles. The tears well up inside of him and Cimmerian lets them fall freely—welcoming their company. His feet drag him across the room in a surreal state. His heart hopes his mind is not just playing a mean trick on him the way Adrinn has so many times in his dreams.

She looks so small and fragile. He reaches out and slips his fingers beneath hers, clasping them in his hands, and replaces their icy coolness with his warm tender offering. His salted lips quiver, shimmering and tear-stained as his eyes memorize her face before she becomes a blur of teary images.

Leaning in, the Elder presses his lips on her temple and whispers, "I am so sorry I failed you." Then he pulls away, shaking his head. His knees go weak and he wavers in his stance, clutching the side of her bedrail for support.

Glancing behind him, he finds a chair and releases her hand to pull it closer to the bed, sinking into it. Gathering her hand back in his own, his eyes lower, bracing his head in his other hand. The subtle familiar smell of a toxic tell—one he knows all too well—alerts him to the fact the Gargons have been here, sniffing around, waiting and wanting, as her health staggers between alive and nearing expiration.

Gritting his teeth with determination, his eyes light with a soft violet hue as does his hands. He promised the covenant he would not ignite his Magik but he cannot allow the Gargons to take from him the only thing that is worth risking his life for. Not again. Not if he has anything to say about it.

Careful not to emit too much, Cimmerian purses his lips and allows the violet strings of his gift to skirt down his legs and coat the floor beneath her bed. His eyes swirl as the Magik wriggles and curls around every edge of darkness within the room. Waves of violet snakes slither up his hand and dance across her flesh, giving her pale colouring a ghostly hue—a gift of protection against those who would snatch her up given the opportunity and pull her back from where she was stolen from.

Hearing footsteps just outside the door, the Guardian nearing to take him back to the Shadows, Cimmerian snaps his fingers and his eyes snuff out any trace of Magik within. The snakes still and fade into an invisible cloak of wards. He draws in a deep breath and exhales—releasing with it a quarter-century of hatred, sadness, and cruel intentions he burned to let free.

SILVER

A knock of three taps sounds just before the door inches open and a soft voice beckons to him that it is time to leave. Cimmerian nods and lifts from his chair, draping his lips over Symone's knuckles, and bids his child adieu with a soft kiss. His mouth, etched for years in folds of sorrow and darkness, now curves upward with soft edges that reach the gleam dwelling in his eyes.

His footsteps trace the path of his entry, stepping over the comforting wards he has cast, and stops at the open door. Peeking over his shoulder, and gathering one last glance at his lost child, he leaves behind the demons of his sins to drown in the wake of his hopeful future.

Cimmerian steps out into the corridor a free man.

Chapter Thirteen

I Am a River

Heart thrumming loudly under her ribs, sending spiky slivers of blood to rush through her tired veins, Gabrian stands face to face with nothing short of a beautiful nightmarish fiend. Unable to escape, and not entirely sure she wants to, she gazes at the form, caught somewhere between terror and complete awe.

With eyes blank and void, white like a snowstorm, the astral being stands unmoving and undaunted by her onlooker. As if guided, Gabrian continues to gaze into the deep emptiness of where her eyes should be. The void becomes filled with swirling light and millions of speckles begin to evolve, filling in the spheres on her face and deepening into an endless jaunt to her soul.

The creature's pale pink lips part, breaking the seal on her perfect and mythically-enchanted mouth. A spill of chaotic low-chiming hums escape on the wind.

Gabrian can only stare in wonderment at the fantastic creature slowly closing the space between them. Flowing sea-green hair intertwined with streaks of daybreak and sunset fire and soft glowing sun-kissed flesh dappled in shiny silver and teal scales scattered at the edges of her face and arms make up the creature—a spectacle of life fused by evolutionary magical bliss.

Gabrian's sense of awe quickly changes into fear. The figure draws nearer, breaching the external layer of her safety bubble. A mental warning blasts an extreme awareness, a reminder of recent changes in her physical form. Normally, her curiosity always wins. Gabrian would never have hesitated to stay, to investigate, shielding herself with her powers, but now, she has nothing in the means of protection.

Frozen in her position, her body betrays her mind's warning to escape and she stands waist-deep in the ocean—merely three feet from this beautifully unsettling image of a woman—she thinks.

Another softly lyrical chime escapes the form as it turns away from Gabrian's star-struck gaze. Peeking over her shoulder, she beckons Gabrian to follow her out further into the water. Gabrian watches the girl, who seems to be harboring no signs of mal-intent, only patiently waiting for her to follow. With nothing left but her instincts for protection, her gut feelings tell her to see what the girl wants.

A far away hushing of words kisses her ear. Rhada's words, '*they will teach you,*' echo through her mind and helps her decide to let go of her doubt. Taking a leap of faith, Gabrian slowly makes her way deeper into the water.

Everything about her is engulfed in electricity. A slow burn of rejuvenation, like having stepped into a hot shower after a long day at work, make her muscles relax and tingle. Gabrian lowers her lids. Her mind surrenders its hold to consciousness and sinks completely unprotected into a watery abyss.

Somewhere in her momentary capture, she loses sight of the girl. Panic strikes through her as she turns to find her. The water swishes in her frantic search, swirling with her movements and begins to whirl. Gabrian stops moving and the water slows its motion, becoming passive again. An odd fascination with the liquid's strange desire to move with her against its natural current stirs her inquisitive nature. She turns around as if on a swivel. The water once more swirls and sparks with tiny dots of light in her wake.

Captivated by this strange phenomenon of the water's complete willingness to follow her movements, she gathers more momentum, twirling round and round, completely unconcerned about the rest of the world around her. Moving her hands, cupping the water as she spins, it begins to rise, only inches at first, then happily rushes upward to meet her subtle commands. A bout of laughter escapes over her lips. No longer sad about what she has lost, this new discovery is enough distraction to lift her spirits from the pits of despair they had fallen into.

A musical giggle, resembling the soft thrumming of a wind-up music box Gabrian once owned as a child, interrupts her playtime. She stops, remembering the girl, and drops her hands, the band of orchestrated water falling with them. Shimmering like a jewel against the white-peaked streams of water, Gabrian involuntarily holds her breath, stunned by the girl's more prominent form. No longer undefined and cloaked in a charmed mirage of light, the girl stands clear and evident in her amusement of Gabrian's display.

It reminds Gabrian of the first time she was first introduced to the Elders of the Covenant of Shadows. The abundance of their powers, even though contained, was a profound feeling of awe, of standing before the greatness of the Gods themselves. This girl dances on her senses like an apparition of Aphrodite but without the weight of goddess intimidation.

This girl exudes nothing but warmth and kindness.

"Come," she giggles, her eyes switching between dark and light swirls of light.

A hypnotic dance, Gabrian thinks to herself, unable to look away and strangely eager to follow.

Gabrian closes the distance between the two, standing silent for a moment. The girl's smile entrances and captivates her attention. Her head slowly bobs from side to side as her eyes scan Gabrian's face—much like Theo's had when he first began to follow her around, trying to assess who she was.

"You remind me so much of a girl I once knew," she chimes out and stares deep into Gabrian's eyes.

Gabrian takes in a sharp breath. The girl's gaze swims into her soul, making her spine tingle, and pulls something from deep within to the forefront. It is an odd, almost nauseating sensation but then it is gone. A soft hum begins to resonate where the tingling had been but spreads to her feet and arms as well.

"This girl spent many hours lingering upon the beach, searching the horizon and waiting for the sun to rise." She smiles and a wave of sadness looms around her in a shroud of blue hazy mist. Gabrian assumes this must be an aura of sorts but less shimmery and more mist-like.

"I am Lyarah," she hums, taking hold of Gabrian by the wrist, the one she had injured before her escape from Uncle Ty's keep. "A sea nymph. And you, I see, are a child of the universe."

Gabrian blinks her eyes, climbing back into the sharpness of the present. "Nymph? A child of the…" She rushes back to a time when her Magik lingered in her veins. "No, not anymore." She frowns, dropping her eyes for a moment.

A song of gentle laughter escapes Lyarah's lips, raising the hum within Gabrian to reach a new level of awareness, and she smiles in the pleasantness of it. "Oh, but it lingers still, daughter of the light," she offers, lifting Gabrian's wrist more closely to her. "A child born with gift will always return where beginnings lie. Your Magik has just begun. Otherwise, we would not be here, and our words never exchanged."

"I don't…" Gabrian squints her eyes, wrinkling her nose at the strange words. "What?"

"Only a rare few have the sight to see the colours of the sea and the children who live beneath its surface."

Gabrian narrows her eyes. *More riddles. Why can't they just say what they mean instead of these twisted words?* She glances down at her wrist still tucked within the stranger's grasp. "Ah, sorry, Lyarah, is it? I have no idea what you are talking about." She raises her free hand to rub at the side of her muddy cheek. "I only went for a run to get out of the house and just ended up here, trying to clean myself up before I head back."

"And cleanse you will." She smiles, undaunted by Gabrian's story. She slowly unwraps the swaddling from Gabrian's wrist, causing her to pull back from her grasp.

"Hey, wait, don't do…" Gabrian's words stick in her throat. The swaddling pulled free from her fresh wound reveals a faint jagged line where her cut should be. She gently traces the mark with her finger. No cut to be found, not even an ounce of tenderness where the glass had broken her skin. "What the…" Gabrian gapes at the non-existent wound, dragging her eyes upward, and is met with a sweet jagged-tooth smile of the sea witch. Gabrian gasps at the exposed lethal grin. "What are you?" she breathes out. "And how did you do that?"

"This was not of my doing, but yours. I am merely a curious friend." Lyarah lifts her eyes to the skies and inhales a deep breath. "So sweet, isn't it?"

She does not hear her. Gabrian's mind is filled with an explosion of wonder. She glances down into the water and wiggles her toes. *Hmm, I wonder.* Lifting her left foot, the one which had been torn from her run, she brings it to surface in the light above the water. Her eyes are wide and unbelieving. No longer are they red and scarred. "How did this happen, what is going on?"

SILVER

The harbor-surfing nymph returns her attention back to Gabrian and giggles, watching the girl caress her healed appendages. "It is simple." She traces her webby digits along the blue veins in Gabrian's wrist. "You and I are rivers. Wild waters rush through our veins."

Gabrian glances up, seeing the flickering swirl of light dance in her eyes.

"Water is the purest of Magik, the very essence of life, and from it all things begin." She gathers one of Gabrian's shredded locks and twirls it around her scaly fingers, grinning. "Would you like to see what else your Magik can do?"

Sweeping a glance to the sparse strand of hair, almost forgetting the monstrous sight she has become and wanting to flinch from the touch, Gabrian looks back to her wrist. The clean line has faded even more than before, making her heart jump into her throat. A swarm of possibilities dance in her head and the hopefulness of the water's spell has her captivated.

The girl who longed to be normal, plain and void of the ancient's gifts is dead, left drifting along the shores of Erebus. Someone new stands waist-deep in the ocean, healing and swelling with the hope Magik has graced her once more, and she is eager to meet it in whatever form it takes. "Yes."

Lyarah's smile widens, spilling an uncharted and strange sensation through her friend's soul. Her scaly hands reach up and trace the edge of her brow, cupping her jaw—soft rows of layered sea flesh tickle her skin.

Gabrian sinks into her eyes, following them, feeling them warm her from beyond a place with earthly bounds. Pulling on her, the nymph slowly dips beneath the water's surface. Gabrian lets the tension in her legs release, feeling the warmth of the water's Magik kiss her chest, then tickle her shoulders and lick her neck as she sinks into its hold. Sucking in one last breath, she submerges her face. Her eyes open in the salty water, searching for the girl.

Face to face, eye to eye, they reach out to hold each other, lost in the womb of a watery world. Lyarah lifts a hand and gently caresses the scarred flakes of skin layered between the scattered remains of Gabrian's hair. Shivers quake over Gabrian in a euphoric caress that makes her eyes roll back in her head as the sea witch works her healing Magik.

Slow caresses from Lyarah's touch lingers over every inch of Gabrian's broken body and encases the girl in a state of utter bliss. The stress in her lungs strangles her serenity, and Gabrian's eyes fly open, feeling their plea for air. She needs to surface but she has no idea which way is up. Lyarah had spun her so gently within her web that now she is lost in shades of muted blues and greens, no longer any light to guide her to the surface.

Her hands swing wildly and her lungs burn to gather air. A stronghold for her footing is nowhere to be found and Gabrian's mind whirls in her torment, a moment of stupidity. Why did she trust that this Magik was good? It never did anything but cause her trouble before, how could she be so stupid as to trust it now?

Stupid, stupid, fool—Magik killed her, brought her back only to be killed again?

Two arms reach out to cease her strife, still buried alive within the waves. Eyes of shimmering wildness stop her in her tracks, easing her will to fight. Her lungs burn, releasing bubbles of the toxins building within her chest. *I am drowning. Slowly dying, again.* "Why?" she gurgles out in bubbled breath to the girl holding her under.

A melodic low song rushes from the nymph's mouth as she laughs. *No, you are not drowning, child. Stop fighting and believe in your Magik. Can't you feel it thriving within?*

Unsure if the few staggering moments of attempted swimming before death's door is the cause for her delirium, Gabrian gives up the fight and plays along. If she is going to die again, she might as well enjoy it.

Relaxing her muscles, and letting the panic release, she slows her inhales. A strange sensation of wetness slips into the canvass of her nose, burning a little at first then cools. A misty spray of oxygen is delivered into her lungs in a slow pull then releases out. In and out, in and out—on it goes, making her feel a little light-headed and high.

Gabrian lets out a bubble-filled giggle. *Is this really happening?*

Lyarah giggles with her and swirls around, releasing bubbles of trapped air to decorate the space around her. She closes in on Gabrian and touches her face once more, met by her friend's hand on hers, and smiles. The soft sounds of the sea woo her and a small shiny school of fish slip by, only pausing for a moment to notice her presence then slip off into the gaining darkness.

Gabrian expects any minute to wake up—this strange watery journey she is on is nothing but a dream—but she does not. She watches Lyarah's hair float poetically around her, moving along the bottom of the harbor in a strange underwater ballet performed in the dusky hours of day. The fading streams of crimson light seep into her consciousness, stealing the serene soft smile painted on her lips. As if reading Gabrian's mind, Lyarah gathers up Gabrian's hand and waltzes toward the lightest part of the water.

"I think it is time for you to start back," she chimes out, glancing over her shoulder. Gabrian nods, knowing she is right, and the dawn of realization jars her from her joyous new adventure. She has been MIA for hours and Tynan is probably tearing up the Earth in a mad search to find her.

They slowly break the surface and tread toward the shore. Gabrian hears a small pop as the last remains of the manifested oxygen is released, trailing a trickle of moisture from her nose as her body readjusts to breathing air.

Gabrian spots her bloody shoes still waiting patiently, as well as her ebony friend at the edge of the beach, and makes her way toward them. Lyarah stops her escort and sends her one last message. "Gabrian."

Gabrian turns to look at her new friend shimmering in her mirage form once more. "You must learn to believe in order to see, and when you see it, guard your secrets well."

Letting out a deep sigh, she releases a breathy chuckle at the nymph's cryptic words. "More rhymes to untangle. Hmm, I get it, I do." She stretches her arms out and riddles her own conclusion back. "Okay, how is this? Wisdom within words, if learned slowly, allows the depths of knowledge to sink deeply," she finishes with a Chessy-cat grin lodged on her face.

Lyarah smiles sweetly at her, releasing a song of melodic joy, then falls back, melting into the watery depths below.

Chapter Fourteen

Into the Woods

Slowly fading behind the horizon, the sun shoots diamonds of fire to surf across the snowy watery wakes as Gabrian plays the day's unfathomable events over in her mind. Her hands coax the foamy edges of water receding with the tide to rush in close. They obey, braver than they should be—obedient currents eager to meet her fingers' command.

The shadows play with her sight. They dance and shift the edges of day's end. Lost in her delight, Gabrian almost misses the movement at the edge of the forest where the sand is left behind by the green grass knolls. She twists quickly, only catching a glimpse of a figure as it slips into the tree line.

Eyes narrowed and a bend in her brow, she recognizes the stranger. "Kaleb." Gathering up her shoes, and quickly retying their crimson remains on her newly-healed flesh, she rushes to her feet and lets out a laugh of disbelief. There is no pain, not even an ounce of fatigue. Placing her toque on her scarred head, she feels the soft bristles of hair lacing the once crusted skin tissue, soft and supple as a newborn babe.

Giddiness bounds within her, forcing her smile to beam with this revelation of awesomeness, more eager than ever to show him her miracle. After a few hurried steps over the beach and through the long grass, she finds an opening in the trees. There is a path marked only by the fallen pine needles that have soured the ground, clearing the way through the twisted woods.

She glances back over her shoulder at the sea and the dwindling light of day's end before hurrying forward, curious as to what he is up to and eager to spill the beans. The roaring hush of the ocean's song is muted by the underbrush of the trees. Listening for footsteps, she hears a soft snap and crunching ahead. Her heart swells with vigor as she starts her journey, but her steps slow. Something flutters in her stomach and stings against her skin.

The odd placement of colour catches her attention through the branches. Inching toward it, a stripe of yellow along the side of a grey shirt stands out. Kaleb's shirt lies on the ground, folded neatly on what looks like pants. *Um, okay. This is a bit weird.* Her eyes lift, scanning the forest for the owner and feeling just a bit awkward doing so.

No more than forty feet away on the twisted earthen path, she sees him. Kaleb stands there. *Bare shoulders, bare back, bare...Oh my.* She gasps. His head shifts to the side and she wonders if he has heard her and holds her breath. But he does not turn around. He stands there, alone in the woods, and lifts his arms wide at his sides, rolling his head back to face the darkening sky.

What on Earth is he doing?

She slides close behind the base of a large pine and watches, feeling a bit like a perv, but this is way too strange not to stare. It is like a train wreck, only there is no train, just Kaleb and his nakedness alone in the woods. Gabrian lets out a stifled giggle, wanting to leave and give Kaleb his privacy to do whatever it is that he is doing, but her inner voice whispers for her to stay. She needs to see this.

Raising his arms over his head, he arches his back then stands upright again, arms stretched out to the side. Kaleb gives his hands a flick and his skin, from the blades of his shoulders to the tips of his fingers, begins to ripple and twist, filling in with bulbous muscles clinging to his misshapen form.

The fade of dusk bends the sharpened edges of reality to soften and blend. Rubbing her eyes, she wonders if what she is seeing is real or a trick as the shadows of night creep in, giving things new shape. *This is getting seriously messed up.*

The thing before her steps away, no longer the man she knew. The soft endearing green of his essences shifts and lightens into streaks of golden fire, swirling around his form. Forcing her eyes to focus, she lowers her stance and edges around the tree to get a better view. Kaleb's form begins to rise. No, not rise, *grow*. His shoulders widen and shift position. His back ripples, revealing a sharp-edged spine with ribs that narrow and curve, forcing him to lean forward and down. The muscles in his arms bulge, flexing in their strain, and hands curl, clenching and clawing at the earth below as they meld, shortening and buckling together. His legs twist and snap, molding into an inverted bend, and stretch to meet his elongating clawed feet which flex and mold into a foundation needed to support his new horizontal form.

The colour of his skin darkens to blend with the forming shadows of night. A manifestation of smooth silky hair erupts from the center of his back and explodes, rushing across his body and shrouding his flesh with a natural means of camouflage—a gift of the Gods, invisibility, to become one with his surroundings. With giant clawed paws, powerful muscular shoulders, and eyes so yellow they shine— reflecting what remains of light within in the darkness—Kaleb turns in her direction and sniffs the air.

Before her stands a terrifyingly beautiful, midnight-coloured beast, shaped to clone the magnificence of a panther, but bigger with longer hair. Its internal essence flares like a golden halo. Gabrian holds her breath, trying not to move as she takes in this phenomenal transformation. A wave of powerful and intoxicating energy stings the surface of her skin as he releases a low guttural growl into the night. She stares, unmoving, as the black stripe of his pupils narrow and hone in, focusing on something.

He gives a shake and tenses his muscles, lowering on his haunches, then darts straight for her. Gabrian digs her nails into the tree in front of her and tries to scream out his name to stop his attack, but the words stay frozen in her fear. Closing her eyes, hearing the pounding drum of her chest, she waits for the inevitable end.

The sound of crushing leaves, loud and nearly upon her, closes in just as a whiff of musk and earth tickles in her nose, caught in the wake of Kaleb's massive form as he rushes past, leaving her clinging for life to the tree, and disappears into the night. Left in the depths of silence, only the soft chittering of disgruntled squirrels nearby keep her company. She opens her eyes, waiting for a face-to-face encounter with the beast, but she is denied. Unhinging her fingers from the bark of the tree, Gabrian steps out to search the shadows for her unusual friend—deciding whether it is worth the risk to follow him.

Her inner dialogue begins its deciphering of logistics from mere curiosity. *It is Kaleb.* She stands, biting her lip, not wanting to make too much noise and a little timid of what may or may not happen if she draws any unwanted attention to her presence. *Loveable, easygoing Kaleb, the one who tended to me with his Magik herbs and soft-spoken words. There is no reason to be afraid unless…* Her internal gut feeling brings its conclusion to surface in her strife. *Unless, the transformation is mental as well as physical. What if Kaleb really is a beast now, a hunter in all its entirety?*

Her decision is made for her. The sound of rustling leaves sends her scurrying back to cling to the shroud of the pine as Kaleb's midnight form appears just as quickly as it has disappeared. Gabrian slinks down behind the tree, hoping she was not seen.

His ears twist as he slows his pace, parading in a measured precise stalk as he sniffs the air around him. Swallowing hard, sharp pins prick at her innards. The bite of fear eats at her from the inside, doped with a massive dose of adrenaline coursing through her. It may be fight or flight time. Even if she could get away without being eaten, how would she explain why she was spying on her friend and his secret?

As if hearing her thoughts, Kaleb's head swivels to the left. His body ripples again and slowly deconstructs from his animal form before he walks past her, naked as a jaybird to retrieve his clothing.

"Full moon tonight," a familiar voice cuts through the darkness and the ringing in her ears as a figure steps out of the shadows and onto the soured path of pine needles. Traces of light allotted from the rising moon above outlines his frame.

Ethan.

"Yes, it is," Kaleb smoothly replies, gathering up his pants from the ground and casually stepping into his faded jeans. The canvas cloth slides up over his taut muscular legs.

Gabrian tries to find any trace of her presence to pull it inward but does not sense anything. She worries Ethan might find a trace of her hiding like a thief in the night and then, she will have two Elders to explain her shady deception to.

Whispers of hushed talk about an ancient Fellowship called the Alakai echo in her mind. They were shapeshifters and Spirit Walkers who once roamed the Realm but she was informed they were long extinct—a race depleted of their existence by higher powers who deemed them responsible for many vicious attacks on humans and Realmsfolk alike. These creatures, beasts of the Fellowships, if hunted down until extinction were endangered. Having just witnessed a full-blown shift by one of the Elders, no less, there may be a slight chance her existence could be endangered as well.

A wave of panic stings her skin and she closes her eyes, drawing in the energies of her surroundings with more intent. Slowly pulling her knees tight up to her chest, Gabrian tries hard to soothe the thrumming beat of her heart. Little strands of green strings dance in her inner sight, and her third eye watches it swirl around her softly, joining an iridescent haze that ignites across her skin. She can feel the gentle caress on her flesh as it clings to her. *Oh no!*

Gabrian's eyes rush open. If she can see these auras, Ethan is sure to spot her a mile away, but there is nothing in the darkness, absolutely nothing. Large leaves of a nearby plant wrap her face and body in a shield of green while vines snake over the rest of her body, hugging her close. Slowly, she lifts her hands and pulls them free from the forest greenery entwined in her fingers.

Slipping her hands under the waxy covering of leaves blocking her view of the Elders, Gabrian finds not only that they have taken no notice of her but she is witnessing an extraordinary evolutionary discovery. Fingers like glass push against the fern in front of her eyes— marbled and melded like liquid in appearance.

The possibility of being discovered slips to the background. She wiggles her fingers before her. A mirage of bended air wobbles in the tangled leaves. Twisting vines on the ground loop and twine around her ankles, tickling her skin, and wrap her in a floral display of nothingness. It seems her swim in the ocean has done more than heal her.

What in the…

The low hum of a familiar voice and scuffing of leaves being disturbed on the ground brings her back to why she is hovelling away in the bushes, cloaked in her airy invisibility.

"I hoped I might find you here." Ethan reaches down and retrieves the grey shirt from the ground, shaking off the clinging pieces of Earth, and offers it to his friend.

Kaleb chuckles, grabbing up his tee and pulls it over his head. His flowy wild aura shifts from brazen gold strands to a soft bending fold that drapes over him in a gentle lime hue against the darkness of the forest. "I just needed a moment to stretch out my muscles."

A quick glance upward through the silhouetted trees, Ethan's eyes pinch at the sides when he glimpses the large glowing rock hovering in the sky overhead. "Yes, I figured as much."

"What has you out wandering in the woods this time of night?" Kaleb widens his arms and spreads his chest for one last stretch of his ribcage. "You know the night is full of strange creatures once the sun goes down."

The softness in Ethan's face fades, darkening in the shadows. "That is what I am afraid of."

Kaleb lets out a coughing chuckle, dropping his arms to his side. "I hardly think you, of all people, fear anything let alone me, being what I am."

"It's not me I am afraid for."

What does that mean? A sting of fear trickles through her.

Ethan's words trail off as he eyes the forest and quiets— searching the edges of shadows. Kaleb's eyes narrow, picking up on his friend's tension, and flares his nostrils, sniffing the air.

A growl rumbles in Kaleb's throat. "We are not alone." Streaks of gold flare out once more, hunting the darkness. Gabrian cannot help but see them through the brush now, hurriedly cloaking her even more. "I am not sure what it is but there is something here."

"I can sense it too," Ethan whispers, sending out a wave of essence to search what his eyes cannot see.

Gabrian watches as his energy surges outward, wrapping each tree, each leave, cutting through the shadowy forest, and leaving nothing unturned. She closes her eyes and pulls herself in tight, holding her breath as the wave cuts right through her.

Ethan opens his eye and sighs. "Huh, that is strange."

"What is it?"

"To tell you the truth, I don't know." Ethan narrows his eyes, still unconvinced of his findings. "Whatever it was is gone now."

"The Veil is thinning, ghosts in the darkness no doubt."

"Maybe." Ethan breaths out. "Enough of this chasing shadows, we have more important things to discuss. That is why I am here."

Kaleb and Ethan make their way toward the edge of the forest, leaving Gabrian alone, lost in her thoughts and still wrapped in her cloak of underbrush. Once she is certain they have gone, she slowly rises and pulls free from her hiding spot, letting out her breath.

Ethan told her she could trust Kaleb, an underlying confession of truths, or so she thought. And now Ethan, obviously undisturbed about Kaleb's little performance, knows who and what he is. The whirlwind of the day's events consume her as she slowly creeps back through the forest, following her Elder's lead. A moment of déjà vu sweeps over her. Once again, she has clearly been left out of the loop of things. Glancing down at her hands, she ponders her own predicament, wondering what other secrets she will discover lying just beneath the surface.

Chapter Fifteen

Lucky Charms

Clear of the woods and back on the road heading home, Gabrian's trek is more like the runs she has come to love. Smooth, pacifying all the demons in her head, and giving her the time to sort through all the information with a calm and clear head, picking out what matters most to attend to. And right now, Gabrian's stomach needs addressing. Briskly making her way back up the gravel driveway to the cottage, she bounds through the door. She pulls on the fridge handle, revealing its innards, and frowns. Her stomach gurgles and growls in concurrence with her findings.

Bottles and bottles of broth—a barren wasteland is what it is. She eyes a white jug of milk on the side door and twists it open, raises it to her lips, and gulps down half of what remains. Swiping the dribbles on her mouth with the back of her arm, she turns and walks toward the cupboard, letting the fridge door slam shut in her absence as she searches for substance.

Setting the milk on the counter, Gabrian lowers to rifle through the empty hollows below. "What on Earth did I eat?" she grumbles, finding nothing but baggies, plastic wrap, and an old box of crackers staring at her mockingly.

Rising back to her feet, she leans on the cupboard and gazes out across the room. A flicker of light catches her eye. Tynan's outside lamp of the guest house reflects through the side door. Gabrian's lips curl in a devious sneer as she glances back down at her half-empty jug of milk, her stomach growling in approval. "I wonder—"

Gathering up her jug, she hurries to the side door and bounds across the yard toward her uncle's abode. Twisting the knob on the door, she frowns. "Bugger, locked."

Her eyes glance at her thwarted hands and her eyes narrow. Pursing her lips, she wiggles her fingers, mischievously curious. "Hmm." She pushes up her sleeve and eyes the door. "I must believe it to see it, eh?" she murmurs and narrows her eyes, focusing on the surface of her flesh, imagining it turning to bended air as it had in the forest. She has breathed water, disappeared off of the Elders' intense and impenetrable radar—surely, she can do this.

Believe, she hums to herself, willing her body to obey.

And so it does.

The pink and smoothen flesh on her newly healed hands wavers in its solidity, fading to dust and then nothing at all. Gabrian's lips curl, her mood giddy, and her stomach growls in her victory as she inches what is left of her arm forward through the wooden door, stopping at the elbow, and twists. Biting her lip, she closes one eye, concentrating on her mission.

"Come on now, just a little more," she says to no one, leaning her head against the barrier and with a low click, her mission is complete. Pulling her arm back from the door, the flesh floods back into its proper form on her hands, and she grabs the knob once more, twisting it. The door releases and swings inward.

"Wicked!" She cloaks her flesh again and pulls it back through the door, picking up the milk from the door step, and opens the door, hoping Uncle Ty will not mind the necessary intrusion. Even though she may have changed and shifted into someone new, she is certain he had not. Or at least she is counting on it, and so is her stomach, as she waltzes through the door, closing it behind her.

***

With a heart filled with despair—his mind spinning to gather all the places Gabrian might be and all the things that may have gone wrong—Tynan emerges from the shadows of Gabrian's room in a desperate effort of starting the search over again, hoping he can find a clue as to where to begin.

He had called on the Elders to help him expand the search. He visited Ethan, hoping she had come to him or Kaleb, but neither of them had any idea that she was missing. With everyone on the lookout for her, searching this world and within the grips of Magik, Tynan wants to start over. There must be something he had overlooked, something in the broken glass and the traces of blood he had found in the bathroom.

Finding nothing different, he descends to the kitchen. The doors on the cupboard are pulled open and the red top of the milk container stands out like a beacon on the countertop. His eyes widen, surveying for anything and everything. A draft sweeps through the room and tickles him with a hint he is getting warmer when he notices the open sliding door in the living room. He skirts to the edge of the door and steps out on the deck, only to see the light of his own home glaring at him. His eyes narrow and he rushes toward it, knowing the answer lies within.

Appearing on the other side of his kitchen door, Tynan's heart stops. His eyes are playing a nasty trick on him. Perched on top of his kitchen counter is the mirage of a hooded girl holding tightly to one of his bowls. Beside her sits the missing milk and his family-sized box of magically delicious cereal.

His face, sunken and drawn, Tynan rubs his eyes, unsure to trust the vision he is being shown. His heart nearly chokes him in his throat.

"Please, don't be mad. I got hungry and all I had in my cupboards were stale crackers," Gabrian squeaks out, slurping another spoonful of colourful cereal into her grinning mouth.

Slowly crossing the room, his steps measured and precise, Tynan stares at the girl. "Gabe, is that you?"

"Of course it's me. Who else knows you have a giant stash of Leprechaun cereal hidden away?"

He sets his gloves down on the edge of the cupboard and circles in front of her, cautious this may be a trick of Magik, a mirage invoked by his sadness. He had seen this before, when Sarapheane and Jarrison died. His heart had been so badly destroyed that his mind manifested their presence, speaking within his misery of their loss.

"Stop looking at me like that, you are creeping me out." She waves her spooned hand and wrinkles her beautifully-healed face at him.

He responds reflexively, not really listening, and closes the gap between them. "Like what?"

"Well, creepy... distrustful and distant," she crunches out between mouthfuls of cereal. She stops chewing for a moment and purses her lips. "Though I have to admit it beats the depressing pity party stares you had going on."

"I don't understand," he says, standing directly before her, and his eyes glisten. His hands tremble as they reach out to touch her face. "What happened to you?"

Tynan's other hand cups the side of her face. Looking her deep in the eyes, he searches for a sign, a truth that she is really who she says she is. She looks so different from the last time he saw her—a fragile shell of a soul merely melded together by flesh and bone, breakable and near death.

He does not fight the waterworks now spilling across his cheeks, seeing her light within the icy blue irises he has watched for so many years. His hands gather at the back of her head, clutching her toque still wound on her scalp. He pulls it free.

Gabrian's eyes shoot to the toque in his hand and shrugs. Feeling the warm graze of her uncle's gentle hands over the fuzz of new growth covering the once scarred tissue, she smiles. "Yeah, it is a work in progress."

Tynan's vision is completely blurred. His hands lunge out and surround Gabrian, pulling her in close and embracing her. A pang of sorrow twists in her chest, feeling the fragility of this tough guardian crumbling all around her. She lays her head on his shoulder and lets him unleash some of the suffering that has been held so tightly and mumbles out her playful discontent with being crushed. "Hey, careful. You are gonna spill my snacks."

Chapter Sixteen

Fairy Tales and Secrets

With her belly full, and her body healed but tired, Gabrian stands before her mirror. Steam from the warm shower casts a cloudy mist around her. She stares at the girl before her, not the monster who lived there only hours before. Sliding her hand across the patch work of hair clinging to her scalp, she crinkles her nose and pulls open the drawer below.

She pulls out a small pair of scissors and pinches them in her fingers, eyes grazing her reflection. "Hmm, nope." Unhappy with her find, she drops them back in the drawer and marches toward the door, making a quick exit. In a flash, she returns, eyes determined and hair clippers in hand. Gabrian plugs the cord into the wall and flicks the switch on.

The low buzz sings with the rushing water of the shower and she grins. Pulling the clipper through the mess of straggling tangles, she shears them away. One by one, they fall to the floor until all that is left are bristles, mere ghosts of the ebony locks that once remained.

She rubs her hand over the soft prickles and smiles. "Much better."

Gathering the mess into the garbage bin, she peels off her jogging clothes and lets them drop to the floor then steps into the hot streaming water. Gabrian releases a moan, rejoicing in the warm splendor of the spray, and soaks it all in, each droplet filled with heavenly energy as soon as it touches her skin.

Showering will never be the same again.

Hesitantly leaving the intoxicating clutch of the shower behind, Gabrian dries off and searches for her nightclothes. Tired but chipper, she pulls them on. No aches, pains, or required assistance necessary to dress and she smiles, grateful for her miracle, grateful for Magik—a blessing she never thought she could ever feel.

Slipping under the covers of her newly-clothed bed and cozying into the pillows, she retrieves a book from her nightstand. It is nearly midnight. The dawn will soon be upon her and tonight, she hopes to find sleep and wake with a rested mind. But the mind does what it does best and drifts over the day's events, shuttling through images to sort through thoughts shifting from the mirrored monster she was before to the nymph—her secret friend who had helped her believe once more in Magik, and allowed it to grow within her, natural and uninhibited. Gabrian's lips grow upward in Lyarah's grace but then flatline on the image of Kaleb staring her down with those golden lethal eyes. Her body shudders, remembering the power he exuded in his transformation.

After finishing her third bowl of cereal, she tried to explain to her uncle what she could about the last twelve hours from the darkest hour in her life to the moment he found her on his cupboard. She had to be creative in her retelling, unsure of how he would react to knowing the keeper of Erebus came to visit her in her bathroom or that she went swimming with a new friend who just happened to be a mythical nymph. Oh and wait—the Elder who rules over the Eorden Realm just happens to be a forbidden Alakai Ancient which were hunted down to extinction.

She had snuck in an inquiry about the legends of the Ancients, all of which only live and breathe within whispered words of fairy tales dwelling on papered pages, the only trace of their past were in books, their existence bound by thread and their undoing bled in ink. They were no secret to anyone from the Realm, especially Tynan, but he assured her they had long passed. All of them had been hunted, exterminated by humans and Realmsfolk alike. Their strange abilities, sometimes feral and misunderstood, reaped fear in the people so many centuries ago.

In a sense, Gabrian thought, they were like Madorrah—a legend—but Gabrian knows Madorrah is very much alive and apparently so were the ancient Alakai.

Tynan's questions probe into why she wants to know so much about them and it strikes a painful sting in her soul that she cannot explain. Taking that as a sign that these were not her secrets to share, Gabrian brushed away their strange importance as only a dream she had the night before. Tynan, just grateful for her reappearance, allowed her that and paid it no mind, continuing to dote on her without a second thought.

No, maybe it was best for now if she left those little tidbits for another day once *he* has recovered. Lost in the day's thoughts, she does not hear her uncle breach the shadows of her doorway until his soft voice does. "May I come in?" he whispers, not wanting to scare her when he notices her clutching a book in her lap.

Gabrian blinks, pulling back from her thoughts, and focuses on the present, smiling. Tynan's hulking form stands meekly in the doorway, holding a glass of water in one hand and a bowl of cut grapes in his other. "You know you don't have to wait on me anymore. I am quite capable of doing things for myself now."

"I know, but I am still your family." He grins, entering the room and setting down the offering on her nightstand. "And family takes care of each other."

Gabrian nods, letting him have his soft moment, and treasures this show of love he has for her. This giant man, so soft and kind, is a mirror of her adopted parent's devotion toward her. She reaches out to touch his arm. "Yes, we do."

"I know that I am not of your blood but I have lived a long life and have learned that family is a bond built not by blood, but by the heart," Tynan says, taking her small hand into his own. He looks down on her face, his emotions getting the best of him as his eyes dew. "I have watched over you since the day Jarrison and Sarapheane took you in their arms and claimed you as their own, dedicating their lives to cradle you in a world built of nothing but love and adoration. They were not alone in their devotion."

His lips tremble as he inhales a breath, and Gabrian mirrors him. His sanded voice whispers directly to her heart. Their loss is still a heavy sadness on both of them. "You may not be linked to the blood running through my veins, but you are the child chosen to linger in my heart." He smiles at her, his cheeks rising to pinch the corners of his eyes and showing the gathered wetness escaping down the edges of his shadowed jawline. "And that is family. You are my family."

Her eyes glaze over and her mouth twists in an awkwardly painful smile. The taste of salt on her lips is strong as tears run over them. Gabrian pulls hard at the man before her and he lets her defeat him, dropping to his knees and lowering over her to sit on her bed. She wraps her arms, as best she can, around his wide shoulders and cradles him close. He is so fragile in her arms.

They are what life made them, but it is the beauty of their hearts that made them who they are.

Chapter Seventeen

Juicy Details

Settling into his cell life, Cimmerian has no issue about serving his time. The sooner he comes to terms with it, the faster he can focus on getting out and taking care of his daughter. She is safe and in good hands. All he has to do is bide his time and stay away from any riffraff that might jeopardize any possibility of early release.

"All settled in, nice and comfy, I see."

Cimmerian's heart drops and he sucks in a breath, facing him. They were friends once. It should not be so hard to deal with him on the inside of the Hollows. "Yes, quite. How are you dealing, Caspyous?"

"Couldn't be better." He snickers, landing himself on the bed beside Cimmerian. Caspyous leans against the wall and folds his hands behind his head.

Raising his brow, the Elder reaches for the book crumpled beneath his visitor and pulls it out from under him, trying to press the forced creases from the pages with his hands. "That is good to hear."

He feels the tension and anxiety in the man beside him. It is a rumbling of darkness that scratches to break loose. "So, how did it feel?"

Placing the book on the shelf, Cimmerian turns to Caspyous, frowning. "Sorry, how did what feel?"

"Ah, come on, you know what I am talking about." A crazed look creeps over Caspyous' face, eyes dilating and his mouth nearly watering as he speaks. He glances around the opening of the cell as if to make sure no one is near.

"No, I am sorry. I have no idea what you are going on about."

"You know, when you killed her." An eerie grin grows on his lips. It is as if he had won first place in a race and could not be more pleased to retell the tale. "Was it exciting? Did she scream?"

Cimmerian's stomach turns at the lust in his voice, his eagerness to know exactly how the cruelty had gone down. "No, she didn't scream, and no, there was no joy in the loss of her life." He rises from the bed, eager to get away from such a fiendish soul. Even Adrinn did not emit this much evil and darkness during their encounters. "What is wrong with you?"

"It's alright," he says, winking his eye at Cimmerian, and unfolds his hands. "I get it. You still have some hope they will let you out of here." He rises from the bed and takes his place beside the Elder, glancing down the corridor filled with cells. "You know where to find me when you realize that might not happen. Trust me, it will feel good to get all the juicy, gory details out. Sharing is caring, you know. See yah around the cell block," Caspyous hums, flicking his brow and claps the Elder on the back before strutting away.

Cimmerian decides this man does not need to know that Gabrian is still somewhat alive nor does he need to know that the title of Elder to Derkaz was not stripped from him, unlike his own. Caspyous' mind is darker and more twisted than he could ever imagine and he wonders about the dark things he is capable of. In here, it may be in his best interest to keep on his good side if he ever plans to leave alive.

Chapter Eighteen

Where There is Smoke

Emotionally worn out and eyes tired of tears and reading, Gabrian slips into slumber with her heart light and at ease for a change. The overload of emotion takes her easily into the mystical realm of slumber.

She wakes to a forest, surrounded by treetops and foggy ferns tickling her feet. A cool damp breeze lingers on her skin as she follows a muddy path to nowhere. Unhurried and peaceful steps pull her forward. Her hands reach out to touch low-lying branches appearing from time to time, close enough to kiss her cheeks as she glides by.

A soft song of a night owl *hoos* in her ears, accompanied by the singing frogs—a lulled tell of happiness sung by the evening choir of amphibians with the cricket percussion section keeping the beat. Everything is so slow and calm. Even the dampness is sweet. Gabrian is at ease and recharging from her hurried introduction into the life of Magik, carrying on unaffected by the growing thickness of the white mist encircling her and cloaking her trodden path.

A sharp snap brings an abrupt end to the night's song, hushing the choir and leaving her in deafening silence. Gabrian's muscles tense in its absence with eyes no longer soft and serene, but piercing and sharp in the remembrance of an uneasy jaunt to this place. The fog is thick now, too thick. She waves her hand before her, barely able to see it within the murky vapors. Something soft, velvety almost, brushes up against her bare thigh. She jumps back, eyes catching on the silhouette of an elongated black form, a long body trailed by a thick ebony tail muted in the vaporous blanket of mist.

Her heart lurches in her chest and the conscious part of Gabrian's brain recalibrates what her eyes remember. She twists in the fog, straining to see, but finds nothing. Worse, there is nowhere to hide. Even the low-lying branches of the trees have vanished and leave her to her own defences.

A low guttural growl in the void wakes her from any confusion of whether she is alone or not. And the answer is not.

Think Gabrian, think. There is new Magik in you. Find what you need, leave the rest for later. Her mind scurries to remember, but her dream state makes her slow to uncover the answer. Finally, it comes. "If I cannot see you, it is not fair that you can see me." Narrowing her eyes, she pulls at the memory of invisibility—the soft airy feeling of becoming nothing but breath upon the wind. Her fingers marvel and bend into distortion but remain flesh-bound, unwilling to assist her in her strife.

Unable to mask her presence, Gabrian panics. Her mind knows it is Kaleb haunting her dreams. Or at least, the essence of his soul transformed into what she fears of him. Another growl, this one closer than the first, reminds her of the stories of what they were. Unmerciful hunters just like the Vapir when they hunted. Fear claws at her wantonness to run away, but she is blind in the vast whiteness that surrounds her. Her only defence is to stand her ground.

Whirling through the panicked thoughts, she becomes frantic and moves forward, hands out in front to feel her way to somewhere, anywhere. A familiar noise cackles ahead, and she calls out his name. "Theo, Theo come here. Help me see when I cannot." The strangely familiar words echo as her words sing out to him. Words that were spoken before by—

Gabrian hears the flutter of wings as he draws near. Whipping at the mist with his wind and clearing the air around her, the bird thins the white barrier and reveals his presence as well as another's landing on her outstretched arm.

Perched on her arm, Gabrian instinctively runs a hand over his midnight coloured suit but her sight is frozen on a vision of the woman before her.

"Cera—" she breathes out, her wind trailing white crystals in the now all too apparent coolness of the air.

Theo cackles a hearty and cheery hello.

"Yes, child it is I." Her lovely slender face is sweet but worn. Her long ebony hair flows against a gentle breeze as she closes the distance between them. A soft silver lining colours against the white, shining in a spectrum of winding strings that hover and dance like waves against the shores.

Gabrian reaches out to touch her arm. It is cold. So very cold. It sends a shiver to rush through her.

"Come sit with me a while my young one." Cera breathes out, gathering Gabrian's hand. Pulling her through the cloud of mist, Cera stops and lowers onto a fallen tree now sleeping in the forest, under a cover of green moss surrounded by crushed decaying branches.

Gabrian lowers beside her and Theo jumps from her arm onto the ground, fluttering his large black wings to clear the space of fog and mist. The long darkened body of a twisted beast is revealed, lying peaceful on the ground in the wake of Theo's wind.

Gabrian gasps in the thinned mist. The creatures massive existence uncloaked, bright golden eyes set within a large majestic and midnight coloured head stares back at her.

Kaleb.

Gathering to his feet, height growing to stand above her, he slowly paces around the log then stands before her. His form resembles a large cat but the edges of his jaws veer out to the side into long broad sharp ends.

Unable to look away, tremors in her body start to build. Her muscles tense, preparing her for escape.

"Don't be afraid." Cera hums, gripping her hand within her frigid grasp.

Really? This is the advice she has.

The large black Kaleb, huffs at her and softens his eyes releasing Gabrian from his trance. He strides by her, leaving her in his immense shadow and circles back around to sit down in front of Cera. Her hand cups him under his jaw and scoops him in to nuzzle nose to nose.

What. Just. Happened. Here? Gabrian sits dumbfound and wide-eyed while her birthmother makes kissy face with Kaleb. Well, not kissy face, but what the hell?

Theo lets out a gurgling coo, a sign that all is well, and Kaleb shakes his large furry feathered—w*ait he has feathers on his head?*

"You have to use your own judgement. Stories are just that—stories—twisted and distorted, from one mouth to another. Fear and hatred are two different powers. Both are strong in their convictions," Cera hums, still staring at Kaleb.

Her image flickers and starts to fade. Her voice breaks up into whispered words. Gabrian reaches out to touch her. "I can't understand what you are saying." Her hand is near ice, frozen and fading. Even with the warmth of the cat's body now settled at Cera's feet, feeding her his body heat is not helping. "You are freezing."

Gabrian's heart sinks. "I can help you. I just need to get you warm." Her eyes jump around the ground, searching for something to burn. Gathering the fallen branches beside the log, she builds a small teepee on the ground. "Just hold on, I will build a fire. I will help you get warm."

Bounding off to gather more of the stray branches, she huddles them closer together in front of her mother. *Fire,* she thinks, *I have to make fire.* Gabrian panics, glancing back at her fading mother. Cera's colours begin to fade out and blend into the mist. "Just hold on, I will fix this."

Gabrian narrows her eyes and stares at her fingers. *Come on work.* She clenches her eyes shut and thinks *FIRE,* imagining the heat within her fingers just like Arramus said she had the night he found her burning outside the building she had destroyed. "Fire," she breathes out, opening her eyes to an orange hue biting the tips of her fingers.

Her eyes sparkle in the glow and she lets out a huffy chuckle, turning to show her mother, but her mother is no more than a sheet of molded ice. "No!" Gabrian yells out, her hands full of flames as she rushes forward. Smoke rolling off her fingers chokes her as she places her hands around the edges of her frozen mother's face.

Her lungs burn and her eyes itch. Gabrian rubs her arm across her view to ease the bite. Blinking hard against the stench of smoke, she brushes away the last remains of her mother, the dark shadow of Kaleb's beast wiped away as well. The cool misty curtain that painted the night is now replaced with shrouds of choking waves of smoke.

Gabrian's lungs fill, burning and rebelling in the vile bitter taste of ash. Tremors of constricting muscles cough, eager to be free of the toxins. Her lungs heave, taking on the attack and replaces the loss of her mother with need for air. Orbs of light spark and dance in her eyes. The world starts to spin, tearing everything away in a blurry haze, and she lurches forward in her attempt to gain control.

Rolling smoke clouds her eyes as she returns to consciousness. Her room, lit with dawn's first dance on the horizon, colours her world in a crimson hue of silhouetted shapes, their edge softened by shadows and smoke.

Smoke!

Her mind rushes awake to hands smoldering over the last remaining pages of her novel burning in her fingers. Lit ashes drop on the plaid duvet, burning into divots, and crusting at the edges with the lit embers. She jolts upward, registering the events.

Gabrian has literally set her world on fire.

Chapter Nineteen

Through the Haze

Patting frantically at the smoldering *City of Ashes*, now merely blackened crumbles of paper clumped together at the spine, Gabrian throws herself out of bed. An annoying high-pitched scream pierces her ears as the fire alarm comes to life. Eyeing the glass of water on her nightstand, she pours it on the smoldering bedspread. Turning to carry the charred novel into the bathroom, she stops. Through the smoky haze, a strange and rather large hole in the wall appears where the bookshelf is supposed to be.

Narrowing her eyes, she stares at it. "What in the world?" No longer hearing the alarm's warning, she inches cautiously toward the opening, no more than a foot from the bathroom door. A soft warm yellowish light glows from within, just beyond the edges of the opening. Rough wooden floorboards lead in but the haze of her burning book, still clutched in her hand, clutters her view of anything else. A waft of smoke irritates her eyes, and she rubs the corners to ease them.

"What in the blazes?" Tynan roars out over the screaming alarm, startling her, and she drops her book. He rushes in and stands before her, gripping her by the shoulders, and blocks the view of the strange room. "Are you alright?"

She squirms to free herself from his grasp. Caught in a trance of urgency to look in the room, she strains her neck to see around the side of his tensed bicep. But the room is gone, the light, the doorway, nothing more than a trick of her imagination. "Where did it go?"

"Where did what go? What are you talking about? Was someone in your room?" Tynan yells, his voice shaking as well as his hands. She feels the tremors ripple through her from his grip. "Gabrian, did someone do this?" He stares frantically into her doe-eyed gaze.

Shaking her head, Gabrian gives up the search for the strange entry and surfaces back to reality. "No, no. No one did anything." She tries to process what just happened. Maybe she was still caught in sleep and just dreamed it. Now, the cloudy haze takes precedence over her search for the room. She ends her fight and relaxes, so does Tynan's grip on her arms. Pulling free, she bends to pick up the abandoned remains of her book. Waving the charred ruins in front of her, smoke still wafting off the blackened pages, she gives him a half-smirk. "Um, I kind of set it on fire."

He frowns and scratches his head. "Why on Earth would you do that?"

"I didn't mean to. It just kind of happened in my sleep." Her nose twists, wrinkling across the bridge. She shoots the small bookshelf a sideways glance as she walks into the bathroom to properly dispose of the book.

Tynan shakes his head in disbelief and wanders around her bed to the window, cracking it open. The black ashes strewn across the top of her duvet draws his eyes, and he looks more closely at the seared holes. He picks up a pillow and waves it at the screaming white demon above until its red eye releases its anger, pacifying it, and turns back to green.

Throwing the pillow back on the bed, he gathers up the damaged blanket and meets Gabrian in the doorway of the bathroom. "So, care to elaborate on this fire-starting thing?" He hums out low. His voice edges with concern but teeters on a just hint of humorous curiosity, lifting the evidence up in front of him so she can clearly understand his meaning. "I need to know that I do not have to worry that you will burn the house down every time you go to bed."

Chapter Twenty

Coffee and Shadows

With the smoke cleared and the evidence of her eventful dream placed properly in the trash, Gabrian jumps into the shower to cleanse herself from the smell of ash. She uses the time to mentally prepare for a walk through the shadows—one Tynan insists they take. A trip to the Covenant of Shadows is on today's agenda. In reality, she should be thrilled to make the visit this time and enjoy the scenery. Her two biggest thorns at the table are gone—held behind the magical binds of the Shadows—incarcerated for their heinous crimes against her. She should relish in the fact that justice has been served.

Exiting the shower and damping the last remains of water from her hair, Gabrian pulls on her clothes and makes her way to the kitchen, following the lure of her favourite elixir wafting in the air. Tynan stands as big as life, leaning over the counter with coffee in hand as she steps from the stairwell and into the light of day.

"I fixed a pot of coffee for us," he says, giving her a wink, and lifts a large black mug to his lips. "Since you seem on the mend, I figured you might like a cup."

Her mouth salivates at the heavenly aroma and grins. "You are the best," she purrs, and heads for the cup steaming with the already poured warm brew waiting for her, properly dressed and tempered. She lifts it to her mouth and lets the nectar of the Gods do its Magik. It lingers in her mouth, just for a moment, and slides down her throat. Her eyes close, savoring the taste. "What time are we leaving?" she hums, almost not caring they have to leave soon.

"As soon as you are ready to go," he says, taking another sip. "It is better to inform all the Elders of what has happened instead of them hearing it in pieces of broken information."

Gabrian nods in accordance and sips her drink. The cup presses against her lips in her daydream.

"Vaeda and Orroryn are gathering everyone now. Ariah was sent to seek out Ethan and Kaleb as they seem to be missing." His voice trails off as he tips the rest of the coffee over his lips. "I am sure they aren't too far. After you went missing, everyone went out of their way to try to help me find you."

Gabrian's heart dips and pinches under her chest. She did not take into consideration how her little disappearing act would affect anyone else. She just wanted to shake off the sadness, to move on and not stay halfway dead forever. And now, after what she witnessed in the forest, how is she supposed to act normal in front of the two Elders who may or may not have some very terrifying secrets that she has stumbled on? Once more she has managed to land herself between a rock and a hard place, placing her life in danger. She is beginning to think she has a real knack for it. She lifts her cup and swallows down all of it. There is no sense in delaying the inevitable. Letting out a loud sigh, she sets it on the counter and turns to her uncle.

"What is the loud sigh for? This will be a walk in the park."

"Sure, it will," she says, forcing herself to smile.

The last time she went for a walk in the park, Gabrian's life turned into a living nightmare—one she still has not found a way to wake up from. Sure, it has had its ups and downs. The trip to Erebus was definitely one for the books. The underwater adventure with the nymph was intriguing as well, especially since it was the Hydor Elder who tried to end her life. Ironically enough, it was the purity of the water that gave it back, filled to the brim with Magik—new healing Magik. The fact her Magik has returned gives her uneasy feelings. In her experience so far, it means that trouble is not far behind. In fact, she is headed straight for it just on the other side of the shadows.

"Relax. The Elders are just curious and eager to see what has happened to you." His large arms snake around her tiny form and pull her into a tender bear hug. She lets Tynan's warm protective embrace coddle her into stillness. The hum of his soul soothes the ruffled nerves of her worrying mind and she clings to it as she has since she was a child. "Who knows, maybe it will be fun."

Gabrian wraps her small arms to hold on to her uncle just a little longer, an attempt to absorb some of his serenity. "Yeah, fun. Maybe no one will try to kill me this time."

Tynan chuckles and rubs his hand over her newly shaven head, soft and warm. Her bristles of hair are marbled in a merle of silver and ebony on her scalp. "You have to admit, at least there is never a dull moment."

Gabrian lets out a breathy laugh and slowly unwinds her arms from Tynan. Standing upright on her own, she grins and shakes her head. "There is that, I guess. Fine, let's go before all the good seats are gone."

"See, now that is the spirit!" Clasping his hand securely around Gabrian's wrist, Tynan pulls them into the edge of the shadows before Gabrian can change her mind.

Chapter Twenty-One

Somewhere in the Darkness

Gabrian's body buzzes with pinpricks of electricity as soon as Tynan pulls them into the Veil. The shadows that cling to her feel alive and a slow pulsing wave of energy pushes against her senses. It is as if the very existence of the darkness is not just mere emptiness but an essence shifting into varying shades of grey the longer they linger.

But why were they lingering?

Normally it was in and out. Today, things are different. The instantaneous journey they usually make is taking quite a bit longer, her mind strangely aware of every second they are consumed by the shadows. Images shift quickly around them—colours, sounds—it is like there is a million bits of everything expanding, contracting, and ushering them at warp speed into a familiar space. Dim light unwraps them from the Schaeduwe jaunt, opening up into the narrow corridor walls of the Covenant, and spits them out.

Gabrian gasps as her stomach flutters in the extraction. Somewhere, in the cusp of returning to the real world her heart squeezes, sensing something, someone so familiar it makes her heart sing and cry out. Only one person has ever done that, the one she left standing in the rain after ripping his heart out with her words.

Her eyes rush to seek what her heart knows to be true.

Shane.

But it is over. Thrust back into the narrow corridor of the Covenant of Shadows leaves the subtle waft of his essence behind in the shadows. Gabrian clutches her chest and her eyes fill with tears as she tenses in her uncle's grasp.

Tynan's hand instinctively tightens around her wrist as they step out into the hallway. "Are you alright?" he inquires, feeling her angst run wild under her pulsing flesh.

She lifts her gaze, a trail of moisture escaping down her cheeks. Not having really pressed the issue of Shane's recovery to anyone, her shame of his damage is too great for her to carry out loud. "I just thought I—" Her breath catches in her throat, words sad and sharp. "Is it possible to feel a soul's essence within the Veil?"

Tynan's brow furrows and he studies her face, feeling a bit relieved that it is just her curiosity which plagues her mind and not something else. His grip had been secure but the Veil can be a vile beast if not treated with respect—one he knows too well from watching Orroryn suffer its consequences for the past few centuries.

His face softens. "You are sure you are alright?"

She nods, her lips quivering and heart still caught within the emotion of the shadows.

The tight straight line drawn on his lips releases and a gentle curve takes its place. "Yes, the essence of a soul is very vivid within the Veil." Tynan steps forward to begin their trek to the Great Hall, and Gabrian follows suit. "Once the trace is learned, anyone can be found or felt within it."

"Would I be able to feel—" Her words choke her and her eyes fill with dew as she longs to hear his name touch her lips.

"Shane, you mean?"

Her eyes drop to her feet. The sound is so painful but the mix of feelings it invokes inside is tangible. For the first time in weeks, she feels alive, feeding off the pain this reality stabs at her. She uses it to fuel her courage, to look her uncle in the eye. "Yes."

He scratches the edge of his jaw and lets his gaze drift to somewhere she cannot see. Exhaling a troubled breath, he returns to her. "I guess there is always that possibility since you are bonded by oath and heart."

They are bonded. Of course, she can feel him. It has to be what it was, the bond. If only she could see him and tell him all the things she has been longing to say. "Is he alright?" she says, her desire to be close to Shane urging her silence about the matter to cease. "Is he going to be okay? You kind of skated around the question when I asked weeks ago."

Her questioning deflates the plumpness in his lips again. A straight line makes its reappearance on Tynan's mouth as his eyes wander for the proper wording to give her. "We normally do not speak of those within the Veil. The Schaeduwe are quiet about things within the shadows. All I can tell you is that he is—" Tynan glances down at her pleading eyes, wetness edging her long black lashes tears with the wish he could tell her all will be well but he cannot.

Because he does not truly know.

No one has ever suffered the wrath of Erebus like Shane has. Well, no one but Gabrian. He still has no answers to explain what miraculous transformation happened there except there is a greater power in charge of her destiny. One that is crueler and yet more devoted to her than he can understand.

He releases the tension in his lips and lets them fill again, arm reaching to wrap around her shoulders, as they walk. "He is where he needs to be."

These words echo in her mind. They are the same words that were told to her by Sarapheane and Jarrison about Cera, words that remind her that he may be there for a very long time. Gabrian bites her lip, painfully trying to push back her emotion. A bitter truth of the world she now belongs to. This world takes prisoners, holds them within its spell until it is good and ready to deal with them. This is her ugly reality. Cera, Rachael, and now Shane are all trapped in the intricate webs of Magik, some of which were spun by her sins.

"I can tell you though, Orroryn will not be here today with the Elders." Gabrian lifts her eyes. His words cut through her sadness and bring her back to their purpose. "He is visiting Shane."

His eyes catch Gabrian's and see them light, a hint of hope dancing in them. Sucking in a long painful truth-filled breath, Gabrian holds the weight of it as long as she can and releases it. She tries to push out her sadness over having no control, letting go of some of the guilt of her doings, and prays she can make amends somehow.

Chapter Twenty-Two

On with the Freak Show

Maybe it was the fact that Gabrian was not facing Cimmerian and Caspyous, or even the guilt of not having to look into Orroryn's eyes, but the binds around her do not feel the same as they usually do. The strangling of her senses is absent, unlike every other time she entered the binds of the Covenant.

Even with the mind-altering knowledge of Kaleb and Ethan, Gabrian is not afraid to face them. Who is she to judge anyone? Maybe Kaleb is an ancient who hunts in the darkness and Ethan his comrade at arms. Even with all their secrets, they are no more evil than the monster she had been only weeks ago.

Hell, even her father, Adrinn, seems to have turned over a new leaf.

Maybe it is time to put all the legends and horror stories of old monsters to bed for a while and find a new chapter to write in this story or be damned trying. Gabrian is not afraid or bogged down with the gut-wrenching despair she always comes with. Something new and strange takes its place. Obliteration, an unusual ease of who she is wells warm in her belly.

She could get used to this.

A strange grin grows at the edges of her lips and her pace slows. The stone walls around her shift and a soft glow hovers around the encrypted etching, melding into an understanding between the two. A soft cue of familiarity welcomes her home.

In this new state of being, Gabrian wonders if this is the way everyone feels entering the sacred space, if it should have always felt this way. The air around her is light and pleasant—a strange phenomenon considering where she is. Stepping out into the great hall of the Covenant of Shadows, Gabrian inhales a sweet scent of summer blossoms and freshly cut grass. She halts, and inhales again. Something else that had been shrouded from her senses, obviously, she concludes.

Tynan ceases his advance into the light and turns back, glancing at his niece over his broad shoulder. "Are you alright? You are beginning to worry me."

A smirk swallows up her serenity, and she exhales a huffy chuckle. "Beginning to…Really?"

She wrinkles her nose at him and tucks her arm under his, gliding them both forward into the masses. Ignoring the sudden wide-eyed glances in their direction—uncaring of what any of the Realmsfolk think of her—Gabrian marches forward, head high and ignited by the subtle energies flowing through the space. She did not ask for anything that she has been made into and everything will work itself out. Rachael will be alright, she will. She is almost certain of it and Shane—well, he will be back, and she will keep him safe and love him with every ounce of her soul. He will come back to her. He will.

And for the first time in a long while she believes it—well, mostly. It is in the ninety-ninth percentile.

"By now I thought it was just a natural state between us," she teases, hugging Tynan's arm, and feeling her new well of bottomless hope.

"I am glad to see you smile. I think it is the first time that has ever happened here."

"You are probably right about that." She grins, eyeing the skyline in the distance. A shimmering sparkle of light dances across the Head Table at the end of the great hall. Layers of wavy mystical and regal hues glow around the Elders' seating area, casting it into a spellbinding presentation of greatness.

For the first time, she harbors no fear of what it represents. The guilt of her strife and her sins plays nice with her today. Whatever Rhada and Lyarah have done to her is exciting—a strange emotion for her, considering everything.

Taking advantage of Gabrian's seemingly light mood, Tynan informs her of a few more details of their visit. "The test is going to be a snap in your elated state."

And goodbye good mood.

Gabrian's happy-go-lucky stride screeches to a halt. Her death lock on Tynan's arms trips him up as she jerks him back, the cheery grin lost somewhere in the Veil of shadows.

"Um, wait a minute. Back up." Gabrian purses her lips and rubs the stubby prickles of newborn hair on her head. "What did you just say?"

"Your test." Tynan's mouth twists, and he scratches the edge of his newly bearded chin.

"What test is this?" she growls out through gritted teeth, loud enough to cause the people around them to slow in their journey and take notice. Grabbing the edge of his shirt, she pulls hard and draws him in closer. "You never mentioned anything about any test."

He presses a smile and looks down at her with soft eyes. "Yeah, about that," he says, biting his lip. "I didn't want you to worry. It is more like research and discovery analysis."

"Uncle Ty, a test is a test no matter how you sugar-coat its name. How could you not tell me?" Gabrian begins to do a three-foot pace,

114

accompanied with a bout of hyperventilation. "You said they just want to see me, to see how I have healed. *Curious* is how you described it, I believe."

He grins. Placing his large hands on her shoulders to stop her march and end her frantic trek, Tynan stares down into her swirling icy blues and tries to settle her building angst. "It is not as bad as your dramatic mind is making it out to be. It is nothing to worry about. Okay?"

"Nothing to worry about? Are you freaking kidding me?" Her eyes widen and shoot around at the onlookers trying not to be obvious in their attempts at eavesdropping. She feels the beat of her heart racing beneath her ribs, each pulse rushing electric waves that sting her.

A warm burn at the edge of her fingers, a familiar sensation that had gone missing in her re-born state of being, has returned. And to her delight, the strange phenomenon wraps her in a distorted sense of comfort. Even if she doesn't truly understand its purpose, she knows it. It is a part of her existence, an early defence and warning sign of trouble to come. No wonder it has returned. Once again, she has been left out of the loop and forced to play by others' rules of conduct.

So much for happy today—on with the freak show.

Chapter Twenty-Three

Rise and Shine☐ Sleepyhead

Down the hall, and to the right of Room 231, the monitor beeps a steady rhythm. Its electrical irregularities play havoc with on duty staff as it spikes and flatlines on a regular basis from the day it was connected. Under the cloak of darkness, a subtle violet haze decorates a small slender frame. Dark chaotic hair drapes across chalky white, sunken skin as Symone's chest slowly rises and falls again.

From the floor, misty black swirls slip beneath the crack of her door, and slither toward the sleeping girl—rising up the side of her bed before halting. Twitching and writhing, the wisps of toxins swoon at her fragile state and release an eerie chuckle.

"Get up, sleepyhead," it coos at her. "Time to rise and shine."

The girl remains still.

Letting out an irritated huff, the smoke swirls again, manifesting into a handsome grinning vaporous form. "Really, Symone, you mustn't be lax on your return." He grins, eyes light. The irises change from hazel to a fiery orange as the colour swirls within. "You have rested long enough. It is time we get you back to Earth."

Closing his lids and dimming the lightshow in his eyes, Adrinn releases his consciousness and enters the girl's. Searching within the chaotic swirls of images, he hunts for a connection to her body, calling out to her in her dreams.

116

"Symone, darling, where are you?"

Within the clouded nightmare, the girl appears. Face sullen and her eyes wide, she searches with unkempt hair flowing wildly, painted within her violet hue. She sees him. Releasing a high-pitch shriek of delight, she rushes forward in the mess of thoughts. Pushing everything and everyone in her path to the side, she clamours to reach him and clings to his form. Clutching hold of his lapel, Symone crushes her tangles of messy hair into his chest with submission to his request.

Adrinn glides his hands around the back of her head and cups her cheeks. Lifting her eyes to meet his, only for an instant, she soaks him in. He allows her this only once to make his message clear to the girl. "It is time."

Symone gasps, her mouth left slightly ajar. Her eyes dilate, gathering all the details of his face, and memorizes it with her soul then drops her head quickly, breaking connection with him and nods in understanding of his command.

"Be a good girl and come along now." He pulls away from her, grinning a devilish smirk, and steps back into the present, letting his image fade ever so slowly.

Her subconscious mind panics upon seeing Adrinn drift into a fading mirage. Suffering from the disconnection, Symone cries out, clutching the emptiness he has left her in. Wrapping her arms violently around herself, and ripping at her own hair, she releases a mind-shattering screech into the void, feeling the sharp-edged pull of her consciousness as he drags her back into the physical world that waits for her final return.

Chapter Twenty-Four

Cimmerian's Child

"Stubborn, pig headed—" Between gritted teeth, Orroryn enters back into the Realm from the Veil, his pulse rapid and his cheeks flush in his frustrated state. But as soon as the soft repetitive beep reminds him of where he is, he quiets and slips across the shadowy room.

His fingers ease their grasp around the stems of the flowers he carries, orange and full of life, not quite of this world. They are a gift from the Veil to brighten up the dim essence of her room. The same flowers that he carried hundreds of years ago to another girl he cared for so long ago.

He looks upon her small frame and sighs, feeling the pressure of the lump in his throat as she lays still, the same as she was when he left her. A need to check on her pulls him. This youngling has become dear to him in a way he cannot understand. A longing to protect her, to be close to her, keeps pulling him back like a magnet.

Removing the dying bouquet from the vase and tossing the old ones in the garbage, he replaces it with his new offering of orange blooms—arranging them to fold out and hang fully over the edge of the vase. Satisfied with the presentation, he slips around the edge of her bed and takes his place at her side. Gently sliding his warm fingers beneath hers, he lays his forehead on their joining hands, closes his eyes, and lets his weariness consume him.

He is truly fond of the girl but his heart can never truly be free. And to lead her to believe otherwise would be cruel, something he would never do to someone. The girl deserves to find someone who can give her their heart wholly and completely—something he can never do.

In his sullen silence, a loud shriek echoes though the shroud of shadows and pulls him back to reality and to his feet. Orroryn swiftly rushes to the door, opening it just as a nurse jogs past.

"Is everything alright?" Orroryn calls out.

"It is the Cole girl. She has just surfaced from the coma and she is in shock."

Cimmerian's child.

With one last glace back at Rachael, Orroryn leaves her to her dreams and follows the footsteps of the orderly heading toward Symone.

Chapter Twenty-Five

Different

Tynan grabs Gabrian's arm and hurries her toward the group of gathered bodies standing beside a giant pillar that climbs endlessly upward. Her eyes dance across their familiar forms and she exhales a furious breath. The only sound she hears is the pounding of fury in her ears. Normally, it would be filled with the murmurs of internal thought whispered unconsciously by the minds of everyone in the marble walls, but since her visit to Erebus, it has been quiet.

Excruciatingly quiet.

And today will be no different. She longs for the soft reassuring *'Just breathe'* of Ethan's silently whispered words, but it is not in the cards. The gift she had tagged for so long as a curse, the one she had wished away, is missed very badly in the moment—not to mention the tall dark shadow she wished was here as well, but that is a missing on an entirely different level.

Her heart twists, and she folds her arms around herself. The hollow ache is cold and feral beneath her arms. Gabrian exhales and pushes the sadness away. There is nothing she can do about wanting Shane here, about wanting to make things right again. It will do her no good to sink into a depression about something out of her control—just like the mindreading or lack thereof. All of it is out of her control.

Maybe its absence is a gift. She was not really sure about Ethan at the moment although her instincts vibrate, urging her to reach out to him and rekindle a spark between their minds regardless of the secrets surrounding him.

Broken bits of random conversations sing merrily around the Elders melded together, unusually mellow and undiplomatic-like. They more closely resembled a group of friends than an Elders' meeting which in normalcy resembles a wake—always dark, intense, and stress-filled. Maybe Tynan is not lying and this would not be the usual gong show she was used to. Not certain how to digest this strange new experience, she shakes out the returned fiery bite at her fingertips and marches forward, head high and defences on high alert waiting the wings.

As she and Tynan near the group, they are welcomed with a mixture of gaped mouths and sincere smiles, playful banter between peers wafting in the air. Gabrian's eyes study the group, still a bit leery. There is a new excitement vibrating around them. She cannot help but feel it and it hums through the walls with a life of its own. A prism of colours sparkles on them like Magik dust. Iridescent auras shimmer and speckle, dancing on their flesh.

What is going on? Gabrian smiles instinctively at the display and lifts her hands in front of her face. She is shimmering with it as well. She twists her hands front to back. It is reflective light and her eyes search for the answer. Even the massive marble cylinders staggering the hall seem to even be decorated. Following the dancing light, she lifts her sight to the ceiling and finds the culprit. The twinkling stars of the Covenant of Shadows pepper the ceiling with otherworldly gems. They light in waves of glowing embers in a display of beauty reminding her of an Aurora Borealis from the Northern skies.

Her breath catches in her lungs. Has it always been this way? Certainly, she would have noticed. Her body treads circles, caught in a trance, and stares into the depths of the ceiling with childlike fascination. She watches the façade of the sky shift and sway until face-planting the back of Ethan's shoulder.

A soft low chuckle escapes him as Gabrian's reality returns to the present. "It is lovely, isn't it?" he whispers to her, mouth wide and curled sweetly. The pinched edges of his eyes warm her heart.

No longer afraid or caring about what she saw in the woods between Ethan and Kaleb, Hell, she is—was—a bigger monster than either of them. Gabrian speaks, needing the company of her friend—her curiosity taking precedence in the situation of her profound and peculiar experience. "Has it always looked like this?" She glances upward to the mock sky then back to her friend. "I mean, everything is so utterly beautiful."

Another soft chuckle escapes him. "Now I understand what Tynan was talking about."

Gabrian, confused, narrows her eyes at Ethan's avoidance of her question. "What?"

"Other than your obvious physical appearance." He smiles, swiping his hand across her shaved marble head. "You really are different."

Chapter Twenty-Six

A Trail of Crumbs

Another steadier but annoying beep sounds in the silence of Rachael's dimly-lit hospital room. The drawn curtain cloaks the faded colours of the dying flowers, their blooms low enough to hang over the edges of the ceramic vase they sit in.

Still swimming within a world neither here nor there, but not lost anymore, strings of her subconscious web tether Rachael to her physical form. A strange beacon of light shines from her chest, and she reaches to touch it, fingers tracing over a soft metal. She lifts the locket. Her eyes swim over the smooth stone, caught in its delicacy, bound with secrets of the universe. The soft glow beams outward, wanting to chase the faded visions dancing in the shadows. It calls for her to follow. Her mind swirls, thoughts of lives lived before pulling her in and out of reality as they busy to reminisce with her soul.

She floats through the memories of her lives, finding friends and family members not seen in centuries. Her heart is tender, feeling all the ties of her soul's encounters, and embraces with lost loves along the way. Drifting inward, through washed out images, she walks through them all. Connections to each of them pull her closer—reminding her of things she is and was. The vividness of her past shifts and clings to her, pushing her forward to a place she has longed to find for so many years—a place her heart longs to remember.

Up ahead, a light grows in its intensity, so bright she has to raise her arm to shield her eyes. It eats up all the colour sweeping around her and blinds her from it. The light rushes through her, tearing at her mind. Soft impulses beg to be remembered and Rachael clutches her head at the strange invasion. The balance between her sense of being fights with her reasoning of existence as the world around her spins. Her stomach flutters as she is zipped through a portal at speeds that send her reeling.

Then it stops, spitting her out, and she falls into a darkness of honey browns and chocolate. The scent of orange blossoms tickles her nose and the soft warmth of velvet caresses her skin. Words of sweet nothings whisper in her ear, and her heart flutters through the muddled words she cannot understand, echoing with endearment that melts her soul.

Sweet flirtatious glances are exchanged with an ebony shadow, cooing with gentle hushes as they pull near then fade away. Rachael gasps at the consumption of this memory. It is hers. She knows it because she can feel it with her entirety. It is clear, euphoric in every measure of its being, and yet, it brings a twinge of sadness. She clamours through her mind in search to find it again, to fall deeper into its embrace.

In a breath of time, she is removed and placed once more in a different fragment of the memory. Windswept leaves and beams of sunlight reach through the tall sycamores dance on her face. She walks down an earthen, flowery aisle. Her body, draped in a white cotton dress, and her hair the colour of sand, is done up behind her head in a crown of wildflowers that frame her smiling face. Chairs set among the trees are filled with bodies of people she doesn't know but loves with all her heart.

Her bare feet drift slowly forward, carrying her closer to an opening in the trees. Tresses of draped flowers sway in the drifts of salt-kissed air rushing in off the ocean, sleeping on the horizon. Every step on the mix of dark, tanned earth and the litter of white sand is a trail of crumbs leading her to the future, bringing her closer to the beach. The sand blushes with hues of crimson and tangerine in her arrival, a wedding blessed by a setting sun.

She remembers the fullness of her heart as it swells, wanting to rush the memory forward to gaze upon the soul that awaits her arrival. The memory fades and Rachael cries out. Her chest contracts, aching as her heart longs to hold on. Tearing at the empty air surrounding her, Rachael tastes the sear in her throat, raw from screams of agony.

A sweet flowery scent pulls her from her tears. The soft gentle coos of a familiar voice whisper *I love you* as kisses touch her neck. A glass of wine is accompanied by the crackle of warm crimson embers within a fireplace, reminding her of the heated sparks which burn between them. Rachael mouths out *I love you, Ry...*

Her mind slips away and bashes her into a fierce battle. Sharp images implode within her eyes. Millions of images bombard her as she slides from his warm fingers, his impenetrable hold on her arm slipping into nothingness. She loses connection to her world as her mind is shred into a million shards of intruding energies. A loud roar rings through her ears, begging her to hold on, to reach out for him while thousands of years of secrets, unknown realities of the universe, surge and overload her mind.

Her ability to comprehend anything is lost and diluted into the mere ability of breath. Floating in a void, alone and uncaring, the severe loss of everything swirls within a body—her body, one which cannot respond. Swallowed up in an abyss filled with her screaming, not one sound escapes her petrified corpse, and she is unable to find her way home again.

Rachael lurches forward and screams, her monitor screeching back at her. The wildness in her chest thrums, forcing adrenaline through her veins and pound in her ears, blocking out the sound of thundering footsteps rushing to get closer. She pants, staring wide-eyed and frightened in the dimly-lit room.

She lost him…she lost him, again.

The doors of her room bust open, two men in blue hurry toward her, frantic in their advance. "Are you alright, Miss?" They scuttle around in a frantic buzz of concern. "Please, lie back down."

Her eyes flutter, sweeping back the tears burning and rushing to the surface. Weeks of being still and unmoving produce unflattering results of aches and pains. Sluggish and malnourished muscles surface their discordance and announce their lack of cooperation.

"How are you feeling? Is there any pain?"

Is there any pain? How can she answer this in truth? These are loaded questions and the answers, like swords, are sharp and double-sided. She has just lost the man she would love forever somewhere within her dreams.

As the orderlies check her pulse, and ease her frigid and exhausted body to lie down, her mind rushes to catch up to her reality. Her mouth relaxes and curves at the edges. Rachael's eyes soften and shine in the dew of her understanding and her heart steadies, easing the duty of the monitor that has been keeping watch on her.

She is not really listening to the people in blue. Her mind whirls with her new discovery of her found past, clutching to the fragments of emotions that sting her soul, manifested nearly half a millennium ago. She may have lost him in her mind, but she is back.

All of her.

Every memory she has ever had is whole. The nagging feeling of misplaced time she had carried with her in every rebirth, the one she could never remember, is found and very much alive.

Chapter Twenty-Seven

Miraculous Transformation

Standing doe-eyed at Ethan's strange words, Gabrian's arrival has been noticed. "Gabrian, dear, we are so happy to see you looking so well," Vaeda chimes, her eyes alight and dreamy as she glances around at the other Elders who nod in accordance to her statement.

Wow, what is going on? Gabrian fumbles with all the new strangeness of her world. Yes, Vaeda has always been airy and glamorously kind to her, but it is like she stepped into a fairy tale and Vaeda exudes an iridescent glow that would make Glinda's sparkling personality pale in comparison. But Gabrian has a hunch that Tynan may be partially to blame for her new leveling up in shimmery awesomeness.

"Your uncle mentioned to us that there had been some new developments in your rehabilitation and recovery, but I never would have guessed this kind of miraculous transformation to be possible."

Gabrian smiles but it resembles more the qualities of a smirk. They are supernatural works of life. *How could something like this be too much to imagine? It was Magik. Anything in this Realm is possible.*

Right?

Or is this just another show of her being a freak of nature? *Ugh, whatever.* She sighs as her eyes roll under her raised brow. The shyness she normally hovers in has dwindled. She has been to Erebus and back, and somewhere in her travels, the meaning of shyness has been lost and does

127

not really fit into her world anymore. Allowing a slight snarky chuckle of distaste for their naivety to escape her lips, she replies, "Thanks, I guess."

Gabrian scans the crowding Elders who are eager to lay eyes on her abnormal recovery. A bit overwhelmed with the intense attention being allotted her way, she runs a reflexive hand over her head, missing the long dark locks that once draped her scalp. The attention is not heavy and deep. It is of awe and curiosity. Gabrian smiles at this new revelation and lets her eyes volley across all those who stand loosely huddled around her.

They are all as different as she is. Their faces are soft and glowing with the gentle hues of their Fellowships, smiling mouths curved upward with playfulness and joy glinting in their eyes. The Zephyr Elder before her is much transformed herself, her eyes light and filled with a girlish glow.

This is really weird.

Gabrian grins as her confidence lifts and lets her guard down. No more hiding who she is. Gabrian is too tired to pretend anymore. The crowd of Elders shift, and she instantly regrets letting herself relax. The strain of her muscles clenching all at once along with her adrenaline is torture and her jaw aches with a reflexive grind of her teeth. Sucking in air, Gabrian gasps as a bright blue hue hovers just behind the Elders, making its way into the circle.

"Hey, Gabrian," he says.

Blinking and trying to regain her composure, she responds, "Hey Manny." Her eyes widen and sparkle as she exhales, trying to hear through the drumming of her heart as it slams in her ears.

He smiles at her as she draws near.

"What are you doing here?"

Glancing nervously around at the Elders listening to their conversation, he straightens his shoulders a little—or as much as his good-natured ways allow him. "I am—" Manny grins, his eyes sparkle with pride. "I was invited."

"Oh?" Her brows lift, happy to see him but still confused.

Ethan steps forward, sporting a grin on his lips. "Maniek is our new elective for the Elder of the Hydor Fellowship," he hums, patting Manny cheerfully on the shoulder.

Manny's grin grows into a full-blown smile.

"Oh." Gabrian exhales, pondering the idea. "That is great. Congratulations, I think," she says, half-happy and half-wondering if he knows what he is getting into with this new level of regard in his life choices. Her lips smile but her mind wanders to a boat trip they once shared and her eyes search his for something—a sign, a glimpse of some unspoken information about someone they share in common.

She longs to ask Orroryn but there is too much shame. Gabrian hurt Shane badly and he still risked everything to save her. No, she cannot look in Orroryn's eyes and see the truth of what she has done— the pain she has inflicted. No, she is not strong enough yet, even with her miraculous transformation. Not while Shane lies heaven knows where, fighting to cling to life. No, she just cannot go there.

But she will ask Manny.

He will know, he has to know, and at the next opportunity, Gabrian will find out.

Chapter Twenty-Eight

Trial and Tribulations

"Alright, shall we get started?" Vaeda hums, addressing the room, but her velvet eyes reach for one soul in particular. Once she finds the large Schaeduwe, a slightly flirtatious grin slides onto her lips as she turns and glides forward, unhurried and touristic almost under her flowy elegant turquois gown. Everyone shuffles to follow her lead, but Tynan drops back to walk with Gabrian. Draping his arm around her, and gathering her small rigid form under his wing, the gentle giant begins his plea and tries to coax her into joining in.

"There no reason for the pouty face," Tynan teases his niece, glancing down and seeing her twisted lips as she tries to fathom what on earth she is in for.

"I am not pouting," she snaps in a hushed tone. "I am merely contemplating."

"Is that right?" He chuckles. "Well then, what is it that you are contemplating?" he says, a grin tugging on his lips. "If it is an escape plan, you might as well forget it. The only way out of here is through the Shadows and unless you have managed to manifest this gift as well you are out of luck."

Gabrian growls at her uncle, rolling her eyes at his suave grin. It is a bit unnerving to see him so cheery. Beautiful, but still unnerving.

"You know what I think you should do?"

"Not sure I really want to know."

Tynan rubs his hand across the top of her head then gives it a kiss, pulling her back into his protective hold as he moves her forward, toward the group that has left them behind. "Relax. Have some fun."

"Fun?" She huffs. "That is not exactly the word I would use to describe my visits here or this place."

Even though she is not officially being seated on the stone chair, as per norm, she is still in the hot seat so to speak. This is no pleasure cruise they are on. "Torturous, unpleasant, mal-intended, yes. That about sums it up."

Tynan's faces lights up. He releases a loud chuckle and pulls her tightly to his side, noogying her head. "Alright, alright, fair enough. I get the point. But I hope today helps to change your opinion of this place and what it represents."

Gabrian wrinkles her nose and smirks at him. "Somehow, I highly doubt it."

Continuing their trek in silence, Gabrian carries on with her gazing. Everything is so different. She cannot fathom it all. Gabrian studies the Great Hall. Her eyes bounce loosely over the walls as they stroll through the edifice. Glowing in the distance are cauldrons burning, warming the cold black and white-speckled stone. Their fires cast soft, welcoming hues of multi-coloured shadows as they draw nearer.

The magical but invisible binds that keeps them all on even playing fields within the sanctity of the Covenant are there, she can feel them, but it is as if today they do not apply to her—making her curious to test this hypothesis. Gabrian drops her eyes to her hands, feeling the familiar tingle at their tips just from her thoughts.

Feeling her uncle's hand on her arm pull her to a stop, Gabrian lets go of her intended experiment and looks up. The group is strangely all spread out, gathered in front of the large stone cauldrons ablaze with the different colours of the Fellowships, well…all but one.

The same cauldron has been barren ever since her first visit here—the one which represents the Silver Mages. The moment her birth mother, Cera, left this world for the Veil, the fire has been absent and today would be no different.

A soft lyrical voice cuts through the hum of souls murmuring all around her. "Gabrian, dear, please come forward." Vaeda holds out her hand, and Tynan gives her a quick hug, smiling down at her wide unknowing eyes.

"It will be fine, trust me."

"I trust you. It is everyone else I am a little leery of."

Dropping a quick peck on her bristled head, and wearing her down with a boyish grin, Tynan releases her from his sheltering arm and guides her forward with a coaxing hand. "You will be fine. I am right here. What could go wrong?"

"Really, you had to ask that?" she grumbles, half teasing, the other half dead serious. She knows exactly how things could go wrong.

Stepping forward, away from her Uncle's safety net, Gabrian's fingers blister. She curls them inward to hide any lightshow they may decide to display. It's not something she cares to explain to anyone right now. Reaching the line of Elders, she steps to the side to see them all, meeting their smiling eyes.

Weird. This it is just too weird. What in the hell are they so cheery about? Gabrian narrows her gaze, and inspects the faces of those gathered beside her. Still no tell signs for her to see what is coming. *Hmm, maybe I don't want to know.*

Vaeda steps out, waltzing to the center of the half circle of Elders, midway between them and the cauldrons. The dark speckled marble floor beneath her sparks then grows into a ring of light. A flare of airy fire ignites around her, matching the shimmery glow of her aura. She peeks over her shoulder at Gabrian and smiles. The Zephyr Elder's eyes light, catching Gabrian's full attention. Their centers glow to match the fire swirling lazily around Vaeda.

Turning back to face the cauldrons, she holds her hand out, facing the ever-watching ceiling stars above. Vaeda focuses on the one with fire that matches her own. It blazes in mere wisps, and traces of light that swirls around within is containment—strong, fearsome, and very much present.

Vaeda's brows pinch just for a moment as she concentrates on the magical fire before her. As if on que, it turns to her, like the fire is alive—a soul built of ancient Magik dwelling within the flame. Gabrian cannot help but gape at the extraordinary display taking place in front of her—awestruck and completely absorbed.

The strange fire flares out at Vaeda's silent summoning of its Magik, but releases its hold on the stone cauldron, and rises. Leaving no trace of existence behind, the enchanting fire lifts upward, floating toward the Mage beckoning for it. Slowly, it inches forward, a defiant child shuffling toward its mother in a show of stubbornness. But with one last express of will, it derails its course and swoops to the right, up and over the crowd.

Mouthfuls of 'Oohs' escape the lips of the gathered crowd standing behind the Elders, curious to watch their leaders at work. The magical entity rushes over them in an exuberant display of acrobatics, catching them all in a spell of exquisite and playful delight, but then turns and makes one last burst forward, stopping just short of landing in Gabrian's face.

Gabrian leans back reflexively at the close proximity of the fire, spirit, or *whatever the hell this thing is.* She ponders this then leans back in, seeing a depth to it—a call to her spirit, like a river calling to a soul, whispering for it to dive in. Before she can get a good look, it whips away and hurries to gather into an orb of bright light set above Vaeda's open palm.

It begins to spin. The orb's shape pulls in at the center, thinning into a tight funnel of light, and lowers to touch down on her flesh. Vaeda closes her fingers, wrapping them gently around the essence, and it disperses into strings of energy, sinking into her like electric blood into her veins. Each entry casts a subtle glow until the light is gone and her body has absorbed it whole.

The Elder turns to Gabrian and smiles, promenading back to her original post in the half circle, then gives a nod in her completion. Standing transfixed, Gabrian has forgotten her angst of being here. This experience is indeed different. Hearing her uncle's words hum over her thoughts, she smiles hearing the words again. He is right, it is fun.

The next to step out of line is Arramus, the Egni Elder who found her in the ruins of fire on the night she had been attacked by Caspyous' compelled minions. Arramus had gathered up her wounded—and still inflamed—body before anyone could see what she really was.

His large frame marches over to the same spot that Vaeda had just stood. Gabrian's heart flutters in anticipation and her eyes narrows, studying the stone beneath his boots. There is a subtle yet distinctive peppering of smaller specks of marbles where they stand. She can see that now. Almost the same colour as his hair. *It must be a hot spot for Magik where the Elders can draw on their gifts with less constraint from the binds that shield this sanctuary.* Gabrian contemplates this theory in her head and determines this to be the logistics of it. She gets it. Strange things have occurred in this area for her as well.

Arramus grants her a smile and follows suit as his peer. With an upturned palm and red glowing eyes to match the fiery cocoon wrapped gently around him, he calls the cauldron's flame. It is not as naughty as Vaeda's fire but it is warm.

Very warm.

Gabrian's brow releases a glistening tell of the immense heat. Beads of sweat trickle down the sides of her temples, dampening the edges of her hair as the fire sways haphazardly through the air toward the Elder's palm. She shields her eyes to its intense flare as it spins, radiating a stifling heatwave in its show of power, and melds into the funnel shape on Arramus's open palm. With a triumphant burst, it disperses into snakes along his skin and then is no more.

"This is incredible," Gabrian whispers to no one.

Chapter Twenty-Nine

Nothing

One by one, the Elders step out of formation and take their place in the center of the enchanted stone, the strange life-like fires releasing their hold on the cauldrons. Each demonstrates quirky and unique personalities as they obey the Elders' request. Gabrian gathers her hands together, fingers clenching in the excitement of this profound display of Magik. The way Ashen's ice sprite dances across the room, dousing out bits of heat in tiny crystalline impressions before curling around her in a lacy print of frost. Mirrored reflective small sheets of light, engrained with memories of the past and future, flash by as Ariah coaxes her cauldron to let go. Gabrian strains to take in any of the thousands of fluttering images cutting through the darkening space between them. A glint of a thought causes her to suck in a gasping breath at what her conscious catches in the flutters. A flash of Jarrison and Sarapheane holding hands rips at her heart before switching to another fraction of memory.

Gabrian's eyes twitch in her strain but close as the entity sinks to touch Ariah. Her eyes swirl with a prism of light as it fades into her body. Even though the glimpse was brief, it was enough to paint a smile on Gabrian's lips—a gift from the whirling spirit, she has no doubt.

The hum of chuckles lighten the room as Manny calls to the Hydor cauldron. Having no real official training or experience at this particular aspect of his duty, the water entity plays an impish trick and raises high above them all before dousing half of them in a bath of vaporous waves then rushes around the room, swirling and weaving in and out of the crowd.

Among the onlookers' humor, Gabrian hears the hint of a more lyrical giggle in the mix. A soft soothing melody of Lyarah's voice memory tickles at her thoughts. This old entity must whisper secrets hidden within the depths of the ocean, that of the nymph, and those gifted with the sight of their existence—a knowledge that lends Gabrian a lighthearted breathy laugh as well.

Manny's face flushes in the outright revealing of his level of inexperience. Furrowing his brow, he lets go of his humiliation and concentrates at the job at hand. His eyes flicker and spark just a little brighter. With one last show of defiance, the water sprite curls around the back of Gabrian's neck, slipping over the top of her head to face her eye to entity. Holding its gaze just a second more than two breaths, it lets go and heads straight for the newly appointed Hydor Elder.

Swirling into a twist, fueled by tidal power, it burns bright blue before washing over Manny's hands and sinking into his soul. The rush of pure Magik presses the wind out of Manny's lungs as he releases a loud sigh. His eyes dim as do the blue haze of flames around him as he glances back at his highly-esteemed peers. Seeing their silent congratulatory smiles, he finds his humor again and bows to the crowd, returning to his place in the semi-circle.

Vaeda's soft but confident voice breaks through the murmuring comments of the new Hydor's show. "Tynan, if you would be so kind," she hums, stretching her arm out toward the center of stone.

"Of course," the large Guardian retorts in a low, sanded tone. Stepping through the half circle of Magik wielders, and slipping Gabrian a wink over his shoulder, he marches into place, taking his position.

In Orroryn's absence, he was asked to assume the position of Schaeduwe Elder to retrieve the silhouetted entity from its cauldron. His hulking form is immediately shrouded in an array of shadowy flames, neither dark nor light, just varying shades of twilight that play hide and seek with his presence. He does not hold his hand out like the rest, for the Schaeduwe are beings made of shadow themselves. The Magik is within them and they with it. The ominous flames of shadow are attentive and obliging to his unspoken demand and rush toward him with no intention of playing games.

The sudden shift of veiled Magik, from the cauldron to her uncle, is swift and nearly missed under her blinking eyes, but the transformation washes a wave of vertigo over her and she feels her stomach turn as the world tilts for a moment. The familiar tingling in her fingers pulls her attention back from Tynan's exchange and returns her momentary lack of balance upright again.

Swallowing down the pool of saliva settling in her mouth, Gabrian glances around at the others. *Anyone else looking like they might throw up? No? Just me? Great!*

Her eyes end their search and return to her uncle as he steps out of the dimming glow on the floor and heads toward her. Handsome as always, mouth twisting in a crooked grin, Tynan delivers a wink. Sidling in to take up position beside her, he leans down and whispers, "Piece of cake."

Ugh, Gabrian thinks, *Cake.* In the strange reaction to his withdraw of Magik, the thought of eating cake makes her queasy, and a trickle of wetness fills her mouth again.

A subtle roar dances on the edge of her ears, distracting her from her unsettled stomach as wispy grey flames rush up around Ethan. His eyes light and his hand slowly lifts to call to the smoky whirling fire that fills the cauldron before him.

A loud snap stings her eardrum and her hand rushes up to defend the opening against the noise. Her sight dances over the others but not one reflects her actions. Either they are all used to the strangeness of this or the high intensity of the Magik is affecting her differently.

Hushed whispers fill the air coloured with strands of greys and antique whites. Strings of energy spring out from the hollow of the cauldron and dance wildly in the space above it like a swarm of fireflies alight and singing songs of the night. Each small fragment of swirling essence rises delicately as if they were spirits of embers, lifting and sparking from the heat of the soul's fire.

Gabrian eyes water in this raw unveiling of Magik, an intense spectacle of emotion moving right through her though it is nowhere near her. It catches on the edges of her senses and pulls her along on its rollercoaster of moods that cling to her insides.

Captivated by this wild Magik, she is completely absorbed—prisoner of its powerful unleashing as it treks back to Ethan. The lethal entity fills the room, but does not defy its mission, and weaves together, orderly and obediently. A definite show of Ethan's many years of struggle to learn his gift and contain its ferocity within.

A ferocity that Gabrian knows all too well.

Clutching his hands into a knotted fist, the Magik is withdrawn and in containment. The Elder's eyes dim just as a glimmer of sweat beads down the side of his temple. The sides of his hair darken, damp from the absolute reign of control over the mighty entity that dwells within him.

Taking a deep, controlled breath, Ethan turns and donates a smile of hope toward his young friend and colleague. It is a glimpse, a show of faith in one's ability to overcome circumstances and to stand resolute in conviction to desired beliefs. Withdrawing from his position, he is met by a friend, one of the remaining Elders to stand and pull back his gifted show.

Giving her head a shake, and letting go of the bombardment of Ethan's turn, Gabrian is curious to see what happens now. Having bared witness to a whole lot of secret Magik, this should be interesting and as Ethan had so nicely said it, *enlightening.*

Whips of pastel greens rise from the floor around Kaleb's feet and twist around his body. His honey-colour skin glows in the lime lighting. He crosses his arms over his chest, wrist touching and fingers extended, and raises his chin. The luminescent glow of hazel from his eyes stands out against the walls of green.

In his still silence, the Eorden cauldron responds. The first stirs and breaks into leafy neon plumes of light mixed with snaking vines that curl and switch as they transform. Nothing unusual in this display compared to all the rest. The shocking yet alluring miracle of seeing real Magik take form is now somehow lost in the repeated ritual being performed for her.

Yet, she keeps her eyes tensed, not lax on her observation as she seeks out another colour that seems to be hiding in the mist of forest greens and lime chiffon wisps swirling its way to Kaleb. She does not care what he is or that he may or may not be a wanted being. Judgement is not something she is at liberty to hold. She just wants to see what her soul so strangely desires to find.

The neon leaves and vinery entity, now settling politely around Kaleb's form, wraps uneventful around his outspread digits and dissolves into his chest. Gabrian exhales a disappointed breath and twists her lips. *No show tonight.* Letting her eyes slip to the others behind him, she waits for the next runner up.

A high-pitch searing roar pummels her backward as a bright yellow fireball lurches forward and hovers in front of her face. No one moves. No one. They all stand staring at Kaleb as he inhales a deep breath, wiggling his fingers.

Gabrian's heart jumps to life. The thing pulsing in front of her wants her attention and hers only. In waves of breathy hummed words, the message comes. "Yhou are the keeper of the soul's secrets. We lives and dies within yhour decision. Our fate is yhour future and our debt in yhour honour."

And with that it was gone.

The sudden void of energy leaves Gabrian cold. Awestruck by the message just given, she turns to Tynan to study his response of the oddity. Surely, he must know what to make of this. But his attention is elsewhere, unmoved and relaxed. Her eyes jump around the space, seeking out anyone who might have seen what she has. But there are no takers. The only one who looks her in the eye is Kaleb.

A strange web of energy floats between them in silence. Strong but serene, it narrows and connects them on a subconscious level of knowing. As their eyes connect, a warm flutter of calm opens up and spreads through her from within. As if feeling it too, his eyes sparkle with flecks of gold haunting the edges of his black dilated pupil. Though they are nowhere near each other, she can see the clarity in each fleck, the sharpness in each cut of colour that lingers in his eyes.

He grants her a smile and she receives it with a light heart. The fear that shadowed her before about the wild beast lingering inside of him just beneath his flesh is no more. Instead, a new curiosity and eagerness to learn more about him germinates and itches at the surface of her mind.

Kaleb's smile turns into a grin and he knows she knows. With a hard blink, he cuts their lingering connection and steps away from the darkened space. No one is any the wiser of what just transpired between the two.

Now, there is only one cauldron left to burn. Violent blackened purple fire swirls and whips wildly within its stone hollow. It casts an ominous shadow of doom over all that lay in its black light. With the beautiful displays of Magik, Gabrian had not really thought about those who had made this place so dark for her. They were banished to the shadows of her mind, cast into darkness by the light of this wondrous show of events.

But her thoughts are back now. And they are very much in the light as the shuffling of feet draws her attention to the crowd parting behind them. Breath strangles her. The familiar and daunting purple haze she knows all too well looms above the bobbing heads, whispering hushes of gossip and truth of his state of being.

The blood thunders in her ears as the Elder's violet aura draws nearer to her. Her eyes rush, scraping over the others but their faces are still painted with creases of serenity and joy. No signs of malice are hidden in their eyes. No disrespect waiting to lurch out and cause disarray. Her mind thrashes a million ways at once, searching for threads of inner strength. She let her guard down and scurries to find the walls of her barriers, her armour to shield her soul.

Her skin burns and her fingers sear as the Elder saunters in her direction. *Why is everyone still smiling?* This is the man who led her to her first death, a prisoner of the Realm. And *Holy crap he is headed right for me.*

A tall, wiry, middle-age man in black—tee-shirt and worn faded jeans—breaks from the crowd. She knows who it is but her eyes deceive her. His long strides, through the huddles of people, bring him toward her. With his presence, electric and way too close, Gabrian steps back to clear the space between them. He slows, hesitating only a fraction of a breath. His eyes meet hers with a nod and a meek but marked smile— one filled with softness, hinting of sadness on the edges.

The strange encounter punches the wind out of her sails, leaving her to drift on an ocean of memories. Within the small exchange of acknowledgement, Gabrian sees something different welling in him. This is not the look of a prisoner. Nor is this the image of a heartless killer. This is the face of a father, lost for decades in sallow gloom, who has finally found his child. The face of a man who merely existed, chosen to live again regardless of his circumstances—a soul once submerged in a suffering of darkness now able to see the light.

Gabrian fights against the throbbing pulse of her angst as much as possible and returns his nod as he walks by.

The Elders shuffle to the side, making room for the Derkaz Elder as he joins the semicircle. "Lady Vaeda," he hums softly, with no malice on his tongue, and bows to her on his entry. "Elders of the Covenant of Shadows."

"Cimmerian," Vaeda chimes back in reply, bowing to meet his. "Thank you for coming."

"It is my honour to be here."

His dark eyes alight with enchantment. His mouth curves with gentle creases, upward and kind. This dark and ominous Elder, who Gabrian has come to know, now looks much like the man who came to the hospital and did not punish her for being there when she was forbidden on the premises—the man who offered to help guide her on the journey of learning Dark Magik.

She narrows her eyes, fascinated by this strange metamorphosis of being that has occurred to Cimmerian. Before her stands a different man. The Derkaz Elder strides into the allotted magical position and the air crackles as he does. Raising his hand, the last lit cauldron responds in whips of violet strands—sizzling and sparking—whirling around in their containment. His eyes shift and are ablaze with haunting darkness. Gabrian shivers at the depth of death control within them.

143

The fire hisses and slithers from the cauldron in strands of dark Magik and snakes across the marble floor. The heavy scent of death and darkness pulls at Gabrian's sense as the thing slithers closely by on its way back to him. Strange memories entangle her mind, images of misty shorelines and beautiful undefined faces dance in the back of her eyes. Rhada's yellow eyes send prickles of knowing across her newly healed skin—this Magik she knows all too well.

A loud snap brings Gabrian back to life, refocusing her eyes to the present as the dark Magik curls upward, funneling like a serpent eager to return to its bidding master, and around his awaiting fingers. He turns his palms toward the hissing entity and it swoons toward his hand, coiling wildly around his lowered arm, and bleeding into his bare white flesh.

As the Magik is retrieved, and the Elder steps from the glow—his moment in the circle—the room dims. All is cast into shadows as the light of all entities dies out. Standing in hushed silence, blending in with the darkness, Gabrian becomes awkwardly aware that all eyes are on her. The unknown expectation of her attendance suddenly is brought back to the forefront and the weight of this elephant in the room weighs heavy on her.

"Gabrian, dear," Vaeda's gentle hum of her name cuts through Gabrian's head like a knitting needle to the brain. "If you will step forward and take your place within the circle?"

Gabrian's face flushes, the prickle of stress biting at the rawness of her severed nerves is horrible. The rush of familiar defences she often wears is back, fingers searing beneath her folded hands. Longing for the comfort of Shane's arms, his soft words, his ability to sooth the rumbling of her uncertainties, Gabrian inhales and does as she is told. Shane cannot help her. No one can. Not even Uncle Ty. He was in on it.

Her mind rushes in its silence, trying to focus and stay upright as the world sways strangely to the right. *Why is my life always like this?*

Mumbling sounds burble around her. Not able to make out any of the words, her face contorts, and everything starts to swirl. Her mind clutches at anything to keep her steady. The Elders should have told her, explained to her why she is here instead of putting on a ruse. Longing for the reassured words of an old friend, she listens intently. Searching within the silence, she scans the edges for any trace of comfort. Echoes of memorized words dance in the halls like ghosts.

Their shape is soft and warm, wanting so badly for them to be real. Then like a dream, the whispered hushes harden. The sound is weak but it is definitely there and her mind rushes toward it, clasping to grab hold with all her conviction. She needs this, however hypocritical it may seem. She pulls at the Magik with her entirety—pulling, fighting for it to be real.

And the sound comes like a rumbling riot, but to her, it sounds like a choir of chanting angels whispering sweet surrender as it gathers all around her. A curse, a gift, caught somewhere in between, she does not care either way, and welcomes it home. And with it comes the break in the dam.

Gabrian's head explodes with sound. Dropping to her knees, she rushes her hands to her ears. Her lids pinch closed in the bombardment of voices, images. She knows the trick of concentration and how to turn down what she does not want, but in the sudden flood, she is overwhelmed and strains to gain control over them. Compartmentalizing and riffling through all that has broken through, she seeks out the one in particular, the one she needs to get her through.

Hey, kiddo,

With wide eyes dewing at the edges, Gabrian stills. Clinging to the familiar wave of energy, she gulps down a hard breath, clearing everything else in her head away with a hard, mental push.

Ethan! she screams out at him as her mind hurries to wrap around his.

Welcome back, he hums, lending her a soothing grin.

Oh, Ethan, I have missed you in my head.

So it seems.

What is going on? I don't understand what is happening.

Just breathe. These are the sweetest words on the planet to Gabrian right now and she lets them ring through her, releasing a bout of fear welling inside of her, and presses her deflated bitten lips into an upward curl. Her eyes close to linger on the sound of his voice. She can hear all the rumbling of muttered words, the high-pitched concerns of Vaeda, but she does not care. She ignores them. Her mind is back and it wants answers—answers that Ethan has always been there to give her—and everyone will wait until she does.

Ethan lifts his hand and pats the air in Vaeda's direction, a sign to the Zephyr Elder and the others, to give them a minute. Vaeda hums to the others the unspoken message of what is taking place and the frantic murmurs outside Gabrian and Ethan's conversation dies down.

There is no need for worry today. For once, Gabrian, this is going to be a joyous and happy meeting that you are in attendance for.

Oh, Ethan… I, Gabrian's bottom lip quivers.

Do you trust me?

Her mind flutters for a moment on the strangeness of his and Kaleb's meeting in the woods but pushes it away with one breath. That was not for her eyes and holds no relevance over their relationship. *You know I do.*

146

Then I need you to get to your feet, put your chin up, and be the stubborn, determined soul I know is in there somewhere.

Gabrian opens her pressed lids and lifts from the cold stone floor. She wipes away the wetness from her eyes and peeks over her shoulder, ignoring the strange stares she is receiving from the onlookers watching her display of oddness—again—and concentrates on her friend.

Do not worry, it will be painless and enlightening for everyone here.

Painless? Enlightening? But what are they looking for? I don't know what they want, Ethan. She bites on her nails, concentrating on her friend and ignoring all the eyes glued to her.

What am I supposed to do?

Nothing.

Her nose twists as she purses her lips and widens her eyes. *What do you mean nothing?*

He grins and repeats his answer. *Exactly what I said, nothing.*

Chapter Thirty

See What You Have Done

Standing alone, wrapped in the shadows dominating the Great Hall, Gabrian clings to the telepathic connection she has managed to rewire with Ethan. Even though cloaked in a level of darkness that hides the quiver in her lip, and the fearful wideness of her eyes from the audience behind her, she feels exposed, in the spotlight, and stares dumbfounded at empty bowls of stone.

Okay, I am on my feet, standing like an idiot in the darkness. Now what?

Ethan cannot help the grin pulling at the edges of his mouth as he gives her directions. *Just relax and all the binds will find you.*

What?

Relax.

Gabrian inhales, shakes the tenseness out of her arms, and flexes the stiffness out of her fingers. Closing her eyes, she tries to quiet her mind…sort of. *Okay, I am relaxing now.*

Gabrian, he scolds.

Ugh, how did I forget you are no fun?

Gabrian.

Fine.

Just think of this as one of your experiments and enjoy the journey. Trust me, kiddo. This will be fun.

Eyes closed, she shakes out her stinging fingers. Inside her mind, she hears everything—every question, every doubt, bits and bobbles of scattered thoughts dribbling through the souls surrounding her in surges of mixed emotions, and surprisingly, even some expressing joy. Then, as if the volume has been disconnected, everyone in the room goes still. The silence is thunderous. Only the steady thrum of her accelerated heartbeat fills the void.

A dim glow lights through the bites of electric currents from her closed lids. Curious as to what it is, she breaches the darkness, opening her eyes to a faded space, a wall coloured in shadows and an eerie glow drawing to life on the floor beneath her feet. The temperature around her drops, prickling at her skin, and the hairs on her arms raises as it creeps up the back of her neck.

Bright flashes of vaporous fires flare up one by one, filling the curved edges of the glowing circle, and wipes away the darkness with an assembly of colours—hues of luminescent souls scurry about, painting the darkened space with smeared light. They hum and murmur in tongues, a formed language she cannot comprehend, and then settle into position alongside the Elders, still standing statuesque along the perimeter of the semicircle behind her.

Yet, none of them turn to see the entities accompanying those who reside there today.

How peculiar, she thinks, awestruck by the spectral phenomenon taking place.

Everything around her glows and swirls in a prismatic array of light—red, green, violet, blue—they all sway, chanting in a unison voice that sings to her soul. Her eyes lower and her body shivers, absorbing a euphoric buzz that fills the space between them.

Lost somewhere in a world of unspoken understanding, rejoicing in her very existence and knowing exactly who she is, Gabrian's tired spirit lifts from her body and dances merrily with the others frolicking, taking no heed of who is watching. Light and unhindered, she revels in the undeniable feeling of complete oneness with it all. Consumed by her soul's restfulness, she lets go of her strings of doubt filled with the knowledge that this is home.

Her stomach plummets, spinning wildly. Her eyes rush open in the sudden silence around her, returning her abruptly to the binds of the covenant and the body now covered with gawking and wide awestricken eyes, awaiting her return. Blinking hard, trying to focus, and hearing Ethan's voice press against her mind, she lands—the connection of her soul to her physical form intact—and turns to let her vision graze over the wall of waiting Elders.

Ever-changing streams of dancing light cascades in waves of glimmering rainbows over the row of smiling eyes and upturned lips. Gabrian's face screws up at the goofy-looking Elders starting back at her, chittering like spring birds in their glee. *What is wrong with these people?*

All done. See now, that wasn't so bad, was it?

What is all done? What in the world are you talking about?

The test. And I must say you passed with flying colours…so to speak.

What?

Ethan breaks formation of the Elders and steps toward Gabrian, her brain still stuck somewhere in neutral. Reaching out, he lays his hand on her shoulders and meets her eyes, gifting her with the warm adoring smile of an old friend. "Turn around, Gabrian, and see what you have done."

She drops her eyes and glances over his shoulder to the stares still clinging to her every move by all those in attendance. Gentle and adoring eyes meet her as she grazes over them. Vaeda dons her with a cheeky grin, twisting her hands together, and presses them to her soft pink lips. With a lifted brow, confused by the strangeness of her Elders,

Gabrian turns to face the marble wall at her back, coaxed by Ethan's hands.

"Well done, Gabrian."

All Gabrian can do is stare, mouth open and wide-eyed. The void of sound around her returns. The crackling of newly born fires raging wildly from within the cauldrons warms against her skin with the heat of their ferocious but loving embrace. Her eyes glaze over and her heart hammers in her ears, the world around her becoming all too vivid as her hand rises to cover her gaping mouth. *Oh no, this cannot be happening.*

"Our Allegiance is yours," Ethan hums to her, dipping his stance to bow his head.

"Um, what are you doing? You are starting to freak me out, Ethan. Get up."

Ethan remains in his dip, but his lips curl just at the edges.

"Why are you bowing? Stop that."

In the shroud of dim shadows, her eyes take in the crowd over Ethan's lowered shoulders. Behind her, painted by flecks of rainbow by the glow of Fellowship fires, every head in the room bows to her. She watches in horror as they all lower in waves, dropping their eyes to study the floor. "Tell them to stop doing that. What in the hell is going on?"

"It is an offering of unspoken respect. You, my young friend, are now the proud new owner of the High Table, my Silver liege." Ethan keeps his head lowered just a bit as he unveils her prize, keeping an eye on her.

"What? No way! No," she hisses out, biting hard at her lip. Her eyes count down the cauldrons, Egni, Isa, Hydor, Derkaz, all the way down to Eorden. The only cauldrons not ignited are the Silver one, as per norm, and Schaeduwe. "No, no, no, I am not a Silver Mage. Two Cauldrons are still empty, see! No fire, no Silver Mage hocus pocus crap. No."

Gabrian begins a frantic march, eyeing the cauldrons, and rakes her fingernails over the top of her bristles, missing her long locks to tangle her burning fingers in. "I am a Grey. That is it, and that is all. I just got lucky. It is a fluke."

"It is only a matter of time and a matter of training, my dear," Vaeda hums, stepping out to gather beside Ethan. The others begin to break formation and chitter amongst themselves in broken agreement with the former head of the Table.

A soft pastel hue of green enters Gabrian's space as Kaleb steps into the light. "And one of belief," he offers her, wearing a sincere smile. Flecks of gold shimmer in his aura as he gazes at her with tender eyes. "One must believe in order to see the truth for what it is.

"We must begin preparations immediately as well the commencement of her training." Vaeda begins rhyming off a list of conventions that must be put into place.

Holy crap, this is really happening.

This is worse than any torturous nightmare she could have imagined. A tsunami of panic unleashes to flood through Gabrian's soul making her legs rubbery. Everything is numbing. Her lungs refuse to take in breath, choking her. Everything around her smears and swirls in slow motion, drowning her with the knowledge that she now owns the weight of the world.

Losing the ability to sort out their words, she no longer takes in any understanding of the chattering whirling around her, biting at the inside her ears. Her heart pounds violently against the innards of her rib cage, and her veins burn with adrenaline as it sears through her.

Instant overload. And now, cue the mental breakdown as the world around her goes to hell—again. Slumping to the ground, Gabrian sits comatose within the circle of stone that has just sealed her fate.

"Is she going to be alright?" Arramus' low words rumble out, cautious and slow. Scratching his head, his brow twists over wide eyes that volley between Gabrian and the other Elders.

Ethan quiets his mind, dancing across the fringes of her consciousness. His pressed lips pinch up at the edges, hearing the barrage of curse words exploding and polluting her mind. Expelling a hearty chuckle, unable to hide his amusement, he reveals his findings. "Yeah, she will be just fine."

Chapter Thirty-One

Last Time I Remembered

Stuck swirling alone in her internal muddling on the dark marble floor, Gabrian finally comes back around. The continuous chatter of plans being made for her life jabs a sharp stick into her ribs at the word confinement. Jumping to her feet, steadying her rubbery legs, she growls out to the Elders as they resolute the actions to be put in place, to be effective immediately. "Excuse me," she interrupts, not interrupting anything at all. The conversations continue as if she is merely one of the entities floating unobserved in the Great Hall.

Hands are flying and words are spewing of a large number of Guardians to be put in place around the training area that is unexposed to the wards in place. "Wait a minute now, I don't think—" Gabrian huffs, her words denied access once more. Watching them huddle together, auras flaring with brilliance in their excited and exhilarated state, she bites the edge of her thumb and narrows her eyes. A flush of rose covers her cheeks as her temper rises.

Having been ignored and excluded in the concerns of her life for as long as her dealings with this group has existed, Gabrian has had enough. Throwing politeness and niceties into the trash, she allows the rising frustration to have a voice. Just a bit more loudly than she had intended, she unleashes, "For frig sakes, will somebody just listen to me!"

The hush is immediate. Her final words ring out and echo across the murmuring crowds still lingering in the background—eager to catch any hint of news and of her new status—and slaps them all hard into silence.

She wanted their attention, now she has it. All of it. Every soul under the shimmering Covenant skies above now lingers to hear her words. And Gabrian wonders if she should have just stood by, per norm, and idly listened to their gabbing before proceeding but she shirks back the alarming wave of attention. This is her life, and by George, she is going to be part of it.

"Oh, Gabrian. What is it, dear?"

"Shouldn't I be a part of this discussion? As in, have a say as to what happens?"

They all look at each other like she has said something so completely odd that they have to decipher the meaning of it. "Yes, of course, but because of this miraculous event, many conventions and securities must transpire and be put into place. It is in your best interest that we act on all of this immediately. Most Silvers have a lifetime to cure and coddle to their powers, but you have been gifted with an abundance of power all at once at full capacity. This cannot be left unguided for everyone's protection."

"Am I a monster all of a sudden?"

"No, not at all." Vaeda closes in on her and drapes a hand on her shoulder. "Completely the opposite. You are our greatest gift, and we will do whatever it takes to ensure your safety and succession in this Realm. You are our utmost priority."

Gabrian shudders at this offering of words. What exactly this entails she is uncertain but has a bad feeling her life is about to become somewhat more difficult as if it had not been that already. "So, what exactly does that mean?"

"Well, since Cera left you surrounded by silver wards, unbreakable and bonded to your home, we have decided that this will be the perfect place of your training."

Gabrian raises her brow, listening. "Okay..."

"And since this place is enchanted and allows no physical harm to come to you, it is the perfect holding place for you until we are confident in your ability to protect yourself from an unwanted harm."

"Sorry, what?" Gabrian cocks her head to the side and wedges her hands on her hips.

Cimmerian edges into the conversation, granting her a soft smile. "In other words, the Elders will be less likely to worry about your safety if you are guarded from those who may wish to extinguish your existence since your rise to such high status."

Still silent, Gabrian slips her eyes across each Elder in attendance to find meaning. "Those as in people with the same mind set of one Caspyous." Cimmerian bows his chin just a bit, feeling the sins of his doing as well.

And the lights of horror come on. "Ah, gotcha!" Gabrian says, nodding, and replays the whole terrifying list of events through her memory.

"This is something we must ensure never happens again," Vaeda hums, her eyes sliding across all in attendance. "We have lost our last known Silver. We will not afford our Realm to lose our chance of finding another."

Vaeda turns her attention back to Gabrian. "And so, you will be limited to the boundaries of your home. Only allotted exit in the accompaniment of a Guardian or an Elder. Training will commence immediately after the leave of the Covenant of Shadows and is hereby decreed by all standing Elders of the Covenant.

"All those in favour say 'I'."

A wave of 'I's' roar over Gabrian's protests.

"All opposed?"

"I oppose… me, the so-called head of the High Table," Gabrian growls out, glaring into the eyes of her newly-found peers, terrified and trembling in waves of anger as she loses control on her life once more. "I oppose this entrapment of my freedom."

"Gabrian, dear, we are sorry for this but it is necessary and is not up for debate. Until the time of your succession of training, and the acceptance of the Cauldron, you will be under our protection and Guidance."

"Please be patient and find your understanding," Ethan steps in and grants her a tender smile. "This means more to the Realm than you can possibly understand right now."

All eyes are pleading but firm. Obviously, her climb to greatness has ultimately led her to the highest status among the people.

Her people.

The magnanimousness of this hollows her, losing the meaning of its importance, and dulls her ability to grasp it. Spoken in Gabrian's terms, it just means she is a prisoner.

Chapter Thirty-Two

Wide Awake

A low groan of soreness escapes Rachael as she rolls on her side, and her eyes flutter. It feels as if a train had been thundering around her head while she was asleep and the light coming through her window burns her eyes. She pulls her arm up to shield her face and hears a shuffle nearby. Pressing her eyes open, she sees a large structure sitting in the chair beside her.

"Oh, Orroryn," she coughs out, still tasting the chalky residue of her absence in her mouth.

"Sorry, did I wake you? I didn't mean to disturb your rest." He leans forward in his chair. "They told me you had woken up and I—"

"No, it is alright," she puffs, trying to sit herself upright, heart thrumming wildly in his presence. She gleams at him and his heart jumps unexpectedly as their eyes lock in a strange dance that he cannot look away from.

"I should go," he rushes out, feeling sweat dew on his brow. The wild pulse in his veins becomes too much and he rises from his chair. "You need your rest."

The thought of him walking out the door and leaving her is too much. After all that she has been through in her journey through the darkness, she cannot bear his absence. Her voice cries out to him just as he opens the door to leave. "Ryn, please don't leave me."

Heart exploding, tears escape and slowly burn down his ebony cheeks—no one has referred to him with that name in centuries. "What did you say?"

Nervous, and bursting to tell him everything but terrified he won't believe who she is, she becomes the girl she was when they had met so many years ago, and slips into that mind frame. "I said, please don't leave me, Ryn."

Orroryn lets the door close in front of him, slowly turning to face her. He dabs the edges of his eyes, where moisture pools, and meets her gaze through his long dark lashes. The hair is a different colour and the skin a shade too pale, but her eyes are alight with a fire he remembers all too well.

Rachael's breath catches in her lungs as her lips curl into a meek but knowing smile—the same smile she has always given him—but today, it holds so much more this time. Pulling the covers away, she slips her slender legs over the side of her bed, eyes never leaving his.

He stares deeper into her eyes and whispers, "Taliyah?"

A flush of rose colours her cheeks. "I have worn many names in my lives, but Taliyah was my first."

Crossing the room with more speed than he is conscious of, Orroryn's soul carries his body, helplessly drawn to stand before her. His mind is lost in a time where he once was married to a spirit so wild and untamed that he could not help but drown in her, heart and soul, a girl he surrendered his life to and vowed to love above all others—one so very much like the girl before him now. "But how?"

"I found my way back home," she says timidly, dying to hold him with the memory of the way the world would stop and she would breathe him in.

A wave of energy shifts the room in a state of vertigo as he falls to his knees. His legs give in, unable to hold the weight of his heart and his desperate need for all of this to be real. Tears glisten over his ebony skin.

Rachael slides her small form from the bed, her bare toes touching on the cool tile floor in front of him. Orroryn pulls her into him, wrapping his arms around her tiny waist, and presses his head against her. His body vibrates in waves of feverish emotion. Rachael weaves her hands around him and tangles her fingers gently into his mess of dark curls, tucking him in tightly—claiming him.

Orroryn's mind relives the night he lost her in the Veil, when his grip slipped on her and she was gone forever. The pain returns so sharp, so severe, he trembles in her hold, remembering the look in her eyes when her mind let go, remembering everything as if it were only yesterday.

"Oh, Tali, I am so sorry I lost you. It was my fault. I should have held on tighter." His words crumble into his sobs. "I should have—"

Rachael hushes him, dying inside as she watches this warrior crumble before her. "It is okay, Ryn. Please don't be sad. It is over, and all that matters is that I am here now."

He draws away quickly, riffling through his pockets, and pulls out a wound ball of metal. He stares at it, heart thundering in his chest just like the very first time he was in this position, and lifts his gaze to the girl. "It seems like a thousand suns have passed since I offered my heart to you."

Rachael's own heart twists in her chest and the room begins to spin in the profound gesture before her, barely able to keep upright.

"It is still yours if you will have it."

Chapter Thirty-Three

Saturday Night Dance Fight

Whirled away and centered in the familiarity of her family cottage, Gabrian stares out through the glass doors separating her from the growing number of bodies appearing on her back lawn. When they said training would commence immediately, they were not kidding. What once held a serene, beautiful, well-kept yard now resembles more of an obstacle course with boundary markers and strangely-positioned half-walls peppering the green grass and aligned against the trees.

Littered along the edges of the property, large bodies stand statuesque, staring outward into the sea. *Guardians*, Gabrian thinks. This must be where the wards are weak and fade into nothingness. Her eyes dance to the garden gate, now worn, aging, and filled with the large presence of her Uncle Ty, arms outstretched and waving to give directions as to where everything needs to be placed in order to not totally destroy the garden.

Memories of a young girl dressed in her night dress tiptoes over her thoughts. Midnight visits to the same faded gate so many years ago, a rendezvous with a friend who would captivate her with his wild adventures to other dimensions, promising to take her along someday. She now knows these were no more than muses to keep her coming back and flood information to him that he was unable to gather himself. Two souls, so completely different in form and expectation, that existed ignorantly within a world which bound them together by fate and blood. Gabrian cannot help but chuckle that her childish fantastical life has become her adult reality.

The daydream vanishes abruptly as Ethan's voice cuts through the muddled silence of her memories. "All set, kiddo?"

Gabrian turns to greet her friend, a half-smile painted on her lips and pressed crooked brow tells him exactly what he expected to hear.

"Not quite the day you were hoping for?"

"Nope, not by a long shot."

He laughs and closes the distance between them. "It is not so bad. You have seen worse."

"You are kidding, right?" Gabrian chokes out, her words catching in her throat. "This is worse than bad. This couldn't have gone more wrong if I had planned it all out myself."

"Oh, it can't be that bad."

"No, really?" She flares her eyes and bites on her thumb, striking into a three-foot march in front of him. "Well, let us recall, shall we? Let's see, first I set my room on fire. Then, I was lied to as to why I had to go to the Covenant, pushed out in front of the whole underground of the Shadows, and put on display like the latest attraction at a freak show."

"You weren't actually pushed."

Gabrian snaps her head around, glaring at him. "You know what I mean."

He grins back. "Just saying."

Ignoring him, she continues her rant. "Then, I'm left in the dark as all the spirits of hell break loose around me, lighting up cauldrons left and right like the fourth of July. You know it would have been nice to have some warning instead of being tossed completely into the fire, frying pan and all."

Ethan's face twists as the list goes on and on. Gabrian's dramatic performances never fail to entertain him, even when she usually is within her right to upscale her overreactions.

"Oh, and here is the best part. Let's keep her in a cage under house arrest."

"Yes, I suppose." Ethan rubs at the edge of his shadowed chin, still sporting the ghost of his grin. "You do have a point."

"A point?" She stops and chirps at his blasé demeanor. "A point? Holy crap, Ethan, I have a whole box full of points, sharp as hell, and I am being buried alive right in the middle of them."

He laughs, her analogy pretty much on point. Placing his hands on her shoulders, he steadies her in her tirade, and offers her some sound advice. "Well, then I guess we need to find you a way to get out of that box. Right?"

She stares him down. His soft warm hazel eyes defuse some of the dynamite inside of her. Maybe he is right. She may not be able to change the fact this is happening, but she can find a way out of the unwanted circumstances.

"First you must discover the limitations of your gifts—understand them—and find your comfort levels. Then learn to master them."

The word *master* is heavy to her soul and sharp in her ears. The weight of it makes her slump a bit. How the hell is she going to master something older than time?

"Mastering your gifts will be your ticket to freedom."

Freedom, the word rings sweet in her ears. "You all don't expect much, do you?"

"It is not about expecting, anything, it is about taking all we know and sharing with you. Helping you place one foot in front of the other, in order to move you forward and keep you safe, even if that means to protect you from yourself."

Gabrian's fuse is out. She cannot argue with Ethan on this. He has a point, and his is sharper than her whole box of points put together as the memory of holding the burning book filters through, so strong that she still feels the sting of smoke in her eyes.

"You are going to be okay. I can't say it will be easy, but you will get through this—I think."

She shakes her head and huffs at his lame attempt at humor. "I see Kaleb hasn't come up with an elixir to fix your bad jokes yet, maybe that will be something I can conjure up. A new special gift to the mission. At least that will be worth it."

Rolling his eyes, Ethan pulls her into a one-armed hug and stares out through the window. The area is nearly finished to start the process of her enlightenment. "Oh, I almost forgot." He steps away and jogs back up into the kitchen, grabbing a bag he left resting on the nook. "This is for you."

"What is it?"

"Training gear."

"Let me guess, spandex and leather?"

His throat releases a hearty chuckle. "No not quite, those are only for Saturday night dance fights."

"Well, at least that is one less worry," she says, walking away to get changed.

"Where do you think we are going? Comic-Con?"

Chapter Thirty-Four

Unearthing, Bad jokes, and Ugliness

Comic-Con would have been a dream, and Gabrian would be completely over the moon if this were the case for her fancy outfit, but it is a far cry from anything that pleasant, not to mention the donated attire would have been acceptable. The bag of 'gear' Ethan handed her was much to be desired. The loose cotton clothes draped over her small form were not what she was expecting but at least they are comfortable, not constraining and restrictive fitting, just odd.

Patting down the side of her grey flowy shirt, Gabrian pushes open the patio French doors, stepping out into the newly reconfigured battle zone. Drawing in a long breath, the sweet smell of autumn and ocean fresh in her lungs, settles her. Wafts of warm of air makes the cloth belt dance on her hip in the ocean's salty breeze.

Bodies turn at her arrival, and the hum of preparations recedes into quick chirps of final necessities put into order. *Ready or not, here we go,* she whispers in a silent voice, clenching and unclenching her now warm fingertips.

This is her world now, like it or not. Fighting it is just a waste of energy she could be using to figure out her plan to push this crap behind her and find a better way of life. Maybe then she can find a way to bring Rachael back and slip into the Veil to see Shane. She does not know the limitations of her gifts, as Ethan so kindly put it, but if any of them lead her toward either of these, she will gladly follow and master them with a vengeance.

This new train of thought washes away some of the bitter taste in her mouth. Unsure of the extent of her entrapment, she makes a mental note to have these rules clearly defined for her so there is no confusion in the boundaries. Maybe this too can become a highly effective motivator. Freedom is worth its weight in gold, or flesh and suffering in this matter.

"Ready to begin?" Kaleb asks, jolting her from her internal architectural scheme of making this work in her favour somehow. His eyes are soft and golden, bright against the afternoon sun and his aura a gentle hue of lime.

Pressing a timid smile across her mouth, Gabrian moves toward him "Ready as I will ever be."

"Nice suit," he says, tugging at her black cloth belt and mirroring her image in his own Gi.

"Not quite what I had expected," she hums shyly as they start down the wooden steps toward the grassy arena.

"I heard the battle cloaks come later. Right now, we need you to be comfortable and relaxed. This is a research and discovery kind of training." He tucks his thumb into his belt as they walk and swings his other arm freely at his side. "Constriction inhibits natural flow, hence the light and airy cloth."

"I figured as much." She squirms in her clothes and a waft of air whipping through an opening in her suit makes her feel exposed and unprotected. This is going to take a bit to get used to. Her eyes dance around the yard, searching for the other Elders, but it is only her and Kaleb along with the nearly invisible outlines of the Schaeduwe Guardians holding the wall of protection to keep them company. "Where are all the others?"

"In conference, I do believe." Kaleb lifts a finger to point at Tynan's small cottage, and she nods in understanding. One gift she is already quite familiar with makes its appearance as she scans the outer layers of Tynan's small abode. Narrowing her eyes, she senses the multitude of energies huddled close inside the walls, their energies large and unbound by any covenant binds. "It is just you and me to start off. I volunteered to go first."

Her eyes rush at him, the words strange off his tongue. A ghost of his inner beast flashes in her mind, stirring her pulse into a more alert pace. "Oh?" she chirps, wondering if he is going to question her on it since this is the first time they have been alone since the transformation of his gift. She bites her thumb, wondering if he knows she saw...*everything*.

"My gift is a bit gentler than some of the others."

Gabrian makes an involuntary squeak. His words, arbitrary and spoken loosely, especially since her recent witness of events, chokes her. He hesitates, twisting his brow, and his eyes pinch at the edges as he watches her. "Are you alright?"

Not ready to confront him on this, she flashes a crooked smile and nods, covering her mouth. "Sorry," she croaks, continuing to cough. "Swallowed a bug." She hopes it is enough to remove any suspicion on his part.

Releasing a soft chuckle, he picks up where he left off before the eating of insects occurred. "And...I thought it would be beneficial for you to find a place to center yourself before we start unleashing all that lies within," he says, halting his steps and donating a slight grin, aura shifting ever so slightly—a trace of amber upon its frayed edges.

He turns to face her, casting her in the shadows of his larger form. "Having no place to go when wars inside you start to rage is not an experience I recommend. It is better to be prepared than left alone without shelter in the storm." Kaleb crouches, lowering to the ground, and sits with his legs criss-cross on the grass, patting the cushy blades of greenery in front of him.

Gabrian follows suit and cops a squat, mirroring her mentor as his continuing soft words flow across her. She hears him, his message, but she still searches for a sign of the beast she knows is in there—sharp, edgy flashes of raw fear of that thing he allowed to form, massive, alert and completely feral. The recollection strikes a chord. The comparison is much like the beast who once stalked beneath her flesh. The one who tore at the binds of her soul from the inside until it escaped and nearly devoured her best friend.

Her eyes glisten as the pain shears through her with claws manifested from sin. Its edges, painted with the poisons of guilt, fester in its swift cuts, bleeding her out in endless suffering—withholding remorse for her feelings.

Seeing the dew in her eyes, Kaleb stops his speech. "Gabrian, are you alright?"

She inhales raggedly, nodding her head. "Yes, I am fine. Long day." Fighting back with all she has left, she forces a smile. She will find redemption, she will bring Rachael and Shane back, righting this wrong she has served them. If she does not possess a gift that can do this for her then come hell or high water, she resolves to find a way to manifest one that will.

"Listen, I know it has been rough on you—all of it. And I would absolutely love to let you off easy and call it a day. But unfortunately, it is my duty and my honour to prepare you for what I am certain will come next."

His breath hesitates, looking out beyond her reach, then returns to his instructions. "I know the ugly in this world, and so do you. But I have seen it in nearly all its earthly forms, and I need you to be able to sort through it for yourself. Find a place just for you when it comes knocking at your door. And it will, I have no doubt."

Gabrian's body revolts, shivering in the levels of ugly knowledge, and releases an uneasy bout of laughter. "Way to sell this whole Silver training thing, Kaleb."

He laughs with her, lowering his eyes to the Earth, then peeks over at the small cottage filled with hope, outrageous expectations, and bits of sadness. "Yeah, pretty bad, eh?"

"You sound more like a demented cheerleader of doom and gloom than the seller of enlightenment."

He rubs the back of his neck and grins a crooked but cautious smirk. "I am not good at candy coating the truth. I don't want to discourage you before we even get started. Listen, I cannot promise this journey will be easy, but I can promise you I will do my best to make it less soul-consuming and prepare you for it. Help drum down the chaos and make it sufferable. Who knows, we might even have a bit of fun in the process. Sounds exciting, right?"

Gabrian laughs, wiping away the blurry Kaleb, and looks at him with clarity. His sincerity resonates through her, and she lets go of seeking out the beast he hides, allowing the friend to take its place. "Right," she hums.

He exhales loudly and shakes out the tension in his arms. "Alright. Now that I have managed to completely bugger that up, let's get started."

"Hey, at least I didn't run away screaming."

"I am not finished yet…give me a few days. You might change your mind."

"Well, from what I gather, changing my mind is not an option."

"Touché." He points his nimble honey brown finger at her. "Well, then. No sense is burying our heads in the sand any longer. I am curious to see what I can unearth within you." His fingers air-quote the word 'unearth' and his mouth twists in an impish smirk.

Gabrian cannot help but chuckle. "It is no wonder you and Ethan get along so well."

"Oh, why is that?"

"You both suffer from the same bad taste in jokes."

And with that, the tension is gone and training begins.

Chapter Thirty-Five

Eyes of Strangers

Kaleb and Gabrian settle into a breathing routine. He asks her to relax and feel the energy of the earth around her, to become comfortable in her surroundings, own the safe space she is quarantined to. She is to become one with the outside world in order to master the internal world he knows rages within her and would undoubtedly devour her if not kept in check.

Dangers of the gifts are unrelenting on a Mage's soul if they cannot learn to control and regulate their desire to consume, running rampant at any given moment—something he knows Gabrian is all too familiar with, as well as himself. This is a must-learn skill for people like them. The only other alternative is oblivion.

This is not an option he will allow.

In the stretched shadows of the evening sun, Gabrian closes out the brightened world around her. All the sounds of life buzzing become nothing more than white noise, a wall of cushioned sound to help guide her inward and onward in search of her quiet space.

"Search for a place that is calm," Kaleb hums, walking through the exercise, and keeps an eye on her facial expressions. "A space that allows for your energy to slow, to quiet, and listen."

Having learned this parlor trick from working with Ethan, Gabrian settles in and steadies her mind. All this leads to is whispered dialogue of the Elders nearby, excitedly chattering on about her next steps of development.

Throw her in head first, trial by fire, Arramus chuckles lightheartedly. *That is the way my father taught me. Nothing wrong with old school teachings.*

Yes, well, I am sure that was fine for you, but...

But nothing. Coddling her won't do her any good if the wrong sorts get wind of her being what she is and all.

He does have a point, Ethan concurs. *It is not like she has never seen the darkness that is out there. Caspyous and Cimmerian have made sure of that.*

Douses of loud mixed arguments going both ways pollute her eavesdropping just as Kaleb whispers her name again, for the second time. "Gabrian, can you hear it?"

Oh, I can hear it alright, she thinks. *No rest for the wicked it seems.*

"Gabrian?"

"What? Oh, sorry, Kaleb. I am trying." She opens her eyes and bunches up her nose. "It is just really hard with all the energy next door buzzing like crazy."

They both turn to peek over at Tynan's—even he can feel the lethal and abundant gathering of Magik under the charcoal roof, wondering if it will hold.

"Mindreading, right. I forgot how sensitive that might be for you." He returns his focus on her and grins. "Well then, I guess we will just have to work harder to ignore them."

"Apparently so from what I hear."

"Sorry, I am not following."

"Never mind. Inside information I just heard." Gabrian raises her brow and thumbs toward the huddled group.

"Ah, gotcha." He nods, knowing the Elders' urgent desire to move her training along as fast as they possibly can. The quicker she learns, the faster they can be assured her succession and her ability to lead her people, not to mention guard herself against those opposed to her rising. "Alright, ready to try again?"

"Do I have a choice?"

"Not really."

"Then yes," she huffs out, settling herself back into position, closed eyes and all. "Let's find this internal safe place of yours so I can prepare myself to hide from the onslaught of craziness they are planning."

"I see you have done some planning yourself."

"Yup, you have no idea."

"Might want to make sure it is solid then."

"Solid as stone."

Kaleb laughs out loud at her unrelenting thread of defiance, something that may serve her well once she can pass the final stages of her testing. So much rests on her small shoulders and her ability to survive. So far in this world, she has been by just hanging on that thread.

Pulling herself out of the chattering in the cottage, Gabrian forces herself to focus. She has to concentrate. Time is of the essence, and she needs to find part of the old Gabrian she knows is in there somewhere. The one who used to grab hold of every learning curve with a vengeance, owned it, and made it her disease until she came out victorious as its master. She needs her help. Then her life will be hers again.

Gabrian struggles at first, but inhales, forcing her lungs to pull hard—no longer afraid of devouring the energy of souls around her. The pull of pure life does not affect her like it had before she died. At least this she can be grateful for. This is indeed a gift.

Quieting herself once more, she trails along the colourful edges of her mind and traces their buoyant hues with her senses, becoming friends with all the dynamisms in attendance. A strange zoo of somewhat feral entities whimper and growl at her as she walks by. They crave attention, unsure of their master's strength of will but eagerly awaiting to be chosen then set free—challenging how far they can press her before she calls them back into her control.

Gabrian feels them, all of them, even the ones she cannot see. And she knows as wild as they may seem, she is the one thing they will all die to protect. She is their preservation. Without her, they are no more, and so, it is with her they find breath to breathe and light to live.

Small strands of energy light her way and wisp out from their cages. Little stings of their tantalising yet delicate ties tickle against her as she lingers by them, trying to study them from a distance and not yet engage their claim to her consciousness. She inhales the quiet calmness as the colours of her gifts settle in their cages, drifting off to slumber in her serene presence.

Kaleb monitors her face as she drifts through her mind, guided by his soft lulling commands. Her eyes shutter gently beneath closed lids, breath soft and repetitive. She has left him behind and is searching on her own, content and calm.

Her body lurches, serenity ripped from her features, and Kaleb's own wind catches, unsure of what to do. Gabrian shivers at a cold breath on the back of her neck and her eyes rush open to darkness. All the day's brightness is banished, taking with it any subtle hues of her gifts. She stands alone. Cold damp grass clings to her feet, and she is merely a ghost cloaked in night's colours.

Shouting from behind grabs her attention and spins her around. Shadows of silhouetted bodies fighting plague every measure of space around a large building crested in stone. Everything is chaotic and oddly familiar. Voices and smells, convoluted with fear and hatred, stifle her in the night air, polluting it with tension.

SILVER

An eerie triumphant laugh scrapes against the inside of her ear, but the words that follow it are unclear. Thunderous pounding erupts from the trees at her back. Gabrian turns to the darkness to see glowing eyes of strangers forming between the densely stalked forest. Large forms take shape, reminding her of Erebus for a moment, but this soon sheds its appeal. Appearing in waves of royal blue and violet arches of light, drones of greyish, shaded skin cling to bulbous, furred limbs—weathered and toughened, void of light and delicate life. More creep out from the folds of water draping along the shore.

Their intent of arrival is not one of kindness and comradery. It is an army of grey knights hellbent on destruction, brought forth by a magic she has not witnessed before now. They rush forward, racing toward her. Screams erupt from within and all around her as they thrash everything that meets them.

A barrage of red, blue, white elemental Magik explodes like fireworks in the darkness in an attempt of defence against the unwanted vessels of war. Blades of fire and ice erupt, streaking across the blackness. Bodies are pummelled and sliced clean through as they close the distance.

Gabrian covers her ears at the sounds of suffering and ultimate death crashing down around her. She watches as the dreary hoard mows down familiar faces, unable to move fast enough to avoid the raised silver and crimson painted axes of their attackers. Gabrian screams just as one of them raises an axe to slay her down.

But the strikes goes amiss, and she is thrust aside by a large feathered paw as its owner's teeth dig deep into the grey attacker's throat, crushing it easily within its jaws. The two bodies mesh in the darkness as they thrash violently, claiming victory over the other. Gabrian clamours from the cold wet grass to her feet and witnesses final stillness as the victor is declared.

"Something is wrong," Kaleb rises from his position on his knees and leans into Gabrian's space. Her eyes are flat and dilated beyond normality. Her breath is ragged and irregular. The ground around her rumbles, and her hands clench into whitened fingers. "Gabrian, can you hear me?" His hands cup her jaw, and he stares into her eyes, distant and locked in another world. "Come on, get back here. This is not a good way to start our sessions. Wherever you have gone, you need to come back. Do you hear me?"

"Ethan…" Kaleb yells out over his shoulder, not taking his eyes off Gabrian's stupefied state. "Ethan, get out here. I need you. Something is going on, and I need you to help me find her." He rises to his knees and shouts toward the cottage. "Ethan, can you hear me?"

Golden eyes turn to capture her. She knows these eyes, wild and terrifying. The large beast made of fur and feather focuses its hunt on her, making her body shiver in fear, muscles taught, and readying for another fight. "Kaleb, no," she screams out. "It's me, Gabrian, your friend. Kaleb, please, you know me," she whimpers to the beast, stumbling backward and onto the grass. "Kaleb, please, remember who you are."

Shards of pain slice through her. Caught between space, the journey overlaps, and the two become one. The creature before her grabs hold of her face, and she cannot escape its clutches.

Hollowed words pound inside her head, over and over, bellowing like a drum without remorse. Each one smashes at her skull until it breaks through to something vivid and brings her back, thrusting her at present company, back to the soft green grass and the heat on her skin in the warm setting sun in her backyard.

She jumps back, digging her nails into the grassy floor beneath to aide her escape, and puts distance between herself and Kaleb. Extreme green and golden flares of intensity flicker as his face and form meld interchangeably with the beast. He lets her, seeing the fear in her eyes and wearing it in his own. It cuts deep, beyond the measure that any word could. He knows that she knows. He knows she can see right through him and knows there is nothing he can do but hope she is the girl he believes her to be. The leader he so desperately needs her to be.

Ethan bounds quickly from the cottage to Kaleb's aide, trailed by the remaining Elders, and drops immediately at Gabrian's side. He clutches her in his arms and attempts to gain command of her mind—to force her acceptance of his wave of calmness into her thoughts.

No deal.

Feeling the rebellion, Ethan clasps his hands with conviction and prepares for the worst. Gabrian, still caught in the delirium of battle, reacts to his act of entrapment and explodes with a wave of massive energy, crushing Ethan as he clings to her form. The burst of energy punches out hard, both, jolting her senses, and breaking her free the last mental strings of claim on her.

Caught in a thunderous boom of voices as they call out broken frantic commands, Gabrian blinks hard, and struggles to pull her hands over her ears. Her face contorts in her failed attempt, due to the odd and impenetrable bear hug Ethan is giving her. With her soul still piecing itself back together, and returning to her physical form, she shifts, feeling the grip around her ease. She realigns focus to her pupils, clinging to her surroundings with much relief.

Ethan's soft words brush against her ears, feeling her return. "Are you alright now, Gabrian?"

She peeks past Ethan, and her pale Eorden tutor sitting wide eyed and edgy, and studies the space behind him. Only translucent traces of Shadow Walkers imprisoning her in the backyard can be detected.

Check.

No signs of any grey monsters armed with battle axes and glowing eyes erupting from the trees.

Check. Check.

Yup, I'm good. She exhales, nodding slowly. "I am good."

Chapter Thirty-Six

Flypaper and Hope

Lost and feeling drained from the strange trip to La-La Land she just endured, Gabrian stares for a minute, letting her thoughts gather their validity and readjust for sanity's sake. She cannot shake the intensity of golden eyes as they dance in the darkness of her mind, the ferocity they held as they ripped apart the grey soldier readying to steal her life.

The vividness of the whole ordeal is unsettling. Dreams are dreams. Even in their fading, she can always shake away their claim on her reality, but this is so entirely different. She had been awake when the images came to haunt her mind. She had a witness. Gabrian immediately bounds to her feet in search of Kaleb.

"Where did Kaleb go?" she asks out loud, striding toward Ethan who stands at the frayed edge of the huddled Elders—eyes seeking out his familiar form among the group cloaked in a smear of dark charcoal-colour clothing.

Something has changed. The whole slow dimension of the evening has shifted, the level of intensity thickening the air with seriousness. Someone has definitely switched on the airstrike sirens to which every Elder is in response, dressed for battle. Only there is no battle gear for her, just a loose-fitting cotton outfit and glances of concern in her direction.

Ethan's grey aura flickers, his words hesitating as he answers, "He left, said something about wanting to gather his resources for tomorrow's session with you."

Gabrian narrows her eyes at this. Only half-truths are spoken here. She can hear it in the whispers of his mind. The uncertainty she witnessed in Kaleb's eyes rubs roughly against her nerves after her weird internal journey. Ethan's strange explanation only validates her whims of suspicion about her friend.

"Hmm," she hums but does not press Ethan further. He does have a point. If she is to be trained in all the Fellowships' Magik then it does stand to reason that not everything would be bombarded on her all in one day. At least she hopes. Although, so far today, they are doing a pretty damn good job of opening the floodgates on her.

"Oh, okay. He just looked strange after our session, and I wanted to talk to him about it."

"He is fine, just wanted to prepare. You know how he is. You will have plenty of time to talk with him tomorrow." Ethan offers her a warm smile, but it does not convince her.

Something is off. Gabrian can feel it. She saw him in her mind as he truly is—raw and unchallenged, frightening and wild—and her curiosity craves to know more about the side of him that he keeps tucked so neatly inside. A forbidden beautiful curse that has caught her attention.

"You are sure?" Narrowing her eyes, she offers Ethan one more chance to come clean.

"Yes, absolutely." No dice. His lips are sealed, sensing her inquisitive mind scratching for scraps of information. "Besides, I think you have bigger things to busy yourself with tonight than worrying about Kaleb."

A large pepper-haired Elder steps into the conversation. "Kaleb is a big boy, just gave him a bit of a start is all. He will be fine." Arramus' energy emanates off him in waves of subtle ferocity. The magnitude of power in each surf pulses, meshing, and pushing against Gabrian's own energy force like the turning of tides. She steps back, giving the seemingly gentle Mage a wider birth in the strange, silent, and not to mention dizzying, evolution of her new reality.

This is really the first time she has stood beside the Egni Elder outside the binds of the Covenant of Shadows where his strength is not harbored within him. Well, other than the night he held her in his arms and carried her from the world of inferno. But that did not count. She had been unconscious then so his magnanimous well of power had gone unnoticed.

That is not the case today. Gabrian's backyard is a smorgasbord of power—counting herself in this mix of things. Out here in the open world, far away from the shield of the Covenant of Shadows, where everyone is fair game and nothing about their internal makeup is altered, Gabrian is now astute to Arramus' overflowing abundance of Magik. His bright fiery aura quickens and switches around him, quite alive and fueled for action.

"So, are you ready to turn the heat up a notch?" With his hands on his hips, and jovial light rising in his eyes, the Elder awaits her readiness.

Her reply to Arramus' question gets caught in her throat with an impromptu cough of nervous laughter.

"Since Tynan has informed us you started the morning off in flames, so to speak," Arramus starts.

Traitor, Gabrian thinks a jest for Tynan's loose lips.

"We thought it's fitting that I would be the one to introduce you to your defensive training." His grin is infectious and unarming.

Stealing a quick glance at Ethan, her brows arch as her words find their way to him. "Sure, why not? No time like the present." She hoots at the Elder, exhaling a defiant breath. "And since I am obviously not going anywhere anytime soon, might as well start the clock on my prison sentence." She shrugs, eyeing the both of them, and does not care if anyone's feelings are slighted or not. "Who knows, maybe if I am a good girl, and try really hard, I might get out on early parole."

The two Elders chuckle at her comment, letting the snarky tone in her meaning slide over their shoulders. "Ah, it won't be so bad." With a grin painted on his lips, Arramus turns away, signalling to others it is time to begin. He peeks over his shoulder and hoots a cheer back at her. "It will be over before you know it."

Ethan pats her on the shoulder and pulls her into a stride next to him, edging her toward the center of her backyard. "Arramus is right, you know. The time will pass quickly, and hey, it is you we are talking about. I have a feeling at least one of two things will happen next."

"Oh really? Please do enlighten me, my all-knowing wise and powerful, Yoda."

Pushing his words through a hopeful chuckle, Ethan knows her sassy remarks are just her defence system kicking in, and a sadness ghosts over his heart. The replay of Gabrian's stolen innocence, replaced by ugly knowledge of this world—her world—flashes in her eyes. They are facts of Magik he himself knows all too well, a bond he and Gabrian both share, separated by centuries of youth.

Life is a journey filled with truths. It cannot always be filled with rainbows and butterflies. And for some, it is within the deepest and darkest hours of strife that one finds strength to stand back up, courage to keep standing, and the brightest strands of light to cling to in order to cast one's own shadows.

Gazing at his brave and feisty little friend, Ethan unveils his forecast. "Well, for one, you will either ace this learning process with flying colours, so to speak and have your freedom returned."

"Or two?"

"Two, knowing you as I do, you will manage to find a way to twist all of it into one of your experiments, as you so like to call them, and change all the rules of this game," he says, giving her a knowing wink.

Ethan tucks her in for a quick one arm hug of support as each of his words stick to her like flies to flypaper. Something about the way they move through her mind gives her hope. She likes it.

Chapter Thirty-Seven

Fire and Ice

Standing before Arramus is one thing. Being watched by a hoard of highly expectant Elders, who just placed a mountain on your head, is quite another. A surreal cloud of fogginess clogs Gabrian's mind and her nerves bite at her from the inside, feeling all eyes glued to her every single move. The burn in her fingertips pulses with each beat of her heart, and she shakes her hands, trying to still their fury.

Her eyes abandon the Egni Elder to watch Ethan take his leave and stand at the edge of the makeshift training perimeter in her backyard, the one created by methodically placed rectangular shielding stations forming a large circle around them.

"Alright, little one, are you ready?"

Gabrian's eyes rush back to study her new mentor. Giving her hands one more shake, she nods and brings her attention to the lesson. Arramus donates a wide smile that pinches the edges of his eyes and nods.

"Excellent," he hums, bringing his hands in front of him, upturned and touching pinky to pinky. "We are going to start slow, and as we progress, I will engage with your gift to its fullest potential."

"What happened to let's throw her in head first, trial by fire, gung-ho whoopla you were spouting earlier?" she offers him, brow twisted and matched by a nervous grin resembling more of a smirk.

"How did you—" Gabrian taps the side of her head and shrugs, watching the Elder as he figures it out. "Ah, you heard that, did you?" He rubs the back of his head and glances back at Tynan's little house.

"It is kind of hard not to hear when the thoughts are so intensely given out."

"Sorry about that, it wasn't intended to be mean. I thought it might be the best way to draw out your gifts, and help you deal. I mean…learn how to wield them. I still hold an old school mentality for some things."

"So, why the start out slowly route, then?"

"I was outvoted." He grins.

"Oh." Gabrian pulls her eyes away from the apologetic Elder and peeks over her shoulder to the crimson setting sun. Its belly dips into the darkened sea, flares of colour dancing across the water, lighting the edges of fleeting waves on fire. The warm glow of the day's end softens her rustling soul, reminding her of better days, of the past and future moments to come. She can do this. Compared to what she has been through, this is a walk in the park.

Ugh, never mind. No parks. Stay away from the park. The thought strangely unearths a giggle from somewhere deep within. As deranged as it is, at least she can laugh about it now, sort of.

"Gabrian, are you alright?"

The voices come from two places at once, inside and out. Arramus hums his request with sound while Ethan does his Magik inside her head. She assures them both with a shake of her head, and a nod, darting her eyes from one concerned Elder to the other. "Yeah, I am good. Just nervous, I guess."

"Don't worry yourself over it. This will be a piece of cake. Or fire I should say," he ruses, bringing his hands to touch together again.

Gabrian settles. It is time to focus and get this prison sentence over with. "Yes, fire. On with the show."

A waft of heat kisses Gabrian's face, brushing her back a step as a large orange ball of flame bursts with a growl and rushes to consume the empty void of Arramus' cupped hands. A blue crust bottoms the beast as it riles and twists, cascading faint shadows to dance over both of them in the depleting light of day.

The fire's alluring intoxication draws Gabrian back in, recovering from her lost step away. She marvels in its splendor of colours and fragrances as it heats the dewing air of dusk.

"Now." Arramus' word breaks the spell, abruptly awaking Gabrian from the soothing trance. "I want you to hold your hands out and cup them together like mine."

Her eyes rip open, wide and alert, and the haziness is gone, bells ringing in her head with alert. "What? I can't do that." Gabrian pulls her arms in close, biting the edge of her thumb.

"Sure, you can."

"No, seriously. I can't."

"Well, let's see. You managed to set a book on fire this morning, so yes, you can. And I have it on good authority that you were once on fire." He offers her with a grin. "You know how I know this? Because I was the one who put out the flames. So, yes, you can."

Her eyes rush to Ethan. *I can't hold fire. Is he insane? I was unconscious the first time and the second time I was asleep.*

Trust, Gabrian. You must have trust. He knows what he is doing. It will be fine, just breathe. Focus and find that stubbornness I know is in there.

"You can," he hums at her, waiting for her to finish her silent conversation with Ethan. "Now stop looking at Ethan for help, 'cause he can't do this for you. Stop biting your fingers and put your hands together. You will be just fine."

She draws her eyes away from her friend and glances up at the Elder's face, coloured by fiery shadows, and whispers a low prayer. "I can do this."

"You can do this. Just don't be afraid of the flame. It will hinder your process."

An awkward chuckle bubbles out from within her. "Oh, excellent…no problem. Don't worry about the massive ball of fire you are about to coddle in your hands. It's all good," she blathers out, not really talking to Arramus. It is more of a half-hearted pep talk for her psyche, an attempt to hear the meaning of the words on a different and deeper level. "I can do this. I can do this." She chants low, over and over, pulling her hands together, and coaxes them slowly toward the flaming ball of Magik. "I can do this. I can…"

Arramus edges his gift of inferno toward the small youngling and holds it to hover over her small trembling hands. "Remember, don't be afraid of it."

Don't be afraid. I can do this. I can do… this. Don't be afraid.

Don't be afraid, Ethan pipes up, offering his silent support.

I'm trying. Okay?

You are afraid. I can feel it.

Why don't you come over here and stretch out your hands in front of this thing, and we will test your fear factor level.

Gabrian, Ethan hums.

Ugh, I'm trying. Get out of my head. You are making me nervous.

Lowering the back of his hands to touch against Gabrian's open vibrating palms, Arramus whispers slow and calm, "Don't be afraid."

Don't be afra—holy hell, that thing is massive.

Breaking the seal, Arramus pulls his hands apart to let the flame descend. Gabrian's flesh stings with agonizing pain as the Magik touches down. *And hot! Sweet mother of…* Instant reflexes kick in as the pain engages with her brain. The flame engorges and flares out, catching the hem of her loose cotton Gi, and sears the edges of her sleeves. *Crap, I am on fire!*

Gabrian breaks from her poetic pose to flap her arms out wildly, dislodging her hands, and beats at the lace of fire eating her clothing. Not making headway in dousing the flames, words taught to her as a child in case of any fire stomp through her mind—*stop, drop, and roll*—and she does as she is commanded.

Rolling around on the grass with conviction, the glow of Gabrian's fiery ensemble writes waves of orange streaks against the blanket of night—much resembling the swish of sparklers in a child's hand on a warm summer night. Gabrian slows her movements, studying her seared black suit—assured the enemy has been destroyed. The failing remains of light turn her world into the supernatural follies in a comic book, its inked characters rumbling with colourful hues of laughter.

Gabrian glances up at the hue of crimson outlining the form of her fiery mentor, her tender fists clenched in soreness. "Well, that couldn't have gone any worse."

Another blast of laughter thunders over her as Arramus lowers down and reaches for her wrists—eyeing what remains of her sleeves. Gently flipping her hands over, he tenderly uncurls her tiny reddened fingers. Peering through the darkness Arramus, determines the level of damage done. Pressing the tender flesh with the tip of his thumb, the soot releases its hold on her flesh and wipes off. Ashes fall unclaimed. Beneath the evidence of failed first attempts unveils soft supple flesh, unmarred and pristine.

His eyes lift to hers, and his hands—warm and gentle—cup her fingers, holding them safe. "Maybe we should start just a bit smaller."

"Do you think?"

Chapter Thirty-Eight

Messages and Ghosts

Arramus finally takes pity on her around midnight, after hours of trying to ignite her fire gifts. She finally manages to draw flame onto her index finger after multiple attempts of him toning it down to end the onslaught of abuse to her poor disintegrating suit.

May it now rest in peace.

After a loud rumble of congratulatory approvals from the remaining Elders, everyone unanimously votes to cease training. The day's unveiling of extraordinary findings depletes much of the buzzing excitement, and they all seemed to be running on reserves at this point, especially Gabrian. It had been a very long day for everyone.

The whole day had been nothing more than a continual whirlwind of life altering events that even in her newly-healed state she is eager to shut down and reboot. After a nice long hot shower, all traces of her first day of training are washed away and thrown rightfully in the trash. Gabrian slides into bed, properly clothed in pink fuzzy jammies printed with yellow giraffes, book in hand, and happily awaiting dreamland. She grins as her fingers run over the soft supple texture of her new purple and silver comforter draped over the bed. She flips the edge over to read the label, curious as to the material used to make it.

A chuckle escapes as she sees the words 'Fire Retardant' in bold print. The lengths her uncle goes to in order to ensure her safety, his unspoken gestures of quiet love for her, warms her heart.

Stuffed into her pillows, and surrounded by soft light, Gabrian's body settles into a blissful rest, but her mind has plans of its own. Her book, which normally holds the mystical power to sooth her wandering thoughts, should have knocked her out cold after the day she just had, but it holds little effect. Her eyes refuse to stay on the pages and drift around the room, catching on the menacing time keeper that ticks out its warning of another hectic day awaiting her in less than seven hours.

Rotten know it all.

A faint ping bounces across the room. Putting her book to the side, she slips out of bed and riffles through the pile of books on the shelf until she finds the culprit of the noise. Snatching up her phone, she flips the cover open and it comes to life as she returns to her bed. She had not paid it any attention in forever, evident by the ton of unread emails in her inbox.

Her fingers slide across the screen, scrolling through the list until a familiar name makes her stop and smile. Taping quickly on the name, her screen opens and her heart lightens, chuckling at his opening words.

To: Gabrian Shadwell

You don't call, you don't write. I am starting to get a complex. Ha ha. Seems like forever. It was great to see you and meet your friend, Ethan. That boyfriend of yours better watch out. The bar is busy as usual. Filled to the brim with life but only one girl has the key to my heart. Miss your smile.

Write me. Better yet, come visit. Feel free to bring Ethan too.

Hugs from your biggest fan, T

Gabrian hugs the phone to her chest, missing the hell out of her friend. It is so easy with him. Thomas is like a missing piece of her life's puzzle she never knew was missing, until after they met. And now, he fits so perfectly into her heart that she cannot imagine not knowing him.

To: Thomas Blackstone

Sorry for not writing. I have been a bit busy the last few weeks. Let's see, where to start? Oh yes, so…I got kidnapped by a Dark Magic Mage stricken with grief for his dead daughter and was being coerced by my father to do his bidding. Who, by the way, is the trapped soul of an evil Vampire. Then let's see, I got pulled into Erebus by soul-sucking Gargons and then sent back to Earth by the Keeper of the Eastern gate of Erebus because I am special and need to help save the world, or something to that effect. Hmm, what else? Oh yes, upon my return to life, I emerged decrepit and useless as the most hideous remanent of a human shell one can possibly become but was healed by a very nice but scary mythical Nymph who lives in the ocean just around the corner from my cottage.

And now, to top it all off, I have been deemed the leader of the High Table—Silver Mage to the people. So, in order to secure my reign, I am a hostage in my own home. I was sent into a terrifying mind-altering trance by an Elder, who's Magik is forbidden and hunted, and set on fire. All activities so far are approved training by the Elders of the Realm because they are hoping to force Magik to appear out of my butt.

Miss your smile more.

And I have a better idea. Come rescue me please, Gabrian.

Hmm, nope. Probably not the best letter to send. Truth, in my case unfortunately, is definitely stranger than fiction, Gabrian thinks, determining this would be an immediate way to get her emails put on Thomas' automatic ignore list. Not to mention an open invitation for a quick call from him to have her put her on the watch list for the looney bin express—the one that arrives with the adjustable white coat, straps, and everything. Gabrian sighs, deleting the truth from the email, and begins candy coating the letter.

To: Thomas Blackstone
Sorry for not writing. I have been a bit busy the last few weeks.
Swamped with work and had a family emergency. No biggy. Then
I managed to come down with a bug, and I was out of commission
for a bit. But I feel much better now.
I met a couple of new people who have friend potential. (Don't
worry they could never replace you…EVER)
And, oh yeah, I got a promotion of sorts. Now Ethan has me busy
training like crazy. No rest for the wicked, I guess.
Miss your smile more. And I have a better idea, come visit me
when you get some vacation time, Gabrian.

There that ought to do it, she hums, pressing the send button, and lets the device fall against her chest. Another ping makes her pull back the phone.

New message from Shane.

"Shane!" she gasps.

Her chest explodes. Clumsy fingers touch the screen, pressing all the wrong buttons and messing with her heart. Finally, she forces them to slow and find the right button.

Shane: I miss you.

Gabrian's eyes burn. Water floods her vision, smearing the words into an unreadable blur on the screen. Frantic to reply, she swabs away the dew with her pajama sleeve and begins to type. But her fingers freeze. Narrowing her eyes, she scrolls up and reveals the last words she had sent. The last time they talked.

Shane: Yah.

        Gabrian: I need you.

Shane: Are you OK?

Gabrian:

Yes, no… Listen, I was wrong.

Everything I said,

Everything I did to push you away.

I was wrong.

Shane: Stop.

Gabrian: No, I need to explain.

Gabrian: I just need to hear the sound of your voice.

Gabrian: Shane, please.

Gabrian: Are you there?

Shane: Just give me a few minutes. Okay?

Gabrian: Okay. Will I see you soon?

Shane: Yah. Soon.

Shane: I miss you.

Her chest wrenches, and she pulls the phone tight against her chest once more. The new message from Shane was not new at all. It just was never seen, never opened because she had been pulled away into Cimmerian and Adrinn's private dark war before it was received—both Gabrian and Shane torn from this world before it could find its way between them.

She glances once more at the phone and crumbles into tiny pieces.

Shane: I miss you.

It is his last words that deplete her will to remain awake. Burying herself within the folds of her comforter, Gabrian clutches the phone tightly in her grip. Tears of remorse and hollowness weigh heavy on her eyes, finally lowering them. Her lips tremble as she breathes out the words, "Gawd, I miss you so much."

A rippling wave of sadness warps the air around her words. The room fills with heaviness as she closes out the world of labored truths, hurrying toward the sweet oblivion of exhaustion, no longer able to hold onto the ghosts haunting today.

As the clock strikes one, today becomes her tomorrow.

Chapter Thirty-Nine

Theory and Orbs

Drained of all energy, Gabrian drifts in the gentle void of slumber when a soft warm glow licks at her closed lids, beckoning them to open. Flickers of candlelight make the furniture in her room dance and sway with jittery shadows, hopping back and forth as the flame shifts on it wick.

She rubs her eyes and peers around the room, noticing the cloak of night still blackening her windows. The light, however dim, emanates a disruptive glow that irritates her enough to lift her head from her pillow. Its location is strange. Centered in the middle of her wall, it is neither in the bathroom nor the hallway. She sits up, more alert, and focuses her eyes. There is an entrance in the wall, just behind her bookshelf, where the light lingers.

Her mind flickers, tracing the start of her day yesterday, back to the mirage that appeared through the smoke when the *City of Ashes* met its untimely demise. Swinging her legs over the side of her bed, Gabrian gets to her feet and crosses the small divide between her and the vision. It is open, inviting, and very unusual. The subtle aroma of paper and patchouli drift on her senses, and she moves toward the phenomenon before her brain registers that she has moved. Her hands reach out to touch the transparent illusion, searching for the tangible proof of the wall that once stood in its place, but her fingers find no evidence. They press clean through. Taking one last glance at the solid wall beside her, she lets go of what she knows to be true and follows behind her curious fingers.

Once across the threshold, her skin, muscles, and everything right down to the core of her bones, are met with a buzz of energy. It reminds her of when she was young and had played inside a netted trampoline, everything filled with static electricity. Even the hair on her head feels like it is growing. Her hands lift to brush over the short bristles on her scalp and find they have not grown at all. Her fingers trace over the ends of phantom hair, leaving a tingling sensation in their wake.

"Weird," she drones out, eyes wide, and scans the contents of the new room. "What the…" Her words fade into a hushed breath as her eyes catch movement on the ceiling. Small wandering orbs of soft light float unhurried across the space above her. Layers of flickering sparks drift along small air currents like mock candles, wicks alight with flame. Their gentle glow casts the room in a warm soft hue and her form shadows the boarded floor below.

As Gabrian steps farther into the room, walls painted with tall shelves emerge from the shadows filled with strange-looking artifacts and books—hundreds upon hundreds of books, all bound with different shades of leather and canvas. Some are smooth and supple while others look torn and tattered—showing their age and wear. She edges toward them, drawn to their shape. Running her fingers delicately along the edges of their spines, the energy in the room shifts in vibration. Each volume of written word seems to exude its own unique identity of being, pulsating with different levels of frequencies.

She slowly drifts along the wall, surfing the different waves of bound knowledge as she goes. The orbs swim in and out of view, following along with her, then wander off into the darkness—flickering in the distance to give glimpses of what lies beyond her sight. Gabrian's eyes follow as far as she can see. A barrage of old books unfolds, placed together in slender rows soldiered in columns cloaked by the absence of light beyond.

Curious of this strange place, she steps toward one of the alleys, eager to explore, and is denied her voyage. A barrier of energy wraps around her then retracts its hold on her and forces her to back-step into the light. Lifting her hands to push out against the invisible threshold, Gabrian meets an intangible force-field that bends slightly with her touch but is unyielding to her request of entry.

Although denied access, she can hear them—the books. They all sing out to her, a silent song of promise, of knowing, of serenity, and of protection. She lingers on her side of the blockade, soaking in their glorious state of existence. Thwarted once again by Magik. This barrier is merely a temporary obstacle. She can feel it—another puzzle piece she will learn how to fit into her life. With a quick inhale of temporary defeat, Gabrian peeks over her shoulder at the space she *is* allotted freedom, and turns to explore.

Her eyes spy a small wooden desk and chair protruding from the wall, snuggly tucked into a cozy nook just around the wall to the right of where the entry of her room still stands erect. It reminds her of an old banker's desk with small slotted shelves lining the top of it. She narrows her eyes, and walks toward it, regarding the more modern constructions of notebooks and sketchpads all neatly lined along the left side of it.

Being the ever-curious mind, Gabrian removes one of them and opens it.

Introduction to understanding Multi-Level Abilities

The secret to handling any variation of a gift is to begin with respecting the element you are working with.

Gabrian inhales, flipping through the pages. Handwritten notes and scratches of unfinished sketches litter the pages, each categorized and highlighted according to the specific magical gift they pertain to. This one just happens to be the Egni Fellowship and their gift of fire.

"Holy crap, these are instructions." Gabrian grins, riffling through them, and replaces the browsed notebook to the shelf, retrieving another for a peek at its insides. "Handwritten, step by step, learning guides of the Realm's Magik. This must have been Cera's room," she whispers, flipping the page over. "Has to be."

She lowers the book onto the desk and pulls the chair out to settle in for a good old-fashioned study session. Unnoticed by Gabrian, who is caught in swirl of curiosity, some of the floating orbs gather near, congregating together and linger gingerly over her, lighting the space more fluidly. She flips it over, reading the spine. Bold printed letters spell out HYDOR. Even just reading the words darkens her inside as the memory of Caspyous' evil mind washes through her. Shaking it off, she lets go of his hatred toward her, not wanting to waste any energy on thinking about him. He got what he deserved—everyone has a choice and he chose poorly. She knows that one day she will have to face him again, being who they think she is, but today is not that day. Today is a day of discovery.

Her pulse quickens as she flips open the cover of the notebook and reads what is scribbled inside the pages. She learns to read the shape and curve of the handwriting, memorizing each letter, and allows her mind to read the information with more fluency and correctness. The first couple of pages are dull and unhelpful, but as she turns to the next page, the inscription of knowledge seems to bleed out, fading off the pages into nothing.

The inked words bled clean of their purpose. She presses her focus to the page—not gone, invisible. "This is kind of strange." Gabrian thumbs through the pages, their pristine condition disrupted by use and inscription. They have been written on, she can make out pressure marks on the pages, but she cannot read the words. Fanning through the book, her eyes catch on some ink within, and she halts her search, hurriedly flipping back to the page where she saw the marks.

Water is the very essence of life. The master of healing and with it brings...

"Well, I know this part. This part is easy. Even Lyarah said as much when the water healed me." A light clicks on in her head. She is about to experiment with the validity of a theory that just dawned on her in the truth of the very words spoken. "Hmm, I may not know the ins and outs of Hydor Magik, but I do believe that I may remember a little something about what Ashen taught me." Laying the Hydor notebook down, she scans the collection of tidy writings in front of her, neatly awaiting her decision. Spying the one labeled ISA, Gabrian pulls it free from its hold and lays it down on the desk in front of her.

The tips of her fingers tingle, and she pulls them in front of her, blowing on their ends to soothe their itch. Shaking them gently at her sides, she slides her thumb to the edge of the ISA notebook and flips over the leather cover to reveal the answer to her anticipated hypothesis.

The page is blank.

Her heart sinks but only for a moment. Shadows dance in her eyes as an orb lowers from above and sweeps down, hovering briefly over the book to lend a bit more light on the matter. Gabrian raises her eyes, blinking to adjust to the lent gift, and gazes at the spark before her just as a waft of air winds over her shoulder and ruffles the edge of the pages. Lost in her wonderment of gazing at this little phenomenon, she pulls her eyes free. The subtle disturbance below reveals what her intuition already knew.

Words.

Tons of them, all the knowledge of Isa she had been given was there, lying in wait to be reviewed in black and white shadows across the page. Curious to test her theory further, Gabrian riffles through the remaining stack of notebooks. Her assumptions are correct. Any knowledge that she has about any given element of Magik, Gabrian is aware of clear as day. Revealed within her books. Those that she knows nothing of lie empty in wait.

Egni, is more or less filled with information that she has not learned yet. Each piece of information seems simplistic and primary as if it is the beginning stepping stones of understanding how the Magik flows and steps to learn how to wield it.

"This is wicked!" She exhales, deciding to settle in and learn what she can about fire Magik. Yesterday's lessons had been a far cry from awesome, but if she has a little inside help, maybe tomorrow's lesson might not be as embarrassing. Flipping a few pages in the beginning of the book, Gabrian finds the perfect place to start and reads the scribbled bold heading out loud. "Here we go. Now this has my name written all over it. Lesson One: Learning how to not fear the fire."

Chapter Forty

Glasses and a Day off

Lost within her disease, Gabrian drowns herself in the pages of her mother's scribbled knowledge, or what the watchful Magik allows her to see—introductory know-how of how some of the elements work, behave, and how to handle them. It is only allotting her the knowledge she requires to move forward—safeguarding her progression from advancement which would undoubtedly get her hurt, not to mention anyone in close proximity of her.

Although frustrated by the limitations set by a higher power, Gabrian happily absorbs what knowledge she is given. Something is better than nothing, especially since she is expected to perform miracles by all the Elders. A light rustling from the corner causes the orbs in the room to flicker and scurry from their soft flowy routine, drawing Gabrian's attention from her studies. Watching them twitch and scurry around the space above her, she is once more captivated by their new strange behaviour.

"Gabrian," a muffled familiar voice echoes into the room, breaking her from her trance. The orbs jitter and dance as she rises from the chair. "Gabrian, are you here?" His voice is louder, hinting with a note of distress.

"Tynan," she hums, turning the corner just as the silhouette of his form rushes by the opening. *Holy crap, how long have I been in here? The sun is already up.* "I am here," she calls out, hearing his thoughts, the worry she has disappeared again. "Tynan, wait." But the Shadow Walker does not reply as he charges into the next room.

She hurries her pace and steps out through the opening, back into her room. The wave of electricity washes over her skin as she crosses the barrier between here and there. She gasps, a wave of shock stinging her, and she immediately looks behind her, afraid the room is gone. But the light remains in the wall. It is faint, but it is still there. She raises her hand and brushes it against the faded illusion, exhaling with relief as her fingers meet no resistance. The buzz of the other side kisses her fingertips and makes her smile.

The thud of worried footsteps brings her attention back to the room, and she calls out to her uncle as his frantic mind debates whether or not to alert the Elders. "Uncle Ty?"

The footsteps halt their descent on the stairwell and hurry back toward her as the large wide eyed Schaeduwe enters her room. "Where were you? I couldn't find you and I thought—"

"I was just in the bathroom," she hums, lying through her teeth.

Tynan's face contorts, scratching his head, and he eyes her confession with a twisted brow. "I just looked in the bathroom, you weren't—"

"Hmm, Uncle Ty, have you thought maybe it might be time for you to look into getting glasses?"

"I am a Shadow Walker. Trust me, I don't need glasses."

"Well, there is always an exception to the rule. I am living proof of that," she teases him, trying to dissuade him from dissecting the lie.

He shakes his head at her. "Yeah, Gabe. That you are."

"Uncle Ty," she says, her voice lowering and losing its sass.

"Yeah, Gabe?"

"Do you notice anything different about my room?"

202

His eyes narrow, studying her for a moment, then releases his gaze, letting it float around the room to try and figure out what in the Realm she is talking about. "Hmm, well, let's see." Rubbing the edge of his soft, bearded chin, Tynan ends his hunt and grins. "You know, if you don't like the blanket then just tell me. I can get a different colour. The other one had burn marks on it and needed to be replaced, not to mention it was highly flammable. I just wanted to eliminate a safety hazard."

"No, no the blanket is fine. Anything else in the room? Like maybe in this location?" she says, swirling her hand over the area near the faint outline of the new opening.

With raised brow, he stares at the spot she refers too but only purses his lips and clicks his teeth, lost for words. "Hmm, you moved the bookshelf?"

He cannot see it. The opening clear as day to Gabrian is lost from Tynan's sight. Clearly, this enchanted room is not meant for him. Time to make something up. "Yup, do you think it looks alright there?" She does not like lying to him, but if she mentions the doorway, and he cannot see it, then he is going to get worried about her mental well-being. And that will just open a big old can of worms that nobody wants to deal with. She has enough on her plate and worms are not on the menu right now.

"Do you like it there?" His words are slow and primary, and he wonders if the pressure being put on her is getting to her. She is not like him—things like the placement of a bookshelf are of little interest to her. She went to hell and back, then was thrown under the bus by him and his obsessive duty to the Realm. She needs a moment or two to recover from everything. He is her family—her only family. It is time to start acting like it.

"Yes," is all Gabrian says, poised with her hands on her hips, and slips a peek at her confused uncle as she pretends to admire the new placement of her books. What else can she say?

Yup, Tynan thinks, time to put in her request for a day off.

Chapter Forty-One

Coffee Hound

After a drawn out debate about giving Gabrian a day off, Tynan finally convinces the Elders to let her have a down day. What that truly consist of is no training for a day while still very much kept under house arrest.

Awesome.

The news of her *day off* is welcome, regardless of the continued jail time. A moment to breathe without having to perform circus acts for the all-seeing eyes of the Elders fills Gabrian with a temporary sense of hope. She is just as curious as the others to find out who she is, but it can wait for one more day.

Brushing the fuzz bunnies from her teeth, Gabrian turns off the tap to hear a rapping on the kitchen door. Spitting out the watery remains of her toothpaste, she wipes her mouth and hurries toward the sound. Stealing a glance at the time keeper on the wall, she frowns. *7:05, who could be here?* Tynan said they had agreed to let her have the day to herself.

Grumbling under her breath, she bounds down the stairs and marches to the kitchen door, feeling the familiar mind of an Elder on the other side. She opens it with an eye roll and sighs. "Good morning, Ethan," she drones out, widening the opening to let him in.

"Well, good morning to you too," he says, passing by her. "I hope you don't greet all your friends this way when they come to visit."

She shakes her head at his blasé entrance and follows behind. "No. But my friends would know better than to show up at…" She glances at the clock on the wall. "7:08 in the morning, emptyhanded."

"Sorry about that, kiddo, but I am sure you will forgive me once we do a session." He grins and takes off his jacket, hanging it on the wall by the door.

"What are you talking about?"

"Don't get mad. I know it is your day off and all. Since we are technically friends…" He turns to eye her reaction, noticing her pursed lips. "We are friends, right?"

Her lips deflate and press into a grin. "Yes, we're friends."

"Excellent, so since we are indeed friends, I had a thought."

"Oh, you did, did you?" She laughs, rolling her eyes.

"Yes, so my thought was what kind of friend would I be if I didn't offer to help you clear your mind—an offering of comradery, so to speak." His hazel eyes warm in the morning light as they pinch at the edges. "And after the strange reaction to Kaleb's meditation, it might not be such a bad idea to start the day off with a good old heart to heart— you know, to sort through the whirlwind of stuff I know is going on in there."

The last forty-eight hours have been something right out of wonderland, that much is certain. As long as he does not go snooping around in her memories, they should be fine. Her eyes dance around the room, contemplating his offer.

"And for a bonus, just because I am such a great guy, I will splurge and take you for a coffee. A real coffee."

Gabrian's eyes widen and light up, hoping his tempting offer is true. Her mouth salivates just thinking of consuming a latte. "We're going to the Coffee Hound?"

"The very one."

"Yes," she rushes out a breathy hiss.

"Now that I have your attention, let's fire up this old relic here—" he says, sliding toward the counter. Wrapping his hands around the black coffee machine, he pulls the top open to look inside. "—then we can get down to business."

Gabrian scrunches her face. Now that she is dreaming of a caramel latte topped with whipped cream, her poor old taste buds cringe at what her coffee machine will offer. "Fine, but when we get to the Coffee Hound, I am ordering an extra-large latte," she warns, a grin creasing her mouth as she reaches for her grinder to whirl up some fresh grinds. "Maybe I will even get C.K. to slip in an extra shot of espresso as well."

"You got it, kiddo."

Ethan knows he has her hooked on his promise of caffeine, now all he needs to do is get her to open up to him. If he was not an honourable man, and she had a normal mind, he could have ripped all of that information from her thoughts easily. But he is noble, and this is not how he works. Besides, he has been inside her head enough to know any wrong move or unwanted prying will only result in an immediate blast of light to the brain, followed by a splitting headache, so for him, not even an option.

Chapter Forty-Two

New Plans

Gabrian willingly recounted her journey through Erebus to Ethan as well as her moments of recovery. She made sure to keep her interaction with Lyarah and the secret room to herself, safely inside her mind and tucked securely behind door number three of her many mental compartments. This trade has always been easy for her. Compartmentalizing everything is just how she works, and how she manages to somewhat stay sane through all of this mess she calls life.

They play around with some training, even though it is her day off, because her curiosity always gets the better of her. Mostly, it is practicing her internal dialogues with Ethan—being shut out from his mind had been a means of sadness for her. The constant thrum of mental noise that they share keeps the rest of the outside noise in check. She had missed him.

With all the people she held dear taken from her, other than Tynan, Gabrian is alone. It is such a comfort to have this little measure of happiness still intact. After two hours of talk, both silent and not, Ethan proposes that he make good on his promise.

"Alright, kiddo, you all set to go for a ride?"

Gabrian jumps up from the couch, scoops up the used coffee mugs, and heads to the kitchen, sliding the cups into the sink. She does not have to be asked twice. "Yup, come on, slowpoke. You have a latte to buy."

"Yes, I do. I—" Ethan's pocket buzzes, and he reaches for the culprit, putting a finger up as he answers it. "I will just be a second," he says, walking away and mumbles words into the phone.

Not wanting to delay their leave after he is finished with his call, Gabrian pulls on a hat and shoes and sits patiently on the small wooden bench beside the kitchen door.

"Sorry about that," he offers her, ending his call, and returns to his duty. "I had to take it, client scheduling conflicts."

Gabrian's smile wipes from her face. She is supposed to be his partner, helping him with his workload, but here she is, going for coffee on holiday. "Ugh, I am sorry, Ethan. I forgot you were carrying all the clients, mine and yours both. I feel so bad."

"Why on Earth would you feel bad? You are doing what you need to do. Once you get a handle on this, trust me, I will put you to good use. Besides, it is just a small issue. You have more important things to take care of."

"Yeah, I know. It's just—I still feel guilty."

"Well, don't. Okay?" She nods, looking down at her feet with guilt still haunting her face. "But I do have some bad news." Gabrian's eyes lift to meet Ethan's. "I can't go to the Coffee Hound. I really do have to get to the office."

"Oh," she says, disappointment looming over her. "It's okay. I understand. I will just fire up another pot of swamp water in my machine and find something else to do around here."

"I said I couldn't go. I didn't say that you couldn't."

Her lips curve upward, studying her mentor's words. "I thought you said you had to work."

"I do, but I have arranged for you to have some company."

"Let me guess, a swarm of coffee loving Schaeduwe guardians?"

He rubs the back of his head and sputters, "Well, yes, unfortunately that was part of the deal I made with the other Elders to allow you this outing."

"Ugh," she grunts, hanging her head. "Really? I mean no offence to them, 'cause, well—they are all pretty good to look at. But I have my own Shadow Walker." Her heart twists, hearing the words slip over her tongue. Shane's ghost forms in her mind, and the guilt of what she has done to him gnaws at her insides, but she pushes it away. "I don't need any more. I might as well stay home."

"Well, Miss Spoiled Sport, if you are done having your rant, I will finish."

Gabrian shrugs, pulling her cap off, and unties her running shoes. "Fine, go ahead."

"Thank you," he hums. "Like I said, I have arranged for you to have some company—other than the Shadow Walkers—and he will meet you there around 9:30 so—"

Gabrian stops, still fiddling with her laces. "He?"

"Just thought that maybe it might be nice for you to see an old friend. And, since his classes don't start until after lunch, he seemed rather eager to take my place as your coffee date."

Chapter Forty-Three

Coffee and Confessions

With her hands tightly wrapped around an oversized Acadian Turtle latte, Gabrian sits quietly at her favourite spot overlooking the sidewalk, and sips the glorious nectar of the Gods from a white cup—Coffee Hound's finest concoction in her opinion.

Her eyes close as the warm liquid slips across her lips and slowly glides over her tongue. She releases a low guttural growl, lost in her euphoric caffeine-induced trance. "Oh, how I have missed thee." Lost in her coffee love affair, the annoying presence of the trio of Guardians at her back—huddled around the table nearest the door—is but a mere blip on her radar.

A black spray of wings descends from the skies and perches on the ground in front of the window. Its ebony sheen washes over his body in a flood of oily colours that meld and shift as he moves against the sunlight.

"Well, good morning, Theo, find any goodies in the waste bin out back?"

The bird fluffs its feathers and calls out a throaty caw. Then clicks and coos, happy to be out and about with its favourite girl. A rustling beside her draws her attention as a young man settles into the seat beside her, his back to her, but she knows who it is. The smoky grey aura flaring wildly around him gives away his nervousness as he looks at his watch and then studies the door.

Gabrian cannot help but giggle, watching him squirm anxiously in his chair. His chatty mind spews out bits of concern that he missed her due to running late. He turns to face her, but his eyes only graze over her to scan the rest of the room, searching the Coffee Hound in the hopes she is up front.

Matthias does not recognize me.

She grins, picking up her latte, and stares back at the black bird picking grass on the other side of the window, wondering how long she should play her game. Matthias turns back around in his stool and sighs, thrumming his fingers on the top of the counter as his giddy mood grows sullen. She feels his energy drop and feels bad—sort of. It is kind of enjoyable to be unseen for a change. But she has had her fun, time to end the poor boy's suffering.

"Looking for someone?" she chimes out through a grin, taking a sip of her drink.

Matthias turns to answer her, certain his movements are disturbing the person next to him. "Yes, sorry, I am supposed to meet my—" He turns to explain but finds the eyes he is searching for. His brow furrows, studying her. His head tilts to the side, just a fraction as if he is figuring out a puzzle. "Gabrian?"

"The one and only," she chirps, peaking at him over her latte, and sports an impish grin.

"But you look," he stutters with his words. "You look so—"

"Different," she finishes his statement. It is the same statement everyone seems to have about her. She knows that she has changed but she really didn't think it had been so drastic. Sure, she has no hair or aura, and sure her skin gleams with life, but she is still the same girl—kind of.

Sliding over a stool, he closes in on her. His eyes continue to wash over her like she is the most incredible thing he has ever seen. "Yes, definitely different. I didn't even recognize you."

"I noticed." She teases, her mouth unable to not smile.

Wasting no time, Matthias reaches his arms around her, pulling Gabrian into a hug—a really tight hug—crushing her to his chest. "You scared the crap out of me. Don't you ever do that again."

"Sorry. I will try not to," she muffles out into his shoulder, still clutched in his embrace.

Loud screeches of unhappy caws sound from the other side of the window. Matthias' advances on his girl woke him from his pecking and have grabbed Theo's full attention. Borrowers are not to be trusted in Theo's mind—none of them—and he lets them know at every opportunity.

The crowd inside the Coffee Hound begins to chatter and rise from their seats, trying to get a look at what all the ruckus is about.

Releasing his hold on her, Matthias sits back in his chair. "I should have known he would be here."

Gabrian laughs and shrugs, then turns to give Theo the reassurance he needs to know she is not in harm. Her eyes dance with the ebony bird's and her soft message of safety enters—settling him into just a staring contest between him and the Borrower sitting too close to his girl.

Matthias pulls at Gabrian's hand and holds it. "You look really good. The hair is—" Gabrian consciously rubs the top of her prickly head, missing her long dark locks. "I like the hair," he says, timidly raising a hand and brushing the tips of his fingers over the edge of her short quills.

Shrugging, she offers him a grin as his hazel eyes dreamily drink her in. "Thanks." Suddenly the words stop. A strange awkwardness steals the noise between them, and she fiddles with her cup. "So, I thought this was a coffee date." Her eyes drop to his empty hands.

"Yes, right," he says, getting to his feet. "I'll be right back. Would you like another?"

"No, I am good, but thanks."

Matthias bounds away, and a shiver runs through her. *What the hell was that? I haven't felt an awkwardness like that between us since—no.* Gabrian bites her lip, returning to a world where she had once had real feelings about Matthias. How he looked at her with complete acceptance and adornment. *I'm not crushing on him, I'm not. I've just missed him, that is all it is.*

The soft scent of summer and earth wafts in the air. A sudden sting to her senses grabs her attention, making her turn and glance behind with the feeling of a familiar presence, one that she longs to hold.

Shane. She gasps.

Her eyes rush over the bodies in the room, but all she sees is the Schaeduwe entourage which had escorted her here. Their conversation ends, and they focus on her strange behaviour, ready to whisk her away at any sign of trouble. Her heart drops. She pulls in a sullen breath, and her eyes addresses their silent concerns with a shake of her head then turns back around in her seat. Her emotions are playing havoc on her mind. Ghosts of their fated meeting still linger here within the walls of the Coffee Hound. She knows he is not here, but it does not stop her heart from wishing he was.

Slipping back into his chair, Matthias leans into her space, chasing away the ghost, and sets down a folded white bag in front of her. "Ethan says you eat everything now so I thought a treat may be in order for you on your day off."

The black bird still on look out, keeping the Borrower in his sights, lets out a squawk as Matthias stretches his free hand to rest over the back of Gabrian's chair. Her eyes catch the reason for his alert, and she settles him with a silent nod of her awareness.

"Oh, you didn't have to do that, but thanks." She grins, peeking into the bag. "It's funny. Since I came back from my visit to Erebus, everything has done a reset, more or less. It is like I am almost my old self again—well, except for all the Magik stuff and all. It is nice not to be a slave to the cravings anymore. The only thing I have to worry about now is my sugary appetite."

Smelling the deliciousness of the treat inside the bag, Gabrian's mouth waters, and she can resist temptation no longer. Peeling back the paper, she peeks inside. She is in heaven, freshly made heavenly Danish delights. Pulling the treat to her face, she stuffs it through her lips. Any sign of fine manners are not to be part of this procedure. Flakes of broken pastry crumble in her bite, coating the edges of her mouth with crumbs and filling it with frosting.

"So, you must be excited to know that Rachael is awake."
With her mouth full of Danish, she nearly chokes on her reply. "What?" Soggy pieces of dessert fly out of her mouth while she coughs, trying to swallow down the rest. Matthias pats her on the back as she coughs, trying to pull air into her lungs though the clumps of pastry in her throat. "What do you mean she is awake?" she nearly screams at him, grabbing one of the napkins in her bag, and wipes away the rest of the smeared Danish from her face. "Are you sure?"

He looks behind him, ominous guardians now on their feet, and turns to settle her discontent. "Yes, I thought you knew."

"No, I didn't know. Ugh, what is with the Elders? They never tell me anything."

"Sorry. Maybe I wasn't supposed to tell you that part."

"Doesn't matter, is she still in the hospital?"

"Yes, she has been awake for a couple days now."

"Son of a—" Jumping to her feet, she grabs her things. "Sorry, I have got to go."

"I can take you there," he says, glancing at his watch again. "I still have some time before my classes start."

"Oh, um, thanks, but my jailers are right over there. Part of the parole agreement."

His eyes slide over to the back door. Picking out the hulking Guardians is like trying to find an elephant in a hay stack—easy peasy. Their largeness and Godly good looks make them stick out like a sore thumb in a crowd of toes.

"Thanks anyway," she hums, leaning in to plant a quick kiss on Matthias's cheek, then heads toward the table behind them, leaving Matthias to his own company. Her mood is chaotic. Caught somewhere between being overjoyed her best friend—who she nearly killed—is now awake, and livid that once again, she has been left out of the loop. This is a pretty big damn loop. Storming up to the table seated by the three large coffee lovers, she delivers her demand. "Please take me to the hospital."

"I am sorry, Miss Gabrian, but we were asked to return you home right after you were done with your *date*." The large blond God in a black tee-shirt informs her, his snarky remark unsettling. *He must know Shane. What am I thinking? Of course they know him. He is a Schaeduwe. They all must know who he is.*

And the fact she is out with a guy who Shane has openly displayed his dislike for—yeah, she can see how it might look.

"Ugh, it's not a date, okay."

"That is not what it looked like from here."

Okay, that is enough of that. "Listen," she snaps at them, seeing red and feeling her insides growing warm as the tips of her fingers start to tingle and burn. Slowing her words to a steady but threatening drone,

"It was not a date. It was just—none of your business. Okay. So, here is the deal. This is my day off, and I need you to take me to the hospital."

"But the Elders said—" the copper-haired Guardian starts.

"You need to take me where I need to go. I will deal with the Elders. Trust me on that."

Chapter Forty-Four

Bobbles and Buddies

Appearing at the edge of the shadows just down the hall from Room 231, Gabrian's hands begin to tremor. Her footsteps are heavy and slow. The thrum of the life force within her buzzes with anxious wanting mixed with fear of the unknown as she prepares to face her friend, but she will reap what she sows, no matter what it is. A wave of nausea washes over her. The smell of death not far away reeks in the hallway as she passes a partially opened door. Her body shudders as she walks past it, and she quickens her pace. The smell recalls the horrific image of Gargons stretched over Rachael's body as they tried to claim her from this world.

But they did not have a chance. Gabrian made sure of it, but it had sent Rachael into a coma, one she has been lost in for a while. Even Ethan could not reach her in the darkness. Would she be the same girl who Gabrian knew before? An ache pulls at her heart, weighing her down with the heavy reality that her best friend's mind might not be the same, and she is the one to blame.

I will make it up to her. I will find a way to make whatever waits for me in that room right again. This is her solemn vow to not only Rachael but herself as well.

With a deep pull of air into her lungs, she presses on the door and peeks through the crack. The familiar beep of the life monitor welcomes her, and a sweet but crackly voice sings into her ears—flooding her eyes with wetness.

"Well hi, you," Rachael whispers, turning her head toward her visitor.

"Is it okay that I am here?" Gabrian's words are soft and unsure. The girl before her, small and fragile, is as pale as the moon's flesh. Her crimson hair hangs messy and undone around her face.

"Of course it is. Get in here."

Gabrian pushes the door wider and reveals another visitor already occupying the chair beside her bed, his hand stretched out and fingers intertwined with Rachael's. "Oh, Orroryn, I am sorry. I didn't know that anyone was here. I can come back."

Lifting from his chair, the Schaeduwe Elder gets to his feet and addresses Gabrian. "No, come in, Gabrian." His voice is much sweeter and endearing than the last time he spoke to her. It is empty of his silent contempt. "I will leave you two alone to catch up."

"Thank you, Ryn," Rachael hums out sweetly.

Gabrian's brow lifts. *Ryn?*

Leaning over her small form tucked securely beneath her freshly laundered hospital sheets, Orroryn kisses the top of her head then dresses the inside of her palm with one more.

Hmm, this is definitely awkward.

Orroryn releases her hand and makes his way toward Gabrian. His large looming form casts shadows over her, blocking out the overhead light. "You are looking—"

"Different, I know."

He smiles at her. Actually smiles. No glare, no discontent, just a smile as warm as the summer sun. "Well, Gabrian—you are looking well." His words ring soft and soothing against her soul. Maybe it isn't so much what he said but how he said it that resonates with her. Maybe he has forgiven her, and maybe, from the looks of things, Gabrian wonders if maybe he has found—*Nah, can't be.*

"Thank you, Orroryn."

He places a large mitt on Gabrian's shoulder and smiles, then peeks over at her friend watching his every move. "I will return shortly."

Rachael's eyes beam and her iridescent aura flutters and sways around her, making her shimmer with the light of an angel. Her pouty lips press wide, and she gathers her wrists to her chest over her heart—obviously drowning in his openly given affection.

Yup, there is definitely some strange stuff happening here. Gabrian grins, watching the two caught in some strange and secret trance she is not privy to.

Orroryn glides out into the hall, closing the door behind him, and Gabrian steals his seat, still warm. "So, how are you feeling?"

"Much better. They said I can leave in a few days."

"Really?" Gabrian wonders how long she has been awake. "That is great news."

"Yup," Rachael chirps, sitting up against her pillow. A low moan escapes her lips as she lies back against it.

Gabrian's heart twists seeing her struggle. "Well, it is settled then. You will stay with me until you are back on your bouncy feet."

Rachael's eyes lower, and she glances toward the door. "Oh, um, thank you, but—"

"Well, you can't very well stay alone, not in your condition."

"Hmm." Her lips curl and a light blush dusts across her cheeks, unable to hide her joy. "I am not going to be alone."

Scratching the side of her head, Gabrian hums. "Then where are you going to stay?"

"I will be staying with Orroryn."

SILVER

"Orroryn. Really?" Gabrian's eyes dart to the door, the strange display of affection she just witnessed bounding to the forefront of her mind.

"Which reminds me, can you push that table over here?" She motions to the lunch tray on wheels, and Gabrian slides it to hover over Rachael. Reaching into the drawer and retrieving a small metal and cloth bundle, she stretches out her hand.

Gabrian lifts from her chair to sit on the side of Rachael's bed and holds out her hand to retrieve whatever is in her friend's fingers. Unfolding her fist, she sees the tightly wound metal bracelet she had tied around Rachael's neck the last time she was here. Her heart's gift that Shane had given her—the Azurite stone.

"Thank you for this."

Gabrian's eyes linger on the gift. Working her fingers over the curled metal, it responds to her touch and releases its bonded form to reveal the smooth sliver of Azurite beneath. She touches it to her wrist. The soft strings of white metal cloak her skin, wrapping lovingly, and entwines itself around her in an intricate intimate embrace. She waits to feel the familiar hum, but it does not come. Her soul sinks at the quietness, but she lets it go.

"I know how much it meant to you, but I don't have any need for this any longer. I have my own."

Lifting her head, her eyes jump to her friend, now holding her arm out—sleeve up and proudly displaying a band of silver, intricately spiraled around her delicate bicep. A black onyx eloquently sits within the middle of the enchanted metal.

"You what?"

Rachael giggles, her face flushes, and she sighs. "Yeah, remember that day that you froze the beer, and I was telling you that there was more to how I felt about Orroryn?" Not taking her eyes off the bracelet,

Gabrian hums her recollection. "And do you ever recall me saying I felt like there was more to my lives, one that I knew was missing, but I could not ever remember anything about it?"

"Yes, I do," Gabrian hum again. "Go on."

"Well, somewhere within the darkness, I found it."

"What do you mean, you found it?"

"When you took all my, well, you know, I left this world for a while."

Gabrian's eyes sting, knowing it was her who stole her life, it was her who had done this. Her own stubbornness to refuse to reach out for help when she needed it most had led Rachael to meet this darkness.

"I know what you are thinking and stop it."

The floodgates open and all the pent-up sadness releases in her confession. "Oh, Rachael, I am so sorry for hurting you. I never meant to—"

Rachael leans forward and pulls her friend in close, wrapping her frail arms around Gabrian's trembling body, and holds her still while she drowns in the darkness of her sins. "It was a blessing in disguise," Rachael says in no more than a whisper, pulling Gabrian back to look at her. "It is within the darkest parts of a storm that you find the brightest light."

Gabrian' wipes the dew pooling at the corner of her eyes and forces a smile, still listening intently.

"It was in that wall of darkness that all those lost memories—everything—all came back to me. And I think, no I am sure of it. It was your stone that found me and led me back to them and eventually back to my body."

Rachael's hand lifts and gathers around her friend's, clutching them with what strength she can muster. "It is because of you that I am whole again. You gave me back the part of me that had been lost."

222

SILVER

They stare at each other, the bond between them reconnecting, and secures between their souls. "So you see, you did this. You helped me find my beginning," Rachael begins, bubbling inside, and rubs her fingers over the black stone coddling her arm. Her crimson curls, although slightly matted and un-kept, bounce in her joy. "Oh, we have so much to talk about."

Chapter Forty-Five

Visiting Hours

Gabrian's mountain of guilt withers down to a hill when she sees her friend's joy. She listens contently as Rachael reveals her life, how she and the Elder of Schaeduwe were once betrothed, and that she was the human he so long ago willingly gave his heart to. The morning burned by quickly. Unable to stop staring at her, Gabrian is overjoyed to have her friend back. The old Rachael she so dearly loves plus a whole lot more. It is fantastic to be lost in her, catching up and forgiving herself for what had happened.

Healing.

She is healing and it feels good, right up until the nurse had finally kicked her out after the fourth warning that visiting hours were long over. Rachael needs her rest. Reluctantly, Gabrian obeys. Giving one last hug and kiss, she wanders into the hall to find her shadow taxi home. Her heart melts at finding Orroryn still there—his arms filled with flowers—patiently waiting to get back in to see his mate, wanting to waste none of the precious time he has left with her.

To him, the few years they will spend together will seem like only mere moments, and precious moments they will be. He turns, hearing Rachael's door close, and stands to hover over Gabrian's small form.

"So, I guess congratulations are in order," Gabrian offers, a little apprehensive that he will accept it.

"She told you?" he hums. "Yes, of course she would, you are her best friend." Orroryn flashes a grin from behind the bouquet, hinting a flush of rose across his cheeks. "Thank you, Gabrian."

"Listen, I know things haven't been that good between us since Shane—" Her insides tremor as she chokes back her sadness "—Well, you know. I just wanted to say I was sorry."

"There is no need to be sorry, child. Shane is Shane, and there is nothing anyone could have done to stop him from going after you."

Gabrian swallows hard against the knot in her throat.

"You are his heart's choice. He would gladly die knowing that he did everything to protect and honour you."

A stream of warmth runs over her black lashes and cuts a crooked line down her cheek as she nods, dying to know where he is and what is happening with him.

"I know, I just—"

"Do not let your guilt eat at you. It will do no one any good, especially him."

Gathering the words she wants to say, she needs to say, Gabrian wipes away the tears and spits them out. "How is he?"

Orroryn purses his lips and looks away.

"I mean, I know that you don't discuss Schaeduwe interests with anyone, but as you just clearly stated, I am his heart's choice and that should count for something." Her words are timid but hold so much truth in them.

Orroryn glances at Rachael's door and huffs, feeling Gabrian's suffering choke the air around him. "He is doing better." He smiles down at her. "And if it helps you to know, he is being Shane. Stubborn and hard to deal with."

Gabrian cannot help but grin and nod. This is good news. Great news. If he has it in him to give people around him a hard time, then he has it in him to fight his way back to her. "Yes, thank you. It does help."

Starting toward the door, Gabrian chirps out her last request. "Do you know when he will come back?" She flushes. "From the Veil, I mean?"

He stops and turns to her. "That is not for me to say," he says, feeling the disappointment sink into her. "All I can offer you is, when he is ready."

"I understand." Gabrian bites on her thumb and nods, knowing what that means. It could be weeks, months, even years. Her own birth mother is still in the Veil healing—only visiting Gabrian in her dreams. Not really much help.

A knowing bow of his head is given, and he turns to enter Rachael's room.

"Oh, you can't go in there. They just kicked me out for violating visiting hours."

He flashes an impish grin. "Visiting hours do not apply to me, I am family," he sings, giving her one last glance over his shoulder, and with a wink, he enters the room.

Chapter Forty-Six

Old Ones and Feathers

Landing back at home, safely delivered as instructed by the Guardians, Gabrian wanders to the sun-filled deck and leans over the railing, watching the boats enter in and out of the harbor. Taking a sip of the first beer in what seems like ages, she closes her eyes and tips her head back, letting the cool liquid quench her thirst and the warm sun kiss her face. A low hum releases from the depths of her soul—happy, content—and feels the urge to celebrate the moment.

Even if it is by herself.

Well, not entirely by herself. She knows that beyond the boundaries of her yard, the nearly invisible collection of Guardians keep watch over her, but they do not count. And Tynan, who is no doubt either with them or tucked away in his small cottage mere feet away, does not count either. Not today.

Today is a one girl kind of hurrah.

Swishing of feathers against the air adds to her quiet moment as a familiar friend descends from the bright sky and perches on the railing a few feet away. She is not by herself anymore. Who better than to celebrate with than her trusty feathered friend—so make that one girl and a bird.

"So, you made it back from town. Did you find anything good?"

The raven gives her a quick double caw and ruffles its feathers.

"Rachael is awake."

The bird only tilts his head and caws.

"I know, exciting, isn't it?" She stares back into the water, pleased to have company to share this good news with.

Another loud swishing of wings catches her by surprise. Theo hardly ever has company other than when Vaeda is around with her guide. But they bicker and moan most of the time, not really what she would call a good visit. But this bird is larger than Theo, quite a bit larger, and nearly towers over him when he lands a few spaces over.

"Hmm, who is your friend?" she asks, raising a brow to Theo, and swills down another sip of her drink.

The big raven glances over at Theo and rumbles out a very loud throaty caw. Gabrian cannot help but laugh. It has been a great day, well other than the fact that the Elders decided to keep important information from her. Again. But overall it has been a pretty damn good day.

"Well now, this makes my day off all the better. You know what they say, two is company, three makes it a party," she sings, cheering the two birds on her deck staring at her. Now it is a one girl, two bird kind of tiny celebration.

Theo turns away and decides now is a good time to preen while the other just sits and watches Gabrian. So, she watches him right back. He is a glorious looking creature. His feathers are glossy and sleek with the prismatic smear of oily sun spun sheen. As she studies him, just as he does her, he spreads his wings out in a stretch and a faint glow of gold hovers around the edges of his feathers, almost like an aura. His outstretched wings fan like long extended feathery fingers.

Her eyes jump to Theo. He displays no extra colours at all. Maybe they are like everything else in this Realm, each soul carrying its own colours depending on what they truly are on the inside. Her eyes pinch, continuing to awe at him. "Fascinating."

The black visitor just gives her a rumble, content to hang out for the moment on her deck.

Gabrian fans her finger out in front of her face and looks through them. Past the solidness of her flesh and bones and into the void around them. Once a grey aura lived there, and a blue, white, and even a violet, but she has not displayed any kind of light since she has been back. She flips her hand around in the sun, but still, there is nothing. Nothing, except strange disfigurations forming at the tips of her fingers. Sharp edges grow outward, pulling her digits into long slender ridged spikes.

"What the—" she hisses out, trying to figure out what the hell is going on now. She sets the beer down on the ledge of the deck and touches the ends of her deformity. It is soft, not sharp, like a feather.

Her eyes rise to the giant bird perched just a little closer than he was moments ago. He seems quite interested in the oddity, as much as she does. Shaking her head, she returns to her dilemma, fingers elongating and flushing out as the feathers take form in her hand. Wiggling her fingers, or strange feather hands, she stares at it, unsure what exactly is taking place.

A loud throaty caw startles her intense trance, and she stumbles backward, glancing up at the bird. "Ah, you bugger."

A low gurgle rumbles in its throat.

She eyes it. It sounds like laughter to her. The bird is actually laughing at her. Gabrian is convinced of it. "Hey, that wasn't funny, you scared me," she says, glancing at her fingers, the strange phenomenon molding back to the formation of her hand into its original design.

Hearing the discontent in Gabrian's voice, Theo scolds the newcomer with loud shrieks, a warning that he is done with his preening and is now paying attention. A bright flare of gold dances across the large bird as he fluffs his feathers. The memory of Kaleb's transformation in the woods plays through her mind. *The old ones*, she hears her mind's voice whisper. *The Alakai*. The ones who can shift and shape their form into the beast that lies beneath the human facade.

"I wonder." Gabrian peers at the bird, its large size, and its ability to laugh at her. "Kaleb, is that you?"

The large bird squawks at her and rushes to the sky.

"Well, that didn't work out very well, did it, Theo?" she says, looking at the remaining bird. He only clicks at her, following up with a consoling coo.

She goes back to trying to replicate the change again, this time concentrating on the remembered shape and length. In a breath, her fingers string out, long and slender, coated with a silvery jagged edge of a feather.

"Well, I have turned into a vampire, an ice mage, a death watcher, and a fire wielder. I guess there is no reason why I can't be an Alakai shifter as well."

A slightly hysterical giggle escapes her. "Now won't this be a hoot." Knowing she has to keep this one under wraps. Being able to shift is labeled right up there with being a vampire, hunted and condemned for what they are by the Realm. Maybe her being nominated to take the place of the Silver Mage might be a great time for her to make some changes in how the Realms treat things. Look at Kaleb. He is one of the sweetest people she has come to know here in the Realm.

There has to be a way to make a difference, a change is possible—that is, if she can hide this long enough to finish her training. She has to talk to Kaleb, to make him understand that she harbors no ill will toward him and what he is. But how? He has made himself busy since the strange visions during meditation that morning. Clearly, he is avoiding her. There must be another way to make him understand things, but to get to him is nearly impossible with the Guardians forming a barrier on the edge of her lawn.

Biting her lip, she paces the deck, the black bird watching her in silence, turning every time she gets close to where he is to keep an eye on her. "Hmm." She stops. "Wait a minute." She looks up at the second-floor windows. "The room. It must have something that will help. I am sure of it," she shouts, loud enough to startle Theo into flight, and heads back into the house for answers.

Chapter Forty-Seven

Orbs, Amulets, and Midnight Joggers

Launching through the house, Gabrian bounds up the stairs to reach her bedroom. Her heart quickens from an anxious fear that the secret room is gone. As if on cue, the wall fades out, and the opening dissolves into fruition. Wasting no time, she enters and slips to the right where the little wooden desk awaits her return—a few of the flickering orbs brighten and chase her along the way. Gabrian pulls out the small chair and settles into it, riffling through the notebooks. Only the names of the Fellowships are present.

"Well, it cannot be just a figment of my imagination. I have heard the whispers of the old ones, surely there has to be something on them. I can't be the only one to have witnessed the transformation."

She lifts from the chair and stalks to the mocking wall of books. Running her fingers along their spines, she tries to read the etchings, what they contain, but mostly, she finds books on Realm policies, territories, and a few large maps. These books come out easily for her, and their words are bold as can be, demanding to be read.

"Boring," she sings, placing them back into the wall. "Aw, come on, I know some stuff," she growls at the room. "Can't you throw me a bone?" A rattle echoes from the little desk. She peeks over her shoulder to the sound. One of the drawers on the left side is open, a soft flickering light beaming from inside. "That is strange, I am sure that wasn't open before.

Edging closer, Gabrian sees one of the little orbs trapped inside, flittering around the small wooden frame. She pulls the drawer open to set the little light free, and it sprints out, but then drops back inside and buzzes around a small wooden box. Reaching in, she gathers it into her hands and sets it on top of the desk. She tries to open it, but it will not budge, even with her strength. Obviously, there are no easy roads in this room. Everything has to be earned to gain access.

The little orb scurries in front of her and blinks frantically. "You want my attention, do you?" she asks and follows it back to the open drawer to another, smaller notebook inside.

Retrieving it, she sets it down in front of her, and the orb lights the top of the notebook. *'Window of Souls'* is scribbled on the cover. Flipping open the leather binding, Gabrian smiles. All the words, much like the boring political books, are there for her viewing, but this she highly doubts will be anything but not boring.

Page after page, she eats up the lesson. It is an instruction manual of sorts to a thing called the Window of Souls—an amulet fashioned centuries ago by someone called William Theron. It has the ability to transport the user from this room to anywhere in the world without leaving a magical trail. And then return again with no one the wiser.

"This is crazy wicked," Gabrian chimes out to the gathering orbs hovering around her, making the lighting more than perfect for reading the entire thing. She grins, reaching for the box, eager to see if she has entry to the treasure it holds within. Pinching her fingers on the corners, she lifts, and with a click, it gives way. Access granted.

This is a beautifully strange looking thing, she thinks as she lifts it gently out of its holding. Two different sized metal ovals made of what looks like white gold are pinned together at the top and bottom of each center, sporting a dark leather strap on opposite sides of the connector pin. The large ring one is more of an oval and the smaller resembles the shape of an eye. The center of the eye is a sleek topaz stone. She flips it over to see the other side. It is brighter with a long dark strip of black running through the center of it muck like that of a tiger's eye.

"Now this is some seriously cool stuff," Gabrian hums, running her fingers across the cool smooth metal. Her eyes pinch and her mouth turns upward impishly. "If I am not allowed to leave on foot, then this may just do the trick. I hope."

Dropping her eyes to the amulet, she leafs through the small book once more to run over the exact instructions of how this thing operates. To return to the room, the eye must point outward to see. To leave the room, it must look inward to your soul.

"Okay, so—" She slips the leather strap over her head and lifts the amulet. "Where do I want to go?" she says, flipping the eye to face inward, and holds her breath as the amulet drops to rest against her chest.

In a blink her body is gone, torn from the room, and rushes into the dark of night in the next—thrown into a mess of bushes that have no love for her exposed arms. "Bugger, ouch," she grumbles, rubbing her arms as thorns slice at her. Her eyes lift, scanning her surroundings. "It worked, wicked," she cheers but then replaces her tone with a growl. "But, where am I?" She pulls herself up out of the brush and looks around. "This definitely does not look like Kaleb's, crap. Who knows where in the Realm I landed?"

A continual slap on the asphalt grows louder, causing Gabrian to slouch back down near the unsympathetic branches. She is not supposed to be out, and getting caught—well, not an option right now. She is on a mission, even if she has no idea where she is. She slinks down farther as the slaps get nearer. *Crap, they are coming this way, bugger, bugger. Hide, you have to hide,* her mind screams.

SILVER

Gabrian's internal mechanics kick in and finds their way to the surface. Her flesh begins to fade and consume the clothing on her back into a mere ripple of melded air. A cloak of the thorny branches wind around her airy form and coddle her, camouflaging any trace of her. She watches the jogger draw near, grateful for the Magik override of her inner instincts, and thankful those rotten thorns are not ripping into her flesh.

Legs stride in front of her, and she gasps—*Kaleb*—and sucks her breath back in, hoping he didn't hear her. His motions waver, and he sniffs at the air as he slows to scout the darkness. Pressing his eyes to study the shadows, a strange grin curls his lips, but he continues his course, turning to the right and into the night.

Chapter Forty-Eight

Old Ones and Feathers

After watching Kaleb turn in the darkness, Gabrian cannot stop herself from launching out of the bushes and following him. This is what she went AWOL for. There is no turning back now. She needs to talk to him. He is her friend, and she does not care what he is. She just wants to know the truth about *what* he is—what she is. Catching him unexpectedly is the only way so he does not have time to make up a story to cover his tracks.

Not wanting to be seen, curious if he is out and about for a reason—to change—she keeps the cloak of invisibility wrapped around her form and bounds after him. A large sign with Cadillac Mountain in bold print announces where she is.

The soft pattering of feet heads up the steep slope, so up, up she follows, keeping a safe distance behind. A low guttural growl rumbles in the darkness ahead of her as he gains speed, leaving her behind. His legs shift, muscles engaging as he pushes his body continually upward. Gritting her teeth, Gabrian draws on her own inner strength, and tears into the side of the mountain trek, trying not to lose sight of him, but she is losing ground. The harder she runs, the faster he gets. If she were a true Zephyr Air Mage, she could have just made a portal like Vaeda does and appeared at the top of the mountain, obviously where he is headed, but she has no knowledge in how it all works and is a little frightened to try.

SILVER

The Window of Souls Magik that brought her here has a manual. One hundred percent different story. So, for now, she is going to have to tough it out the old-fashioned way. Sweat and tears, and luckily, being supernatural does come with some perks. So onward and upward it is. Reaching the peak of the mountain, there is no sign of Kaleb. He left her in the dust easily a half mile back. Catching her breath, she searches the darkness for any clue as to where he is just as the sky opens up and releases its bounty.

Great, just great, she growls, and in retort, the sky rumbles back a loud clap of thunder to keep her in check. Her skin tingles and the back of her neck buzzes, feeling an abundance of electricity building in the clouds nearby. The night lights up as the first strike of lightning lunges forth a few miles away, making Gabrian shiver with energy.

The storm looks like it might move this way, so she needs to find her friend and quickly. Another loud roar echoes around her, but this time, it comes from a different source. It's the large malformed shape of her friend as he runs toward the edge of the cliff and jumps—arms wide and outstretched.

Gabrian's throat closes in, stifling her scream. She rushes across the opening and falls to her knees, peering over the edge just as a fan of large feathery wings soar up from the depths of the cliff, releasing an ear piercing screak of freedom, then veers left to glide low just over the treetops. Still cloaked in her invisible armour, Gabrian watches the giant bird glide and stretch out the golden shimmer of its wildness, the untamed feral need to be let loose. She smiles, knowing how he feels.

She sets herself down on the edge, letting her feet dangle over the side, and watches her friend breathe under the shroud of darkness and storm. With a few more passes over the mountain top, he opts to return, gliding to the left of her among the clutch of thick bushes. The guttural growl as he transforms back into his human form meshes with the next roll of thunder, making his change seem otherworldly.

Gathering her courage, she lets go of the invisibility cloak as he emerges from the bushes and announces her presence. "Hello, Kaleb."

Chapter Forty-Nine

I, Mother Earth

Kaleb turns quickly at the sound of the familiar voice. His aura switches from green to yellow once more. Having left his clothes in the bushes just beside her, he stands before her in all his glory. Gabrian wonders if he will run, but where would he go? She knows him. A terrifying thought grabs hold of her. What if he decides to destroy her because of what she knows, what she has witnessed? *Maybe I didn't quite think this thing completely through.*

A cold tingle on her chest reminds her she has an option if things turn ugly—The Window of Souls. She can disappear at any sign of aggression. So, she decides to see the plan through.

Kaleb's aura fades from gold to green as he glances her way. "Huh, so you saw that, did you?" he simply says, sauntering to the bushes, unbothered by his nakedness.

Gabrian remains seated on the ground, her arms hugging her knees. "Yup," she says, not really knowing what else to say. She watches him retrieve his clothes, captivated by his machine-like build, every muscle tone and responsive to his movements.

"So, how did I do?" He chuckles.

Her face flushes in an immediate awareness that she is staring at her friend's naked body, and he is trying to say something to her. "What?" She hides her eyes, looking away while Kaleb pulls on his loose pants and shirt.

"How did I do?" he repeats. "I have been trying to perfect my dives among the treetops and since I have a feeling you watched the entire show, how did I do?"

He is not mad. Not even a hint of anger or fear resonates from him. *Wicked*. "You were—incredible."

He pulls the white shirt over his head and smooths it over his ripped muscles hugging his midsection. Then gathers his shoes and saunters over to her. She peeks up at him, checking to make sure he is clothed, then returns her stare as he drops down in front of her and slips on his shoes. They sit in silence for a moment while Kaleb watches her face contort, trying to find words deemed appropriate. He laughs out loud, watching her pick at the grass beside her, still quietly contemplating.

"You might as well just come out and say what you want to say before your head explodes."

She has seen all that he is, but she hesitates for a moment. "Are you a shapeshifter?"

His sweet smile broadens. He nods his head and turns to gaze out into the night, watching the storm change course for the moment. "I guess you can call it that," he starts. "I am a descendant of an old clan. The one that is only whispered amongst the Fellowships."

"The Alakai?"

His brow crooks at the mention of the name. "So, you have heard of them?"

"I was told a little, but the story I heard was that all of the Old Ones were extinct."

He smiles again. The moon slips out from behind Gabrian, catching in Kaleb's eyes. The centers change, lit with a haunting glow around his irises, much like that of an animal when caught in the light at night. "That is what we hope everyone believes."

Her eyes lift. "We?"

"There are just a handful of us left." He runs his hands through his brown messy hair. "But we remain in control and hidden among the others."

"Are the stories true that you are worse than the vampires?" Gabrian wonders if her candidness is too much as a slight wave of gold runs through his naturally calm green aura.

"Let me guess, this story was told to you by a certain vampire or a Borrower?"

Unsure she wants to reveal her source, she lowers her eyes and shakes her head. She will not tell him it was her Uncle Ty who told her about them, she will not have him looked upon with unkind eyes by one of the Elders. She pretends she cannot remember who told her just that she remembers hearing the story somewhere in her journeys.

The gold flecks dissolve from his aura as he inhales a deep breath. "Our existence has been the blame for so many innocents being mangled and desiccated for centuries. I will admit our feeding habits do sometimes get a little heated at times but only in the frenzy of the kill.

Gabrian gasps at this. Kaleb quickly reaches out and places a tender hand on her shoulder. "Relax, it's not what it sounds like. We do not hunt people like the legends say. We hunt like who we are—natural predators. We are brothers with nature and hunt as other wild things do," he says, with a grin, then lets it drop. "But accidents have happened."

Gabrian sits quietly as she learns a different side of the tale, seeing the sadness creep into Kaleb's eyes.

"The stories quickly spread, and the incidents became a scapegoat for those who would use it for their own discrepancies. Feverish killing benders were tainted and blamed on our animalistic nature. Soon after, we became hunted by those who twisted the minds of the people naïve and scared enough to believe them.

"Many of us were hunted down and destroyed by the Peace Keepers. Whole communities were obliterated. The rest of us went into hiding, pulling in our inner beast and learning to contain it, vowing never to show our true selves to anyone, and only allowing our Magik to manifest in complete secrecy. Very few could see what we were."

"That explains a few things."

He chuckles at her words. "It does, does it?

"Yes," she hums. "I saw you. I followed you into the woods a few days ago."

Kaleb's brow twists, his mouth curving into an impish grin.

"Only to tell you I was healed, that is all."

"Mm, hm," he teases.

"Anyway, I watched you shift in the darkness. I thought about leaving, but I couldn't. I had never witnessed anything like it, so I stayed." Gabrian hugs her knees a little more. "I tried to keep myself hidden, but I felt as if you looked right at me."

His face lightens, and his arms relax as he leans back onto them. "I knew you were there."

"How? I pulled in my aura and tried to silence my presence."

"I could smell you." He taps the side of his nose. "I didn't hear you, but I caught a subtle waft of your new scent briefly."

"I'm sorry."

His face twists. "Why?"

"Well, when I saw you on the beach, I wanted to ask you a question, but then you disappeared so quickly into the woods. And then, once I started following you, I forgot why I was there and became curious as to why you were sneaking around in the underbrush. When I saw you change, it frightened me—the stories and all."

"I should have said something. I feel bad, but I didn't know what to do. Then, Ethen showed up right before I could get my courage up to say anything."

Stopping for a moment, something dawns on her.

"Wait a minute. You said Borrowers started the story and you hid from them."

"Yes, them and the rest of the world that wanted us gone."

"Ethan saw you."

"Ethan and I go back a long way. We have seen each other's darkest hours and have come to build an alliance."

"Oh," she announces, picking at the grass.

"Oh." Kaleb leans back into his arms.

"Well, I want you to know that I won't tell anyone either."

"I know." He grins.

Their eyes meet, and she can see the resolution in his gaze. Happy that he has so easily accepted her vow of silence, she picks at the grass, confused by his easiness about it. She knows his secrets, his life is in her hands and her ability to keep her mouth shut about it, and her mind.

"So, how is your shifting coming along?"

She glares at him, biting her lip, and he just gives her a lazy knowing grin, pointing down at her hands. Gabrian eyes her fingers and notices her hands have melded into the undergrowth that she has been playing with the entire conversation. Long slender blades of grass entwine and envelope her hands. Vines slink and twist upward along her wrists. Her eyes grow wide, inspecting the phenomenon, and she pulls free, revealing the shape of her fingers, green and lush like the very grass they were just entwined beneath. She pushes the foliage away and gathers her hands back to clutch around her knees, watching the green of her Magik fade back to her human flesh.

"This is how I didn't hear or see you in the woods. The earth Magik dwells within you. I didn't need the cauldron to confirm it. I kind of had my suspicions for a while."

Gabrian shoots him a quizzical glance.

"You look at me like no one else does. You see me, the real me yet you say nothing."

Gabrian purses her lips, listening, and curious to where he is going.

"Your birth mother did the same thing."

"You knew Cera?" She shakes her head, hearing her words. "Of course you did. She was the head of the table in the Covenant of Shadows."

"Yes, but she was also my friend." He offers her a sweet smile, his eyes shining as the moon peeks out from behind another cloud. "A friend who kept my secrets as well."

"I didn't know any of this." She drops her eyes.

"How could you?" Feeling a strained and uncomfortable ripple of energy surge around his young friend, Kaleb tries to end on a good note. "You are very much like her, you know."

Gabrian looks up again, meeting his soft gaze, and the sincerity within.

"And because of that I ask again, how is your shifting coming along?"

"How did you—"

"Did Theo have a friend over earlier?"

"Ah, it was you. I knew it."

"Maybe, maybe not," he teases. "If it was me, would you be mad?"

Gabrian laughs out loud, releasing her hold on her legs, and leans back on her arm in the grass. "Now you are in cahoots with my already obsessive stalking Raven?"

She sits up with a quick jerk, her face wiped clean of humor, and her eyes wide. "Wait, is he a shifter too?"

"No, he is what he is, no worries."

Her face heats against the night's coolness, and she purses her lips at his inquiry. "Um,"

"Seriously you just watched me reveal myself as one of the most wanted poster boys in the Realm and you are holding back on me? Really?" He clicks his tongue and shakes his head, trying to look offended.

She sighs, rolling her eyes at him, and realizes how foolish she is being. The trust factor is no longer an issue.

Chapter Fifty

Inside Scoop

Gabrian explains how she only changes the smallest parts of her body—she is not sure how much she can do or if she can do more.

"That is because you are thinking and not feeling," he explains. "Every one of earth's creatures knows who they are because they feel it. You have to *feel* the fire inside. It will respond and show you what your true inner shape is. Once you find it, the animal awakens, and all you have to do is let it out."

"You make it sound so easy."

"Awakening it is the easy part. Keeping it in check? Not so much, and there are those who would end you without question if they found out."

Gabrian shudders at the thought. She remembers all too well what that is all about, the scene of Caspyous leaping over the Head Table in his last effort to end her coming to mind.

Kaleb looks away, studying the stars. Only a few more hours before daybreak. Gabrian's thoughts race with all the new firsthand information. She continues to play around, reshaping the formation of her hands. It feels nice to be let in and have the inside scoop on what is going on with her.

"Well, we should probably head back down the mountain before the rangers find us here and start questioning our intentions," Kaleb says, interrupting her experiments. "No need in starting any rumors."

Gabrian chuckles. "No, that is the last thing I need."

"Do you have time for tea?" he asks, getting to his feet and reaching out his arm, offering her a hand up.

Her face scrunches, clasping onto his hand as she gets to her feet. "It is probably midnight, Kaleb, and you want to have tea?"

"Is there some place else you need to be?"

She hears his jab though he makes no mention he will snitch about her escape. There are tons of other places she would rather go than back to being a captive. So, tea it is. "Nope, tea sounds like a great idea."

"Excellent, also I thought it would be fun to let you in on a couple secrets that you might like to know."

"Okay, sure. Like what?"

"Like how to talk to your black feathery friend."

"You can actually talk to him?"

"Every creature has a voice. You just have to know how to listen to it. Kind of like your mindreading skill."

Gabrian grins. This kind of learning is helpful and fun. Kaleb reminds her of Ethan, Ashen, and well…even Arramus does in their instruction. They all seem to be so patient with her learning. It could be worse. They could all be like Cimmerian, although, she had been sucked into Erebus before any of her training with him had commenced.

Kaleb's soft low voice stirs her from her pondering. "Do you want to race down the mountain?"

Turning quickly, she stares at him and the cheeky grin painted on his lips. "What?" She had a hard time trying to keep up with him going *up* the mountain, but since they are going down, surely she has some chance of winning. "You got it," she cheers, running off into the darkness, back toward the road.

Kaleb laughs at her and easily catches up. Gabrian pushes her legs to go faster, only to see him gaining ground as she peeks over her shoulder. Kaleb's eyes gleam in the partial moonlight, form shivering and shifting, *lengthening*. He lunges forward and lands on his front hands—*paws*—body slender and sleek followed by a strong black tail swishing behind. His face is feral, feline-like, and edged with feathery points. His mouth is wide, wadded full of cloth—no doubt his clothing.

His wild form is the one from woods and the one she saw in her dream with Cera. She laughs, no longer afraid of what she sees—no longer terrified of him attacking her. Tonight, it is exciting and fun.

"Hey, no fair," she shouts at his tail as he passes her once more.

"You try," is all he says, leaving her in the dust.

A strong stir in the pit of her stomach flutters. She tries to run faster in order to catch his black phantom, but it is no use. He is winning. The fluttering turns to a warm burn, begging her to acknowledge it.

So she does.

Stretching her arms wide at her sides, she submits to the animal inside of her scratching to get out. The ridge of her spine warms, and her entire body burns the same way the tips of her fingers usually do. Vibrations tremor through her extremities. Long feathers sprout out of her extended arms as they elongate and narrow, marbled in silver and black to resemble the colour of her hair.

The pounding of her feet against asphalt becomes less jarring, smoothening out. The stormy night air catches under her form, giving her a lift from the ground. Her toes no longer touch the earth as she glides inches above the road on newly sharpened wings at her sides. The weight of her body, fully air born, strains her arms in this unknown use of muscles. She waves them just the same, lifting herself higher, and tries her hardest to stay centered on the narrowing space of the road. Hitting something this low would provide an abrupt halt and damage. There is no room for quick maneuvers of recovery here.

Her eyesight sharpens, and the darkness melts away like the Derkaz gift of night vision. Nightfall and shadows are no longer an obstacle. She might not be able to catch him down the winding road without maiming herself, but she can still win. Taking an alternative route, she turns against the course, the wind catching her wings, pulling her upward, and over the treetops. Gabrian inhales the cool ocean air and gasps at the view from her new vantage point. It is nothing less than stunning. With miles and miles of boundless freedom, she has a new appreciation for her friend and a sadness that he must hide within his skin.

A slip in the shadows below catches her attention and regains her reason for shifting in the first place. Her eyes narrow in, watching the Elder nearing the bottom turn on the mountain road. She yells out '*bugger*' but a loud screech shrills through the night instead. *Cool.*

Dipping low, her feathery body cuts through the air, faster and faster. Her balance falters. Gabrian's mind cannot catch up with her eyes. The air currents play havoc on her descent, shifting her side to side as they push against her tiring arms. The continual strain is a throbbing ache that depletes her momentary confidence. She falls, her height too low, and the sting of the treetops nicks at her, knocking her off course into an inevitable collision with the uprising ground.

Kaleb watches, helpless from the ground as she falls from the sky, and pushes his shifted form into overdrive, racing to find her, hoping she has not managed to hurt herself too badly. Gabrian lands with a heavy, painful thud. Her world spins, and she hurts everywhere upon making contact with the ground. Her body twitches violently as it rolls into the ditch and finally stops as a thorny bush ends her journey.

Hearing the quick smacking of footsteps nearing, she opens her eyes. Gabrian pushes away from the sharpness of the bushy entrapment and sits up, grateful to have her fleshy arms again even with the new scratches she is given. A familiar voice calls out her name. She exhales, thankful it is not a park ranger who she would have to explain just how she managed to fall from the sky. Kaleb's bellows continue until he is at the edge of the ditch.

"Stop yelling," she croaks out, winded from the fall. "You are hurting my ears."

Scurrying down into the ditch, back in human form and clothed, Kaleb surveys the damage. "Are you alright?"

She moves her newly transformed arms, and nods, knowing that it might be sore now but it is going to really hurt later. "Yeah, I'm good."

"Well, that is one way to come down the mountain."

They both let out a howl of laughter. Every move jars her torso, yelling out its need for her to end the madness. "Hey, I still beat you, so there."

Kaleb sits back on his legs and exhales, patting her on the head sweetly. "That you did."

Chapter Fifty-One

Midnight Tea

Taking the conventional way of transportation, Gabrian climbs inside the cab of Kaleb's aging quarter-ton pickup truck, parked just around the bend, and he drives them to his home. She bellies up to the pine-board bar as he sets the kettle on the stove to heat.

Two cups, a glass infuser, and some loose burgundy tea leaves are set in front of her. "Now, are you going to tell me how you escaped the wall of Guardians surrounding your house or do I have to ask you?" he says, attending to the whistling on the stove. "And don't tell me that they just let you go."

Gabrian knew it was too good to be true. The silence he had kept on the mountain about her presence there was just a ruse. Of course he was going to eventually ask her. He would not be a responsible Elder if he had not. Gabrian bites her lip and looks away, studying the glass infuser as it fills with hot water. The steaming liquid transforms from clear to crimson, reminding her of blood.

They have a bond now, more so than before, and are dependent on each other not to spill the beans about who and what they are. Secrets are a thing of the Realm, and she has managed to rack up a few of them. What is one more, shared among silent tongues? She slips her hands inside the neck of her shirt and pulls out the white metal amulet.

"Hm, I thought as much."

Gabrian shoots him a wide-eyed stare of wonder. "You knew about this thing?"

He chuckles in his soft hearty way and returns the kettle back to the stove, passing her a cup of the midnight blood-coloured brew. "Your mother used to play the same tricks on her father."

"She did?" Gabrian never knew her mother really, just knew *of* her, and some strange encounters with her essence or spirit, or whatever it is that keeps showing up.

Kaleb leans into the counter and picks up his cup, blowing away the steam misting over the top. "Yes, she lived in the same home, and under the same kind of 'home captive' life that you are doing now while she grew up training to take her father's seat at the covenant."

"Oh," is all she can say, feeling a twinge of sadness wash over her—sorry for her mother. She had only been under house arrest for a few days. She cannot fathom living a life that way. No wonder why she chose a wreck like her father as her mate. First class teenage rebellion case if Gabrian ever saw one. Good girl, bad—really bad—boy. It makes perfect sense to her.

"Don't feel too bad," Kaleb continues, taking a sip of the crimson tea. "She was very resourceful and enjoyed her life like most teenagers, only with a touch more excitement and danger involved." He chuckles as if he is remembering something that is not privy to Gabrian. "I knew that if she still had it, eventually you would come across it. I am sure there are a few other interesting things hidden away within the walls just waiting to be found."

She nods, not ready to divulge to him that she has already found something. Her mind lingers along the edges of the walls in her secret room. Raising her cup, hints of a peppery cinnamon scent tickles her nose as she sniffs the edge of the white porcelain mug, and peers over at him through the steam. "What kind of tea is this?"

He grins as if he has another secret of his own. "Do you remember the bright red flower in my greenhouse? The one that I kind of overreacted to you touching?"

How could she not? The image of him rushing through the greenery and yelling at her like a crazed lunatic was pretty hard to forget. "Yes, I remember."

"Well, this is made from its blossoms."

"The ones you told me would completely destroy the insides of a Borrower?"

"Hmm, maybe not destroy exactly, but wreak massive havoc on. But yes, the very one."

She sets the cup down and grimaces. "First, you say don't touch it and now you want me to ingest it? Are you trying to get rid of me?"

A rumble of laughter echoes through the small earthy kitchen as Gabrian pushes away the cup. "No, no, nothing like that." Setting his cup down, Kaleb leans in on his elbow, wanting nothing more than to see this open-minded youngling excel. Maybe with her sitting at the High Table, the fear of what he is, of what *she* is, can finally be put away. "You, obviously, are immune to its ill effects, or at least you were. And it not only repels Borrower and Vampire bites, it actually has a property in it that helps keep the animal inside in submission."

Narrowing her gaze, she glances from Kaleb's serene green to the deceptive tincture awaiting her in the cup.

"Seriously look, it is harmless, I think." Picking his cup back up and taking a large sip, he grins at her cautious stare. "See? No harm, no foul. Only a nice warm sip of animal control."

"Alright," she says, a little leery. "If you say so."

"Just try it. If it didn't burn you then, chances are, you are immune."

She gathers the mug back in her hand and slowly raises it to her lips, letting a small amount of the warm bloodlike liquid slide across her tongue and down her throat.

"And hey, it will either help you control your urge to shift or it will cause massive internal paralysis," he teases, watching her eyes flare wide open as she chokes on her mouthful of tea. "Sorry, maybe I should have started with that tidbit."

Chapter Fifty-Two

Nothing but a Monster

Having survived the tea, Gabrian takes her leave and flips the eye of the Window of Souls to face inward to her chest as the manual had instructed. The solid edges of her form pull into her center, and within a blink, she is standing beside the small wooden desk in the secret room. Flickering orbs end their wandering and scurry to circle her in a frenzy. Gabrian's sudden appearance is an exciting event for them, it seems.

Once they have their fun swirling around her form, they lose interest and are on their way back to the places between here and there. All except one. It hovers near while Gabrian slips off the amulet and tucks it safely away within the box and the drawer she had found it in.

A wide yawn reminds her that it is late, and that sleep is going to feel really good after the day's events. So, off to the shower for a quick rinse and then to bed it is. If she knows anything about this world, Gabrian is certain that tomorrow will hold much more of the unexpected so she better get some rest in the hopes of surviving it.

***

The morning light breaking through the window is a soft yellow through her lids, still heavy with sleep, and the need for coffee overrides the desire to remain in bed any longer. The buzzing of her phone on her nightstand jars her sleepy eyes to open. It has been silent as a ghost for weeks. She peeks over at the timekeeper on the wall. 6 AM it mocks.

"Now who in the world would be calling this early?" Gathering the phone, she reads the message. It's Rachael. She is home and wants her to come over. She has a surprise for her.

"She is home already?" Punching a quick reply to her friend, Gabrian hurries to find her clothes and searches for her keys, then stops, remembering she is not technically allowed to leave the premises. Her eyes rush to the fade in the bedroom wall, and she grins. "Problem solved," she hums, pulling her clothes on, and strides through the wall. Retrieving the amulet, she pulls it over her neck and wonders if the Shadow Walkers loved their means of instantaneous travel as much as she is starting to love hers.

Appearing just outside Rachael's apartment door, Gabrian tucks away her Magikal contraption and slides it beneath her shirt. Then, with three light raps on the wooden door, she waits. Light footsteps on the other side grow louder as the click of the lock is undone.

Rachael's small form pulls open the door, and Gabrian cannot help but shudder at her pale sickly look. *Why would they let her out of the hospital in this condition? She looks as if she is half dead.*

"Gabrian, you're here," she croaks out, pulling the door wide. "Get in here."

Gabrian forces a smile and walks in, giving her friend a peck on the cheek as she passes. As the door clicks shut, she notices the smell of orange blossoms and the frame of a large man lurking in the frame Rachael's bedroom doorway. "How are you feeling?" Gabrian asks her, turning back to her friend.

"Wonderful, never been better." Rachael gives her a wide smile and closes in for a hug, but her face is wrong, smell sickly, like death is hiding under her skin.

Gabrian searches for the shadow in the room again. Orroryn finally steps out into the light. His face is drawn and tired with circles of purple under his eyes but serene just the same. "It is good to see you, Gabrian."

"You as well, Orroryn." Gabrian cannot help but feel a tension in the room. Something is off, but she cannot figure out quite what. Orroryn's eyes leave Gabrian, settling on Rachael, and he disappears from the doorway to appear at her side, an arm draping around her small form. The room is silent. Eerie silent. Gabrian cannot stand the oddness of it. "Okay, so what is this big surprise that you so desperately needed me here for?"

Both Rachael and Orroryn grin, and they point at the space where Orroryn had just been standing. Turning to search the doorway once more, another large form silhouettes the doorframe, only this one makes her pulse stir. The azurite stone lying flush with her skin comes alive with prickles of awareness, and butterflies warm her belly. She knows this shape, this buzz of electricity as the scent of summer fills the room, drowning her heart in its purity. A sea green glow breaches the darkness of the shadows and sets her world to spin.

A boyish grin pulls crookedly at his lip as he steps out into the light. "I missed you," he breathes out, low and sultry.

Gabrian's vision blurs, but her body does not wait for her to clear her sight. She bounds across the room and jumps into his open arms. Her muscles burn as she clings to him, refusing to pull away, terrified he will disappear at any moment if she lets go. Burying her head in the crook of his neck, she weeps, missing the song his soul sings to hers, feeling the words of their bond speak their secret language of forever. She wants to live in this space, forever surrounded in what he is, in what they are—two pieces of fate's puzzle reconnected.

His heartbeat thrums through her ears as her angst slows, the warmth of his flesh against her own coddling her fears, and she finally draws back enough to gaze into the sea of green she has longed to see.

"Gabrian I—" he whispers low and soft, but she covers his words with her full lips, pressing soft with precious sweetness at first until the fire within them both ignites.

Stepping back into the room, Shane closes the door with Gabrian still wrapped tightly around him. Their tongues hunger for more, their hands reach beneath the cloth on their bodies in a fever to search, to explore. Sparks of their passion sting the darkness of the room, and Gabrian growls as her desire for this man grows in it intensity. She cannot see straight, everything shifting in a bounty of colour. Her mouth waters, and her teeth begin to ache. Every inch of her skin buzzes with excitement as the dark room lights with an amber glow. His feverish kisses along her neck cause her to growl again, louder and untamed.

Gabrian pushes hard against Shane's chest and rolls him over onto his back, perching above him. Her turn to take control. Ripping his shirt off and throwing it to the floor, the curves of his well-maintained muscular torso are bared, and Gabrian's eyes sharpen, taking in every shadowy bend in his flesh.

She lowers and kisses him, biting his bottom lip, and his approval is given in a low moan. Her bite intensifies as the sweet tang of copper dances over her tongue giving her a stir of elation. Releasing his lip, she hovers over his soft shadowy jaw, nipping along the edge as she goes, and inhales the scent of his earthy-salted flesh, licking it with her tongue. She bites again, her jaws aching to clench, teeth gnawing to draw deeper into his flesh just as the warm tang of copper bursts into her mouth.

It is exquisite and exciting. Her pulse quickens with the sudden outcry of noise in her ears. She bites harder, pulling the warm taste deeper into her mouth. Loud rumbling only dances on the edge of her acknowledgement as the body below her squirms and pushes against her, but her fingers grip hard into his flesh. She clings to his neck, letting the savory flow of his life fill her mouth.

This is like nothing else she has ever tasted before. Her tongue urges the flowing ooze of blood to continue on and on until the movement below stills. Her hands reflexively unclench from their impenetrable hold, and she eases back now that the liquid is nothing more than a slow drip. Lost within the euphoria, Gabrian sits up and licks her lips, enjoying this strange elation just as the bedroom door flies open, flooding light into the room.

Rachael's high pitch screams echo and bounce off the wall of the small space as two bodies rush in. "Oh my—what have you done, Gabrian?" Orroryn cries out.

Gabrian open her eyes and looks over her shoulder, confused by the intrusion and the chaotic display. Her eyes catch on the mirror. The reflection staring back is a charcoal and crimson smeared feral creature, with icy glowing eyes. Her face is stained in streaks of red and her aura flickers in a golden hue. All she can do is grin.

She twists her head, taking it all in with admiration. From a dark corner, a vaporous form claps slowly with his applause, his approval of her performance. "That is my girl," he jeers. "Since you have no problem killing the Shadow Walkers you love, killing the rest will be easy. Well done, my dear."

Gabrian pulls her eyes away from the mirror—and the ghost in the mist—and looks down to gaze at the still body, a torn jagged mess of flesh staring back at her from the base of Shane's neck. His eyes are drawn and blank, life gone from this world. The high of the blood rush leaves her soul bare—another innocent life stolen on her watch by her very hands.

The snide chittering of a familiar voice punches her hard from behind as the Eorden Elder steps into the room and stands beside Orroryn and Rachael. "Cimmerian was right to hate you," Kaleb hisses out at her. "We should have let Caspyous kill you." He hisses again, pointing to the shadowy corner. "You are nothing like me. You are just like him. Nothing but a monster."

Chapter Fifty-Three

Nightmares and Fire

A large frantic form bursts out from the corner of Gabrian's room, rushing to her thrashing body as screams fill the air around them. Draping his hand over her forehead to check her temperature, but finding none, he sets his hands on her shoulders to hold her still. Tynan whispers low, trying to lore her out of the nightmare she is drowning in.

"Gabe, wake up. Please, wake up," he says, hoping that it is only a nightmare and not something else. He is not sure he can handle seeing her go through another bout of internal damnation to her soul. "Gabe, please wake up."

The softness of Tynan's words breaks through her screams. Gabrian's arms flail widely as she fights her way back to consciousness and clammy sweat dews on her skin. Wide, frantic eyes scan the room, and her chest heaves, desperate for air not filled with copper and the tell of her monstrous actions.

"I killed him," she whimpers, tears running down her cheeks. "How could I kill him like that?"

Wiping the tearstains from her face, Tynan tries to reason with her. "Who did you kill?"

"Shane," she can barely say his name. The vividness of the act and of what she is, is so real—too real to her. "I killed Shane."

"No, Gabe," he assures her, assuming she is still living the night they were both in Erebus. "You didn't kill him. You both made it back from Erebus."

"I don't mean—" she quiets herself as the lucidness of her mind slowly wakes up and brings her back from the nightmare. "I mean, I killed him...myself. I took his life, I bit him, and—"

A softer tone slips over his lips, knowing how much she misses him even though she barely asks. He can feel the sadness reek from her, and he wants to tell her everything will be okay, but he just does not know himself. It is not his place to discuss Shane's progress or his decisions, and there is no sense in giving her false hope. It is cruel, he knows, but it is better this way.

"Gabe, it was only a nightmare." He cups her chin and gently coaxes her to look at him. "You did not kill him. Okay?"

Gabrian sinks into his deep green gaze. The softness they hold gathers her in them and settles the wildness in her mind, slowly reassuring her that Shane is indeed still alive. She looks down at the azurite stone. Although there is no hum, she is still connected to his soul, and she exhales with a nod, trying to let go, and knows Tynan would tell her if anything had happened to him.

He takes her tiny hands in his own, heat warming her fingers. "Better now?"

"Yeah, I guess."

Leaning in, Tynan kisses her forehead gently and gets up from the bed. "The sun is about to rise. I am going to go put some coffee on. Sound good?"

"That sounds awesome, Uncle Ty."

"Go have a shower. It will help make you feel better before the Elders get here."

"Elders?"

"I could only convince them to give you one day, so it is back to training today."

"Ugh, I was hoping they would forget all about me." She exhales, falling back into her pillow. "Maybe I will get lucky today and Arramus will set my whole body on fire."

"I think that is part of his plan." Tynan chuckles, heading for the door.

"What? Seriously?"

Chapter Fifty-Four

Forgiveness

It was nice to spend the last free moments of her day off with her Uncle Ty. It was also nice for her to see him actually smiling and joking around again like his old self—the playful man-boy who had always come to visit her while she was growing up. *So much has changed. So much has happened. Even in their strange Magikal world, he had to admit Gabrian's circumstances are the extreme.*

A light rapping at the kitchen door stirs Gabrian and her uncle from their quiet moment. They both let out a whoop at the same time. "Come in." A release of humor fills the room with their laughter.

The door swings wide then closes. Only the shuffling of shoes being removed can be heard. "Good morning, I hope I am not too early," calls out a familiar voice. The lime green aura floats above the Elder as he makes his way through the kitchen. Gabrian and Tynan glance up to see Kaleb standing bright-eyed and bushy-tailed on the other side of the counter.

"No, not at all. We have been up for hours." Gabrian cheers, sipping the remains of her brew. Kaleb's presence had been scarce since the strange vision, but after last night, they have obviously crossed over a bridge of understanding, and he is back, to her delight.

"Really?" Kaleb's brow twists, surprised since he figured she would have slept in a bit due to her forbidden adventures a few hours

SILVER

earlier. "Well, that is inspiring news. I always believed that watching the sun rise is good for the soul."

Her heart twists a little. Sunrises had become a Shane thing for her. The thought of him lying dead in her dreams beneath her runs a shiver through Gabrian, but she forces a smile to her guest just the same.

"Help yourself to the coffee if you like, we made plenty." Gabrian nods, hearing her Uncle's words as he rises from his chair and heads back up to the kitchen. She has got to pull herself out of her funk.

"Thanks, but I already had some tea. Speaking of which, Gabrian, I brought you a little something."

"Oh," she says, her mind resurfacing. Unfolding her legs, and getting to her feet, she bounds for the kitchen as well. "What did you bring me?"

"Tea," he chimes, holding up the small bag made of folded parchment in front of her. "I thought it might be a good routine to get into before we start your day."

Tynan rinses out the remains of his cup and sets it into the sink. "What does the tea do?"

"Oh, well, this particular tea helps with concentration and clarity of mind," he says, turning to face Gabrian, a grin edging at his lips—one built from secrets between friends. "And, it is high in vitamin C so it helps to keep you from getting run down."

"That is very thoughtful of you, Kaleb," Tynan say, wiping his hands. "Thank you for looking after Gabrian."

"It is no trouble, really." Kaleb's eyes brighten. Last night unloaded a mountain of stress. He found another friend who he knows he does not have to hide from, not anymore, and it is a breath of fresh air to him in a world stifled with toxin.

"Alright, I am off," Tynan announces. "The others are probably going to arrive soon, and we have some things to discuss so I will leave you to it."

"Alright, Uncle Ty. I will catch up with you later."

After the tea is brewed, Gabrian and Kaleb gather on the deck and watch the morning sun cast diamonds over the water.

"So, are you okay?" Kaleb asks, feeling a little strangeness flowing around Gabrian.

"Yeah, why?"

"Well, you seem a little off. The light in your eyes is dimmed."

"Oh." She deflates in her chair, sinking back into the pillow. "Well, I felt great after we talked, and I came home, but then I woke to my own screams. It must have been really bad because when I woke up, Uncle Ty was already in my room, wearing the same look he used to when I was sick."

"Did you talk to Tynan about it?

"A little," she hums.

"Look, I know you are the doctor here, but if you want, maybe it might help to talk about it. Just to get it out of your head."

"Yeah, maybe." Gabrian retells the dream to Kaleb, all of it— even the mushy parts. She has seen him naked, twice, so a little story about her kissing her mate is nothing. She tells him what he said to her about Caspyous and Cimmerian, and about her father being in the room. All of the bizarre details were divulged.

Kaleb sits silent for a moment, pursing his lips. "Well, first off, what do you think it means?"

"I think it means I am capable of everything everyone has ever said about me, the bad things. All I ever seem to do is hurt those closest to me."

"Okay, yes, I can see that." He scratches his jaw and takes a sip of the blood tea. "Now, do you want to know what I see?"

"Yes, of course."

"Even though all of those things you just said are true, and are part of who you are, I also see a girl drowning within her own self-loathing."

Gabrian grimaces at his words, the same words Matthias has used when they first started training together.

"Now before you shoot the messenger," he says, holding up his hands, "all I am saying is, maybe the real problem is, you haven't forgiven yourself. You are holding on to your guilt, and not only your guilt, but of all those who have tried to harm you."

She nods, sipping on her own tea, and lets the words sink in.

"Maybe I am just shooting bullets in the dark here, but for me, the only way I have learned to move on, to carry on, is let go of the sins. Give forgiveness to those who would harm you. More importantly, give forgiveness to yourself. If you don't, it will continue to haunt you, slowly eating you up inside. Yes, things have gone badly, and yes, life is full of crappy things, but you don't need to carry them with you for the rest of your life taking up precious energy and space. You owe yourself that much."

Still she sits in her silence, gripping the edges of her cup. "But what if I don't know how?"

"Then you must learn how, or else I can guarantee you are in for a rough eternity."

"Even, Caspyous?"

Kaleb cannot help but chuckle. "Yes, even Caspyous. Be better than him and let his sins go. You must learn to forgive for your own good. It might be a good idea to face him and the fear head on. It is not like he is getting out anytime soon. This would be the time to do it."

"But I don't know how to forget what he tried to do."

"I never said anything about forgetting—that stuff you keep to remain strong and alive."

Chapter Fifty-Five

I See Fire

A flicker of red catches her eye as the Egni Elder approaches the deck. Tea time is over, and it is time to get back to training. "Good morning," he cheers out.

"Morning," they both reply.

The sinking feeling in her stomach releases strangely at the thought of training—a better focal point than the one she and Kaleb had been discussing.

Arramus claps his hands together and rubs them. "Kaleb, it is nice to see you back and feeling better."

Gabrian glances over at her friend, unaware that he had been ill. He hadn't said anything to her about it.

"Yes, much better. Thank you for asking, Arramus." He smiles, picking up his tea, and sips at it, flashing Gabrian a wink.

"Alright, Miss, whenever you are ready," Arramus cheers, moving his attention to address Gabrian.

"Oh, um, yeah, can I have just a second?"

"Sure thing, I will meet you at the center mark."

"Great. Thank you. I will be there shortly," she hums, waiting for him to take his leave then turns to eye Kaleb. "Why didn't you tell me you were ill? I thought you were just avoiding me."

A crooked grin tips his mouth. "I was, but last night remedied that."

"Oh," she says, "but why were you avoiding me?"

"Because after you slipped into that trance, you looked at me, and you knew what I was. I saw it in your eyes. The fear of what lingers inside of me. You saw past the human form, and I was unsure of how to approach the subject. I wanted to know my next move in case your reception to my secret was unfavourable."

"What were you going to do if it had gone another way?"

Kaleb stands, clearing the table of tea cups and grins at her. "Doesn't matter now, does it? Don't you have a lesson to get to?" he says, edging toward the door.

"Hey, you are avoiding my question."

He gives her a wink over his shoulder. "Yes I am."

"Ugh." She sighs. "Kaleb."

She gets up to follow him but a large arm waving from the center of her lawn flags the fact that her few minutes to finish up are over. She smiles, returning the wave, and heads to the center, calling out her dislike of Kaleb's vagueness over her shoulder. "I am not done talking about this."

A faint reply starts Gabrian on her trek. "I didn't expect so."

Leaving the warmth of the deck, she jogs toward the center mark of the training area, baggy clothes flapping in the breeze. Irritation already starts to nick at her nerves. *Seriously, can't they train in something more streamline?*

"Sorry about that. I just had something to discuss with Kaleb."

"No worries, Miss." The heavy look of frustration he had carried at the end of their last session is gone, void of existence. Today is a new day and a great time to put things into perspective, and since she found the cheat booklet in her secret room, maybe today's lesson might not go as badly as last time.

"So, what am I going to be doing today?"

"Same as last time, only this time it won't hurt," he hums. "I think." He chuckles, rubbing his hands together, then turns them palms up. "Now place your hands over the top of mine."

She shrugs and steps in front of him, doing as he asks.

"Ready?"

"Sure, ready as I will ever be."

"Just relax. I am not going to blast you into a ball of inferno."

"Like last time you mean?"

"That was a slight oversight on my part. Sorry about that."

"Mmhmm." she teases, eyes wide with a pinch of fear.

"I just want to see if you can accept the ignition from me. I brought a fire extinguisher this time in case it gets out of hand." Arramus nods his head to the left and grins.

"What? This is not a great way to settle my nerves." Gabrian searches the ground for the extinguisher.

"Just kidding. It will be fine."

"Can I have your word on that?"

Rolling his eyes at her, he sighs and flashes a grin. "Okay, ready? Here we go."

She nods, losing her sarcasm, and focuses on the Elder. The center of his eyes brighten and light up like embers in the ashes. Small warm tingles itch the palms of her hands as Arramus engages his Magik. His eyes swirl backwards—a trick to engage her mind into paying attention.

Her palms grow warmer and warmer. She lowers her lids, feeling the soft heat flowing between their hands, and releases a low hum. "Whenever you are ready," she says, waiting for the sting of fire to bite.

A low chuckle jars her eyes wide as Arramus takes a step back.

"What the—" she reflexively waves her hands, but he grabs her wrists. With a grin painted on his lips, he holds her hand in front of her face so that she can see the Magik burning in splendor at the tips of her fingers. "It is beautiful," she coos, enchanted by the orange glow.

"Sure is, Miss. Welcome to Egni."

Chapter Fifty-Six

Unorthodox Training

The next few weeks are more of a blur than anything else. Between the all-day training sessions, and after supper study time in her secret room, Gabrian is starting to learn so much. The books are playing nice and showing most of their hidden words. Even the invisible blockades have pushed back some and allowed her entry farther into the halls. Not much but some. It has been a steep learning curve, but she is starting to enjoy it. Now, if she could just stop sleeping, everything would be perfect.

The nightmares have arrived again and show no signs of leaving anytime soon. Even after hours of brutal, intensified training they find a way to creep into her slumber and deny her any rest—or peace, more like it. Dark hours filled with the same horrors of Caspyous and Cimmerian's hatred as well as her blood-filled evil and monstrous acts against her loved ones. Last night's episode involved Jarrison and Sarapheane being shredded apart because they could not reach the Veil in time to escape her.

Every morning, she wakes to Tynan holding her down, trying to sooth her screams, and the fear in his eyes grows darker as the days pass. At least she is not setting things on fire—only a few ripped pillows and shredded blankets are victimized.

On the upside of things, Matthias is granted access to the grounds to train her in hand-to-hand combat during the mornings before his classes. It is a welcome distraction to flush out her jittery nerves from the night terrors. Each afternoon, Gabrian is acquainted, met to bind, and trained with all the rest of the gifts in the Fellowship. She manages to keep her own special gift under wraps, thanks to Kaleb's tea, and only explores that avenue under his supervision on occasional night treks.

All the elements are addressed except Cimmerian's Derkaz gift. That kind of Magik is a one-on-one interaction due to its sensitiveness and need for minimal distraction—and the fact he is still incarcerated. She knows she will have to face Cimmerian soon to do it. Even though his act against her was not as malicious as Caspyous', he still managed to destroy her, and she would have to deal with being in front of the man who sent her to Erebus. This alone is enough to trigger the nightmares.

Maybe Kaleb is right. Maybe it is time to try the forgiveness thing. If it will help her in the long run, then it is worth the short-term suffrage. But that will have to wait for just a bit longer.

Today Gabrian's testing begins. It is decided that it is time she learns to defend herself against the forces she has summoned. She is not sure if it is the tea or extra circular study sessions in her secret room, but it feels like she is gaining control of her new world. Probably a little of both, and either way, she is glad to have it.

Having thrown the flowy and annoying cloth gi in the trash, Gabrian opted for her own kind of training wears. More sleek and snug, easy to maneuver without flapping sleeves that could slow her down or catch on fire. Crouched in the center of the training area, dews of perspiration bead on her brow, and Gabrian waits the next trial. Her eyes are pinched and senses on high alert. The first couple of tests are just a warm up. She knows they will progressively accelerate as she learns to respond.

Her skin tingles as the first strike comes. She dips to the left, feeling the heat of fire as a streak blasts by her. Grabbing hold of the flame, she spins within its momentum, absorbing its power, and wills it into ice. Whipping her body around, Gabrian thrusts the melded Isa

274

Magik back at her opponent in a handful of jagged edged frozen daggers, sending them slicing in Arramus' direction. Shifting quickly, he avoids the icy shards—pushing out a wave of flame to wash over them as they pass, turning them to liquid.

"Nice try, Miss, but I am fire. Those icy claws will never scratch me."

Gabrian purses her lips, scratches the edge of her pixie-length hair, and watches the dust at his feet puff into the air as he marches around, gloating. A grin crawls onto her lips, and she rubs her hands together. A new plan hatches, and she is ready to try his hand. "Okay, again. This time I am ready."

"Alright, here it comes."

His hands face the sky as two spirals of fire spin off and shoot straight at Gabrian. She slips between them, catching them both in her hands, and thrusts them back from where they came, in swords built of long slim pointed ice. She flips her palms outward.

"I told you that won't—" Arramus starts to complain just as the ground rumbles beneath him. A cloud of dust whips around his feet then climbs upward, cloaking his stumbling form. The Eorden Magik blasts his eyes with its tiny bombardment of ammunition, blinding him. His entire body shakes, and he falters to his knees. The earth beneath opens and consumes him in a thick layer of pebbles and sand, burying him alive in her strike.

Gabrian lowers her hands and tucks them on her hips, listening to the Elder curse, coughing out the grit and dirt lodged in his lungs. He rises to his feet, dusting off the debris, and rubs the grit out of his eyes.

"I win?" she chirps at him with a smirk.

Coughing up what sounds like a lung, he replies begrudgingly, "Yes." Another loud cough. "You win."

"Next!" she cheers out, feeling the joys of her victory over the Egni Elder.

Arramus takes his leave just as another Elder steps into position, grumbling to him over his shoulder, "Watch her. She cheats."

"Hey, now, don't be a spoiled sport," Gabrian taunts him as he goes.

One by one, they test her ability to defend and offend, and one by one she figures the best counter action to display. Each one of her successes builds her confidence until Ethan takes his turn and steps into the ring. Her lips quiver, unsure of how this will play out. The only gift she knows that can outplay a Borrower gift is that of the Schaeduwe. Borrowers can only attack the auras, but the Shadow Walkers have none which makes them tolerant to the Boragen threat.

Are you ready? Ethan hums to her silently.

She nods, having no idea what to do.

Ethan's eyes darken. The hazel of his irises are no more, the pupils dilating to consume his eyes in blackness. A shiver runs down her spine as she watches her dearest friend transform into something eerie and dark, wondering if this is what she looked like when she stole life essence. She weakens in his pull. Feeling him draw harder at the life force, Gabrian stumbles, unable to push him away, unable to hold onto her soul.

Fight back Gabrian, Ethan's words bounce through the hollows of her mind.

I'm trying, she hisses back.

Lightening in the distance dances across the sky, catching her eye. This is a light of hope, not despair, as the air thickens with wild energy. She closes her eyes and draws in a deep breath, searching for the familiar sizzle, and holds her hands outward at her sides. It is different from the everyday household power. This one is cleaner and more eager to be beckoned.

Slender snakes of the sky's Magik whip across the distance, meeting her demand, and crackle around her. Gabrian feels the intensity build within and lifts her hands up, watching the electricity construct a nest of pure power in her fingers. Spinning and binding, it materializes into a mini electrical storm. Darkened clouds rush in above her and release a loud crack that shakes the ground beneath their feet.

Eyes of the group volley back and forth then up to the sky, feeling the tingle of electricity in the air intensify. Something completely unanticipated is taking place. The hair on their heads begins to rise and stand on end. Whispers hiss over the training area.

"What the—" Ethan breathes out just before Gabrian claps her hands, releasing her hold on the Magik, and pushes it forward. It flares out in a wave of white, blinding him as it strikes him and everyone else close by.

The air surges with heat, and she grins, knowing it's a direct hit with Ethan and that he will recover quickly. "I might not be able to stop you, my friend, but I sure as hell can slow you down."

A white sizzling chain of light plummets from the skies, snapping loudly as it strikes Gabrian's tiny form. Her body lights, throwing her across the grass, and she quakes on the ground as the remains of electricity sear through her entire body, leaving her nothing more than a smoking gun. Horrified Elders rush to her side. Kaleb and Vaeda step around the huddle to create barriers, using their earthly gifts to urge the skies to move along and carry their own Magik with them.

"Gabrian, Gabrian," Tynan yells emerging from the shadows, laying his ear on her chest, and presses his trembling fingers to her neck, waiting. "There is a pulse," he hisses, lifting her into his arms.

Ethan hobbles to the blackened center and hovers over the two. He stumbles but steadies his footing and lays his hands on her, gauging her energy level. "Gabrian, can you hear me?"

Tynan pushes everyone but Ethan away from her and cradles her gently in his arms, the tears already streaming down his cheek. Her body lights. Small sparks of the lightning strike bite at Ethan's and Tynan's skin from her as the smoky streams of her own Boragen Magik swarm around her. Her mouth falls open and a stream of it enters. Her eyes open but are unresponsive.

"Gabe, please, honey. Please be okay," Tynan whimpers out.

She blinks and jerks upright, drawing in a loud gulp of air—eyes wide and wild. "Holy crap, that was some blast," she croaks out, her voice sanded and hoarse. "Did I win?"

The crowd exhales the breath they had been holding. Tynan pulls her in tight and kisses her forehead as the others unclench and unleash their fears in a bout of grateful laughter. "Yes, Gabe, honey. You win."

Chapter Fifty-Seven

Sickly Sweet Visit

Screams fill the darkness as well as a crackling light just as Tynan reaches Gabrian's side. Her pixie long locks are damp with fear as she reaches out and clings to her uncle's large form.

"Are they getting worse?"

She nods in in his arms, hearing her heart pound from within her trembling shell. Her wide eyes search the darkness for her mirror, desperate to see her face, and hoping it is not the horrific thing she becomes in her dreams.

"Oh, Gabe, I wish I could help you make them go away."

Gabrian pulls his warmth in closer and mumbles into his shoulder. "You can. You can take me to the Hollows in the Covenant."

He slips back from her and crooks his brow. "The Hollows? Why on Earth would you want to go there?"

"I need to find forgiveness. It is time to deal with my demons."

"Are you sure?"

"Yes."

"I will make it happen."

"Thanks, Uncle Ty." She looks away, rubbing the soft flat stone on her wrist. "Can we make one pit stop on the way?"

"Sure, Gabe. Whatever you need."

**

The slow beep that had kept the small Vindere youngling company is silent today as Gabrian peeks her head through the opening

279

in the doorway of room 231. Already awake and reading a book, Rachael's sweet smile welcomes her friend.

"Is this a good time?"

"It is always a good time to see your beautiful face. Get in here."

Sauntering across the space between them, Gabrian sinks into Rachael's outstretched arms and falls into her friend—grateful for her forgiveness and trying really hard to forgive herself. "How are you feeling?" Gabrian pulls away and settles on the side of the hospital bed.

"I'm great, still a little weak, but other than that perfect."

"Good," is all Gabrian can say. "I know it is early, and I am not going stay long. I just wanted to see you."

"Well, I am glad you popped by. I heard the Elders have big plans for you." She grins and clasps one of Gabrian's hands with delicate icy fingers. "Silver Mage, so I hear?"

"Yeah, something like that. They are suffering from some kind of delusional high expectations."

"Don't put yourself down like that, you are special, Gabrian. Embrace it like the workaholic I know."

"That is my plan. I am hoping to razzle and dazzle them all so they will release me from house arrest."

"Yeah, I heard about that too." Rachael bunches her nose, her body shivering, and goosebumps rise across her arms. "Sorry about that."

"It is fine," she hums, scanning the room. Lifting from the bed, Gabrian fetches a folded white blanket from the back of the visitor's chair and lets her Egni Magik sink over the cloth. A delicate hue of her crimson gift spirals out in snaky streams, warming it, then Gabrian drapes the heated fabric across Racheal's shoulders. Rachael purrs as the warmth coddles her chilled body.

"Now that is cool."

"Yeah, I guess Magik does have its perks sometimes." A click of the door crackles in Gabrian's ears, and a chill of her own runs up the back of her neck, sensing an intense and eerie strain of darkness nearing.

"Symone," Rachael cheers out.

"Sorry, I didn't know you had company." A tall slender girl stands in the opening with dark hair, wild and unruly. The hint of an arrogant smirk rides on the plumpness of her lips, and her black pensive eyes bore into Gabrian, already irritating her patience, knowing exactly who this girl is.

"No worries, come in."

Gabrian's senses sting as the girl enters the space. Her purple aura flares in bursts with each slow stride she takes, reminding Gabrian of a predator. There is a strange darkness to her, different from the aura she saw on the girl's father. Where his is bright and vibrant hers is potent and murky. The girl smiles sweetly, eyeing the two friends as she approaches, but it is sickly-sweet, and it gnaws at Gabrian's core.

"Gabrian, this is Symone, Cimmerian's daughter," Rachael chimes out.

Gathering her manners, and her self-control, Gabrian returns the smile. "Hi."

"Hi," she softly hisses.

Did she just hiss at me? Gabrian pinches the edges of her eyes for a second. The dark aura around the girl grows in its murkiness and whips out, violently sending strands of its presence to lurch and wind invasively around Gabrian's form. Irritated, Gabrian purses her lips and pushes her own energy out. A strange wave of sizzling light blocks the intrusion and sends the invasive strands of light to scurry back to its owner.

Symone's sickly-sweet smile flinches in the retraction, and she flexes a twisted brow. "So, you are the girl all the fuss is about."

"Um, pardon me? Sorry?"

"Adrinn and Cera's child," she tries to spit out politely, but Gabrian can hear the disdain through her nearly gritted teeth.

"Yes, I guess I am."

Symone glides over and sits on the side of Rachael's bed, almost in the same spot Gabrian had just vacated. Gabrian's skin crawls at her close proximity to her friend, and a growl grows just beneath her throat as she cozies up to Rachael.

"You two know each other?"

"Oh, sorry, yes. Symone is in the room just down the hall, and we met a couple weeks ago."

"Ah, right." The odd sting to her senses, from the day she found out Rachael was awake, ghosts over her. Remembering passing by the room, and its familiar offence lingers over the girl only mere feet away from her. It must have been her room that she had passed by on the way here.

Symone paints a bigger smile, more sickly-sweet than before—one that curdles in the pit of Gabrian's stomach. "You know," she says. "I think I am going to go."

Rachael smile dips as the words leave Gabrian's mouth.

"You don't have to go on my account," the girl taunts.

Gabrian forces a polite smile. "Oh, it's not, trust me." She makes the point clear to the girl. "I have some things I need to take care of."

"Oh, okay," Rachael hums.

"I will come back. Maybe tomorrow." Gabrian slides in and leans down, wrapping her arms around Rachael, and feels the light of her soul burn brightly in contrast to the girl beside her. She whispers a soft 'I love you' before letting go.

"I love you too, Gabe," Rachael replies, letting Gabrian slip out of her arms, and starts for the door.

"It was nice to finally meet you," Symone says, way too chipper for Gabrian's liking.

"Yeah, you too," Gabrian lies, not even bothering to pretend to smile this time.

As she steps through the door, and it slips closed, a wave of high-pitch giggles stings her ears. The heat from her boiling blood flushes her cheeks. Her fists clench, aching to punch clean through that smiling rat sitting on Rachael's bed.

"There is something not right with that girl." Gabrian purses her lips, looking back at the door. "I am not jealous. I'm not."

Chapter Fifty-Eight

Forgiveness is a Four‑Letter Word

The sun drifts through the clouds like a ghost in the darkness when they enter the Covenant of Shadows. Its faded light mixes with the colours of the cauldron's fiery prismatic glow, flickering in Gabrian's presence, but nothing more. One remains just as barren as the day she first saw it.

Tynan releases her wrist and drapes his arm around her as they walk through the corridor, sensing the frayed edge of Gabrian's nerves as she bites the tip of her thumb. "Are you sure you want to do this?

She looks straight ahead, gearing up for the encounter, and unsure of how it will all play out. She needs to do this, regardless of her own sanity. She must face her fears before they consume her. "No, I'm not, but I have to, Uncle Ty. I can't go on living this way—afraid to close my eyes because of all the monsters that wait for me when I do." She tucks her arm around him and takes in his strength. "I have to let go or at least try to."

He knows she is right. Tynan has witnessed firsthand the flood of terror her eyes hold when she wakes. Instead of going to the left, as usual when entering, they take a right and walk through the giant pillars and into the center of a large oval opening in the marble wall. She has never seen this part of the Covenant, her desire to look farther into the place tainted.

On the other side, small vendor kiosks are scattered in a chaotic order. Different colours of their banners breach the boredom of the white and black speckled floors. People are busy straightening displays and chatting gainfully with potential buyers—that is until Tynan and Gabrian stride through the middle of it. Voices cut out mid-sentence and switch to hisses of whispers and pointed fingers—not to mention the mixture of dirty looks with hopeful but meek smiles under nodding heads.

Gabrian's head fills with the internal dialogue of the people scurrying about to catch a glimpse of her. Words like *'not much to look at'* to *'she is too young to be trusted'* flair through her mind. She lifts her chin as she has before, blocks out the barrage of mental murmurs, and looks straight ahead, not wanting to see or hear anymore. She is here for a reason and will not let the doubts of unfamiliar people waver her determination to see this through.

Feeling her tension, Tynan guides her through the market with more hurriedness toward a large slab of dark marble just a few meters away. Gabrian stares as the darkness shifts and sways within the wall. Two large forms stand on either side. Their serious faces ease in to smiles as the large Guardian closes the distance between them. "Tynan, it is good to see you," one says. The other, "Where have you been hiding?"

His inner glow bubbles out over his tongue as he speaks with kindness to his friends—both of them no doubt having trained under the Shadow Walker. Standing patiently, Gabrian waits for the pleasantries to subside and lets her uncle get down to the reason for the visit. "Guardians, this is my niece, Gabrian."

Their eyes lower to the small woman and dip their heads, knowing exactly whom and what she is rumored to be. *I wish people would stop doing that here.*

"Gabrian requests a visit with the Elder of Derkaz, Cimmerian Cole."

"Of course. He should be in his chamber. Just tell Murphy inside. He knows which row he is in."

"Thank you, gentlemen. I will see her in."

Tynan grips hold of Gabrian's wrist, and she follows her Uncle's lead, fading in the shadowy wisps of the space between the two men. On the other side, they step out into a narrow hallway, take a left, and step out into an open space filled with rows upon rows of small open cubicles. An array of different Fellowship colours lightly drift in front of them. A few people dressed in light blue common tees and jeans come and go as they please in and out of cells.

A wave of nervousness flips her stomach, and she tugs on her uncle's shirt. "This is where you keep all the prisoners?"

"Yes, most. Why?"

"Where are the locks and keys? There are no bars or doors on the cells."

"It is okay, don't worry. The people here are under strict monitored watch by Guardians just within the Veil. No one steps out of line before they are quickly put back in and given a proper reminder that there are other places they can be kept. It is just an illusion. Some small freedoms given help keep the prisoners' mental state a little more intact."

"Oh," she says, not feeling any better about the set up.

"Being caged like an animal isn't good for anyone's state of mind. Besides, where are they going to go? No one gets in or out unless it is through the shadows."

"Okay, if you say so." She raises her brow and keeps her hold on his shirt.

A tall young man greets the two, and Tynan makes his request, pointing to the row of cells where Cimmerian calls home. They both thank him and head in that direction. Not everyone seems to be awake. Only the early risers are up and moving, she notices, taking a quick peek into the open cells as she glides by, closely shadowing her uncle's large form.

Tynan slows his stride, making Gabrian suck in her breath. A haze of purple light drifts out from the cell. Sitting up against the pillows of his already made bed, the dark Elder peers up at them above his glasses. A snug grey tee hugs his torso, matched with a pair of faded black jeans. His hands hold the leather-bound edges of a book. Her heart rattles her chest, and a rush of stinging heat flushes her face as she meets his black eyes. He looks way too content to be a prisoner in Gabrian's opinion.

"Good morning," he says, sliding a strip of paper into the cream-coloured pages of his book, and closes it, resting it on the bed beside him. "To what do I owe this pleasure, young Gabrian?"

Tynan steps back, eyeing the Elder, and senses his energy levels for any signs of aggression then looks at his niece. "Would you like some privacy or do you want me to stay?"

"Do you mind if I speak to him alone for a few minutes?" She wants him to stay but with him physically lurking over her shoulder, she is not sure she will find the right words. But the Veil will do. She knows there are others watching, so privacy isn't really a big concern right now.

"Sure thing. I will be just on the other side if you need me."

"Thanks." She watches his physical form fade into nothing. Even though she has seen this parlor trick a hundred times now, it is still fascinating to watch it happen.

"So, I say again. What do I owe this pleasure to?"

Inhaling, she turns to face her fears—well, at least one of them. "I just wanted to talk to you about some things."

"Certainly, my dear," he offers, getting up from his bed and stepping out of his cell. "Shall we take a walk then?"

Is he serious? We are in a prison full of bad guys, and he want to go traipsing through the muck of them. "Sure, okay."

He tucks his hands behind his back and starts to go, but Gabrian's feet are stuck to the floor, paralyzed by the very thought of perusing nonchalantly through the prison.

"Don't worry, it will be fine. I have no desire to hurt you. If it makes you feel better there is a constant watch on all of the inmates."

"Yes, Uncle—I mean Tynan mentioned that." She sucks up her hesitation and starts after him.

"Before you say what you have come to say, I just want to tell you that I am sorry. I feel horrible for what I let happen to you," he says, his words soft and sincere.

Her body almost jerks to a stop at his unprovoked confession. "But why did you do it then?"

"It was never really about you, child." He slows his stride, letting her catch up. "I will admit that I did not hold any concern for you and your Borrower beginnings. You were just a pawn. A disposable player in the game I had chosen to play with your father."

My father. Another demon she must soon face on her trek of forgiveness.

"I will make no excuses for what I have done. And I deserve to be here. It is just, sometimes life offers you an unorthodox opportunity to obtain what you want. But, in return, it creates a tunnel vision, blinding out all the wrongdoings of your actions, only allowing focus on how to achieve that one thing you so desperately desire to have.

"For me, it was the chance of getting my daughter back." His eyes graze down the small girl at his side. "I held no regard for what it may have been doing to you or your loved ones." Cimmerian still feels the sting of casting the blocked shadows around Gabrian's adoptive parents. His tunnel vision had cost them their lives, but he will never speak of it. He wants to eventually be released from this prison and if this secret were to be let out, his chances would be slim to none. "Unfortunately, this kind of thinking can make you very dangerous."

Gabrian purses her lips, listening to the Derkaz Elder explain his reasons for his actions—his words earnest and heartfelt. Understanding completely what he is saying, she is not here to cast judgement, only to find forgiveness. She has her own demons to slay when it comes to doing what she needed in order to survive. At least he is coming clean on his own, and the pill he offers is easier to swallow.

"The same kind of blindness, I do believe, was the undoing of Caspyous as well."

Hearing the name sends shivers down her spine, a replay of his heinous acts toward her setting her skin to crawl. Gabrian does a scan over every face they meet on their walk, knowing he is here somewhere, and prepares herself for an encounter.

Seeing the youngling shudder, Cimmerian curves away from the ex-Elder's mention. His intention is not to burn the bridge before he can build it. He needs to move forward and strengthen his frayed connection with her, especially if she is to be the new head of the Table. "Anyway, all I am trying to say is that I am sorry. I know we are scheduled to work together in the near future, once I have served the mandatory amount of time of my sentence, and I am hoping that I can redeem myself in your eyes."

This Cimmerian that is before her is not the man she came to forgive. It is like all the darkness that had loomed over him like a cloud is gone. The anger and the hatred that seeped from his soul toward her is nothing more than a distant memory, another life. Gabrian turns to face the Elder, letting go of her fear of the man, and finds a meek smile.

"Alright. I have said my peace, and I will reap what I have sowed. The stage is yours," he says, guiding them toward a large open area of the

Hollows, and stops before a table. He slides into one of the chairs, offering the other to Gabrian.

Slipping her small form into the stone chair, she exhales. All the words she so carefully cultivated in her mind, everything she had wanted to scream at him, hold no meaning anymore. Her heart is lighter and the twisted knot of stress she had carried in here with her unwinds as forgiveness is lent to the man who sent her to Erebus. "So, um, I was just wondering if there is anything I should be doing to prepare for our sessions together." The words ring easy on her tongue. Not hatred, no malice, the hatchet has been buried in her mind, handle and all.

The two sit for a few moments, discussing some small pointers she could work on while waiting his clearance for temporary leave. A few inquisitive stares float over them as they speak, but no one approaches, not even Tynan who is just on the cusp of the Veil.

Gabrian's skin prickles as one prisoner closes in and interrupts her visit. "Well, well, well, what do we have here?"

Cimmerian tenses. His violet aura stops its flowy display and switches over his form, snaking out to shield the girl, knowing the boiling hatred that runs rampant within the intruder. "Caspyous, do you mind?"

"Oh no, I don't mind at all, Cimmerian," he spits out. "It is not every day we are privileged with a visit from such an esteemed new member of the Covenant."

Gabrian's fingers burn like wildfire biting at the ends. Her body tingles with the stream of adrenaline pumping through her veins and shadows shift in her peripheral. She knows the shadows are watching now.

"Caspyous, we are in the middle of a lesson, could you please move on."

"It is alright, Cimmerian." Gabrian clenches her burning hands and finds her voice. "I came here to see Caspyous as well."

The Hydor member switches his brow at her, his eyes digging into her to try to stir her fears, and steps in to invade their small bubble of comfort. Gabrian's breath hitches, and she cannot seem to find enough air to fill her lungs.

"Is that so? Alright, you came to see me so here I am. What do you want?" he hisses, sliding his hand around the back of his hip, tapping his side, then brings his hand forward again.

"Well," she croaks out, her eyes sneak a peek at Cimmerian then around at the shifting shadows just within reach, and finally land on Caspyous. "I just wanted to tell you that I want to forgive you for—"

A loud crack of haughty laughter claps in her ears. His eyes burn wild with the same glare of hatred he has always shown her. There is no guilt in his eyes for the attack he had orchestrated, nor a plea for sympathy in his attempted murder. No there is nothing good or kind in those eyes. He leers at her and steps in. Cimmerian rises from his chair and blocks the wild man's advances on his young visitor. "Forgive? I don't want your forgiveness. I meant every single vile act toward erasing you from this Realm."

Cimmerian pulls Gabrian behind his back and puts a hand out to the ranting ex-Elder. "That is quite enough, Caspyous."

"I hardly think it is," he continues his tirade. "You are the spawn of evilness, an abomination of existence. These people are stupid to stand by and watch you claim the throne of their world. The Elders are so eager to pass the torch, and when they do, you will burn them all to the ground. Even if no one else can see the truth for what it is, I can."

Cimmerian, steps away from the irate man and tries to pull Gabrian along with him, placing her out of Caspyous' reach. "Come on. I think it is time for us to go."

Tears well at the edges of Gabrian's eyes as she glances back at the seething glare being thrown her way, then moves along with Cimmerian's demanding tug to leave.

Caspyous sneers at her as the two walk away. "You will be nothing more than a monster just like him. His darkness lies too deep in your veins. He took everything, *everything* I loved, and destroyed it with his evilness," he continues to mumble under his breath. "I won't let his spawn do the same."

Her eyes tingle to match the ends of her fingers, and everything slips into a slow pull in time. Her mind's eyes watches as Caspyous slides his hand behind his back again and pulls out a small jagged object clutched tightly in his hand. Gabrian ducks under Cimmerian's protective arm and whips herself around. Her body buzzes, alert of the slow-moving oncoming assault as Caspyous lunges toward her.

Raising her hand to block the blow, a scream escapes her throat. Light rushes in around Gabrian, a wave of winding energy consuming Caspyous just before he strikes, and slams him backward against the marble wall behind. Sizzling sparks of energy release from her hand, tracing around his form and pinning him still. Gabrian's eyes burn, and her irises spin wildly in an electrical blue ice storm. Her free hand burns, and she closes her fingers around the heat growing in her palm. A white blade of light surges out from within and pushes along the edge of her folded hand into a shard of pure wild energy. *Another gift from the Gods, no less*, she thinks.

Time starts to move again inside her as everything unlocks from slow-motion. Cimmerian turns toward the screaming body of light that has Gabrian and Caspyous pressed on the wall. Figures blip on the radar around her as Guardians make their presence known and rush toward the light, unsure of what to do. Gabrian's form stands as still as death, holding the white dagger at his throat. All the fear this man has made her suffer floods in, and her mind drowns in the hatred he feels for her, making Gabrian's body tremble as she holds him in the rage.

Three times this man has tried to kill her. Three times. Large hulking Guardians move to close in to stop the strange interface but the light emanating around her allows them no access. She cannot be reached by them or anyone.

Caspyous squirms in the sting of her light, small snaps of her energy biting at his helpless paralyzed body. "How the—the binds of the Covenant—this isn't possible."

She stares at his wide eyes, her anger shifting to observe with a more lucid mind, a little surprised herself. "Apparently, the binds of the Covenant don't apply to me today."

A soft voice from somewhere on the other side breaks through. "Gabrian, this is not who you are. Don't let his hatred become your undoing."

Tears run over her eyes, blurring her vision. "Do you know how easy it would be to end you right now?" Gabrian steps into him as she whispers the threat, her power intensifying as it sears through him.

"Then do it," Caspyous hisses at her, his blue aura switching between his pain and delight in watching her become the abomination he sees her to be. "Do it."

She can hear the wheels of minds turning outside the light. Her display of power ignites a mix of fear and awe to sweep through the crowd of prisoners slowly edging in to take in the show. A show of powers so strong that it has broken through the binds, defying the stronghold which has kept the Covenant a peaceful place. Familiar voices sing inside her, "You are better than this, Gabrian. Let him go. He will be dealt with."

"Do it, Monster!" Caspyous screams at her, knowing things are on the precipice of going either way. "Show them who you really are."

Monster.

The word stings her. Gabrian's own mental beast laughs at her from within the memories of her dreams. Refusing to become what Caspyous longs for her to be, her heart and her mind release the Magik. The white dagger disappears as she releases the Magik, and the barrier of light is gone. Time rushes in and returns to normal as the onlookers watch Caspyous drop like a stone on the floor.

"I will not, because I am not like you. I will show you mercy and forgiveness," she says, looking straight at him as he gathers to his feet. She turns her back to him, ready to leave her guilt here in the Hollows to keep him company.

"Forgiveness from the likes of you? Ha! That is where your mistake lies." He rushes forward. His fingers just inches from her throat before the onslaught of Guardians stop him. She looks back as he struggles in their arms, still fighting to get at her—looking down on her like she is nothing. "Scum," he hisses, spitting in her face. The Guardians crumple him to the ground.

Wiping away the spittle from her face, her soul releases another ton of weight with it. "To Hell with forgiveness, you can rot in here for an eternity for all I care."

Chapter Fifty-Nine

Coffee and Kisses

Adrenaline courses through Gabrian's veins, and she forces herself to stand tall and walk out of the Covenant of Shadows with her head held high, no longer caring whether she was stared at, or whether her show of power is acceptable. If she is to become their leader, then they will just have to get over it. It is not like she is doing all of this on purpose or asked for any of this. She is just trying to survive in the world she was thrown into.

"Can we go home now?" she murmurs quietly over her shoulder to her Uncle at her side.

"Yes, Gabe, we can go home."

Pacing the wooden floor in her living room, urgently waiting for the coffee to brew, Gabrian decidedly sorts through the wreckage of her mind. She pulls away all the garbage of the morning fiasco and tries to compartmentalize everything. The last gurgle of the coffee machine growls from the kitchen above, and she bounds for it—eager to embrace the nectar of the gods once more. Holding the warm cup in her hands, she sips at it, and slows her mind down. A tear of emotion bubbles over and surfaces to run down her cheek from earlier events, defying her need to remain in control.

Her hands tighten around the cup, and she stares blankly at the wall, barely hearing the rap on the door. Blinking her eyes, she sets down the cup and wipes away the wetness from her face before she answers the door. A tall handsome Matthias carrying to-go cups in each hand awaits her like a silhouetted angel against the light of the morning sun just on the other side of the archway.

Her heart bursts open, tears flood her eyes, and she reaches for him, wrapping her arms around his waist, not caring how she looks. The episode at the Hollows drained her. She is empty and needs someone to hold onto. Caught off guard by her sudden show of affection, Matthias looks down at the small girl who has captured all his affection. Slipping the coffee one hand at a time to rest on the bench on the inside of the door, he wraps his arms around her trembling body.

"Woah, what is this all about?" he coos softly to her, still cradling her in his arms.

She clings to him, feeling the heat of his flesh sink into her own—needing this embrace, needing this more than she knew. She misses Shane like the flowers miss the sun, and she needs him more, but he is gone. Maybe forever. Right now, she just needs someone to touch her like she is not the monster in her dreams.

Matthias holds her in a silent embrace, running his hand up and down her back until she stops shivering. Feeling her hold on him relinquish, he cups the sides of her head. She looks up at him with such strange and alluring sadness in her eyes it is all he can do not to bend down and kiss her.

Her stomach swirls as his hazel eyes sparkle like a warm summer fire drawing her in like a moth to the flame. *The closeness is so easy, so inviting, and so wrong,* she thinks as a wave in the shadows nearby sends a familiar scent wafting over her. She turns, narrowing her eyes to study the faint corner of darkness, her senses returning to her and killing the strange pull between herself and her sparring partner.

"Gabrian, are you okay?"

A strange drift floats between them as Gabrian pulls away, still staring at nothing. "Um, yeah. Sorry, I don't know what came over me. It has been a rough day."

Matthias sighs, knowing the moment has passed but is happy to be here anyway. "It is only nine in the morning."

"Yup, I know. It is going to be one hell of a day," she chuckles, glancing over to the corner, and once more rubs the smooth azurite stone on her wrist.

"Well, I brought you something that might make you feel better." He reaches down and picks up the coffee from the bench, handing it to her with a grin.

Her eyes light up, and she reaches for it, smelling the top of the cap. "Is this what I think it is?"

"The one and only," he chirps victoriously.

"Oh, you are an angel," she sings and pulls him into another hug, this time only without the tears and less desire to kiss his soft tender lips.

"Well, I wouldn't go that far."

She grins and tips back the cup, sipping on the latte her friend has brought her from the Coffee Hound. Her eyes close as the flavours dance over her tongue, reveling in the euphoria of this Magikal elixir.

"So, are you okay?" he asks, now that she seems to be herself again.

"Yeah, much better now, thanks to your impeccable good timing."

He furrows his brow and sips on his own cup. "I don't understand."

She explains the trip to the Covenant to her friend as he slides into the counter beside her and slips his arm around her back as she unloads on him. It is nice talking to Matthias. It is different than with her uncle—it is freeing. There is an underlying connection between them that makes their conversations intimate and close. And right now, she can't help but lap up his easiness with a spoon as she leans into him while they talk.

The sudden opening of the kitchen door takes them by surprise as a large form fills the entryway. Tynan gives the two a watchful glare and enters the space. Gabrian slides to her feet and pulls away from Matthias, throwing her empty cup into the garbage. "Hi, Uncle Ty," she hums, trying to erase the near frown from his lips.

"If you two are planning to train this morning, you might want to get to it. The Elders are already arriving for the afternoon session."

"Already? Ugh, don't they have other priorities to attend to?"

"No," is all he says, flaring his brow at Gabrian. "Matthias," he half-grumbles, nodding his head in acknowledgement as he heads back outside.

"Well, you heard the grouchy Schaeduwe. Time to train."

Chapter Sixty

Secret Plans

After changing, and helping the Elders clear the morning snow away from the sparing area with Magik, Gabrian had spent the rest of the morning duking it out with Matthias. His physical workouts always make her feel better—his crooked smile and warm playful banter do not hurt either. And she is thankful for it. The strings of her sorrow this morning had been cut and burned away by the presence of her handsome friend. Cooldown time is spent in a perimeter run, overseen by her black bandit who had decided to join them and caw out his dislike for her company any time they got too close.

Ignoring the irritating warnings of Gabrian's guard dog, or Raven in this case, Matthias begins to make idle chatter. "So, since you are on a mission to redeem your soul, are you going to face the biggest test?"

"What do you mean?" Gabrian throws Matthias a peek over her shoulder, her brow bunched. "What test?"

"Your father."

Gabrian halts her run, and bends down, hands on her knees, and catches her breath. Matthias stops, regretting his big mouth already. She had been in a good place, why does he always seem to say things to ruin it?

"Sorry, I didn't mean to—" he says, lowering down to look her in the eyes.

"No, you are right. I have to." She straightens her back and stretches her arms over her head, looking out across the ocean, and feels a wave of dread wash over her. "If I am going to get all the garbage out of my system, I have to face him and let everything go. Good or bad, come what may." She flashes him a smile that ends at her cheeks. Her eyes are somewhere else, trying to figure out how to go about it."

"Are you going to go to Thunderhole?"

"Probably, maybe. I don't know."

"Did you want me to see if the Elders will let me take you?"

"No," she chirps, grabbing his arm. "Please, don't mention anything about me going there. They will have a cow. That is a definite no-no in their book. He is bad news in their eyes. If they thought I was going to attempt to go there, they would double my surveillance and bind me to my bed."

"I suppose you are right. Although, he did technically save you all from dying in Erebus, they may be a bit more lenient."

Her mind whirls and her voice is silent as the plan of escape shapes in her mind. The amulet. No trace of Magik, no witnesses to her indiscretion. It is perfect. She only needs to talk with him, nothing more, nothing less. It will work.

"Are you sure you don't want me to—"

A rustling of leaves disturbs their secret discussion as Vaeda's iridescent form manifests in front of the two within a bend of icy fall air. "Sorry to interrupt you, but Tynan would like a moment to speak with Gabrian," she chimes.

Gabrian smiles and glances up at Matthias. "Sure, okay. Thank you, Vaeda."

Vaeda's warm smile spreads wide across her lips as she nods and fades back into the fold of air before them.

"I seriously need to learn how to do that." Gabrian turns to her friend. "Well, so much for our session. Will I see you tomorrow?"

"Of course." He grins. "Wouldn't miss it for the world."

Her face flushes as he lightly brushes his hand across her shoulder, letting the heat in his summer eyes warm her in the cool morning breeze. "Uh, great. Alright, I need to go." She starts toward the house and stops, softly calling over her shoulder, "Don't say anything about me going to see Adrinn, okay?"

"Nope. Mum's the word." He zips his fingers over his fleshy lips. "You have my promise."

She rushes back, lifts to her toes, and pulls him into her, pecking him on the cheek. "You are the best. You know that, right?"

"Yeah, I know," he says, watching her turn away and bound across the snow-covered ground toward her home, the ebony bird following her from above.

His hand rises to touch the ghost of where her soft rosy lips had kissed him, still feeling their warm caress on his cheek. With the Shadow Walker MIA, and out of the picture for the time being, now is his time to make her see that he is the best for her.

Chapter Sixty-One

Dinner discussions

Hurry up and wait is the motto in this Realm. Gabrian knows this all too well as she stands in her kitchen, waiting for her uncle to come see her. She had been shooed away while he discussed something with the Elders in his home, and she couldn't be bothered to stand outside in the freezing cold until he got around to letting her in.

Half-way through a lightly toasted BLT sandwich, Tynan appears at her door. "Sorry it took so long, Gabe, we just discussing the misfortunate events that occurred this morning with Caspyous."

Gabrian stops mid-bite and sets her sandwich down, no longer hungry. Even though she is determined to let go as much as she can—to stop the demons inside her head from playing havoc on her mind—the ex-Hydor Elder is going to take a little time.

"It is fine," she hums, pushing the plate to the side. "What did you want to talk about?"

Tynan exhales and dips his head. "This morning in the Hollows."

Gabrian bites her lip but keeps her uncle's gaze. "Yeah."

"What happened in there?"

Gabrian lowers her eyes, chewing harder.

"I mean, I know a lot of changes have been happening, but I have never in all my years seen something so—"

"So awful?" she says, feeling just a twinge of guilt for wanting to end Caspyous and his evilness from this world.

"So pure and uncontested."

"What?" Her eyes bounce from the floor, surprised by his words. She had expected him to give her the third degree about the strange Magik.

"I don't know what happened inside the bright flash of light you were surrounded by but—"

"Just another parlor trick, I guess, aided a little from good old mother nature I suspect as well. Ever since that lightning hit me, I have felt little buzzes of electricity running all through me," she says, not wanting to reveal to her uncle the ugliness that swelled within her during that moment. If no one saw anything, then he does not need to know what she came close to doing even if it was justified.

"Huh, well, that is one for the book. Definitely explains the purity of it." Dragging his fingers over the edge of his beard, he grins at her. "Anyway, I just wanted to make sure that you were okay, you know, since he tried to attack you again."

"Yeah, I am fine," she says, trying to believe it.

"Oh, before I forget to tell you. Vaeda and Orroryn would like to see everyone in the Covenant of Shadows and—"

Okay, here it comes. I am in trouble now. Gabrian's mouth pulls down at the edges, appetite non-existent, and she's even a bit nauseous now.

"Don't worry, this meeting doesn't really involve you. Just a matter of tidying up some of the loose ends of everything," he says, scratching the edge of his bearded chin.

"Sweet," she chirps, ecstatic to not be returning. She has had enough for one day.

"So, the rest of the day is yours. Try to get some rest."

"Are you taking the rest of the Guardians with you?"

Tynan flares his brow and rolls his eyes. "No." Shaking his head, he turns to leave.

"Hey, so," she says, biting her thumb, "the holidays are coming up soon." He stops and turns to her, his face a little drawn thinking about it. "And I was thinking that maybe we could step away from all the training stuff for a minute and have a dinner." She looks away just for a breath, then looks back. "You know. The way Mom and Dad used to do, and invite everyone? What do you think?"

He smiles, letting the pain settle, and steps toward her. Cupping her chin in his hand, he leans in and kisses her gently on the top of her head. "I think they would like that."

She looks up at the gentle giant and sees the dew of his emotion trace the corner of his eyes. "It is gonna be okay, right, Uncle Ty?"

"Yes, Gabe. It will be alright." He pulls her into a hug, thankful for all that he has left in this world. "So, who is doing the cooking?"

She looks up as he lets her go and starts toward the door again. "Well, I thought I would."

A cunning grin creeps across his face. "May the Gods help us."

Chapter Sixty-Two

Romeo and Juliet

Now that her afternoon is free, Gabrian finds herself up in her secret room, flipping through her studies. More and more books reveal their secrets to her, and she hungrily eats it up. The orbs swarm around her to keep her company for a while, curious of her interests, then float away, continuing on their leisurely course—all except the one that normally stays by her side and patiently waits while she flips through the pages of the leather binds.

Reaching for the Zephyr notebook, hoping to find transcripts on how Vaeda creates her air portals, a loose folded page flutters to the desk. She flips it open and reads the note.

My dearest Cera▯

The stars of the heavens hold no beauty in your presence▯ and I would wait a thousand years in the darkest of hours just for one small glimpse of your inner light▯ to be gifted one tender forbidden kiss from your lips▯ Say you will meet me tonight under the fool's moon so I may look upon the keeper of my heart, if only just for one breath of time.

Forever yours, A

Gabrian reads the note over and over again. The words bring tears to her eyes for the parents she has never really known. Sweet vows of endearment from a man so clearly enamored by this girl who owns his heart.

Pulling the other books away from the shelf, she sees something tucked behind them. It is another leather-bound book, only this one is lighter in colour and tied with thin leather straps, gathered together by ivory beads to keep the cover closed. Gently removing the straps, she opens it to discover the hidden world of Cera and Adrinn's forbidden love—pages and pages of their meetings, handwritten by her mother herself. Dozens of love letters like the one she just found are folded between the pages of their story.

Feeling strange about unearthing all the intimate details of her parents, Gabrian hesitates but gathers it back up, needing to know. It is the closest she has ever been to both of them, seeing them exactly as they were in the years before she was born. No second-hand deliverance of what people saw or were told. This is a first-hand account of who they were together.

Hours fly by, and tears redden her eyes as her heart is filled with raw emotion. This love story unfolding in front of her is breathtaking and Magikal, making her fall in love with them both, but it soon reveals the trial and tribulation of their struggle to be together. A mystical modern-day Romeo and Juliet, deny thy father and refuse thy name kind of tragedy.

It is all Gabrian can do to breathe.

Staring at the wall through blurry eyes, a light sparks to her left. The little orb that so faithfully remains at her side hovers over the drawer where her amulet lays safely away.

"You are absolutely right, little one." She wipes away the sadness from her eyes and sets the book down, tucking all the love letters back between the pages. Pulling open the drawer, she removes the box, sets it on the desk, and opens it. Staring at it for a moment, and rubbing her fingers along its soft metal, Gabrian pulls the leather bind over her head. "He may have not been perfect, but he is my father. And if my mother loved him, then maybe I should try too."

With a twist of the eye within the Window of Souls, Gabrian is no more. All that remains is her secret room and a book full of tearstained love letters from the ghosts of her past.

Chapter Sixty-Three

Letting Go

With her heart full and ready to forgive, Gabrian appears beside the large amethyst rock that overlooks the place of her father's undoing. As soon as her eyes focus, everything collides at once—all her memories against the truth of what really happened the night Adrinn stole her and tried to take her power. The lies, the innocent people she had put at risk and nearly killed, along with the wild dangerous glow of her father's eyes as he willed her to give up her life for his own.

Her thoughts defuse the twisted compulsion she had been under. There had been no attack on him by Shane, or Ethan, or anyone. It was all a lie. They had come to save her. Shane had come to save her. A trickle of electricity bites over her flesh and climbs up the back of her neck, her fingers burning at the tips as she senses the presence of the vaporous form she came to see appear behind her.

"Hello, Gabrian."

She turns to peek over her shoulder, clenching her fists to contain the energy raging to get out. "You," she hisses, turning to face him, and no longer feeling the love she had held just moments ago for this man. "You lied about everything."

He grins at her, twisting his brow. "I am sorry, dear, but you will have to be a bit more specific. Which lie in particular are you speaking of?"

Storming towards him, warm surges of electricity sting through her veins, biting at the palms of her hands, and letting off a crackling of sparks in her closed fists. "That night that you told me they tried to send you back, it was all a lie."

She waits for him to deny it like he had before, but it doesn't come.

"Yes, I suppose it was." His grin vanishes with a soft sigh.

"But why?" she grumbles. "Why would you do that to me?"

He glides away and looks out over the edge of the cliff. "I didn't know who you were."

"What do you mean you didn't know? You came to me for years when I was young. You knew me, and I thought we were friends."

"Now don't get yourself into a tizzy," he says, waving his hand at her. "What I mean is, I didn't know you were my daughter, and at the time, it was merely an effort to preserve my existence and ensure my survival until I found a way out of my bodiless predicament. It wasn't like I set out to kill my own daughter or anything."

She fights back the urge to lash out and rip him to pieces for his actions. She did not come here to make their relationship worse. She had known deep down that there was verity to Ethan and Shane's retelling of the kidnapping, but she did not want to believe it. Today, the truth had been delivered like a stinging slap across the face for being so naïve. She can either deal with it, and put it behind her, or reap more of the infernal suffrage of nightmares.

With a loud sigh, she lets her grievance go. "Seriously, what is wrong with you?"

Adrinn's grin returns. "More than you want to know."

"You are insufferable."

"It seems that I have that effect on a lot of people." Gabrian rolls her eyes. "Anyway, for what it is worth, I am sorry. If I would have known—"

"You would have what?"

"Well, not tried to kill you, of course." He chuckles. His hazel eyes soften and pinch at the side as his smile lights up his face. Seeing him like this brings Cera's heartfelt written words dancing over her thoughts. He is breathtakingly handsome—she had never really noticed before now—and she can see why her mother had fallen so deeply into his eyes.

The bitterness on her tongue is gone, and she sighs. "Anyway, whatever." She steps back and leans against the amethyst stone, folding her arms over her chest, and kicks at the dirt. "It doesn't matter now."

"No, I suppose not. So, tell me, is this what you came for? To scold me for my un-father like behaviour?"

"No, that was just a bonus."

His translucent form sweeps back from the edge and slides over to her side. "Well then, do tell what I owe this wonderful surprise to?"

"I came to—" Her words soften. The bravery she coveted falters as the truth of her mission has been brought forth. Caspyous's response to her mission had been less than encouraging.

"To what, dear? Come on spit it out. It is best to just rip off the Band-Aid quickly than to doddle and suffer."

He is right. Even for a deceiving backstabbing friend, father—whatever—he usually is right about a lot of things. "Well, it has come to my attention that maybe I need to face my demons."

"I, being one of them?

She nods. "I need to let go of my past in order to deal with my future. And since you are part of both, I am trying to find a way to deal with the fact that my only blood relative in this Realm is a Spector."

"Spectors are dead, my dear. I, on the other hand, am very much alive," he hums, looking down at her with a boyish grin, "just indisposed at the moment."

"Mmhmm, whatever makes you feel better." She rushes her hands over the top of her head, clutching at the wisps of short marble-coloured hair. "Anyway, I have come to find forgiveness—for you and myself. I am just hoping that this goes a little better than the last try."

"Well, your sullen expression betrays your façade of hopefulness."

She exhales, biting her lip. "It has been a bit of a rollercoaster day."

"Would you like to talk about it?"

She makes a face at him. "You don't want to hear about it."

"Oh, on the contrary, I would love to hear every last detail."

Gabrian walks over to the ledge of Thunder-hole and sits down, letting her legs hang over the side. Adrinn does the same, as best he can. She retells the events of her day, letting the tears flow unhindered in front of her father. It feels good to talk to him again, like they used to when she was young, and when he had helped her find peace in the world when everything was on fire.

It feels good to let go.

Once she unloads her day, she ends with the toughened retelling of Caspyous' tertiary attempt to kill her and notices something different in Adrinn's eyes. The softness he had displayed earlier is replaced by a hint of concern. She can see wheels turning in his head, and from her experience with the man, it usually means he is planning something.

She lifts from the ledge, seeing the sun lower in the sky and the hints of red paint edging the clouds across the water. "Anyway, I should be heading back before someone comes looking for me. I am not supposed to be out."

"Yes, it is probably best that no one knows of our visit."

"Thank you." Gabrian's voice is soft and serene against the hushing of the waves below.

"You are welcome, of course, but for what?"

"Just thank you." Feeling a weight lift from the center of her soul even though the strain of the day had been heavy and uncharted, Gabrian is hopeful. For the first time in a long time, she feels a little more like her old self.

"Of course. Now, run along. I have some things I must attend to." He starts to fade into oblivion but reappears to stand in front of her. "Maybe we can do this again sometime?"

Her cheeks rise, and she gives him a smile that shines in her eyes. "Maybe."

And with that they both slip back into their bounds of confinements.

Chapter Sixty-Four

Cheeky Smiles

Feeling good about a lot of things is strange for Gabrian, but she lets the sweetness of it flow through her soul as she stares out across the backyard, feeling the cool night air creeping in.

Appearing through a spin of light, Vaeda appears at the edge of her snow-covered lawn. "Hi, Vaeda," she calls out to the Elder.

Looking a bit awkward, she recovers her smile, answering the girl, "How was your day?"

"It was pretty good actually. Did you need to talk about something?"

Her face blushes. Maybe it is from the cold or maybe it is something else, Gabrian is not sure. "Um, no." The magnificent-looking woman stands shyly as she glances over at Tynan's small cottage. "I am here to see your Uncle. Is he home yet?"

"He was a few minutes ago." Gabrian grins sheepishly, knowing exactly why her cheeks are rosy. "I am sure he is not too far."

"Okay, thank you, Gabrian." The Zephyr Elder turns away quickly and heads toward Tynan's.

"Have a nice visit," Gabrian sings out into the night. *Ah, young love*, she thinks, happy her uncle has finally found someone to give his heart to.

Chapter Sixty-Five

A New Ally

Finished with his classes, and still daydreaming of his morning with Gabrian, Matthias gets in his car and goes for a drive. Stepping out into the evening, and leaving his car behind, he hikes the path leading into the woods and stops to looks around, perplexed by Gabrian's fascination with this place.

Examining the darkened spot on the ground, his memory replays the night he joined the others in attempt to help Gabrian. Although he had been knocked unconscious for most of it, and missed the action, he does remember the dark creature of a man who had her convinced she was being a hero.

In the shadows of the trees, Adrinn watches the visitor as he investigates. Curious about the grey aura floating around him, he decides to get better look. Gently, he searches the stranger's mind, a discreet and unguarded entry into his thoughts.

Matthias, continuing his study and completely consumed by his thoughts of her, is oblivious to the intrusion but stops. His face curls, and he turns around, sensing a presence. "So, it's you who brings her here."

Adrinn stops moving as well, realizing that his presence has not gone unnoticed.

"I kept wondering what was so special about this place that she kept wanting to come back here, but now, I guess I know."

SILVER

Adrinn pushes roughly at the boundaries of Matthias's mind, preparing to compel him into forgetting, but Matthias only grins, feeling the urgent need flood through him. "Save your efforts, Adrinn. There is no need for compulsion. I am not your enemy."

Matthias searches the empty forest, waiting for Adrinn to show himself. The air around Matthias becomes heavy and weighted, his throat tightening, and he swallows, losing some of the arrogance he had just held in his words and turns to face the darkness he has just got the attention of.

Appearing on the edge of the trees before Matthias, he makes himself known. "Why are you here?"

"I am only curious," he continues. "Feel free to read my mind if you are unsure of my intentions."

Adrinn quickly gathers up his thoughts, combing through them to see this Borrower's truths. Seeing the image of his newly discovered daughter consumes most of the boy's consciousness and the Vampire smirks, knowing he has discovered a very strong point of vantage for him.

Score one, Adrinn.

Diving a bit deeper, he finds a similar distrust for the Elders but becomes ecstatic at true full-blown distaste for the Schaeduwe. Adrinn grins, deciding today could very well be one of his favourite days. All the odds are beginning to stack in his favour, and with some careful encouragement, he may have just found a new counterpart.

Chapter Sixty-Six

Unexpected Visitor

Large feathery snowflakes fall outside Gabrian's windows as she stares at the orange and blue hue of the crackling fire burning in the heart of her living room. Warm, loving heat sinks into her bones as she sips a cup of Kaleb's special tea and replays her visit with her father. The soft lull of newfound contentment slows her soul.

It had been a good visit. A normal visit, sort of, for her world, and she drifts in the daydream of having a connection with the man Cera so clearly adored in her journal.

A knock on the door gives her a start, and her eyes rush to the timekeeper on the wall. Nine. "Who on earth?" she mumbles, sets her tea down, and gets up from the couch to answer it. "Whatever it is, can't it wait until tomorrow?" she grumbles, marching across the kitchen, almost certain it is one of the Elders. Swinging the door wide, her breath hitches in her lungs, and a high-pitched squeal escapes from her lips.

Leaping, Gabrian wraps her arms around the neck of a tall orange-hued surfer wearing a crooked grin, carrying a bag in each of his hands. "What are you doing here?" she sings into the night, releasing her bear hug on him and bouncing on her toes.

Snow whips in around the form of the beautiful traveler. His face is warm like the fire as he holds out his bags. "Well, if you invite me in, I will tell you. It is freezing out here, and these bags are getting heavy."

Shaking her head, still in shock, she backs out of the way. "Yes, of course. Get in here." She pushes the door wide, grabs hold of his sleeve with her free hand, and pulls him inside. Thomas' grin grows wide as he walks across the threshold, giving her a kiss on the top of her head on the way by. Gabrian promptly closes the door to shut out the coldness of winter's breath behind him.

Dropping the bags on the floor, he turns to her. His orange hue flares out like a beacon of hope on a dark stormy night. "Now, get over here so I can hug you properly," he says, holding his arms open wide.

Gabrian runs willingly toward him. Thomas holds her gently yet securely in his arms, and she welcomes his warm embrace. "I had a few weeks of vacation to spare, and you said if I ever had the time, that I should come visit."

She holds onto him like he is going to disappear. It feels like a hundred years since she had seen him. Even though she emailed and texted whenever she could, everything has changed so much that this little piece of her life still seems very much the same, and she clings to it.

"And," he continues, "something in the back of my mind kept telling me that you could use a hug. So, here I am."

Her arms instinctively cling tighter, fighting back the urge to cry. He had become her sounding board and confidant, not to mention the string that kept her from becoming completely unraveled. Never judging, never prying, only gladly lending her an ear to listen. He once thought they might become romantic, but after time, his feelings for her became that of something different—a friendship found by chance and forged by a stronger connection than either of them can understand.

Finally, Gabrian lets go of Thomas, steps back, and smiles at the breath of fresh air standing in her kitchen. "Yes, so here you are."

After Gabrian gets Thomas all settled in, she finds him sitting in front of the fireplace, watching the embers crackle and spark, casting a soft rose to kiss his honey brown skin.

"Are you hungry?" she calls down from the kitchen.

"No, I am good." He turns her way and flashes her a smile.

"Alright, how about a beer?"

"Now that sounds like a plan." He grins over his shoulder at her, holding his hands out against the flame.

Gathering two of her favourite clear bottles of beer from the fridge, she joins him on the floor in front of the fire. "So how long are you going to stay?"

Tipping the bottle, he takes a long sip and exhales a happy sigh. "I am not really sure. I hadn't planned that far. I just packed my bag and jumped on a bus. The rest is dependent on you."

"On me?"

"It is your home. How long I stay is up to you."

"Well, then I have made a decision."

"And what is that?" He laughs, taking another drink.

"I would love for you to stay for the holidays. That is, if you have no other plans." She studies his face. A glimpse of sadness washes over him but is gone in a breath.

"Are you sure? I don't want to intrude."

"I wouldn't ask if I didn't want you here. And besides, you can help me cook."

"Now that I can do."

Gabrian sighs in relief. She had wondered how she was going to pull it all together. She had helped her mom do it year after year, but this year it would only be her.

"So, tell me all about this new promotion and job you are training for. Sounds like it is quite exciting."

"Exciting is one way of describing it." She glances at the fire and takes a sip of her drink, pondering how she is going to explain all the special particularities of her life to Thomas. "Thomas."

"Yeah," he hums watching the fire.

"How good are you with weird and unusual things?"

"Pretty good I guess, I have you for a friend so—" He nudges her with his arm.

"Hey now," she chirps at him, grinning. "No, I mean really weird and hard to explain."

"You mean like supernatural, auras, and ghost things."

"Yes, something like that."

"Well, from what I can remember, my mom was a healer and helped people realign their energies. She said she could talk to the dead as well. And my dad, well it is kind of hard to describe, but he kind of dealt with more scientific things. He supported the claim there was Magik in this world, and that the mind, if open and accepting, could do anything."

"And you?"

The firelight makes his eyes sparkle as he talks about his past. "I have seen some pretty crazy things that make you question the boundaries of your existence, so I guess, yeah. I believe there is a lot more going on then what is on the surface."

"Good," is all she says, sighing, and rubs her fingers over the label of the beer, hoping he keeps his open mind when it is time for her to train tomorrow.

Chapter Sixty-Seven

Things to do

The morning light has barely breeched the sky when Symone is woken by a soft humming beside her bed. Rubbing the sleep from her eyes, she grins and sits up in bed.

"Good morning, my dear. Sleep well?"

She nods and stretches her arms. "I was hoping you would stop by today."

"Yes, well, I couldn't miss you getting out of the hospital now, could I?"

"What? I am getting out?"

"Yes, everything is taken care of, and you are free as a bird," Adrinn chirps, his eyes bright and cheery. "I even convinced a nurse to bring you some new clothes."

"But I thought the doctor said he wanted me to stay for—" Symone says, pulling on one of her loose tangles of hair.

"Come now, you can't really want to stay any longer in this drab place?"

"No, but—"

He rises from the bed and floats over to chair where the new pile of clothes awaits her. "And besides, there is something I need you to do."

Symone hurriedly pulls back the covers of her bed, the morning chill forming goosebumps on her bare slender legs. Grabbing the small bag of toiletries from the table, she heads toward the bathroom. "What exactly am I doing?"

"You, my dear, are going to pay a visit to dear old Dad."

Her eyes widen, and her smile vanishes, wiped clean from her face. "Are you crazy?"

"Crazy like a fox, my dear." He grins, waving her into the bathroom. "Now, do hurry, it is going to be quite the day."

Chapter Sixty-Eight

Wicked Grin

A light rapping outside Rachael's door quiets the room. The sweet tender giggles of rekindled love hush as Rachael lifts from Orroryn's lap and slips back onto the side of her bed. Hoping her cheeks are not a flushed as they feel, Rachael answers the knock. "Come in."

Symone pushes the door open, and her mouth twist awkwardly into a knowing smirk. "Interrupt something, have I?"

Rachael peeks over at the love of her life, and Orroryn only grins, his eyes filled with his unrelenting devotion to his heart's choice. "No, it is alright. Come in."

Striding into the room, Symone flicks her eyebrow at the dark handsome Shadow Walker gathering to his feet. "I will give you some privacy," he hums taking Racheal's hand in his own and brushing his lips against her fingers. She gleams, his touch sending warm shivers through her soul.

"That won't be necessary," Symone says, pursing her lips. "You see, it is you I have actually come to see."

"Oh?" Orroryn turns to face the girl.

"Yes, I am being released today, and I would like to request a visit with my father."

"I thought you said you would be here for another couple of weeks," Rachael chimes in, certain that is what Symone had told her yesterday.

"No, you must have misunderstood," she quickly corrects and turns her focus back on Orroryn. "I knew that you would be here, and who better to ask then the head of the Covenant of Shadows."

"Well, I—" The Elder rubs the edge of his jaw, contemplating her request. After the upset he was told of yesterday between Cimmerian, Gabrian, and Caspyous he is not certain about the visit.

"Oh, please say you will help me. I won't stay long, I promise. I just need to discuss a couple things with him. Then, I will leave."

His face lightens as he looks to Rachael. She nods her support for her new friend's request, and his heart melts in her soft green eyes. "Alright, fine, but it must be quick. I don't need any more upsets like the one we had yesterday."

"Oh, of course. Trust me, it won't take long."

Orroryn leans down and kisses Rachael. Their lips linger in a soft tender silent vow of forever. Leaving his heart behind, he closes the space between him and the Derkaz girl and wraps his hand securely around her wrist. He looks down at Symone, and she grins. A wicked grin. Orroryn swears he can see something in her eyes that makes the hair on the back of his neck rise as they fade into the shadows, heading for the Hollows.

Chapter Sixty-Nine

Into the Hollows

Symone's heart pounds as she walks along the corridor. She squirms, waiting for Orroryn to address the Guardian of their appearance in the Hollows.

Be a good girl, Symone. No need to fret. It will be a quick in and out, he whispers to her, inside her head. *I only need a moment to do what I need to do.* Adrinn's voice echoes from the place his essence is neatly tucked inside her mind.

She nods nervously, but no one notices. Orroryn turns. "This way," he says, and she follows behind him.

"Make it quick, I don't know how long I can stand to be here," she mumbles under her breath.

"Sorry, did you say something?" Orroryn asks over his shoulder, continuing on his way.

"Um, no, nothing."

"Hmm," is all he says, facing back to his front.

She forces a smile, striding behind, and tries to keep up. Peering into the open cages filled with the Realm's most wanted criminals, she wonders what they did to get put here. A few more steps, and she stands before her father. Symone's hands clench as she tries to hide her displeasure of being here. Cimmerian looks up from his book to see

Orroryn and greets him with a smile, but his mouth drops as soon as the girl appears from behind the large Schaeduwe, stepping out into the light.

"Hi, father," she grunts. "I have come to see you."

Tears fill Cimmerian's wide eyes, and he rushes to his feet, letting the book drop haphazardly on the bed. "Symone."

"I will leave you now," Orroryn announces, just before he disappears.

Cimmerian only glances quickly at the Elder and reaches out to touch her face. "You look well," he hums, taking her in. She looks so much better than the last time he had been allowed to visit.

Just keep him talking. Let him blather on, but mind your tongue. I can't have you being escorted out of here before I return. Although, I must say, starting an uprise here in the Hollows would be quite fun. Her body shivers as the hitchhiker takes his leave from her form.

"Come sit down," Cimmerian says, noticing the quake in his daughter's slender form. He clears away the book back to his table and ushers the girl to the bed. "I had no idea you had been released, I would have requested to come help you."

Symone looks around, sporting a bored look on her face, and hopes Adrinn does not take too long. There is only so much of her father's bland prattling she can take.

Adrinn floats unseen through the rows of incarcerated souls, and peers into each and every cell. "Come out, come out, wherever you are." Three rows down, he stops, and grins, slipping inside the cell. His eyes narrow on the ex-Hydor Elder still tucked beneath his covers as he sleeps.

"Wakey, wakey, sleepyhead."

Caspyous stirs, hearing the voice in his cell. Blinking away the sleep, he rubs his eyes. The translucent form of the man who stole Cera and killed his father leers down at him. "You," he croaks out, "but how?"

"Well, I can't very well tell you all my secrets. You might snitch on me, but I doubt after I am done with you that that will be an issue. I hear you are trying to take away what is mine again. Well, we can't have that now, can we?"

Caspyous jolts upright in his bed, his eyes wide and searching the shadows behind Adrinn's translucent form. "Listen if this is about that girl—"

"That girl is mine and Cera's daughter. You remember her, don't you? My Cera. And as for Gabrian, I won't let you destroy her future like you tried to with mine. She might be above destroying you, but I can assure you that I am not." An eerie ring of fire dances around his irises and a grin melts into pure hatred on Adrinn's lips. "Let's have some fun, shall we?"

Symone taps her foot on the floor as Cimmerian explains to her the events that took place yesterday. Caspyous had been taken on a tour of the shadows in a swift reminder of where inmates of the Hollows go when they do not conform to the rules—the black parts where only the dark souls are kept. She yawns and watches the opening of the cell for any traces of Adrinn.

Screams echo through the halls. On and on they continue, filling the Hollows. Inmates gather in the space between the rows as Shadow Walkers appear from within the Veil, hurrying to quiet the disruption. A familiar form of energy fills her mind, and she grins, missing his presence.

Alright, love, time to go.

Her eyebrow flicks as she rises from the bed and turns to her father. "I need to go."

"Yes, of course." Cimmerian rises and searches the hallway. "Ask Orroryn to take you home. Everything has been prepared."

Moments later, Orroryn's large form slices through the crowd of inmates as they hover the halls, chattering, and eager to get the girl out. "Visiting time is over. Time to leave."

"What is going on?" Cimmerian asks, seeing the frustration in his friend's eyes.

"It is Caspyous," Orroryn frowns. "I think he has gone mad."

Now that is truly music to my ears, Adrinn sings inside of Symone's head, making her grin. *Let's celebrate.*

Chapter Seventy

Coffee Grinds and Compulsion

Gabrian rises to the sound of gurgling, coffee already brewing in her machine from downstairs. Her mouth curls into a smile, feeling the slow wave of happiness drift over her. Lifting up on her side, she checks the timekeeper barely visible on her wall, and bunches her brow, wondering what on earth Tynan is doing in her kitchen so early.

Pulling her robe over her fuzzy giraffe pajamas, she slips on her slippers and trudges toward the smell of heaven. Hitting the bottom stairs, she stops abruptly at the sight of Ethan grinning from ear to ear at a tall familiar form standing at her kitchen counter.

That is not Tynan, she puzzles just as the remembrance of Thomas' arrival last night surfaces in her sleepy brain. Gabrian steps out into the dim light of the morning and twists her brow, grumbling, "Good morning."

The two men turn to her and cheer a merry good morning back to her. Gabrian cannot help but smile as she weaves her body between the two overgrown boys and grabs a cup full of coffee. She feels groggy but good. As the warm coffee dances over her tongue, she begins to welcome the day. Not sure if it is the arrival of Thomas to fill the void in her home, or the letting go of demons yesterday, all she knows is that the heavy weight has been lifted and a bounty of peace settles in her soul.

"What brings you so early in the morning? Did you fall out of bed?"

Ethan flashes Gabrian a fake disapproving look but waves her away. "Not quite. I have been to the Cov...the office."

The sleep vanishes from Gabrian's eyes. "Oh?"

Ethan glides an arm around her to herd her away. "It is about Caspyous." She grinds her teeth at the sound of his name. Folding her arms across her chest, she narrows her eyes at him. "Something has happened. He has suffered some kind of mental breakdown—one of the worst cases I have ever seen—and has been removed from the open part of the...facilities to a more secure location."

Gabrian hears the words, hollow in her ears, but that is all. She wants to feel something, but she cannot find even a small glimpse of sadness for this man. Any resemblance of compassion for him had been murdered in the Hollows that day, buried deep within the Shadows where she left it. Inhaling a deep breath, she purses her lips and gives Ethan a quick nod. The ghosted burn of the white knife tingles in her palm and her stomach flutters remembering how good it felt as she held it to his throat. "Pity."

Ethan pats her on the shoulder, understanding where she is. He knows the walls that he has built himself in order to keep going. "Yes, well. I just thought you should know."

"Thank you," is all she can say.

"Of course," he says, flashing a meager smile, and turns back toward the kitchen counter. "And, I wanted to let you know that I am officially on vacation from the office and decided to stop by with a holiday treat." He grins, pointing at the bag of grounds from the Coffee Hound sitting beside the machine.

The heaviness in the room evaporates. Any thought of Caspyous is expelled from her existence, and she welcomes the freedom of it. "Oh, you are my hero. Thank you, Ethan."

"Although, I was a bit surprised when this handsome young man greeted me at the door."

A slight flush washes across both men's faces and Gabrian grins, wondering why had she not noticed this connection before. "Yes, I got a big surprise last night, and I have convinced him to stay for the holidays."

Ethan glances at Thomas, his eyes pinching at the edges as his smile widens. "So, I have heard."

"Ethan has invited me to spend the day touring the area with him if we don't have any plans."

Gabrian's eyes light up as she cheers, "That is perfect." She can avoid explaining everything to Thomas about the Magik, at least for another day, until she can come up with a way to let him in easy. "Thank you, Ethan."

Worst case, if he freaks out, there is always compelling the crap out of his memory.

Chapter Seventy-One

No Rest for the Wicked

Everything about Gabrian's world over the next couple of days just seems to fall into place. Ethan has spent the days with Thomas while she trains, keeping her from having to explain the supernatural smorgasbord taking place in her snowy backyard, and Matthias has stopped pouting about her having a male friend stay in her home. Not that it is any of his concern anyway, but she knows that he is jealous. If he only knew what she could see developing, he would welcome the tan visitor with open arms.

Gabrian wakes to a bright and cheery Saturday morning. She glances at the dim light drifting into her window as a gentle cascade of snow falls like feathers just outside. Thomas and Ethan had stayed late last night to help her put up the decorations for the holiday, and it had been a joyous occasion, but now, lying in bed while the house lies quiet in the still of morning light, her mind drifts to the year prior.

Her heart sinks just a bit, feeling the loss of two special souls that will not be joining her this year. She lies silent in the memories of her mom and dad, and how much they loved the holidays. With all the strange and unusual things she has experienced, she chuckles and thinks, *Who knows, maybe Santa Clause is even real here too.*

Not wanting to lie in bed feeling sorry for herself, she dresses for the morning and heads out into the hall, exhaling deeply. Through all the pain, all the misery, and all the ghosts it may upheave, the holidays are going to happen whether she likes it or not so she might as well embrace it. She forces a smile to replace the placid look she had worn.

The house is quiet, even Thomas is still in bed, and she tries to step lightly down the stairs to put on the coffee and start the day. Staring at the festive decorations strung about, she feels something is missing. Wandering to the basement, Gabrian digs out all her mother's boxes and sets them in front of her. Tears start to well in her eyes. Everything becomes overwhelming, and she feels like it is just too much to handle in her coffee-depleted state.

Coffee first. Finish decorating after the caffeine kicks in.

Somewhere between the three cups of coffee, and the touching up of the mantle decorations, she realizes she had forgotten to send out the invites. Hurrying past a sleepy-eyed, messy hair Thomas, she rushes up the stairs to her phone and texts out her invites right away, not sure of who will be able to make it since it is such short notice. Even if it is just her and Thomas, it is better than sitting in an empty house, eating junk food and watching sappy holiday movies that are supposed to bring her a miraculous epiphany to her life. And so, she decides to throw the pebble into the pond and see what happens.

After becoming fully caffeinated, she wanders back to the basement to dig out her mother's centerpiece for the table. Now, everything is perfect. Well, almost. Now, all she needs is food. After convincing her Uncle Ty that nothing is going to happen to her, she grabs the keys to her car, giddy to be actually let loose from her captivity, and takes off for Bar Harbor with Thomas in tow.

It is Magikal for her—a little taste of freedom without having to be deceitful—and the company is more than awesome. They spend the morning picking up everything on the list, even making a special stop at her favourite place for a Turtle Mocha Latte that CK insisted be on the house with it being the holidays and all. So, without much fight, she humbly accepts, repaying him with a hug and sweet kiss on the cheek.

Placing the car in park, they gather the groceries from the trunk. Gabrian's hair stands up on the back of her neck at the sight of large footprints around the side of her cottage in the layer of newly fallen snow. Not only footprints but door ornaments knocked to the side and markings that look like there may have been a struggle.

Dropping the groceries, her senses flare into overload, and she leaves Thomas behind, rushing toward the door, an unsettling feeling that whatever did this is still inside her home. All she can think of is her Uncle Ty home alone. "Sweet Mother of Pearl, what now?" she curses under her breath. "Can't evil take a break for one day?"

Shielding herself, she slowly unlatches the kitchen door, pushing it open just enough to peek inside. Her heart pounds loudly in her ears. Searching the kitchen for energy, she finds nothing. Something is going on, she can feel it. Pushing the door a little wider, she slides the rest of her body inside.

A loud voice calls out to her, nearly making her jump out of her skin. "Hey, it is about time you two got back. What do you think?" Tynan bellows out from the living room below.

She leans up against the wall, clutching the cloth above the racing pulse in her chest. "Seriously, Uncle Ty, you nearly gave me a heart attack."

"No, I didn't, don't be so dramatic. You are from the Realm, we don't get heart attacks."

Gabrian picks up a shoe and biffs it at him over the counter, rolling her eyes. "You know what I mean."

"Oh, Tynan, you shouldn't tease the poor girl," Vaeda hums, rising from the living room into view. "She might very well take you down one of these days."

Tynan waves his hand at the two girls standing side by side in the kitchen above and goes back to decorating the biggest tree Gabrian has ever seen inside a house.

Vaeda leans in and gives Gabrian a hug. "Happy Holidays, Gabrian."

"Thanks, Vaeda. Same to you."

"I hope you don't mind, we brought you a tree and used the decorations that were in the boxes in the basement. Tynan thought it would be a nice surprise for you."

Gabrian's heart tugs at her. The memory of youth flashes before her, standing around the tree while her mom and dad handed her the delicate ornaments to be hung. She smiles, wiping a tear from her eyes. "Not at all, Vaeda, it is lovely. Thank you."

Noise from behind crashes through the kitchen as Thomas erupts from the other side of the door, carrying the bags of groceries that Gabrian had dropped on the ground. "Don't worry, I've got the bags."

Gabrian laughs, turning to help unload them from his arms. "Sorry, Thomas, I—"

"No worries, little one. It's all good."

Yes, it is, isn't? she thinks. *Maybe things will be alright.*

Chapter Seventy-Two

Holiday Blues

As the day goes on, Gabrian's house becomes filled with laughter and talk of joyous events to accompany the beautiful tree and decorations. One by one, each invitee she had reached out to had reached back. Every knock on the door proves to be inviting and full of love. Each one lends a hand with dinner and preparations. Once they are all seated at the table, Gabrian, who had been too busy to feel sad anymore about missing her family, looks around to see she is already surrounded by a new family.

Matthias sits to her right, smiling at her. Thomas, on her left, exchanges interesting glances Ethan's way, those of which do not go unnoticed by her. Orroryn and Rachael sit snuggly together, lost in conversation of long-ago holidays past while Tynan hangs on to the edge of the table listening, even sporting a smile as he and Vaeda retell stories of some holiday follies they have endured.

Tynan even proposes the motions that her training subside for a few days until the turn of the year has come, which after some sideways glances and some shrugging of shoulders, is passed by those present. Gabrian watches as all the auras mix and mingle throughout the room, creating a prism effect over the table. She isn't sure if anyone else noticed, but she is pleased, honoured to have them all at her table. For the first holiday spent without her mom and dad, overall it is quite wonderful.

Feeling the room swell with the heat of numerous bodies, the air grows stuffy. Grabbing a warm cider from the cupboard, she quietly slips outside and stands on her front step, hands around her cup, and watches the steam rise and float into the cool approaching night.

Seeing Gabrian's cheery demeanor fade from across the room, Rachael excuses herself and slips across the kitchen to check on her friend. She opens the door and peeks outside. Cuddling up beside her friend, she wraps a warm arm around her. "You okay, Gabe?"

"Yeah, I am fine."

"Are you sure?"

"Yeah." She nods and looks away. "It's just that I miss them so much." Pulling her tighter, Rachael leans her crimson curls against Gabrian's shoulder and rubs her arms. "And, I miss him." Gabrian's voice trembles as the truth of her sadness unfolds.

"Oh, Gabe. I wish I could make the pain go, but he will be back. You'll see. He loves you too much to be gone too long."

"Cera loved me too, and she has been gone my entire life."

Rachael turns and looks her in the eyes. "He'll be back. He will. Give him some time to recover. He is not super woman like you."

Gabrian laughs and pulls Rachael into a bear hug. "I have missed you more than you will ever know."

"I have missed you too, Gabe," she says, pulling away and rubbing her arms from the cold.

"Go back inside before you catch a cold. I will not have you getting ill on my account."

"Are you sure you don't need company?"

"I am sure. I will be in in a minute. Now go, before you catch your death."

Rachael smiles and gives Gabrian a kiss on the cheek. "It will be alright, trust me."

"Thanks, Rach." The moment Rachael steps back inside the house, the flutter of black wings grows louder until Theo makes his appearance, landing at her side. He cackles a low rumble and struts in front of her, gathering all her attention. Gabrian laughs. "Happy Holidays to you too. I was wondering when you were going to show up."

With a sharp caw, he culls his feathers, fluffing them. Taking a sip of her cider, she exhales, traces of crystals forming on her breath in front of her. In the silence, the thought of her parents once again enters her mind. "I don't know exactly how this works, but wherever you are, I miss you." She sighs. "I wish you were here to see everyone."

She stands there a little while longer as the sun begins to set. Theo rustles at her side, but then he shrieks, jumping up and down, and calls out in to the night, searching the direction of the garden gate. His wings flutter, and he continues warning of an intruding force that Gabrian cannot see. Pushing her senses out into the fading light of day, she finds nothing. Theo is highly agitated, and from past experiences, it is best to listen to him when he is talking.

Something shifts in the oncoming darkness, and a cold chill climbs up her spine. She steps out into the night. Theo flutters the sky, shrieking out his last warning as he flies off to take cover. She tilts her head and follows the shoveled path that leads to the gate—the same path she had journeyed so many times as a child. A dark figure emerges from the side of the gate and greets her with a smile.

"What are you doing? You shouldn't be here," Gabrian hushes, glancing around the invisible wall of Guardians she knows is not far away.

Adrinn transforms as clearly as his vaporish form will allow, eyeing the house behind her. "I know, but I just wanted to check in on you and wish you a blessed holiday."

"Oh," Gabrian gasps. The familiarity of speaking to him here is overwhelming, clinging to her like she had been a child only yesterday.

But she is not a child any longer, nor is she naïve or ignorant in the way the world works.

"I know things between us are rocky at best, but in the season of forgiveness, I come in hopes that we can start anew."

She sucks in a small breath. Somehow, in all the misery over the last year, things seem to be turning around again. "I would like that, thank you."

"You are welcome," Adrinn hums, looking deep into her eyes, then looks back to the houseful of Elders behind her. "You have guests, and you should get back to them before they come looking for you."

She nods and turns to leave, but stops, turning to him over her shoulder. "Happy holidays Adrinn."

He smiles and starts to fade. "Happy holidays, my dear."

She watches him vanish then turns back to the house, rushing to the front door. Reaching the bottom steps of the porch, Matthias opens the door, and stands in the entryway, leaning against the frame. "Hey there, what are you doing? I was just coming to find you."

"Oh, sorry," she says, reaching him. "I was just taking a breather. I'm good now." She gives him a smile as she slips under his outstretched arm and back into the house.

Matthias senses an elevate surge in her energy as she passes him and turns back to glance quickly over the darkness where she had come from. A strange shift in the shadows down by the gate catches his attention. Not noticing the quick flutter of black wings, Theo makes one last fly by the doorway, cawing his dislike for the Borrower.

"Get lost." He snickers, frowns, and gives the bird a menacing glare, partly from the fact he is not a big animal lover, and partly due to the fact the bird is a busybody who seems to always be in his way.

SILVER

Turning his back, he rejoins the party, shutting the door on the annoying bird, and hears the cheer in Gabrian's voice. "Happy Holidays, everyone. Who is ready for a drink?"

Chapter Seventy-Three

Pandora's Box

After waving goodbye, and wishing the last of her guests a fond farewell, Gabrian looks up into the clear wintery sky. Orion the Hunter greets her heavenly gaze with a shimmery twinkle. A sullen shift in her mood takes her far away, back to the night she laid beneath the stars with someone who had not been with her tonight. All the light happy moments move into the shadows of her mind as she touches the Azurite stone, quiet on her wrist.

"I miss you so much." She sighs. Stepping in from the chill, Gabrian turns off all the lights and heads for bed. There is no one left to tend to. Ethan had invited Thomas to take some festivities in town so it is just her and her ghosts tonight.

With slow heavy steps, she creeps up the stairs and runs a finger along the edge of each of her mother's paintings, saying goodnight to each and every one. Maybe it is the business of her day or the loss of so much this past year, but Gabrian is empty. Riffling through her things, she finds a grey cotton T-shirt and pulls it to her nose. The scent of him still lingers on the cloth, and she holds it close, feeling the loss of his presence sink in, and longs to be close to him.

Her lips purse, and she gazes at the wall, watching it fade into a doorway filled with light and choices. She sets the shirt down and hurriedly enters the room. The flickering orbs dance around her as she enters. Gabrian reaches out and pulls open the drawer that holds the Window of Souls and retrieves the amulet. Stringing it over her neck, she prepares to turn the eye, but her constant companion who always greets her flutters in her face before she can.

Gabrian's eyes draw to the little light and follows it to the chair. A small wooden chest sits on the seat, engraved with markings that remind her of those etched along the wall in the Covenant of Shadows. Stepping toward the box, the little orb moves out of the way. She purses her lips again, tapping her finger on them, then bites their edges. Knowing that these things, these incredibly wondrous things, are not hers, she should probably leave well enough alone. But hey, she already walked into a wall filled with Magik. What could opening a simple box do?

Her conscience jests, *Ever hear of a little thing called Pandora's box?* "Yes, I have, but this is highly unlikely to be hers. And if you recall, I have already been to Erebus and back. They don't want me. I think I can handle whatever is waiting inside this box."

Sliding the tips of her fingers gently under the lip of the cover, she lifts the top off and peers inside. Silvery charcoal scales shimmer back at her, catching her breath. Slipping her fingers into the box, Gabrian runs her fingers along the edges of the smooth and delicate folds. A soft supple texture meets her touch, igniting a gentle burn in her fingertips as it makes contact. "And I probably shouldn't reach in and take this out of the box, either," she whispers. Her hands slip under the cloth and slowly lift it out. "Ah, hell, Gabrian, live a little. What is the worst thing that could happen? Besides, the little orb obviously wants me to, so who am I to disappoint?"

Gabrian glances up for a minute and laughs, realizing that she is engaging herself into conversational back up, but she doesn't care. The cloth drapes down, unfolding in her hands. She holds it out in front of her. The markings unveil a majestic pattern, caught between what she would imagine a dragon's scale would look like and feathers, all meticulously interwoven to create this masterful creation of wardrobe. It is some kind of suit.

Holding it out in front of her, the colours meld together like the sheen of an oil spill—prismatic and slick. Turning it around, a small rectangular piece of parchment comes loose and falls to the wooden floor. Gabrian hurries to scoop it up and flips it over to read an inscription.

My child,

A gift to help assist you along your journey. Wear this in health and may it serve you well.

Her heart warms. This is a gift from her mother, and she wonders if she had actually been here. *She had to*, Gabrian decides. This special space must be some kind of pocket where Gabrian's dimension and hers can connect. Gabrian's thoughts slow. Or maybe this is something that had been left for her long ago before Cera left. Either way, it does not matter. This is perfect, and she will use it well. Folding it, and placing the gift back within its box, Gabrian closes the top and pats it, knowing she will have to try this out on her next practice.

Tonight, she has other plans.

Chapter Seventy-Four

Can You See the Stars☐

Flipping the eye of the Window of Souls inward, Gabrian's form erases from the secret room and reappears somewhere cold. The bite of the night's chill stings her bare arms, but she does not care. Careful footsteps take her across the snowy lane to stand in front of a rustic-looking cabin, tucked snuggly into the woods.

A soft light beckons to her from inside and the smell of smoke tells her there is warmth that awaits her inside. Climbing the stairs, her heart pounds in her chest, getting louder with each step she takes. Pulling the latch on the door, the heat from inside swims around her, knowing Manny must have been here not long ago to put the fire on to keep the pipes from freezing while Shane is gone.

Slipping off her boots, and carrying them across the floor, she peeks inside the fridge, hoping for a beer to grab and then continues her trek into the living room. Replacing her boots, Gabrian grabs the patchwork duvet folded just on the back of the couch and pulls it across her shoulders.

Her heart twists as the summery scent clinging to the blanket triggers the replay of the night Shane had whisked her away. The night he devoted his heart to her and she accepted. The night they laid quiet under the stars within their own little world, watching the heavens roll past while they held each other close. Her mouth trembles as she wipes a tear free. Spying the large familiar book sitting neatly on the end table, she gathers it under her arm and climbs the ladder to the hobbit-like hatchet door.

Pushing the hatch open, the chill of the night licks away the brief moment of warmth that surrounded her inside. She climbs out and kicks away the snow then hunkers down on the open spot of the deck. Unfolding the book, she lays it on her lap and twists open her beer, taking a sip. Lying back into the duvet to watch the heavens sparkle above her, Gabrian's eyes dew over, blurring a fallen star as it streaks across the sky.

A torturous bout of laugher bubbles up inside of her, remembering Shane's fumbling attempts to impress her with his stargazing date night. The laughter soon turns to sadness. Her bottom lips trembles as she looks out into the night and the sky becomes nothing more than a blur of lost moments. "I'm sorry. I am so sorry I pushed you away. I am sorry I hurt you so much." Her words become whimpers of pain as she rolls to her side, unable to keep her eyes open. "I wish you could hear me. I am so sorry. Everything is all my fault." Her body shakes as the tears rolls down the edges of her cheeks and the night consumes her into slumber.

Chapter Seventy-Five

Of Earth, of Life, of Summer

Deep sea green eyes drape over Gabrian's small form, watching from just within the thinnest membrane of the Veil, longing to be near her and touch her soft alabaster skin. "I know you are sorry, and I am sorry too. The fault is not all yours to bear."

Shane's body tremors. The pain of seeing her this way, of letting her lay there in her misery is worse than dying in Erebus, but it is the only way right now. It would hurt too much. It is better for everyone. She does not need to see what he has become. He will watch over her from the safety of the shadows as he has done before. The Elders will protect her when he cannot, and her friend Thomas will keep her from sadness until he can return.

Only for a moment does he dare to breech the divide. Just for a breath to breathe her in. The scent of earth, of life, and of summer floods through the darkness and drowns out the crisp coolness of winter. Ripples in the night surround her as his fingers lightly trace across the edge of her jaw and smiles. She is peaceful now, no screaming, no teary dreams, just the slow steady rise of her chest and the soft hushing of her breath while her body and soul finally rest in unison for the first time in months.

Gabrian stirs in her sleep, caught somewhere between the surface of consciousness and the pull of slumber, but close enough to feel the hum of her bracelet spring to life as her Guardian lingers too close to her world.

Her eyes flutter, and he steps back into the Shadows. Torn whispers of his name cross over her lips, calling out to him as her consciousness consumes his familiar scent and pulls her deeper within the dream to chase after a boy with eyes the colour of the sea.

To Continue the journey click here:

https://www.amazon.com/Kade-Cook/e/B01M64VACI/

Join the newsletter at kadecook.author@gmail.com

to keep up with inside current events and promotions.

One last message to all you amazing readers, if you like a book and wish for more adventures by your favorite authors then please take a couple moments and leave a review. It means the world to us. Big hugs and bigger dreams – Kade

About the Author

Kade Cook

Kade Cook is an IT Professional and major fangirl. Her love of Twilight and The Mortal Instruments inspired her to begin her journey and write her own fantasy book series, The Covenant of Shadows.

Book one, GREY, was Shortlisted for the 2017 Emerging Writer's Prize on June 27th for Canada's best new books in Speculative Fiction.

Born and raised as a 'Maritimer' through and through, Kade will always be at home around good times and kind hearts, proud to be a daydreamer with a story to tell.

Theo & Quinn Creative Works
Shediac River, New Brunswick E4R 6A7, Canada

Or come visit her at https://www.facebook.com/kadecook.author
https://kadecookbooks.wordpress.com/
twitter.com/CovOfShadows

To Continue the journey click here:

https://www.amazon.com/Kade-Cook/e/B01M64VACI/

by KADE COOK

The Covenant of Shadows Series

GREY

Her path was already chosen. How she walks upon it is still up to her.

CALICO

Everyone has darkness within them. It is a choice to be wicked.

SILVER

Sometimes you must face your demons—even if they try to kill you...again.

TBD
-BOOK 4

Printed in Great Britain
by Amazon

53120464R00208